SOULMATED

Shaila Patel

Month9Books

SOULMATED by Shaila Patel
All rights reserved. Published in the United States of America by Month9Books, LLC.
No part of this book may be used or reproduced in any manner whatsoever without written permission of the publisher, except in the case of brief quotations embodied in critical articles and reviews.

EPub ISBN: 978-1-944816-87-2 Mobi ISBN: 978-1-944816-88-9
Paperback ISBN: 978-1-944816-64-3

Published by Month9Books, Raleigh, NC 27609
Cover design by Amanda Matthews of AM Design Studios

Month9Books

To my husband and son for all their support.

To Kirsten, the first person who ever loved my story.

To Purvi, who I wish could've read this.

SOULMATED

Happy Reading!

CHAPTER 1

Liam

They're calling this a test?
    Not even a ping grazed my mind as the five Elders tried to slip past my mental blocks and into my emotions. A sheen of sweat over William's lip proved he wasn't faring as well. Of all the cousins now come of age, William and I were the last to be sitting before the Elders. I'd have felt guilty for his not doing so well had he ever shown an interest in leading the family. But, we all knew he'd rather have his head in a library. Now his heart was with his wife Colleen. He at least seemed to have a choice about his fate.

I sighed. *Not so for me.*

"Are we boring you, Prince Liam?"

I snapped my eyes up to Elder Adebayo. He wore his trademark bow tie with a traditional fila atop his head. In the fraction of a second it took me to untangle the meaning from his heavy Nigerian accent, I'd blanked my expression and sat upright. The Elders sat along one side of an antique conference table, facing William and myself. The manor staff had rearranged the study to hold both the testing and signing-over ceremonies. Gone were the leather club chairs and stained glass lamps normally dotting the large space, giving it the air of a posh library. Now it seemed more an election-night headquarters, like the sort you saw on the telly, with bright lights and a gathering of family strewn about, waiting for the results. A photographer hung about in one corner, camera in hand. Not far from him stood a team of solicitors guarding rolling briefcases that were no doubt stuffed with legal documents for the victor to sign.

My throat-clearing echoed in the now silent room, and my cheeks warmed. "No, sir, not at all. Although, uh ... I'd like to know when it is you'll begin with me." I pasted on an oh-so-innocent smirk and watched William shake his head and smother a grin. I shrugged at him, hoping to lighten the mood.

Four of the Elders cocked an eyebrow—all except for Elder Claire Brennan, our lone Irish representative. She leaned ever so slightly forward from where she sat at the center of the group.

So much for having a bit of craic.

The familiar knocking on my brain—like the distant sound of drums—told me someone had got past my first line of defenses with their probe. The rest of my mental blocks held up though. The corner of Brennan's lip stretched upward. Toying with me, was she? I leaned back with a matching smile and loosened my tie. Mum and I were the only ones in the family who'd mastered the skill of probing and manipulation. A handy skill that, especially when the burden of the entire clan's financial success might well be resting on my shoulders.

As if sensing the end of the ritual, Mum whispered to the house staff and pointed toward the main doors, directing them to begin preparations, most likely. She turned and nearly ran into a Mediterranean-looking man with a grotesque mole on his left cheek. He wasn't a relation or a solicitor, so I assumed he was a council minister. Their stances were stiff, and despite being too far for me to hear, Mum's replies seemed short and clipped. He moved around her, and on his way out, his eyes met mine. He lifted his lips in a smirk.

Arse.

My attention darted to Mum. She was smoothing out the front of her dress, and her shoulders heaved a time or two before she turned back to face the room. I mentally sent her my curiosity, but she ignored me with a smile. She did at least send me her love before she weaved herself into the crowd.

Within a few minutes, Elder Brennan squared her shoulders and opened the portfolio in front of her. The rest of the Elders relaxed back in their seats and passed her folded slips of paper.

Jaysus Christ. Thank you. This bleedin' muck-up was about done.

After tallying the results, she stood with the help of a finely carved cane. Rumors about her age had always been entertaining—the last one I'd heard was that Claire Brennan was well over 140 years old. Apparently, documents as to her history had disappeared. Her regal manner and piercing blue eyes—the sort that'd make a gutless gobshite piss his pants—set her apart from the rest of the Elders. She now set those sights on me.

"Prince Liam, please stand. It is our unanimous decision that the Royal Empath House of O'Connor will now be led by you, Prince Liam Joseph O'Connor-Whelan, on this day, the sixth of June, in the year 2015." Flashes from the camera punctuated every other word, and spots began to form in front of my eyes. "You have proven your worth to lead your clan by exhibiting the strength of your empath skills to the satisfaction of the presiding group and by extension, the Council of Ministers."

Brennan rattled on about allegiances and legal mandates, all of which bore down on me like the weight of history, dry and inescapable, yet ... a bit liberating. Now we could stop our search and stay in Ireland—better of two evils and all that. I could make that happen now.

An explosion of clapping hands, and thumps on my back from

a relieved-looking William, forced me to plaster a smile on my face.

Mum hurried over with open arms. "Darling! We're so happy for you." Da and my older brother Ciarán, a non-empath, followed, both decked out in a suit and tie. After her hug and kiss and Da's pat on my back, they congratulated William on his effort and made room for the Elders to come around with their well-wishing. Ciarán smirked and punched my shoulder. The strobe-light effect of the flashes had me squinting.

Elder Santiago from Spain shook my hand. He sported a thick mustache and proudly wore his Catalonian flag pin on his lapel. He'd been wooing our clan for support in Catalonia's bid for secession from Spain. Ciarán had thought it a good cause to be getting behind—especially if we beat another royal clan from doing so first. We had several holdings in Barcelona, after all. Now that it was my call to be making, a hasty decision didn't seem wise. Santiago always had the look about him of a tapas dish drowning in olive oil.

He sidled closer. "Your strength is most impressive. And at the age of eighteen too. It is not hard to believe you will be the next soulmated empath, in truth. Some have doubts though, eh?"

He wants to discuss this now?

Da pointed to his own temple, stabbing at an unruly black curl. "No need for doubts. If I've seen it, it's as good as true."

I resisted rolling my eyes. Admitting I had my own doubts about Da's visions wouldn't be wise. "Time will tell, yeah?" *No point kissing Elder arse.*

The other Elders came one by one, congratulating me and posing for photos. Brennan was last. The crowd dispersed enough to give us a bubble of privacy. She tipped her head back and studied my face.

Without being able to read her blocked emotions, her body language was all I had to go on. A smile like before tugged at her lips.

I leaned in. "So were you toying with me earlier?" My bold question would either be living up to the liberties given to the heads of the four remaining Irish royal houses, or it'd be taken as the yipping of a whelp learning to growl. I hoped for the former and straightened up just in case.

"The test need only be as strong as the weakest candidate." She curved her gloved hand around the crook of my elbow and turned me to face the patio. "Come now. Walk me outside."

Leading an Elder outside for a private conversation wasn't as nerve-racking as I'd thought. With her hand resting on my arm, she exuded an unexpected grandmotherly warmth. The stone patio ran the length of the building on this side of our manor home. It overlooked the meadows of our property—now mine—and with the cloudless days we'd had of late, the scent of heated earth surrounded us. I inhaled deeply. *Definitely better here than returning to the States.*

The few who lingered outside turned and meandered back to the study once they spotted us. Elder Brennan patted my arm, then released it, flattening her palms upon the balustrade, her ever-present white gloves in sharp contrast to the weathered stone.

Her gaze floated over the view. "It seems you are to have a very interesting future ahead of you."

"Possibly."

Her features relaxed with another one of her enigmatic smiles. "When will you be returning to America?"

"I'm thinking to stay here," I said.

A disapproving frown appeared, and she tapped a sole finger on the stone.

How the hell was this any of her bloody business? I forced my expression to remain neutral and unclenched the hands I'd not realized I'd fisted. If only Da had kept his mouth shut over the years.

"Choices are a funny thing, Prince Liam. We often treat them as black and white, but rarely are they."

I pocketed my hands. What was I meant to say? Yes, Zen Master Brennan.

A breeze picked up and coaxed a few strands of her silver hair across her cheek. She tilted her face into the wind and closed her eyes. "You should return to your search." She turned and pinned me with a stare.

"What? Why? Are you trying to boot me from Ireland? Away from the estate? Is something happening you're hiding from me?"

She held up her hand. "The demesne will be in capable hands. Go now. Enjoy your celebration. Congratulations and happy eighteenth birthday." With a nod, she summoned two of her gendarmes, who came to her side and escorted her down the patio.

Mum must have been watching because she rushed outside. "What did she want?" Her concerned gaze scanned my face as if to get a read on my emotions, but as usual, I had them blocked.

I rolled my shoulders and took a breath. "She wants us to go back to the States."

Her mouth opened and closed.

I knew that look. "Just say it, Mum."

"Your father had another vision during the night."

I snorted. "Where now? Alaska?"

"Liam, you used to believe—"

"Do you think we'll be seeing some actual igloos? We could even go to the North Pole and watch the ice cap melt—"

"What harm could one more year—?"

"Have you tried whale blubber, Mum? I hear it's a right treat."

An elderly couple came out onto the patio. With a huff, Mum crossed her arms and broadcast her emotions as clearly as any mother's scowl would convey. Waves of her irritation registered in my mind like seaweed washing in and wrapping around my toes. I moved a few steps away and leaned over the balustrade, resting my forearms on the sunbaked stone. A good fifty yards out, a hare popped up to scan its surroundings and then chased a second one into the shrubbery.

After a few moments, Mum joined me. "We know this isn't

easy, Liam, but we're doing it for you. We've sacrificed so much. Please understand."

I ground my back teeth and straightened. So much for making it happen my way. "Fine. One more year."

I stormed back into the study so the signing could begin, passing by several girls in long glittering dresses, tittering behind their fingers. No doubt my pain-in-the-arse brother had arranged for them to be here.

If the Elders knew about our search, so did the rest of the empath community. Speculation would be flowing like whiskey tonight, but it didn't change the fact we'd not be finding our target in Ireland.

CHAPTER 2

Laxshmi

The longer I stared at the words, the faster my ability to read left me. With my mom and Mrs. Beacham staring at me, I was in the Indian-American version of hell.

I slid the Wake County Public High School Planning Guide back to the guidance counselor, a rush of air escaping my lips. School started on Monday, and Mrs. Beacham's desk was as clutter-free as I'd ever seen it. Her letter trays didn't look like our pot-bellied principal yet, and a green ficus tree, still sporting a dangling how-to-care-for-me label, had replaced the wilted brown one from the end of my sophomore year. With the halls devoid of students, the only sound came from the generic school clock ticking away. There wasn't even a window I could make a visual escape through.

I clenched my hands together in my lap.

Mrs. Beacham gave me a tight-lipped smile. Mom flicked her

long braid over her shoulder and leaned forward in the chair beside me. Her face could've been one of those *I Gave You Life and I Can Take It Away* memes.

How could this be happening? I blinked back tears.

"If you're set on this course of action, Mrs. Kapadia, Laxshmi will have quite a bit of testing to show curricular competency before next June. But she'll also miss out on the social aspect of having a senior year."

"That is not important." Mom raised her chin. "This is what she needs to do."

"She could still finish out her last two years in high school and apply before her senior year," Mrs. Beacham said. "She seems to want—"

"Laxshmi will do what is expected of her."

Gee. Play the culture card, why don't you?

Mrs. Beacham gave me a what-else-can-I-do look with a tiny shrug.

"What do we need to do to start?" With Mom's accent, all her *w*'s became *v*'s. Most of those sitcom caricatures of Indian people weren't too far off. Was it terrible to think that? Maybe I *was* too Americanized, just like Mom had always said.

Mrs. Beacham told us about the letter Mom would have to write to declare her intent—one I'd have to draft and type up for her to sign, of course. She could speak English and read it well enough, but having to write anything more complicated than a grocery list was a chore for her. Mrs. Beacham pulled out what had to be the manila folder version of my life from her squeaky filing cabinet and began making a timeline of what I'd have to do to graduate early.

I ducked my head toward Mom and lowered my voice. "I don't want to do this, Mom. Please."

She stared at whatever Mrs. Beacham was writing, acting like I hadn't even uttered a word.

The air-conditioning in Mom's Camry had stopped working long ago. With the windows open, the wind had been whipping the loose end of the soft fabric headliner against my head—until I slammed my hand up to pin it in place. Mom spared a glance in my direction, but kept humming along with a stupid Bollywood movie tune as if she'd done me the world's biggest favor.

I sighed. "I don't want to miss my senior year. Why can't you understand that?"

"If you don't do this, then you will have to get married."

"God, Mom! What kind of choices are those? I'm only—"

"*Choop.* Quiet. Be thanking God, *hunh*? You won't have to worry about money every day like your mummy."

The culture card and now the money card. Lovely.

She hooked a right into our gravel driveway, and I looked past her to see a moving truck two doors down. As we pulled farther in, our house blocked my view. I dashed out and climbed the front porch steps, hoping to spot our new neighbors, but despite the truck, the house looked as abandoned as when it had stood empty all summer. *They must be inside.* Mom all but pushed me into the house.

She dropped her purse and keys on the dining table. "Did you make the *batata nu shaak*?"

"Yeah, but I didn't use all the potatoes." I stomped up the stairs.

"Then come back down and make the *rotlis* for lunch."

"Can't. Have to finish my summer reading," I called back down with my lie. She mumbled something in Gujarati while I climbed the pull-down stairs to my attic bedroom and yanked them back up like they were a shield protecting me from all evil. My butt hit the carpet hard enough for a shudder to reverberate through the floor and furniture.

Mom's voice echoed in my head. "*What good Indian girl would study dance in the college? You will make no money. You are too smart to do dancing.*" With a flick of a tear, I dragged myself up to my window seat and dropped my head back against one of the bookcases that created my nook.

Four burly movers were unloading the truck on the other side of Mrs. Robertson's house. The faint sound of them hollering instructions at each other reached my ears. From my third-floor perch, the chance our new neighbors would see me spying on them was slim, which I liked just fine.

A man with a mop of curly, salt-and-pepper hair directed the team. Dressed in a blue sweater vest and white T-shirt over gray Bermuda shorts, he kept clapping his hands and rubbing them together. He completed his ensemble with white tube socks and some sort of brown sandals. I smiled for the first time today.

A shiny black Audi parked behind the moving truck, blocking an old-model Mercedes and some expensive-looking, white SUV in their driveway. An elegantly dressed blond woman and a dark-haired guy in shorts and a black T-shirt got out. From this distance he looked like he was about my age, but I couldn't tell for sure. He took a soccer ball out of the trunk.

Great. Just what the world needed—another jock.

But what were a Mercedes, some expensive SUV, and an Audi doing on our street? We lived in a neighborhood of small single-family homes, the kind with carports or the odd detached garage, like ours. It was homey. Our neighbors took care of their shrubs, put up holiday decorations, and carried pooper-scoopers for their dogs. It was rare to find a house whose paint wasn't peeling, whose gutters weren't blackened, or whose sidewalks weren't christened with initials whenever cracks were sealed over.

A newer Mercedes pulled up and parked in Mrs. Robertson's

gravel driveway. A uniformed chauffeur got out and opened the back door. A young man in slacks and a button-down shirt stepped out. He hugged the adults and grabbed the soccer guy— *his brother?*—in a headlock. They knocked each other around for a bit while the chauffeur lifted a small suitcase and a messenger bag from the trunk before getting back into the Mercedes and leaving.

I hugged a cushion to my chest and settled in to spy. With the air-conditioning vents blowing right above my window seat, goose bumps chased each other across my arms.

The mother and the dressed-up young man moved toward the house and out of my view, leaving Mr. Clappy-Hands and the jock outside. Jock still hadn't turned around. He kicked the soccer ball between his knees and feet with almost dance-like skills. The few times he struggled to control the ball, I'd hold my breath until he resumed his self-assured, lazy rhythm. I was impressed with his dexterity and pressed my nose to the window to watch. Something about his movements warmed me, like the moment the morning sun burst above the horizon. I didn't dare turn away for a second in case I missed anything.

I wondered how tall he was compared to me and how broad his shoulders were. What color were his eyes? Was he a junior like me? And where would he be going to school?

The soccer ball flew into the air. He bounced it off his head and let it drop to his foot, and in one lithe movement, kicked it back to his knee, turning enough for me to get a good look at the front of him.

A black V-neck T-shirt stretched snug across his muscular chest. While his feet did their thing, he balanced himself with his arms outstretched, the curves of his biceps clearly visible. What would they feel like under my fingers? My hand went up to the window on its own, and a sizzle shot up my arm and settled behind my eyes. I yanked my hand back down with a yelp. Soccer guy jerked around as if he'd heard me, and I shrank back, my heart racing.

Don't be stupid. He can't see you. Maybe a noise had startled him.

He scanned his surroundings, but never looked up. He ran a hand through his dark hair, pushing back what fell over his forehead, and rubbed the back of his neck. What was he thinking about? He faced his front lawn again, and my shoulders slumped. The urge to touch the window again overwhelmed me. *What is wrong with me?*

I shook out my hand, balling it into a fist, and squeezed the cushion tighter against my chest. Falling for a neighbor when I was being forced to graduate early wasn't a choice I could afford to make.

CHAPTER 3

Liam

We'd parked on yet another dull street, in another dull neighborhood, of another dull city. *Ah, sure look it.* At least it was something new to see—a new state. North Carolina.

I stepped out of Mum's Audi and stretched. It felt good to be walking around since our last stop was more than three hours ago, back in a place called Asheville. We'd taken a self-guided sightseeing tour for three days, from our last house in Memphis to Cary, and if I never saw another Cracker Barrel, I'd die a happy man. Since Da had gone on ahead to meet the movers, he'd missed all the fun.

I reached for the football I'd tossed in the boot back in Memphis and spun it on my finger. *Agh, they call it a soccer ball in the States, Liam.* For as many years as we'd been returning here, each autumn was like the first time—relearning American English and trying not to be standing out like a tourist. Except now, I didn't find myself much caring.

The sounds of a lived-in neighborhood met my ears—dogs barking, lawn mowers running, and kids laughing. The street offered up more trees than in our last few neighborhoods, but their thick, dark green canopies felt oppressive to me, nothing like the lively greens from home.

Da stood on the porch, rubbing his hands together, a smile glued to his face. He was always excited by the prospect of a new lead from another one of his visions.

"Isn't this grand?" he asked. "The mountains, did you see 'em on the drive? Fantastic, weren't they?"

I ignored him and bounced the football between my knees and feet.

My brother arrived minutes later, having flown into the Raleigh-Durham airport an hour ago. Ciarán would be staying only the weekend to help us with the unpacking. Wherever we'd moved, finding movers cleared by the empath government was brutal. It meant that every year, we had to pack and unpack our personal possessions on our own, in case outsiders saw something they shouldn't. Ciarán would be flying back home early Monday, and I'd be starting as a senior at a new high school, looking for my next target—again. If I'd been at home, I'd have been done with my Senior Cycle and have gone on to university by now.

As I concentrated on keeping my balance, I sensed a fleeting presence touch my mind, like fingers pressed against my skin. I jerked around, but saw not a soul. It took a moment to settle back into reality, as if I'd just woken and was trying to call to mind a dream.

The sensation stuck around like an itch I'd never be able to reach. Even though it wasn't an empathic projection, I reinforced the mental blocks guarding my mind. Now that I was head of our clan and refused bodyguards while in the States, I'd want to be careful.

We made a quick supper of sandwiches around our kitchen table. I hadn't much of an appetite. Each time we returned to the States, it was the same. I'd miss my cousins and the calm of the countryside something fierce. Wherever we'd lived here, I could never walk more than ten feet before I'd be staring at a chain-link fence, a dying patch of grass, or a rattling air-conditioning unit. Compared to our estate, everywhere here felt like the devil's closet.

Mum waved her hand in front of my face. "You know, darling, you're making it worse by brooding."

"Stop trying to read me, yeah?" I must've relaxed my block, so I closed my mind off tighter.

"I don't have to. Anyone can see what you're feeling."

Da and Ciarán were arguing about something useless, so I popped in my earbuds to drown them out and picked up my paper plate to throw it away. Splender's "Yeah, Whatever" blared from my eighties and nineties playlist. *How fitting.* Mum frowned and shook her head.

I excused myself to go and unpack my room. The first thing to set up was my stereo, which already had Twenty One Pilots in the disc changer. In the coffin that was now my room, I fell back onto my bare mattress, staring at the ceiling, wondering how my last year in the States would be. If the drywall nails popping out around the ceiling fan were any indication, life would be grand.

Just grand.

Ciarán stuck his head around the door.

"What's craic?" I asked. Hiding my sarcasm would've been pointless.

"Just checking on my little brother … the prince." He waved his fingers in the air.

"Little? I'm tall enough to be stopping your cakehole, boy." Ciarán stepped into the room and leaned a shoulder against the wall. He'd changed into some girlie-looking T-shirt and a pair of Da's safari shorts. *Smooth.* "Couldn't find a tie in Da's room to go with that?"

"You're in a maggoty mood." He turned down my stereo and glanced into a box of books.

"Registered for your modules at Trinity, have you?"

"I have. When do your classes start here?"

"Monday. New school, same old shite." I pushed off the mattress to unpack.

"Think you'll be finding this soul mate in some little girl still in school? It's a woman you're needing." He wiggled his eyebrows at me and shoved some books on a shelf.

"School means the girls are the same age as me, moron. I'm not a perv."

"'*I'm not a perv.*' Jaysus, you're even sounding like a Yank."

I ignored him, flattened emptied boxes, and threw them into the corner. If the room were any smaller, it'd be regurgitating all the furniture stuffed in here.

"*Oh, Ciarán,*" he mimicked. "*These girls can't flirt, they've no sense of humor, and not a one can snog worth hell.*" He laughed. "Did I sum up the last few years well enough for ya, dear brother? What you keep on about is a girl in pigtails. Now the women I'd shown you this summer, there'd been a few there worth a shag. But no, you've got this soul mate blather stuck in your head. What happened to you needing an outlet?"

"Don't be making shite up now." I'd never admit to needing an outlet to him. Those girls he'd put my way had been too old for my taste—or even younger than my targets here. Listening to him whine on about how I needed to find a *right-now* girl aggravated me to no end.

"Mother of Jaysus." Ciarán shook his head. "You don't shag a girl with your brain. A right poof romantic, you are. One of these days you'll dive too deep into these visions of Da's, and you'll never come up again."

I shoved a pile of my jeans into a drawer and slammed it shut.

"You're chasing clouds here, Liam. To hell with Da. Come back with me, yeah? Screw these arseways visions and start living your life." He reached into his back pocket and pulled out a thumb drive. "Your latest estate reports." With his eyebrows raised, he tossed me the reminder of the life waiting for me in Ireland.

Why had I come back here to the States after my summer at home? I ran my hand through my hair and sighed. I was eighteen now. I could leave and quit the search. Maybe I *was* some teary-eyed romantic looking for my damsel in distress. But there'd be no chance I'd be admitting that to Ciarán.

"I promised Mum," I said, defending my decision.

"Ma's boy," he muttered.

"Why the bleedin' hell are you even lurking about? Is it for the pure enjoyment of being a pissing arse?"

He fanned his face with a kid's book about the fifty states. Our little cousin, Ian, had bought it for me as a birthday gift so I'd not "lose my way."

I pointed to it. "Maybe you need to be finding your way to Maine if you're having trouble with the heat down here."

He frowned at the cover. "Who's being an arse now?"

An hour later, we had most of my room sorted. Ciarán studied a photo from the box he'd just opened by my dresser. His back was to me, but in the mirror's reflection, I could see the look of disgust flash across his face, leaving it pinched. I'd never have seen it if he weren't standing where he was. He wasn't an empath like me and Mum, but he'd learned how to block his emotions. Once he had, he never wanted to stop.

"I'll bring up some Guinness later, yeah?" He dropped the photo back on the pile and left.

I maneuvered around boxes and picked up the photo. It showed the four of us not long after I'd felt my first empath ripple. So why was I getting Ciarán's disgust? Hell if I knew how to figure him. I flung it back into the box.

I yanked up the silver metallic blinds over my window and stared out. My room had a view of our driveway and detached garage. Several of our neighbor's overgrown trees hung heavy, leaning over the fence between. As if on cue, someone's air-conditioning unit rattled to life, reminding me again we weren't in Ireland.

I braced my hands on either side of the window and rested my forehead against the warm, west-facing glass. Why the hell was I back here again? I'd rather boil off my skin than have to be faking enthusiasm again for a target when I knew she wasn't The One— all while we waited for Da's next vision to confirm it. And dealing with the emotional drama when I'd break up with them? It was like throwing salt in the boiling water with me. No, I'd not let myself get sucked in to Da's excitement like every year past. Of that, I'd make certain.

The back of my neck tingled, reminding me that the itch from earlier hadn't ever left.

CHAPTER 4

Laxshmi

Between bites of our *dal dhokli* and rice at dinner, Mom spewed more of the same drivel she had all week. She'd found out about early graduation last Sunday from some woman at the *mandir*. To her, it was the answer to her prayers, the reason she'd gone to the temple in the first place.

She served herself more rice and let the spoon clunk against the pot. "If you graduate early next summer and go to the faster medical school like Bhavna*ben*'s son, you will be done in six years. Six, not eight, *hunh?* If you don't want to do that, then I will start looking for a boy for you to marry. You want a choice? That is your choice."

Whatever. The spoon's handle dug into my tightening fingers. I *could* forget to tell her college applications would be due in November.

"Once you become a doctor, you can find a good Indian boy. And see, if you finish early, you will be younger and more pretty than the other girls."

Wow. Apparently, beauty years were now like dog years—girls one year older than me would look a whole seven years older. Mom smiled like some evil genius. *Where does she come up with this stuff?*

Her idea of a good Indian suitor was a mama's boy who thought flirting was pulling a girl's hair. *As if.* The boys at the temple were the worst. They'd parrot their parents' criticisms of Americanized girls and then fall all over themselves when one of those girls flipped her hair back and flashed a flirty smile. I'd gag every time I'd see it.

My ears stung with Mom's litany of her friends' daughters who were more Indian than I was, who cared more about their future, and who would have better marriage prospects. I could go to school every day with a freaking *chandlo* on my forehead, and she still wouldn't think I was Indian enough. When would I ever get to make my own decisions?

I bit back tears. *God! Why do I always let her get to me?* I couldn't stomach any more food.

Making the only choice I could, I pushed back, dumped my dishes into the sink, and muttered something about finishing my summer reading as I fled upstairs.

I settled into my window seat and began rereading *Wuthering Heights* by the light of the setting sun, opening the window just a crack. A humid breeze fluttered the sheer curtains, and with it came the smell of someone barbecuing. The sound of two kids laughing floated up as they enjoyed the last bit of light. Mrs. Robertson's sprinklers were on, making a tinkling sound as it hit her windows, and from a distance, two dogs were barking. I took a deep breath, letting my muscles relax.

After skimming a few chapters, I spied two of our new neighbors climbing onto their roof, tools in hand. I barely saw more than their darkened silhouettes bathed in halos, so I raised my hand to shield my eyes against the sun and watched while they fiddled with something that looked like a fan. The dad seemed busy at his task, and the son sat, leaning against the chimney. He occasionally left his perch to help his dad, but otherwise, he'd just stare off at the horizon.

When the last light of day filtered over the treetops and my pages were a dull orange brown, I reached up and flicked on my reading light. It was a good time to take a break.

Turning on my CD player, I did some ballet turns to one of my favorite songs by Mindy Gledhill, "Bring Me Close." After years of taking lessons, resisting the urge to dance was never an option. It put me in my happy place, the place where I could forget about the world and get lost in whatever emotion needed expressing. When Mom had forbidden me to audition for the University of North Carolina School of the Arts' high school diploma in dance, I had quit ballet. There didn't seem to be a point anymore. I'd focused on my Indian dancing, *Bharatanatyam,* instead, hoping she'd let me apply and audition for an undergraduate degree in dance. That wouldn't happen now.

Before Daddy had died five years ago, he'd set up an account only I could access, but I couldn't touch it until I turned eighteen. A yearly allowance from the funds helped pay for my dance lessons. I'd dubbed it my Princess Fund, after his nickname for me. Mom and I weren't allowed to know how much was in it, though, which was weird. It wasn't like we were rich. I'd always assumed Dad locked the money away so Mom wouldn't use it on bills instead of my dance lessons.

The plaque above my dresser mirror was my focal point for my turns. "*The whole is greater than the sum of its parts.*" The Aristotle quotation kept me believing I could be part of something extraordinary someday, something *greater.* Mom and Dad's arranged marriage had been far from extraordinary, so why did she keep threatening to saddle me with one?

After letting the song repeat several times, I got a drink from downstairs and returned to the window seat.

Twilight bathed the neighborhood now. The dad and his

tools were gone, but the son had stayed behind. He sat there in the darkening shadows as still as the chimney behind him. Had he fallen asleep? It didn't seem real to have company up here. I wondered whose vantage point was better.

Intrigued by this muscular and admirably agile guy who now shared my world, I narrowed my eyes to see if he was moving and detected a flicker of light in his lap. *Probably a cell phone.* It illuminated his sagging shoulders and head, bowed down as if in defeat. He seemed deep in thought, sad even. His edges were soft and vulnerable there in the shadows. With an occasional heave of his chest, it seemed like some kind of hopelessness weighed on his mind. Somehow, it made me ache.

My hand was resting on the window again, my fingers itching to touch him. I shook out my hand. *Geez. Not again.*

I wondered if he'd be going to my school. Would he be walking like the rest of us this Monday?

After a few more minutes, the shadows swallowed my view completely. I returned to my book, flipping to one of my favorite parts.

Another flicker of light from the roof caught my attention. He was holding the device closer to his face, and it provided enough brightness for me to see he was looking right at me. When the white of his teeth lit up the night with his smile, I slammed myself into the back of my seat.

Crap!

With my overhead reading light, I'd been in plain view while he'd been sitting in obscurity. I pulled the sheers closed, turned off the light, and flew off the window seat. My heart was drumming against my chest. I crouched on the floor, afraid he could still see me.

He'd been watching me!

For how long? *Oh God.* Had he seen me picking my teeth? We'd had blackberries with dinner, and the seeds were driving me bananas. My blood was pulsing behind my left ear, and my fingers were trembling.

What do I do now? Had he seen me watching him?

I found enough strength in my wobbly legs to stumble to the door and switch off the main ceiling light I'd turned on earlier. I crawled back to the window seat, inching away the sheers for a peek. With the moon hidden behind clouds, darkness had swallowed up his roof. At least he couldn't see me now.

My breath rushed out, and I shook out my fingers. I didn't dare turn the lights back on. *Yup. Time for bed.*

I fumbled for my pajamas in the dark and dived under the covers. I stared at the closed window for what had to be hours. My mind was too wired to sleep. His smile kept flashing in my head. It felt comforting, but unnerving—like performing my favorite dance on stage in front of an audience.

I took out my poetry journal from beneath my pillow—the one marked *Math* to disguise it from Mom—and scribbled out another one of my corny couplets to relax me.

Shoulders slumped, heart so sad,
A wondrous smile that made me glad.

I crossed out the word *glad* and changed it to *mad*. It wasn't Shakespeare, but my poems were like my diary.

And today felt like a day worth remembering.

CHAPTER 5

Liam

I'd unpacked more boxes and had set up my seventh room in as many years. The summer had ended far too fast. As always, the first part of it had been spent on our royal estate outside Dublin with Ciarán and the rest of the family. This year, instead of finishing up the summer in Wales, where Mum's parents had another home, I'd visited Ciarán's flat in the city to check out Trinity University, since I was hoping to be enrolled there next year. I'd finally be moving on with my life and damn if that wasn't a relief.

My summers back home had always been the recharge I'd needed before returning to the States. Each time I'd meet a new target here, I couldn't help but catch some of Da's excitement over finding my soul mate. I'd let myself get wrapped up in the idea, only to be disappointed by another false lead. It was hard to shake the idea of finding The One when it'd been a part of my life since Da's first vision about me. I'd been only six, for Christ's sake.

Would this time be any different? Or would I fall for the excitement again, despite my intention not to?

Da knocked on my door and let himself in. "So are you sorted then?"

"I am. Can't you tell?"

He walked over to the dresser and took up the photo Ciarán had been looking at. I'd wedged it between the frame and the mirror along with the rest.

"Ahh," he said. "That's a special one, isn't it? Your ma was happy as the day you were born."

I was only four in the photo. Da was wearing these God-awful neon-yellow and orange striped swim trunks. Ciarán and I had been wrapped in tacky Aladdin towels.

"I still have those swim trunks."

I laughed. "Please, Da, don't wear them, yeah? You could get deported. Fashion crime and all that."

"Oh, go on with you. They're not as bad as all that."

He tapped the photo against the palm of his hand a few times and wedged it back. He seemed a bit wistful, but I couldn't be sure why. As a non-empath, he'd also been taught how to block his emotions. Grandma Whelan and Da's siblings were all empaths—it was probably a matter of sanity to keep his feelings to himself, given how rowdy Da's side of the family could be. Unlike Ciarán though, Da often slipped and relaxed his guard—especially after a pint or two at the local.

In the picture, Mum was kneeling down beside me with a love in her eyes that, thanks to the photo, I'd not be soon forgetting. I remembered her smoothing my wet hair and telling me how proud she was of me. I smiled at the memory. I'd sensed my first outside emotion that afternoon. From then on, I was an empath like her. And Ciarán had called me a ma's boy ever since. It annoyed me, but what brotherly slagging didn't?

Da reminisced while I sorted my desk. His trips down memory lane were easy to follow, as worn as the path was. He kept stopping to ask if I was listening.

Before he could do it again, I interrupted him. "Da! Was there a reason for coming in here?"

"Sure. Your ma's got herself a migraine. The attic fan is *kerplunking* like it's on its last gasp, and she's seeing red and green spots. Let's see what can be done about it, yeah? Her poor head can't wait for a repairman come Monday."

He grabbed a newly emptied box and dropped it out in the hallway. "Here. Bring this." He gave me the ladder that he'd left out there, and I followed him as he carried the toolbox.

We used the top-floor veranda off my parents' bedroom to climb up to the roof. A small nook by the chimney became the perfect seat while I'd be waiting to do what he asked of me. I surveyed the neighborhood and wondered where this next potential soul mate could be.

"Here we are above the treetops, just like I'd said we'd be."

"There are no girls on the roof. In case I needed to point that out."

He huffed. "My visions aren't always literal, Liam. You know that better than any."

Most of what he saw was more than vague. At least knowing she was Indian helped narrow down the options when we came to a new location. How he used his visions to drag us from city to city was a mystery to the likes of me. Too many "clues" seemed to have been misinterpreted over the years.

"How can you not understand?" he asked. "The signs I get, they're all meant to be put together like a puzzle. With the pieces we have, we're getting closer, yeah?" He pointed a pair of pliers at me and then all around us. "We might be right at her doorstep."

Yeah, whatever.

I helped him take apart the fan, and he whistled old drinking songs while he worked. As cheesy as the tunes were, the sound of them made me miss home even more.

"Don't forget the other puzzle pieces, Liam. She'll be bighearted, dances like an angel—"

"I know. I know. Shining black hair, smart as a whip, powerful empath. Yeah, yeah. You seem to forget every target had most of those traits—and they never amounted to much now, did they?" He'd always made this girl sound perfect, like she was better than the Virgin Mary and St. Bridget rolled into one. "Ciarán thinks there's no point to this bloody search. I'm beginning to agree."

"Now you listen—" The hammer slipped. Da cursed under his breath, shaking his hand and leaving off whatever he'd been wanting to say. He went back to work, but after a few minutes of blessed silence, his sigh drew me back to himself. His head was bowed, and he shook it ever so slightly.

"How many times do I need to be telling you?" He cleared his throat. Looking up, his gaze met mine. Fear flashed across his eyes before he masked it with steely determination and a clenched jaw.

That was his reaction of late, whenever we discussed ending the search. We'd had quite a row about it over the summer. Something had him rattled, but he'd not share a bit of it. *Whatever.* It was his problem then.

"I'm giving you a way into the Group of Elders," he continued with another defeated sigh. "Or at the very least, a higher starting position in the Council of Ministers. You could even be first in the Line of Ascension, and once one of those Elders turns up his toes, you're in. Your future would be set, son. *A soulmated union.* Think of the power, the prestige, the rare honor. Who wouldn't be wanting that, yeah? Hand me the screwdriver, will you now?"

"And for how long have I been telling you that I'll not be going into politics?" I slapped the handle of the screwdriver into his palm. I had to admit, the special powers bit always piqued my interest, but it was a legend, nothing more. There hadn't been a documented soulmated union in centuries. Aside from that, why the hell would I want to be joining a group of old wankers who got off on control issues? The council members were no better. Made up of representatives from each country, all they did was kiss Elder arse and claw and manipulate their way up the Line of Ascension—all so they might be an Elder one day.

Da slammed his palm down on a shingle. "Don't be wasting opportunity like this. I didn't raise you to ignore your destiny." His tone had a hard edge to it, almost as if he were getting desperate.

Just grand. There was no point arguing when he'd be getting like this.

It took everything I had not to up and leave him there.

Off to my right, the sun sat low in the sky. When I turned back toward Da, a window two doors down caught my eye. Someone was there, but the glare coming off the glass blinded my eyes. When a cloud passed over, giving a bit of shade, it was clear a girl sat watching us. She had dark hair, but since her hand was up, shielding her eyes from the sun, I couldn't see her face.

What could she be thinking about each time she looked over our way? At this distance, she was a bit too far for me to feel empathically, not that it'd tell me her thoughts.

The sun soon fell below the tree line, and I was able to make out a pair of legs framed by the wide window. They were some damn fine looking legs too. She sat propped up against the side of the window, and as high up as she was, she must have been on a window seat. Thank God for my heightened vision. I'd been lucky enough to inherit an enhanced sense, though no one else in my family had. I always thought of it like winning the genetic lottery.

Even without the glare of the sun, a shadow still masked her face, but her shapely legs kept me looking her way. I adjusted my shorts and then rubbed the back of my neck. To say this soul mate business was brutal on my sex life—or lack of one—was an understatement.

Going beyond just fooling around with any of the targets left me feeling uncomfortable. I'd play the part of a loving boyfriend, sure, but I couldn't take advantage of them, knowing I'd be moving along as soon as Da's next vision confirmed what I already knew—

that I hadn't found The One yet. But why should I go about at my age thinking of every girl I took a gander to as a potential mate for life? Who could have a bit of fun with that sort of pressure?

I left to get a bottle of water and came back to find Da packing up. The girl had turned on a reading lamp above her, but a shadow still covered her face.

"Leave the ladder, yeah? I'm going to stay up here and listen to some music."

Da shrugged and left.

"Crash Into Me" by the Dave Matthews Band played from the eighties and nineties playlist on my mobile. The raw quality of the song appealed to me. It was how I'd always imagined feeling about this soul mate Da kept harping about. Maybe I was just a romantic like Ciarán had said—one who was waiting for the right girl to come along but couldn't admit it.

I huffed.

That ended here. After twelve years of this—the last six far enough away from home—I was done.

I wasn't eager to find another false lead, but damn if the curiosity about our neighbor didn't needle me. I'd guard myself against getting my hopes up too high. No point repeating the disasters I'd had with my past targets. Finding and getting to know the girl would be a job and nothing more. I looked into the sky and smiled. Why hadn't I thought to do this before?

The girl stepped away from her window seat, swaying to some music she must be playing in the background. Before long, she was dancing around, slipping in and out of my view. Soft and graceful were the words coming to mind. I craned my neck to follow her when I could.

Ah, she's a dancer. That explains those fine legs of hers. She finally disappeared from view altogether. Oddly disappointed, I leaned back, closed my eyes, and listened to the lyrics. Even behind my closed eyes, I couldn't stop imagining her dancing in my arms.

The neighborhood sounds had died away, so I opened my eyes. It was time to head back down into the house to finish the unpacking. Dark as it was now, the girl showed up plain in the window, illuminated by an overhead lamp. She was reading and talking at the same time, like she was reciting lines. Glossy black hair, almond eyes, and a dancer. I snorted. She could be my next target—a dancer found up in the treetops no less.

I groaned. Da was right. Again.

I pulled out my earbuds and turned off the music. When I looked back her way, her gaze was fixed on me. An unexpected smile exploded onto my face, and a wave of her panic crashed into my mind.

Mother of Jaysus! She was projecting her feelings—and at this distance too. Not only was she the first target to do *that,* she was better at it than most lifelong empaths. Was she already one of us? But she couldn't be. The empath community here didn't have anyone registered as living on this street.

She threw her curtains together and shut off her light, breaking the connection between us. I laughed out loud at her reaction, rubbed my hand down my face, and groaned again.

Was I ready to go through this shite once more? I hated having my hopes going up and then dashing down like a bleedin' carnival ride, leaving me sick at the end of it. But I didn't have much of a choice in it. It was one last try at fulfilling Da's visions—or failing to.

She'd be nothing but a last chance try. Nothing more. Then I could go home.

CHAPTER 6

Laxshmi

I bolted upright in bed and threw my arms out to brace myself. My chest heaved. *Calm down, Laxshmi.*

It was six in the morning on Monday, and as the dream faded, I looked toward the window and remembered his smile again. Darkness still clung to the glass, which made the memory seem like it had happened minutes ago instead of three nights before. I rubbed my palms over my eyes, hoping it would wipe away his smile.

What was my dream about anyway? Vague scenes of falling toward something—while screaming and then laughing—floated around in my head. I'd had the distinct feeling of someone catching me, a set of arms wrapping around me protectively.

In fifteen minutes, my alarm clock would be going off for the first day of school. I dropped my face into the pillow and groaned. What was fifteen minutes when I hadn't slept well for the last three nights? How irrational was I to be obsessed over a new neighbor? I hadn't even gotten a good look at him.

I showered, dressed, and made my way down for breakfast, none too eager to drop pancakes upon the nervous swarm of butterflies flitting about my stomach. Obsessing about whether I'd meet Soccer Jock on my way to school was obviously not good for my digestive health.

The slamming of pots and pans halted my steps, but reminded me it was probably Mom's reaction to our latest family drama. At least it wasn't about me this time. If I could push aside my anxiety about meeting our neighbor and ignore Mom's lunacy, I might just be able to enjoy what the first day of school meant—escape.

As expected, Mom was starring in her own Indian soap opera, the kind with melodramatic sighs and spectacular hand gestures involving a spatula. The only thing needed now was obnoxious sound effects and exaggerated camera angles. Her sister-in-law had broken the news yesterday that my cousin, Sujata, was dating a white boy. I couldn't have been more thrilled. I'd known Sujata and Michael had been dating for two years at Georgetown, but my surprise-face when Mom told me the news could've won me an Oscar.

All in the name of self-preservation.

I plopped down at the old Formica table my parents had gotten from a thrift shop when they'd first moved to the States. It was surrounded by three mismatched chairs. We could probably afford a new dinette set, but Mom wouldn't hear of it. The table was shoved against the wall between the entry to the kitchen and a metal bookcase that served as our pantry. She'd paid a whole dollar for it at a yard sale. The side was now covered in magnets.

Mom took my entrance as an invitation to speak. "Harshna*ben* should have made Sujata stay close to home and not let her go to the Georgetown."

"It's a prestigious university, Mom."

She huffed and poured pancake batter on the griddle.

Sujata had sent me an email yesterday morning to warn me

about the upcoming fallout. Mom would see Sujata's defection as the worst kind of influence on me. Chernobyl was nothing compared to the plume now hovering over our little street in Cary.

By the time I'd eaten half my pancakes, Mom's tirade about how Sujata was ruining her life expanded to include me—how I was wasting my potential, how I was becoming too Americanized, and how I was disrespecting all the sacrifices Mom had made. If there wasn't a button she could push, she created one.

Yup. Fallout.

I let the fork fall to the plate. A sharp edge on the chrome lip of my chair dug into the back of my legs. "This stupid chair is going to rip a hole in my jeans. God! You need to get rid of this ugly thing."

She turned to stare at me, holding the batter bowl midair, brow wrinkled. I pushed back from the table, scraping the chair legs along the linoleum, and chucked my dishes into the sink. If I stayed here any longer, she'd wrench out my tears, for sure, and who'd want to start their first day of school with puffy eyes?

I had bigger things to worry about.

The walk to school would take exactly fifteen minutes at full speed. At half past seven, I bolted downstairs, yelled a goodbye, and ignored Mom's blessings for a good first day. She used to make a whole religious production out of it until I told her I always rubbed off the red *kanku* from my forehead so I wouldn't get made fun of. It had taken years of whining, but she'd finally stopped.

I casually walked off our porch and glanced in either direction for our new neighbor. Except for Mrs. Tolbert walking her dog and the sound of a distant lawn mower, a hollow emptiness surrounded me. I exhaled sharply, not realizing I'd held my breath.

I peeked over my shoulder several times while walking but never saw him. The back entrance of the school and parking lot were crowded, and my eyes darted from face to face, visually barging in on students reuniting with friends. A strange sense of excitement surged through me at the idea of seeing him. Would he be late for his first day at a new school? Could he already be here? The house had been sold in early August, so his parents would've already enrolled him somewhere. Maybe he'd be going to a private school. I bit my lip at the thought and rubbed my chest.

What is wrong with me? I didn't even know what he looked like up close or what grade he'd be in. He could be in college, for all I knew.

His smile flashed across my mind. Would I ever get to see it again?

God, Laxshmi. Get a grip.

I'd memorized my schedule weeks ago—school was my thing, after all. First period was AP U.S. History, which was right around the corner from my bank of beige, paint-chipped lockers. With all the first day reunions, the main artery of the school was crowded and noisy. The familiar smell of locker-room mildew, over-perfumed teenagers, and a faint smell of new pencils tickled my nose.

I waved to two good friends and dancing buddies, Caitlyn and Bailey. They were twins, and the combo of their pale blond hair and willowy frames turned heads wherever they went.

I bopped Bailey on the arm. "I heard you're moving ballet studios."

"Yeah, I am." We hugged each other. "Don't you want to join me?" She, in particular, had taken my quitting hard. We both had dreams of auditioning for UNCSA and transferring for our last two years of high school. Her audition hadn't gone so well though, and now she'd set her sights on majoring in dance in college. She was getting to live my dream.

"You know I can't," I said. "It'll all be about Indian dancing this year. Sorry. But I can still help with drill team, if you need me to."

"Now that I'm captain, we're counting on it," Caitlyn said, giving me a hug.

The five-minute warning bell rang, and we said our goodbyes.

I maneuvered around the cliques of students and throngs of clueless freshmen and found my class. Colonial posters with white men in wigs, black slaves, and women in pouffed dresses had been tacked up everywhere. I slid into a middle desk in the row closest to the door. It wasn't too eager of a seat, nor did it scream slacker. Being by the door meant I could make a quick exit and avoid the bottleneck of students when class let out. I didn't like crowds. They always made me feel awkward and self-conscious, as if they could somehow do more than just invade my personal space.

At the sound of the bell, Mr. Owens closed the door at the back of the room and walked to the front, sharing his class rules along the way. Since taking AP U.S. History was considered an elective, both juniors and seniors filled the class.

Roll call began, and when the teacher paused, I knew it was my name he was stuck on. "Lax ... my—me?" Mr. Owens said.

I rolled my eyes and raised my hand, in case he couldn't see the only Indian girl in the room. Hiding in a deep, dark hole sounded good right about now. "It's Luck-shmee, Laxshmi Kapadia," I pronounced for him. "Here."

After a few more names, he called Jack Thomas. Jack had been part of my life since his sister Shiney and I had become best friends in fifth grade. They were South Indian Christians, and because of that and my friendship with Shiney, Mom tolerated Jack's presence. Otherwise, the mere mention of a boy's name would send her on an anti-male campaign to protect her precious daughter's virginity.

Jack had his irritating, frat boy-like moments, but his older brother routine was sweet—when he wasn't bossing me around. His ever-present rugby or soccer jerseys paired with longboard or cargo shorts—worn spring, summer, fall or winter—always made me shake my head. He'd even told me he'd marry me if Mom kept up with her ranting. We'd always had a good laugh about that. Mom randomly spewed garbage about how no one would marry me since she was a widow and considered unlucky. Even in India she'd be old-school.

The teacher finished roll call and scanned the room. "Anyone else?"

From the back of the class, a strong, deep voice with an Irish accent resonated through the room. "There is. The front office told me to give this to you."

Everyone turned to follow the new kid as he came up my aisle to meet the teacher. He smiled at me, and a funny blip in my chest bubbled up and became a lump lodged in my throat.

It was *him*.

He wore a brand of jeans I'd never seen before, and they fit him the way a pair should fit a guy—good enough to make me bite my lip and take notice. Several girls *ooo*'d and *ahh*'d, and it made me grit my teeth. *What am I jealous for?*

"Liam Whelan, right?" Mr. Owens looked at the transfer paperwork. "Welcome to Cary and your first period homeroom."

Liam thanked him and turned to come back up the aisle, and gorgeous, pale-green eyes locked onto mine.

Oh, God. Look away. Look away. But I couldn't. He was absolutely divine, like one of those Michelangelo statues we'd learned about in Art History.

Was he trying to hide a smile? *Ugh. How arrogant.* He obviously recognized me. Hadn't my reading light been shining on my face? The thought made me sink deeper into my seat. *Breathe in, breathe out.*

I had yet to get a good look at his other features, but at first glance, his dark brown hair clashed with my idea of what an Irish guy should look like. He did have a kind of international swagger separating him from the boys at our school. Most of them were lumbering goofballs, walking around like they didn't fit into their legs.

Mr. Owens handed each student in the front row a stack of history books. As they got passed to me, I turned halfway in my seat to continue sending them down, one at a time. With my breathing under control, I glanced in Liam's direction with a flick of my eyes. He was talking to Jack on the other side of him, who was probably assigned to show him around. Jack loved volunteering for stuff like that. It gave me a good chance to observe Liam while he wasn't looking my way.

With the way he leaned back in the seat with his legs spread out, he showed a confidence I didn't see in the other boys. A small Adam's apple interrupted the line of his throat. I imagined touching the little speed bump and the stubble around it and shivered. Thick, brown eyebrows framed his eyes, but didn't overpower them in an old-man way. A slight scruff shadowed Liam's defined chin and jaw, surrounding full, pink lips. He was animated as he chatted, showing more personality than the boys who tried to act cool. I almost envied Jack. Liam laughed at something and raised his muscular arms to run his hands through his hair.

I gasped at the gorgeous image it created, and my lower abdomen clenched without warning. I spun back around in my desk. What the hell was that? I covered my stomach with my hand, wondering if it would happen again. I waited before turning back around. When my gaze settled on Liam, he was looking down with his shoulders shaking. *Jack must really be a riot today.*

Mr. Owens passed out some paperwork, and it gave me a chance to study Liam again. I'd had countless crushes over the years, but no guy had ever made my heart jump. Even my lip hurt from biting it so hard. I wanted to scream at myself for acting so stupid about a guy. Whatever this was, my reaction wasn't normal. Maybe those pancakes were bad this morning.

Mr. Owens cleared his throat, grabbing Liam's attention, and I whirled around to avoid getting caught gawking.

Liam definitely had the jock-bad-boy vibe going, and I was too timid to tame a wild animal.

When the end-of-class bell rang, I took my time gathering my things. I didn't want to run into Liam in case Jack had kept him by the door to talk. They'd been pretty chatty during the lulls in class. If they were out there, Jack would pull me into an annoying headlock, like he always did. My heart couldn't take any embarrassment today. I entered the hallway, peeking left and right, but there was no sign of them. I sighed. Both relief and disappointment swamped my senses, confusing me even more.

I walked around the corner to my locker and froze. Apparently, Fate loved a joke at my expense. Jack was standing with Liam at his new locker, which was two down from mine. Two doors down from me at home *and* here?

Could my life get any weirder?

I quickly debated whether I needed to drop off my history book at all and decided to carry it for a period or two until I could gather enough courage to return. I darted to the other side of the main artery, but Jack spotted me. *Crap.*

"Hey, girl!" he bellowed.

Seriously? He always called himself a brown Ryan Gosling. I waved halfheartedly and sped up.

"Wait up, Laxshmi."

I stopped and then inched around. *Please don't bring Liam. Please don't bring Liam.*

He was bringing Liam.

"Dude, this is Laxshmi. She lives on your street. You haven't met, right?"

"No," Liam said. "We haven't met—formally." His lip curled up slightly.

Not formally? Ha! My stomach was twisting in knots, and he looked *amused*. I almost snorted out loud.

"Hey, Lucky. I'm Liam." He reached out his hand to shake mine, changing his amused smile into a businesslike one. The nickname sounded flattering coming from him, even though I never let anyone call me Lucky. But the way he lilted the *L* sound …

I widened my stance a bit to keep my balance. My mouth was so dry I cleared my throat to say hello. I reached for his hand, and a spark flared when we touched, like a static charge on a dry, winter day. Both our gazes shot down to our hands before our eyes met again. His forehead wrinkled for a second before he smoothed it out.

I felt oddly comforted by his strong hands, like turning on the light in a dark room, and my heart slowed its pounding. His eyes kept me hostage, or maybe I was just stupid enough to stare.

This is bad. Really bad.

Jack gave him a you-don't-want-to-mess-with-her chuckle. "Nah, man, she doesn't like being called Lucky."

"Ah, sure." Liam kept his focus on me when he spoke.

Our hands slid apart slowly. They'd fit together perfectly, and I missed the comfort. My heart protested the loss by throwing a tantrum against my chest. I stretched out my hand at my side. My fingers tingled. *Weird.* Out of the corner of my eye, I noticed he flexed his fingers too.

"Uh, yeah, it's Laxshmi. Not Lucky." My voice squeaked. I averted my gaze. *Wow. That should set him straight.*

While Jack was telling Liam how to get to his second period class, I casually raised my eyes to Liam. He was studying my face instead of listening to Jack, and he grinned when our eyes met. *Oh. Wow.* This smile was wider, with dimples, and seemed genuine, not like his other smiles. Surprise flashed across his face, and then he schooled his features, probably realizing he didn't want to turn on the charm for a girl like me.

"I'll be seeing you around then," Liam said to me. The businesslike smile returned. "Jack, meet up with you later, yeah?"

Why couldn't I breathe? I'd never acted like such a dunce around a guy I was crushing on, but then again, none of them had ever really spoken to me.

"Yeah, see you later, man." Jack said. "'Bye, Laxshmi." He threw a soft punch at my shoulder before leaving, jarring me out of my stupor.

At least he didn't put me in a headlock.

I took a deep breath and let it out slowly. My heart wouldn't stop pounding. I glanced down and wiggled my fingers. The tingling was fading, and I missed it. So did my subconscious, apparently.

And with one smile, he stole my heart,
Its beat, a wail, at being apart.

Ugh. I managed to start walking, but kept remembering his eyes and how he'd studied me. When was I ever going to learn? My first crush was in second grade. Nicholas Basel. Unrequited—like all the rest since. It was as if there was something unlikeable about me, something so different that I was an anomaly needing to be ignored.

"*I'll be seeing you around then.*" Liam's voice echoed in my head.

CHAPTER 7

Liam

I left second period French, glanced at the map Jack had given me, and headed to calculus.

I'd gotten some Secondary schooling at home because of all the moving about. I'd already studied calculus, American and European literature, several history intensives, some of them in Irish, business classes to help manage the estate, and European poetry, thanks to Da claiming verse as a building block for love. I'd seen it as preparation for my role as clan leader. If not, I'd have spent the summers there hanging about with my cousins causing trouble, no doubt.

I didn't mind the poetry as much as I let on, and I suspected Da of knowing that too. On the rare occasion we got hammered down at our family's pub, we'd start reciting Thomas Moore or Yeats, each of us trying to top the other for a better quote. Those were some of my favorite nights.

Every other memory was soul mate, soul mate, soul mate. *Mo shíorghrá,* Da called it in the Gaelic. My eternal love.

I stepped into my calculus class. The teacher, Mrs. Lenko, was explaining the seating chart in a heavy, Russian accent. Her tight bun and drawn face wouldn't be brooking any arguments. A seating chart was being passed around the room, and once I filled out my name, it'd be my assigned spot for the year. I glanced around the room. An empty desk stood right behind Lucky.

Lucky. I'd been feeling exactly that when Jack introduced her to me. The nickname suited her. I'd wanted to touch her something fierce and had held out my hand, hoping she'd take it. I'd not expected the sizzle up my arm. At first, I'd thought it was static, but what sort of static kept on for several minutes?

I slid in behind Lucky and waited to make myself known to her. When the seating chart came to me, I filled it out and held it over her shoulder. She bolted upright. A wave of her anxiety washed over me. My empath interpretations were mental metaphors where I experienced the emotion, and Lucky's anxiety felt like I was floating on a raft over choppy waters. As with Mum, our readings always expressed themselves through water imagery.

Lucky whipped her head around, and strands of hair framed her face as if they'd been windblown. I could well imagine her in a skimpy bikini on a breezy day. I was hoping it'd not be long before she'd learn to relax around me.

"How lucky to see you again." I flashed her a smile. Her cheeks reddened as if she were flattered. Jack saying she didn't like the nickname tugged at my memory. I got the feeling she didn't much mean it.

But then her eyes narrowed, and she studied my face. "Ha, ha. You're lucky to be so funny." She spun back around.

Christ. I shook my head, laughing to myself. I actually liked the sarcastic lip she was giving me. Maybe she'd have a good sense of humor too. I hoped so. But when the hell was a target ever suspicious of me? They'd giggle, blush, or look behind them to see if I was speaking to someone else, but never question if they could trust me. Maybe Lucky could sense an ulterior motive coming from me.

Sensing someone versus being projected upon was a bit like reading body language instead of being told how someone was feeling. She'd projected her panic that first night on the rooftop as loudly as if she'd been cheering at a rugby match. Accidental, no doubt. Even now, without her projecting her emotions, the body of water carrying her feelings to me was clear and pure—easier to read than most. Not like the muddied shite I was always having to block out from the people around me.

Her projections had rivaled any empath's, but she didn't seem to notice my blocked mind here at school. If she had, she certainly would've recognized me as an empath and raised her guard, giving herself away as she protected herself.

If she was strong enough to be projecting accidentally, once she broke through and became an empath—if she broke through—I wondered if she'd also be having the skill like me and Mum to probe and manipulate emotions. Manipulating wasn't what you'd call an exact science. A manipulated emotion wouldn't last but for a few seconds, but it was a powerful tool that. As clan leader, it'd definitely be giving me the upper hand in negotiations.

I thought I'd push Lucky's latent empath abilities by mucking about a bit. Being exposed to my empathic energy could help break out her abilities, and wouldn't that be nice? With enough exposure, it'd feed the dormant part of her brain, initiating a breakthrough— if she had the genetic potential, that was. Something that never happened with the others. I'd caught a shiver of a chance with the last target, Sejal, but after an entire, frustrating school year, she'd never broken through. Would Lucky be like that—another failure?

I looked at my fingers, remembering the tingling from when we'd shaken hands. Could that mean something? Or was I falling in with Da's useless dreams again? I pushed aside my thoughts and started on my schoolwork while projecting different feelings at

Lucky. Each time she'd stiffen, and she'd scratch her neck as if the sensation were physical. It probably felt like distracting background noise in her head.

I rubbed my palm along my jaw. *Damn.* I shouldn't be messing with her, but how else could I keep this from dragging out a whole year like with Sejal? Memphis had been brutal, and the longer I'd tried to make it work for Da's sake, the harder it had been to lead her on. No doubt Lucky intrigued me, but what if nothing ever came of her potential? Or what if she did break through, but she wasn't my soul mate? Another waste of time it would be.

My mind wandered to a vision of what Laxshmi's eyes would look like if I kissed her. It caught me by surprise, making me cough. *Grand.* Now I was the one with the concentration problem. If I kept this up, I'd have a hard time blocking out my classmates' feelings. I stretched my legs a bit and tugged at my jeans. *Jaysus.* Was I thirteen again?

Keeping other people's emotions out of my head was like blocking calls on my mobile. Normally, most empaths had about a ten- to twenty-foot reading range, so it wasn't too taxing on me, having been an empath since childhood. Unless my concentration was shot to hell, blocking was as simple as breathing. Soon, staying open to Lucky meant she'd have her own ringtone in my head, and I'd be able to lock on to her feelings without having to do anything at all.

When the class bell rang, Lucky bent to pick up a small pile of textbooks from the floor. I hoped she wasn't one of those geeks who carried her books around with her all day. Then again, maybe she was avoiding her locker because of me. The thought left me frowning.

As she got ready to leave, I waited for her. "Going to your locker?" I pointed at her books.

Her surprise came over to me in a gentler ripple than had her other emotions. The gentleness reminded me of a calm day on

Galway Bay—the sand, small waves nipping at my toes, and the sun, glorious on my back. The surprise felt like a warm ocean spray I hadn't been expecting.

"Yeah," she said with a sheepish grin.

"Brilliant. I'm heading there too."

She bit back a smile, her excitement feeling like a frothy surf tickling my toes.

When we approached the door, she rushed to catch it before it shut, almost dropping her books. Most girls would've stood back and waited for me to make a dash to open it, making sure I was being attentive. Lucky didn't seem to want any such nonsense, and I felt a bit off, like I'd put my trainers on the wrong feet. I couldn't shake the feeling of being in unchartered waters.

She stepped to the side and held the door open for me—for *me*—and I had to dive forward to help her steady the load of books threatening to fall.

"Here," I said. "I'll help you carry these—"

"No. I mean, that's okay. You've got your own to carry."

I sensed a genuine concern from her, as if she were afraid to be imposing on me, not something I'd been expecting. I stepped closer, meaning to convince her to let me help, but then her eyes snapped up and met mine. The softness and sincerity in them froze me to the spot. Lighter and more vibrant than the other brown eyes I'd forced myself to stare into—all in the name of being romantic— her eyes drew me in like a kaleidoscope, with amber and black flecks peppering her irises. A soft gasp escaped her lips, and I understood how she felt. With each blink of her long eyelashes, it felt like an eternity before I'd see her eyes again. I had a strange urge to brush my finger over the tips of her lashes.

I swallowed against the dryness in my throat. "I—I just have one book. In my bag." *Jaysus Christ. What is she doing to me?* I couldn't get sucked in. I wouldn't. If I expected anything, it'd only turn into another disappointment.

She stood there, blinking, and dropped the weight of her books into my arms. She was throwing out all kinds of emotions, enough so that I couldn't concentrate on a single one.

"Thanks," she said. Her cheeks became rosy, and she averted her eyes. "I, uh, didn't get a chance to get back to my locker."

A wavy vision of her, like a reflection in disturbed water, told me she was holding back the whole truth. It only confirmed she was avoiding her locker because of me.

We headed toward the main artery of the school, as they called it, back to our lockers. She followed while I led the way through the crowd so she'd not get jostled. When I couldn't sense her clearly, I turned around to make sure she was still there. A small smile played on her lips, but then she looked down and a curtain of silky, black hair hid her face. When the crowd thinned, I turned and waited for her again. She tried to hide another smile, but wasn't fast enough this time. I nearly returned the smile, but I kept my expression impassive.

"I can take it from here if you have to get to class," she said.

Why was she fighting me? Was she trying to get away from me? Had I misread her attraction to me?

"Is it that bad to accept my help?" I asked, genuinely curious.

"What? I mean, no. Thank you. I just, uh, thought you might have to get to class." She bit her lip and fidgeted on sandal-clad feet, obviously embarrassed. I also felt some regret coming off her now. Did she think she'd insulted me?

"Relax, Lucky." Her nickname had the effect I'd been after. She let go of the chaos in her mind and focused on me.

Amazing.

She had pretty decent control of her emotions if she focused. We started down the hall again, this time side by side.

"So, do you always read the lines of your books out loud?" I asked.

Her eyes widened, and I sensed her shock, as if I'd stepped into frigid water.

I was about to continue, but Jack called over from the lockers. "Hey guys, what's up?"

He moved over to Lucky and slung his arm around her shoulder. She flinched and spun out from underneath his arm, pointing a finger in what I assumed was some silent warning. She muttered something about headlocks. Jack laughed and held up his hands in surrender.

She darted a glance at me, and an awkwardness rippled outward. Was I making her feel that way, or was Jack stirring her up? I hated not knowing the reasons behind an emotion. It was the most frustrating thing about being an empath.

Lucky sorted away the books I'd returned and blushed when she caught me studying her. Jack was still hanging about behind us. He mentioned having the next class with Lucky, and I gathered he'd be walking her there. I wondered if I'd be seeing Lucky in any of my other classes.

We closed our lockers at the same time, but she left her hand on the lock like she was needing support.

I leaned in to keep my voice from Jack. "I expect an answer later, yeah?" The way her eyes bored into mine tightened my throat.

"Later, then." She blinked her gorgeous eyes and looked at me as if all her hopes were resting on my shoulders. The weight of it felt comfortable, like I was invincible. It surprised the bloody hell out of me. All I could do was nod and watch her walk away.

Damn. She's a target like all the rest, Liam. You'll do well to remember that.

CHAPTER 8

Lucky

I left for lunch from AP Biology with a textbook at least four inches thick. Would Liam be there at the lockers? Did he have someone to eat with today? I didn't like thinking he'd be alone on his first day of school, but with his smile—his real smile—he could sit on the garbage can, and girls would be lining up to eat with him. I pushed away a pang of jealousy at the thought.

Jack had to talk to the teacher about this year's science fair, so I went on ahead. He was going to meet me by the lockers, and then we'd pick up his sister by the elevators.

Should I ask Liam to join us if I see him? Would I even have the courage? Ugh. Why was I even thinking like this? He was as healthy as eating a bag of chips for dinner, but who cared about being healthy when seeing dimples like his? When he'd leaned in close earlier, all I could think of was touching him and feeling that tingle again. *Stupid, stupid hormones.*

I sneaked a peek before turning the corner and spied Liam leaning against the lockers. He had one foot propped against the metal and was fiddling with his phone. Sunlight streamed from the windows at the end of the hallway, illuminating him from the side like a halo in one of those Renaissance paintings. I couldn't catch my breath. Would my heart ever beat normally around him? I was sure a heart machine would show permanent damage to the way mine worked.

All my familiar anxieties whirled around in my head like leaves caught in cross winds. This would never be a simple crush. No way. He was affecting me physically, for crying out loud.

I wiped a clammy hand against my hip and walked up to Liam, searching for every ounce of confidence I had. He gave me a grin, showing off his dimples, and turned his body toward me. He was even closer to my locker now—close enough for me to touch those dimples, or his lips, or his hair …

Breathe, Laxshmi. I refused to sound like a breathless fangirl.

He waited for me to open my locker. "So?"

"So … what?"

"Are you going to answer my question?"

I looked at his phone. "What were you listening to the other night?"

He slipped it into his pocket. "No fair now, not when I was asking you first." He stared at me with a smug grin and crossed his arms.

"I wasn't talking to myself." I finished with my locker and slammed it shut a little too hard, startling myself. "I was reading certain passages out loud." He didn't need to know I enjoyed practicing my British accent.

He narrowed his eyes like he doubted me.

Whatever. I crossed my arms and turned away from him to wait for Jack. Liam had his answer, so why was he still standing behind me? My guilt got the better of me though, and I bit my lips together. What if he didn't know where to go? Should I ask him to lunch? I looked over my shoulder. Out of the corner of my eye, I saw him looking at me with a devilish grin.

Ugh.

"And by the way," I said. "You still haven't answered *my* question." I didn't dare turn around to face him.

Liam stepped forward, close enough that I could feel his heat warm my back. Before I could move away, he leaned over my shoulder, his lips brushing my hair and the edge of my ear.

"I was listening to music," he said, his voice soft.

His scent overwhelmed me. He smelled like the fresh crisp air after a rainstorm. All I wanted to do was nuzzle his neck and take a deep breath. On an inhale, I inched my face around, met his beautiful light-green eyes, and gasped for the second time today. He was so close I could've kissed him. My face probably looked like a blotchy tomato. His eyes darted to my lips, and I reflexively jerked back, bashing my head against the lockers with a loud clang.

Ow. Klutz. Klutz. Klutz! The other students turned to look at us, and I imagined their thoughts like headlines: *Gorgeous Guy Looks at Bumbling Brown Girl Near Locker.*

We both reached for my throbbing head, but he stopped short of touching me. It was like he'd made a conscious decision not to touch the weird girl.

"Mind yourself," he said, his voice raspy.

I stared into his eyes and froze. They weren't filled with the cocky playfulness from before. They looked concerned, which made me feel worse. How was I supposed to avoid getting my heart crushed if he was nice on top of everything else?

He studied my face, focusing on my lips. The thing with my lower abdomen happened again, just like before, and I swallowed my gasp.

His after-a-rainstorm fragrance, or pheromone, or whatever it was, obliterated what senses were still working, making me feel more naked than if I had taken my clothes off. I tried my best to push oxygen into my body so I could regain some control, but it was useless. I was floating on a cloud of *eau de Liam.*

Somehow I sidestepped him and caught sight of Jack speeding toward us.

"Are you okay?" Jack asked, glancing from me to Liam, his eyebrows gathered tight. Jack must have seen what had happened. "I thought we were meeting by the elevator," he said to Liam.

"Got done with gym early," Liam said, shrugging. "So I came here."

Liam's joining us for lunch? I reined in my excitement. Jack turned back to me, waiting for an answer.

"Yeah, I'm fine. Just bumped my head. Let's go get Shiney." Something had to distract me from Liam's scent before I threw myself at him. In a desperate move, I linked arms with Jack and dragged him down the hallway with me. Liam followed, but my eyes stayed glued straight ahead.

We met Shiney at the elevator. She waved to me in her usual flinging-her-hand-about motion and widened her eyes when she saw Liam. *Oh, this'll be interesting.*

"Liam," Jack said. "This is my little sister, Shiney, and yes, that's her actual name. Shiney, this is Liam."

"Hey," she squealed, lending credence to the nickname Jack had given her years ago—Piggy. A huge smile appeared on her face, and her black curls bobbed. "Although, I'm not *that* little. I'm only a year younger." She let out a high-pitched cackle. Was she nervous? "I mean, I am little, like short little, but I guess you can see that for yourself."

Yup, definitely nervous. Even Jack shoved his hands in the pockets of his cargo shorts and shook his head.

"A pleasure to meet you," Liam said, offering a tight-lipped smile. I wondered why he didn't shake her hand.

"Oh, you're Irish?" She giggled.

"That I am." He shot me a sideways glance, catching me staring, and his lips turned up slightly. My cheeks warmed, making me bow my head and check out the carpet stains.

"That's so cool." Shiney drew out the word *so* and giggled again. *Geez.* No chance she'd tone it down now, but it didn't bother me. She'd had a major crush on a guy from her Bible study group for years.

Did I really just think that? I shook my head clear.

We split off in pairs when we got to the lunch line, and all Shiney could talk about was Liam's Irish accent. I gave her a brief rundown of the moving truck and how his locker happened to be near mine too. I left out the rooftop and the unexpected heart palpitations. The lunch line really wasn't the place for that kind of analysis.

"It's a sign," she whispered.

I grimaced. If it were, it'd be a *bad* sign. I knew where this was headed. Months of parsing his every stray word, sentence, and gesture, months of longing and daydreaming, and months of thinking I wasn't good enough for him.

I touched my ear, remembering how close he'd been.

We all took our food to the tables nearest the tray return. Shiney and Jack sat on one side, leaving me and Liam to the other. Jack and Liam were talking about soccer, and I watched as Shiney made some futile attempts to join in. She would unleash a million questions any moment now. I was almost embarrassed for her.

When the conversation lulled, she exploded. "So, Liam, where did you move from? And are you a senior like Jack?"

"Memphis. Atlanta before that. And, uh, I'm a senior, minus a credit or two." He shrugged. "Transfer issues."

Undaunted, she continued. "Oh. So you move around a lot? Why did you move here? What do your parents do?"

I'd seen this side of her. She wasn't going to stop. I wondered idly if she should consider journalism as a career.

Shiney stopped for a breath after a dozen more questions and then continued, asking about Irish sayings, leprechauns, and the difference between clovers and shamrocks. Liam squirmed in his seat, and I wanted to burst into laughter. I took a bite of my apple pie, wondering if I should save him.

"If you stay in America, will you go to college here?" she asked.

"My heart's set on going back," Liam said. "I've got loads of family waiting on me to return."

Oh. My bite of pie felt as heavy as lead, dropping into my stomach after a hard swallow. *Seriously, Laxshmi. You hardly know him.*

Jack put an unopened vanilla pudding on my tray. I scrunched up my nose and threw it back with a bit too much force. "Why are you giving it to me? You know I hate vanilla." The snap in my voice surprised me.

"Since when?" he asked.

"Duh, since always, stupid," Shiney chimed in.

Jack shrugged one shoulder, peeled back the lid, and began eating. Liam turned to me, concern like before back on his face. I focused on my pie and ignored him. Why was he affecting me so much? I took a deep breath to relax.

Shiney leaned forward, as if getting ready to start her questioning again. Out of the corner of my eye, I saw Liam fidget, and a strange awkwardness blew through me. I held my fork midair for a moment. Why would *I* feel awkward? Liam and I turned to each other, his head tilted as if he were curious.

"So, Li—"

"Hey, Shiney?" I interrupted. "Weren't you going to the mall this weekend?" Liam obviously needed saving.

She took the bait, and I thought I heard Liam sigh in relief. My strange mood lifted at his relief, and I wanted to laugh.

"Oh, yeah," she said. "On Saturday though. We have a church

thing on Sunday. Don't forget, Jack. You promised to take me."

"I haven't forgotten," he said, his mouth full.

"Ooo, Liam, why don't you come? You too, Laxshmi," Shiney said.

I choked on my water. *Crap.* Let the weeklong obsess-fest begin.

"Ahh, the mall." Liam's eyes were fixed on me. "Will you be going, Lucky?"

Jack and Shiney fell silent. An understatement really. It felt like they'd stopped breathing too. Liam didn't seem fazed though. Shiney stared at him, and Jack smirked with his I-warned-you face. They knew I didn't react well to people calling me Lucky. Well, *other* people. The way Liam said it seemed to connect us. Judging by how I was reacting to him, I wouldn't be surprised if it was just wishful thinking.

He leaned over, his well-defined biceps propped on the table, and looked right into my eyes. I had no doubt he was taking full advantage of his good looks, and—*God*—was it unnerving. I wondered if he could tell my heart was racing.

"Lucky?"

"Why do you ask?" I felt my eyes narrow. If he kept staring me down, my food was going to lurch back up.

"Just curious."

Shiney broke the spell. "*Pft.* Of course she is."

He turned to Jack and Shiney. "Can I get back to you on it?"

That settled it. If he was remotely interested in me—one iota interested—he would've jumped at the chance of coming with us. But he didn't, which had to mean he was only being nice to me. *Doesn't it?* Or maybe he was just being diplomatic.

Great. Let the parsing begin.

We started talking about colleges, and Jack mentioned my mom had called his mom last week and asked about accelerated med school programs.

"Wonderful." I groaned, my appetite destroyed.

Liam looked a bit left out, so I filled him in. "My mom expects me to go to medical school. I pretty much have no choice about it."

He gave me an earnest look. "I know the feeling—of not having a choice, I mean." The gravity with how he said it gave me chills. It was our first time sharing anything personal. When I tore my gaze away from Liam, Jack was watching us.

The fifth period bell would ring soon. Jack and Liam got up to leave. Shiney stopped her brother to ask him something, so Liam turned to me. He placed a hand beside me on the table and leaned in. "I'll be seeing you later at the lockers, yeah?"

I looked up into his pale-green eyes. "If that gets you through the rest of your day, sure." *Oh. My. God. Did I just say that?* I stifled a nervous laugh-whimper.

His eyes widened, and another one of his dimpled grins lit up his face. He rubbed his hand across his jaw while he shook his head. I was running on pure adrenaline at this point.

"It'll have to now, won't it?" he asked.

All I could do was turn to my tray and press my lips together to keep from smiling like a loon. I didn't have to watch to know he'd left. The magnetic pull was gone.

"He keeps looking back at you." Shiney squealed and bounced in her seat. "Oh, and his accent is like ... well it's like butter. He's so cute. Don't you think so ... *Lucky?*"

I rolled my eyes. "Well, yeah, sort of, but come on. He's a senior, and he'll probably have the entire cheerleading squad drooling over him by tomorrow."

Shiney and I saw Liam again at the start of last period in the language arts hallway. He and Jack had English right next door to our own English class. Shiney thought it was kismet, but the more I saw him, the more trouble it would mean. After class ended, I scrambled my things together. Liam was expecting to see me at the lockers, and my stomach had fluttered all through class in anticipation.

I turned the corner and bumped right into him.

"Look at you there," he said.

"You were waiting for me?" I hoped I didn't sound too excited.

His eyes twinkled as if he were thinking of a private joke. "We're going along in the same direction, now aren't we?"

"I suppose," I said slowly.

"Relax, Lucky. Are you always this suspicious of people?"

I felt my eyes narrowing again, so I relaxed my face. "Nope, apparently it's just you."

"Meself?" He slapped his hand to his heart playfully. "Shouldn't I be wary of you? You were the one spying on me first off."

My face burned. "Well, it's not like I could really see you in the dark. Anyone would've been curious about a guy hanging out up there. Who does that?" A group of a dozen or so students barreled toward us. He grabbed my bag strap and steered me around them while I babbled on. "You, on the other hand, could watch me like … like my window was a movie screen. So who was the one spying, hmm?"

"Is this you slagging me a bit?"

"Depends. What's slagging?"

"Making fun of me, of course."

I laughed out loud. "I guess I am."

We got to the lockers to find an end-of-day crowd blocking the way. We waited our turn and when the area thinned out, we stepped up to our lockers. Between us, a tiny ninth-grader was decorating the outside of hers with pink stickers. Once Liam was done, he came over to my side and studied me while I finished.

"What?" I asked.

"Just waiting on you. We'll be heading in the same direction, yeah?"

He wanted to walk home with me?

It had to be because he didn't know anyone else. In a few days, he'd likely be watching the cheerleaders practice after school anyway.

Temper your heart, and take it slow,
He's just being nice, so let it go.

He stood there watching me while I'd zoned out. Why did these couplets pop into my head at the most God-awful times?

He wants to walk me home! I allowed myself to grin.

"What is it you're thinking?" he asked. "Is it other plans you've got?"

"Me? No. No other plans. Just curious about you."

"Curious? Ah, sure you mean suspicious, yeah?"

"Uh ... yeah, that too." I suppressed the urge to giggle nervously. "So, I, uh, see you made it through your day." I raised an eyebrow, trying to be smug like him.

He let out an exaggerated breath. "It was brutal, but that I did."

I stifled a snort. "Yeah, right." I put my thinner textbooks and notebooks in my messenger bag so they wouldn't be slipping out of my hands. Thank God I could leave most of them at home.

He studied me for a moment. "I'm thinking I like it when you're a touch more relaxed."

My heart jumped into my throat, probably bulging through my skin like that thing in the movie *Aliens*.

Breathe, Laxshmi.

"Thanks, I guess. So, uh, you never really answered my question earlier ... when I hit my head." I scrunched my eyes closed behind the locker door. Did I really just remind him how klutzy I'd been? I peeked out to see his reaction.

He had his fist covering his mouth, trying to hide his laughter. "Oh, I believe that I already did right enough."

I shot him a ha-ha-you're-so-funny look. "Music? That's hardly an answer." Nothing more would fit in my bag, so I held the rest and closed my locker.

"But now it'd be my turn—what was it you were reading?"

"Fine. *Wuthering Heights*." We turned toward the stairs.

"And why were you reading out—?"

"Hey! My turn."

He put his hands up in the air and laughed. "You've got the right of it. Go on."

"What music were you listening to? Be specific."

"Dave Matthews Band, their 'Crash Into Me.'"

"Nice." I nodded, smiling and remembering the lyrics. "Too bad I'm not wearing a skirt to hike up." My face heated. Where was my filter?

"Sorry?" He opened the door to the stairwell for me. Even confused, he looked hot.

I stopped right in front of him and tilted my head back to meet his eyes, trying to look calmer than I felt. "The lyrics?"

He narrowed his eyes, but didn't seem to catch on.

"Never mind. It's not like I'd show you my world anyway." I chuckled. Caitlyn and Bailey's parents worshipped the Dave Matthews Band, and they'd played DMB in the car on the way to and from dance practices for years.

Liam must have realized which line I was referring to, and his mouth made a little *O*. The blood rushed to his face.

Ha! I just made him blush.

He stood there, shaking his head and scratching the bridge of his nose as if he could make it stop. I studied his face, and when he showed me his dimples, I couldn't help but giggle. I covered my lips with my fingers to keep from gloating.

"Don't worry. I happen to love the song." I turned and flew

down the stairs as carefully as I could with four textbooks locked in my arms. I had to leave before I blurted out something stupid, like the song was how I wanted a guy to feel about me.

Twice now, he'd gotten me to say something I'd never imagined coming out of my mouth. At this rate, I'd commit social suicide by tomorrow.

Liam caught up with me, but I couldn't even face him. We walked side by side through the parking lot without saying a word. Between the blacktop and all the metal, the August sun made it feel like an oven. It wasn't helped by the stench of heated asphalt either. We reached the back of the school property and paused to let a car pass. Its blaring stereo made our silence more awkward. I turned to find the corners of his lips turned up, his eyes twinkling as if he found all of this amusing. *Figures.* His smile was contagious though.

"So why would you be reading *Wuthering Heights* to yourself?" Hearing his voice was as soothing as the shade from the surrounding trees.

"I was trying to read Joseph's accent. Well, *hear* it, actually. Now my turn. When did you know I was watching you?"

"Shortly after getting on the roof. It wasn't until later I could see much of you—the sun's glare, you know."

He'd probably wondered who his rude, nosy neighbor was.

"Sorry. I didn't mean to invade your privacy or anything."

"No worries, yeah? Now, do you know what your question says about you?"

I stopped at the first intersection we came to and faced him. "What?"

"You could've asked what it was that I was seeing," he said. "Or if I'd caught you doing anything strange. But you didn't." He laughed when I groaned.

Yup, he saw me picking my teeth.

He nudged my elbow. "Means you're a fine girl, one who's worrying about others more than herself. We'd be calling that bighearted in my family." His brow wrinkled as if he remembered something.

Bighearted? My forehead itched. I turned to cross the street. Liam followed. Shiney had always warned how people might take advantage of me for being too nice. Even Jack agreed, telling me it was why Mom walked all over me. It was a weakness, and I wasn't exactly jumping up and down that Liam had picked up on it. Would he take advantage of me? Flash me a grin and get me to do his homework for him?

"Lucky, did I say something wrong?" He stopped, so I did too. "I was only meaning it as a compliment, yeah?"

Damn him. The sweet, concerned expression was back again. I sighed. I didn't want him to feel bad—obviously, an effect of being too bighearted—so I gave him my best attempt at a flirty-smile instead. "Is that your question?"

"It is. I'm wanting to know whatever's going through your head just now."

Nobody I knew would be so direct. I liked it because it felt genuine and honest, despite the cocky and flirtatious side of him that I'd seen today. He didn't seem nervous about being himself. *This* Liam was the real one. The one hidden behind the businesslike smile and smug good looks.

"No." I cleared my throat. "You didn't say anything wrong. It was like you read me, but you barely know me." I shrugged. "I'm used to my anonymity, I guess."

Liam studied me, and I wondered if he scrutinized everyone like this. What could he be thinking?

"I suppose I'm after the same." His gaze followed a car down the street, and he turned to continue down the sidewalk.

With a few quick steps, I caught up to him. "Okay, so why do you like your anonymity? You don't seem the shy type."

He shrugged. "We've moved around more than a good bit. It's easier to, well … to hold back when it's a dead certainty you'll be uprooted in no time at all."

A strange feeling blew through me, making me desperate to chase after it, like something was being kept from me. I rolled my neck, thinking the heat was probably getting to me, but the sensation persisted.

"What's troubling you?" he asked.

"I–I feel like … like you're leaving something out. I mean, I don't doubt it's hard moving around, but … " His eyes widened for a brief second before he smoothed away the expression. *Crap.* "I'm sorry, Liam. I didn't mean to pry."

"It's not … not that. It's just turnabout and all, I suppose."

"I don't understand."

We crossed another small street and only had one more block to walk before we reached our homes. I'd carry my entire locker full of books every day to keep walking with him.

His mouth curved up. "It's an odd feeling this. I'm not used to anyone reading me, and certainly not as well as you've been doing anyhow."

"Really? Wait. As well as I've been? When did I read you before?"

"That's more like three questions you're asking, isn't it now?"

"Just the one, smarty-pants. You got to ask two in a row. If this wasn't my first time, then when?"

He laughed. "No, this wasn't your first time, and something tells me it'll not be the last."

"You still haven't answered me," I said, raising my eyebrows.

He scrunched up his face like he was embarrassed. "You stepped in, saving me from Shiney. At lunch. I know she's your mate—"

I giggled. "You should've seen yourself squirming."

He grinned, and my giggles turned into full-blown laughter, making him laugh too. We laughed so hard we had to stop walking. When I finally got myself under control, I caught Liam studying my face again with a small smile and one of those far-off looks. I used my shoulder to dry my tears, and felt the alternating warmth and coolness as sunlight filtered through the swaying branches overhead.

He must have realized he was staring at me and looked down.

"Christ, Lucky." He jerked forward and grabbed the books from me. "I should've taken these from you earlier. I'm sorry. Why didn't you give me a word over it?"

I didn't complain this time. The muscles in my shoulders felt instant relief. I rubbed at the red crease marks embedded into my forearms.

"Don't be sorry, Liam. They're not your books."

"I'm such a git," he whispered. He held my entire pile of books with one arm, while I'd needed both. "Sorry. I'd not meant to grab them." He pointed at my arms. "You sure you're right enough?"

"I'm fine. Thank you, by the way." We started walking again. "Oh, and I count that as your question."

His eyes twinkled as he muttered the word *greedy*. "Well, go on with you then."

"On the roof Saturday, why did you look so sad? I couldn't really see your face, but you almost seemed ... hopeless."

He ran his free hand through his hair and sighed. *Oh no.* I was prying again. We hardly knew each other, and here I was asking something personal. "If you don't want to—"

"No, no, it's not a bother. At times it seems the moving will never end. That the search—well, it's brutal. That's all."

We'd reached my house, and I wanted to ask so many more questions. Liam gave me my books back. Having to leave him left a pit in my stomach.

"Take care of yourself, then," he said. His eyes locked onto mine. "I'll see you tomorrow, yeah?"

I nodded. "Wait. You're not feeling that hopelessness now, are you?" Why I'd blurted that out, I didn't know, but something about it felt right.

He stared at me for a long moment before his face relaxed. His grin was all I could see now. "Lucky, Lucky, Lucky. Like I said, not your first time, and it'll not be your last."

CHAPTER 9

Liam

I jogged across Lucky's front garden and turned back when I reached the pavement. She was leaning against the railing of her front porch, a brilliant smile warm on her face.

I had to force my feet to move, realizing it was too late—I'd been sucked in by Lucky's charm.

Damn, and all in one day.

I couldn't believe how much I already liked being with her. The purity of her emotions was a rare thing. Like a prisoner being set free, I could take my first deep breath. She'd had me admitting to things I'd never thought I'd say to a girl. Jaysus, I never expected one I was after to leave me speechless either. I'd lost count of the number of times she'd surprised me. None of the other targets had ever read me like Lucky could—not a one had even come close.

When she was laughing, I'd not been able to take my eyes off the curve of her neck or how carefree her expression could turn. I looked over my shoulder to see if she was still there, but she'd gone inside.

Ciarán would be saying I'd started thinking with the wrong head. Maybe he had the right of it.

I reached our front porch. Flattened boxes were being held down by a large empty planter, and a faint smell of bleach clung to the air. Cleaners must have come by today to deal with the built-up grime and mildew on the outside of the house. With each new home we'd lived in, Mum and Da had fixed it up proper and when we traveled on, they'd donate it to a local charity. It reminded me how another of Da's visions could take me away tomorrow or in a week if Lucky wasn't my soul mate.

For the first time, the idea bothered me and not because I was that tired of moving.

Starving, I headed inside and to the kitchen, one recently refurbished by the previous owners. They'd seemed to have no other idea than to be putting white on white with more white. It was bloody eye-blinding.

A roast beef sandwich waited for me in the fridge, made the way I liked—crusty bread, Gouda cheese, lettuce, and tomato. The faint smell of grainy mustard had my mouth watering. I poured out some milk, sat at our maple kitchen table—an invader from the past in the stark, too-modern white—and devoured the first half of my sandwich. Now that my stomach was no longer possessed, I had to figure out what to do about Lucky.

Could she really be The One—would this end the blasted search? Or was she simply the next puzzle piece—another close miss? Each of the targets had matched up to Da's visions in one way or another, but none of them had ever matched so close as Lucky. That had to mean something. Then why wasn't I sure as certain? Why didn't I know down to my bones that she was the end of our quest? Why wasn't I getting a bleedin' sign about it?

I supposed if there had been one, Da would've told me already.

Hard as I tried, I could never feel anything more than friendship for Sejal back in Memphis. I'd had to string her along for the entire school year before Da finally had himself another vision, confirming what I'd already come to know—Sejal wasn't The One. There had to be something more than just gut instinct at work here. Knowing how Sejal had felt about me and knowing I'd have to break her heart in the end had been bloody torture. She'd seemed to have all the traits, save one—she'd not been strong enough. In a battle of wills, my money would be on Lucky.

I snorted. Like I'd let the two of them ever meet up.

More importantly, what was I going to be telling my parents about Lucky? I didn't want the pressure from Da.

Mum brought a small box into the kitchen, kissing the top of my head as she passed. "So, darling, how was your first day?" she asked, setting the box on the counter.

"Grand."

"Did you meet the potential candidate?"

I let out a small laugh. She hated using the word *target*. "That I did."

Mum smiled. "Lovely, darling. And her name?"

"Luck—Laxshmi Kapadia. She lives not two doors down, on the other side of Mrs. Robertson."

Mum pulled some magnets from the box and put them onto the fridge. She'd acquired a collection over the years, one from everywhere we'd lived and visited. "Did you get to spend some time with her then?"

"Some." Lucky's smile at the end of the day flashed across my mind, and I barely kept myself from grinning.

She turned to me just as I masked my expression. "And? What are your impressions?"

I thought of Lucky's legs and had to stop myself from rubbing my neck. I blocked my emotions from Mum most of the time, so she'd analyze my body language like it was the key to the universe.

"Don't have any yet—" *Damn.* She'd take that as no more than an invitation to pry, to be sure. With each target, I'd always come home with something to say.

She's quiet, but I'll get her to talking.

She's an easy one to talk to—and she's got potential enough.

She's a nervous one, but I'll get her to relax.

I probably said more than most guys would tell their mums, but this quest of mine made the bloody situation a bit different than normal dating.

I'd been excited about it in the beginning, giving each of the targets a hand-carved gift. Woodworking was a hobby Great-Granddad O'Connor and I had shared. It'd been naive of me to think the gift would mark some important moment. By the time we reached Memphis, carving one had become a chore. I did it anyhow.

And damn if I wasn't already imagining what I'd be carving for Lucky.

Mum raised an eyebrow and took a long look at me, giving me the I-really-want-to-read-you glance I knew all too well. She sighed and put a kettle on to boil. *Thank God.*

"Is she an empath yet?" she asked.

"No, she wasn't sensing my blocking her."

Two things had to happen for Lucky to become a full empath. First, she had to sense emotions, which she seemed to be doing a fair bit of already. Second, she had to be able to sense another empath's mental block. I'd be testing Lucky as much as possible to see if she had the gifts to make such a leap.

"What of her potential then?" Mum asked.

Good. A safe topic. "You'll love this—it's off the charts."

Mum raised her eyebrows. "Really?"

She headed into the front room, brought back one of her spiral research notebooks and settled herself into the chair beside me. Her specialty was studying empaths, and we'd been rating the targets' empathic potential from the beginning. Back then, she'd call me her little grad student. I pushed my bread crumbs around the plate, waiting for her to finish jotting down her notes. When she was ready, I described the three times Lucky had read me, telling Mum the last emotion was optimism instead of the hope I'd felt. Anything to sound like less of a sap.

"And how would you rate the last one, darling?"

"Clear ten. She was plucking the feeling right out of my head when I hadn't even got around to acknowledging it myself." That was a lie. I'd known it was there, buried under six years of wasted time.

Mum wagged her pen at me. "That is impressive. She definitely shows more promise than the others. Your father did say she'd be a strong empath."

"Yeah, but that's after we've joined and become soulmated," I said. "And has Da come any closer to finding out what the hell this joining is meant to be?" I pushed back my chair and crossed my arms. It probably meant sex, which was fine by me, but the parents weren't so convinced as of yet.

She frowned. "Watch your language. Laxshmi couldn't become a strong empath if she didn't have a high EQ potential to begin with, now could she?" She got up and began steeping her tea.

Years ago, Mum had developed the test to determine an empath's empathic quotient, like an IQ test. It made her a big deal in the empath community.

I stared out the kitchen window. The view of our neighbor's chain-link fence and his tangled garden hose reminded me how much I missed the views from home. *Home.* I thought about Lucky and what had happened at the lockers before lunch. I'd only meant to taunt her when I crowded close, but her scent had been overwhelming. It caught me off guard and took me back to my summers in Ireland, where I'd hang about in the meadows behind our home, laughing, talking, and having a grand old hooley with the cousins.

The neighbor's air-conditioning unit whirled on, and I slumped in my chair.

Lucky's scent seemed close, like she was right in front of me, and that made me think on her eyes and those long, dark lashes of hers. They were so inviting. I'd almost leaned in to kiss her, but then she'd freaked and banged her head on the lockers. The urge to touch and comfort would've won its way with me had she not slipped out of my grasp. I couldn't lose control like that again. How could I be focusing on the job while acting like a lovesick puppy at the same time?

The smell of Darjeeling filled the kitchen and drew me out of my daydream.

"Your father and I still haven't discovered what the joining entails, but we don't suspect it will be a simple process. He's working on it every day, however. We think we know what it is *not*, but if it is sex, well … then … you'll have to wait until you both are married." Mum sat with her teapot, cup, and saucer and gave me the all-too-familiar look that threatened she'd drag me to confession if necessary.

Was she bloody serious?

"What is she like?" She poured herself some tea.

I scrubbed my hands over my face. I knew she'd find her way back to finding out more. I had to be giving her something, or I'd not hear the end of the matter.

"I could see dating her, I suppose." I shrugged.

Mum raised her eyebrows. "That's new, isn't it? I'm happy for you, darling. I would like for you to have a normal relationship for once." She took a sip of her tea. "Is she pretty?"

I thought of her eyes and my face warmed. I looked down a tad too late.

Mum laughed. "I'll take that as a yes, then."

"Jaysus, Mum. Can you not understand I don't want to talk to my *mother* about this?" What was I meant to tell her? That Lucky was topping with an eleven out of ten on my rating scale?

"Come now and out with it. Tell me about her."

"Fine. She projects. She'll send out several feelings all at once in a blast almost. It was … actually entertaining."

"She projects? Already? Interesting." She took another sip and then gasped, narrowing her eyes at me. "Liam, you weren't projecting on her to push her, were you?"

Shite. I looked at the checkerboard pattern the grout lines made with the tile floor and scratched the side of my head.

She clinked her cup down onto the saucer. "Liam Whelan, did you or did you not?"

"A bit, all right?" I raised my hands. "I'll not be waiting a year like in Memphis to find out if she's my soul mate, so I pushed a little, tested her, and I was right to do so."

"You know how I feel about that. I don't like manipulating a non-empath."

"I know and I'm sorry enough for it. But no worries. No manipulation was involved. And she handled my projections, she did. No harm done. She even embarrassed me later, giving me back some of me own—in a good way, of course." I tried to hide a smile.

She shook her head, but she was fighting a smile too. "Is she in any of your classes?"

"Two of them."

"Which ones?"

"History and calculus."

She pushed a wavy lock of her blond hair out of her face. "Those are your AP classes, are they not?"

Mum and Da loved nothing more than to match each target with descriptions from his visions. Comparing Lucky to those bleedin' visions didn't feel right—Lucky was just … Lucky. For once, I was wishing they'd leave me be. "She's smart as a whip. Isn't that what the old man always says? Should I be sending out wedding invites now?"

"Liam, why are you acting like this?"

"You're the shrink, yeah? You'll be telling me, won't you?"

Her brow furrowed. She finished her tea and rose to wash her cup, taking my plate with her. Even though I wasn't trying to read her, I was sensing her disappointment. She hated when I didn't respect what she did. *Well, bloody hell and damn me hide.*

I went up to her and rested my chin on her shoulder. "I'm sorry, Mum."

She turned off the faucet and leaned her head against mine. "You know I'm on your side. I love you."

I took a deep breath and caved. "Fine enough. Yes, Lucky's beautiful and brilliant."

She turned to me, her eyes wide. "You call her Lucky? Tell me more about her, or I'll die of curiosity."

Jaysus, why had I ever opened my trap? "Sorry you don't have a girl, Mum."

Straightening, she pursed her lips. "Nonsense." She dried her hands and turned to face me. "Did you learn anything about her family? Does she have siblings? What does she want to do with her life?"

And I'd thought Shiney's interrogation had been bad.

I answered as many of Mum's questions as I could, but for the most part, I was clueless. Each one kept reminding me how little I knew about Lucky. Several dozen rapid-fire questions later, I was ready to gouge out my eyes. I groaned, realizing Da would be worse.

"Mum! Like I'd said before, I didn't ask. Are you done now with your inquisition?"

"Liam Whelan, this could be important. We didn't uproot ourselves time and again for the last six years only for you to shut yourself off like this. My shrinky powers—as you call them—are telling me you took a shine to her. So, yes, I would like to know more about her." She sounded stern, but her eyes were soft. "This time next year, she could very well be my daughter-in-law."

Whoa. "Next year? For Christ's sake, can you not cut me

some slack here? I'm not doing all of this to get myself shackled at eighteen." I stormed out of the kitchen, kicking a chair out of my way. This conversation had gone on long enough.

She followed after me. "Liam, don't you dare take the Lord's name in vain in this house. I've taught you better."

I grabbed my bag, ran upstairs, and slammed my bedroom door. Thankfully, she stayed downstairs.

I blared the stereo, looping "Crash Into Me" on repeat, and lay back on my bed. It was a live recording, and with my eyes closed, I imagined I was at the concert. When he sang the line Lucky had quoted, I felt my cheeks stretch into a smile.

Could Lucky be The One?

She was different—*real*. She could flirt too. Who the hell had ever made me blush before? Once she relaxed, she was a right bit of fun. The line she'd laid on me at lunch had almost made me piss my pants. "*If that gets you through the rest of your day, sure.*" I couldn't wait to see what she'd be like tomorrow.

But I'd have to be careful.

Sejal had been promising at first too. What if Lucky turned out like Sejal? What if she was another brilliant display of fireworks that fizzled out in time?

Glancing at the clock, I wondered how Ciarán would be keeping himself. Was it too early to be telling him about Lucky? *Yeah, probably.* I already knew what he'd say. He'd say something about the novelty wearing off and the targets being so useless that not even the tide would take them out. I could always count on him being crass.

But if Lucky wasn't my soul mate, what was I going to do? Screw the search and stay behind to date her for no better reason than my liking her? Or keep searching until I graduated? I covered my face with a pillow and groaned.

If Lucky was The One, I wanted to start living my life—return home to Ireland, go to university, and start heading up the estate.

But even with Lucky there with me, I surely couldn't see myself in love, starting up a family, and all that shite. Not yet, anyhow. Empath politics was out of the question as well. Uncle Nigel could keep holding those reins, as far as I was concerned.

I got up, cracked open my physics book, and began doing my schoolwork. Two hours later, Mum called me down for supper. Da had brought take-out Chinese, and Mum was setting it up in the dining room, now that all the boxes were off the oak table. It was the one room downstairs with enough uninterrupted wall space to hang all the family photos. Between Granddad Whelan's family manor in Waterford, Great-Granddad O'Connor's estate outside of Dublin, and Granddad O'Connor's estate in Wales, we had more family reunions crammed into each summer than most did in a decade, and we had the pictures to prove the fact of it. That was the life waiting for me.

Da's questions about Lucky would surely make the meal a nightmare. If I'd not been so damned hungry, I'd have skipped the whole bloody supper.

He came out of the kitchen drying his hands on one of Mum's dainty towels. "So what's the story? Have you met the target then?"

My attention jerked to Mum who was putting serving spoons in the take-out. *She hasn't told him.* For the first time ever, she'd left it up to me.

"No, not yet." The lie came out as easily as my smile. Would Mum rat on me? She wouldn't look my way, so I assumed she was right enough with me not telling Da anything for now. For once, he'd not be plaguing me by going on and on about my soul mate. I rolled my shoulders, not realizing how tense they'd been. Or had I been tense because I didn't want to be thinking of Lucky as a target?

"No worries. It'll be happening soon enough." He sat down to eat but stared off for a moment. "Yes, it must. It must." He rubbed his stubble. "Pass the soy sauce, if you'll be so kind?" He doused his food and cleared his throat. "Moira, love, an email came in today." He shoved some noodles in his mouth.

"From?"

He swallowed and took a swig of his Guinness. "The Elders."

She put down the container of sesame chicken and stared at Da.

"What's wrong?" I asked, looking from one to the other. The tension felt like the humidity outside.

Mum went back to serving herself chicken, and Da's mind was closed off to me as usual. I slapped down my chopsticks. "I'm not a child, for Christ's sake. So will someone please be telling me what the hell is going on?"

"Liam, language! How many—?"

"Leave him be, love," Da said. "One of their ministers will be flying into Charlotte. They're wanting a meeting with me."

"When?" she asked, her fork suspended midair. It looked like she was holding her breath.

He wiped his mouth. "Sunday."

"I'm coming with," I said.

Mum shook her head. "You most certainly will not. Tell him, Patrick. Pass me the beef, please."

"Mum—"

She clenched her hands together, as if in prayer. "Liam, the testing was different. You have no experience with this brand of politics, and I'll not have you dragged into anything. You will allow your father to handle this."

"If this concerns me, I will be going along," I said.

Da cleared his throat. "Let him, Moira." He averted his eyes and shrugged. "They may not be coming about the visions." He sounded as if he were convincing himself. "If they are ... well, we have time yet, we do."

Time?

Mum distracted me with an empathic warning that felt like hot water scalding my skin. Her intention was clear—my little lie to Da could backfire.

We normally blocked our own emotions as a rule, unless we had to project an emotion to send a message. To accept messages from those closest to us, we kept our minds open, but only in one direction—to accept incoming calls.

"Of course, that's what they're coming for, Patrick. If the top-ranking members in the Line of Ascension think Liam—soulmated or not—is a threat to their positions, I've no doubt they'll try to silence him or manipulate him for their own gain. The Elders are not getting any younger. If one of them should pass soon, Liam could get caught up in a feeding frenzy to rival those sharks you're so fond of on the telly. He's not ready for that."

I didn't know if I should be upset at Mum's lack of faith in me or if I should just be thankful she didn't want me in politics.

Mum's lineage came from one of the five original royal empath houses of Ireland—only four of which were still around. Since we didn't follow the rules of primogeniture, once Great-Granddad O'Connor had passed, the Elders had scheduled the test to determine the strongest empath in our family. Those of us over eighteen had taken part in it. I beat out all the eligible cousins, along with granddad, Mum, and both of her brothers, Nigel and Henry.

As the new clan head, getting my arse dragged into empath politics would come about sooner or later. Empaths could live to be well over 120 years, and I'd been hoping it'd be much *much* later before I'd have more to do with the Council. Besides, with Uncle Nigel taking our family's seat in the Council, there'd be no need to be rushing into anything. I could spend years at university getting several degrees before I even began taking up my clan's duties.

Da shrugged one shoulder as if he couldn't be worried, but the tightness in his face told a story otherwise. No doubt, he was trying to keep Mum from fretting. "Pass me the rice, son."

With a huffed breath, Mum crossed her arms.

"I have it handled, love." He drank from his bottle. "You need to be having some faith. While there's sure to be a power struggle, it'll not be anything Liam here can't handle."

Jaysus. Was I meant to be thankful for *his* faith in me? I certainly wasn't surprised he'd be thinking I'd want any part of a power struggle.

"When will we be leaving on Sunday?" I asked.

"You're not going," Mum said.

"Moira, it'll be good for him to go. He needs to learn how to get on with the Elders, and one testing wasn't enough time to learn what he needs to know."

I cringed at the thought of spending more time with them. "No, Da, I need to know whose arse we'll be kicking if they're coming after me and—"

Mum slammed her glass down, and I coughed to hide my near-slip. Her glare told me well enough that I'd best keep my gob shut if I wasn't going to be telling Da about Lucky. Da didn't seem to catch what I'd been about to say.

He pointed his bottle toward Mum. "If you're right, love, and they're coming because of my visions, well, I've not given anyone specifics, which is probably what they're wanting now. We'll tell them we've been chasing a ghost these past twelve years, and that's not a lie, is it? That'll buy us some time, it will."

Mum's eyes narrowed. "Who are they sending?"

Da cleared his throat and took a long drink of his Guinness. "Minister Gagliardi."

"Drago?" She paled, and I sensed ripples of her concern. She turned to me and then quickly glanced at the window facing Mrs. Robertson's house, showing me she was thinking of Lucky. She sent a stronger warning this time—hotter water than before, and it caught my breath. *What the hell?* I shot her my irritation.

A knot formed in my chest. How was it that Lucky might be

in danger? How in the bloody hell could this Drago Gagliardi be a threat to her? I pushed away my plate.

"Patrick, I told you this would happen one day. You'll have to put off Drago however you can." She turned to look at me. "Otherwise we'll all be in danger."

"Now love, you're overreacting," he said, waving his chopsticks dismissively. But he wouldn't look at her.

Mum took a deep breath. "Patrick, Drago is fanatical, and his EQ is as high as Liam's. It's no coincidence he's the one chosen to come see you. His family has made it well known they want representation within the Group of Elders, and Drago has been moving up the ranks in the Line of Ascension with a fury." She pushed her food around her plate, then froze. "It's why he was there at the signing. He was most likely waiting for Liam to turn eighteen and prove himself before the community—prove he indeed had the potential to become a soulmated empath." She turned her gaze to me. "Drago will do what he can to stop you from becoming more powerful than himself. Stopping the joining will be his first priority." She glanced out the window and back at me. The knot in my chest grew tighter, and the memory of the Mediterranean man Mum spoke with flashed across my mind.

"And how would you be knowing all this?" Da asked. "From thirty-some years ago when his family wanted you married to this Drago of theirs? I've not once heard you mention Gagliardi or his family's name since."

My head snapped in her direction. "What? You were going to marry him?"

"No, darling. I had no interest, but my parents considered their proposal—how could they not? He comes from a powerful family in his own right. His family wanted a seat on the Council. They thought if Drago married into my family, he'd be guaranteed one." She faced Da, her eyes sparkling. "But I refused and married your father instead. The only reason my parents entertained the idea at all was because your father wasn't an empath." Her smile faded. "I have no idea how Drago finally became a Minister, and I think I don't want to know."

Da pointed his chopsticks at me. "You wouldn't be sitting here if your ma hadn't made such a wise choice." He let out a burp and rubbed his stomach.

Mum fought down a smile.

If she was right about Drago Gagliardi, I'd need to know more about him. Whatever it was between Lucky and me, I'd be damned if I let anyone touch her.

Mum and I were cleaning up after supper when she leaned over and lowered her voice. "If Laxshmi is half as good as you say she is, Drago will see her potential immediately and assume she's The One. We have to keep him away from her. If she breaks through to become a full empath, I'll take her on as my apprentice and train her until she can protect her own mind. I'll delay presenting her to the Elders to avoid drawing any attention to her."

The Elders required an initiation ceremony for empaths who broke through after the age of twelve. They'd insist on Lucky pledging her loyalty to our laws and way of life. In my mind, it was little more than an excuse for a party where the old farts could probe the mind of a new initiate. I'd not be subjecting Lucky to that.

I stopped drying a plate and turned to Mum. "*You'd* be her mentor? Why not me?" Being an apprentice to a royal was a rare honor. It was better than becoming an A-list actor in Hollywood overnight. To be the soul mate to the heir of a royal line was an even bigger deal. Lucky might as well be the *only* one on that list—ever.

"You have no experience in such matters, Liam. Besides, you're too young to mentor a new empath." She pointed a wet finger at me. "Being a royal will show its advantages. It will mean the Elders will not dare to question my reasons for postponing her initiation. But it will bring undue attention to her, especially if we must move on from here to continue our search, leaving her behind."

A bubble of anger surfaced at the thought of moving on. No doubt in protest, but of what? Moving yet again … or leaving Lucky? The sound of her laughing was echoing in my mind.

Mum handed me a wet dish. "If Laxshmi does turn out to be The One, our main focus will be developing your new powers after you join. I'll feel better about her chances against someone like Drago then. I'll talk to your Uncle Henry and tell him to make sure everyone remains tightlipped back home, just in case."

"How is Lucky in danger from Gagliardi? Or am I meant to be in the dark about everything, for Chr—crying out loud?"

She scrubbed the serving spoons with a little too much attention. She stopped abruptly and then stared into the sink. "He was one of our first subjects for the EQ test. We gave him an intensive psychological analysis at the same time." She rinsed off the spoon, gave it to me to dry, and met my gaze. "He had some strong antisocial tendencies and skirted the line of psychopathic behavior. It was as if he knew how to beat the test and was taking pleasure in toying with us. Not all my colleagues agreed with me on the matter, however. I suppose his charm helped with that. The only reason I'm able to warn you now is because his results had to be disclosed publicly for his ministerial position. I suspect the Elders ignored my concerns or were influenced somehow."

A deranged council minister with designs on Lucky? Not good that.

She pulled the plug from the other half of the sink, draining the soapy water with a gurgle. A film of brownish oil and suds clung to the sides. She never did manual labor back home, but here, she seemed to enjoy it. It made her feel normal, she'd said.

"I'm concerned he would try to usurp my claim to mentor her. The red tape alone would leave her vulnerable. He'd no doubt use that time to lure her away from you, brainwash her against our family, or pervert her emerging powers for his sick gain." Her voice steadily increased in pitch.

Damn.

She took a deep breath in, then exhaled slowly before continuing. "If it wasn't for meeting your father ... Well, since you insist on going with him this Sunday, I thought you should know. Keep Drago away from here and be careful. For Laxshmi's sake."

I rubbed my right temple, hoping to ward off a headache. I thought Da would've been the one giving me a migraine.

Mum rinsed off the sides of the sink. If only keeping Lucky out of these complications would be as easy as cleaning up had been.

"Liam, I know you're not going to like this, but I'll need to meet her." I opened my mouth, but she shot up a hand to stop my protesting. "The sooner I can sense her in person, the easier it'll be for me to home in on her state of mind and help protect her." She studied me for a moment. "You know, darling, she must like you if she made you blush, which I assumed is what you meant by being embarrassed in a *good* way."

Jaysus. How does she always know? I sighed. "And why would you be saying something like that?"

"Because we women don't wield our charms to make just anyone blush. Besides, who could resist my baby boy?"

I groaned, and she giggled. Thankfully, we finished up in silence. After I had the leftovers sorted and stored, I leaned against the counter. "For once, I don't want my life to be about finding a soul mate."

"I know." She cupped my cheeks in her hands. "Why do you think I didn't protest when you chose not to tell your father, love?"

CHAPTER 10

Lucky

I woke the next morning and stared at my ceiling, trying to bubble wrap yesterday's memories of Liam and store them someplace special.

Would he be awake yet? I glanced toward the window. "Crash Into Me" was still stuck in my head from playing it on repeat all afternoon. I imagined Liam and me sitting on the window seat in the moonlight, talking for hours, and not caring about school, mothers, or the future. It was how a connection between two people ought to be … carefree. But, surprise, surprise, I was getting ahead of myself.

I yanked my poetry journal out from under my pillow and read what my insomnia had inspired last night.

I wish my hand would dare,
To memorize your face,
To run its fingers through your hair
Then feel your heartbeat race.

Sap. My heart was definitely vulnerable to being ripped apart by hope. I was already hoping to walk to school with him, hoping to have lunch with him, and hoping the tingling would return.

Yup. I was a hopeless cause.

I did some deep stretches on the floor, reading my plaque with Aristotle's quote again. Would Liam and I together be greater than our sum? Was it asking too much to want that? To marry for love? I imagined centuries of girls asking the same question.

Mom's words echoed in my head. *"Passion goes away, and love won't pay your bills. Dancing won't either. Remember that, hunh?"*

After showering, I headed downstairs to the usual morning sounds of pots and pans clanking in our small kitchen. Even the noise couldn't distract me from thoughts of Liam. At least I'd see him soon.

"Hey, Mom."

She popped some bread in the toaster. "I was so busy on the phone with your Harshna *Mami* yesterday, I forgot to ask you about the school. How was your first day, *beta*?" she asked, using a term of endearment. I guessed things with Sujata's drama had blown over for now.

"It was fine. How's everything at the travel agency?" I sat down at the kitchen table, switching chairs to avoid the one with the sharp chrome lip.

"Good. Good."

"So how's *Mama* and *Mami*?" Had they killed Sujata yet? I had to be careful asking about my uncle and aunt. I couldn't let on that I'd known anything about Sujata and Michael dating.

"They're fine."

Liar.

She finished slicing a banana and moved to the sink to put the peel in the large yogurt container she used for kitchen scraps.

"Laxshmi," she said, nonchalantly. "Mrs. Robertson said there is a new high school boy on the other side of her. Is he in your classes?"

"Liam's in two of them." *Damn. Damn. Damn.* I shouldn't have said his name. "But he's a senior, so I don't see him a lot," I added quickly.

One of her lectures on "what all boys wanted" was sure to follow.

"Oh? Which classes?"

"AP History and AP Calculus." I didn't know why I cared, but I added the AP to impress her. I doubted it would work.

She stayed silent, so I picked up a pencil and doodled on the message pad. Her thoughts had to be marinating. The idea of fighting with her about Liam made my heart race.

"You know, *deeku,*" she said.

Great. Here we go. Toast, bananas, and a side order of paranoia wrapped up with another term of endearment.

"It doesn't matter how smart boys are, they all—"

"God, Mom. Please give it a rest. I know. All boys are bad. You don't have to lecture me every time the name of one comes up." My gut twisted for jumping down her throat, but I'd heard every version of her spiel since Daddy had died. She glared at me like I'd just poked a hornet's nest, and she was the queen. Blood pulsed behind my ears.

"You don't know everything, okay?" she said. "What happens if you get pregnant, *hunh*? Are you going to raise the baby on your own? Do you think some American boy will marry you and take care of you?"

He's Irish, not American, so, ha!

"You will be struggling all your life. Struggling. Okay? It's all over the TV. Watch those people on Jerry Springer. Do you think their life is so easy? Do you want to be like them? *Hunh?*" She scraped the butter on the toast with a little too much gusto.

"I'm not going to end up on Springer just because I talked to a boy." Why bother explaining? I looked away, toward the dining room, and blinked back tears. Why did she always get to me like this? Sujata would've reminded me to be brave.

"Do you think you will become a doctor when you cannot sleep and have to clean up the diapers and vomit? *Hunh?* Do you want to be like Sujata? She's bringing shame to the family."

Shame?

"Mom, give Sujata some credit. She's dating a smart guy. He's at Georgetown too, you know." I should've kept my mouth shut, but I couldn't. The message pad now sported Liam's name with swirls around it. Maybe I'd be fighting for him someday.

Yeah, right. I frantically erased his name.

She plunked down my toast in front of me on a green-flower-rimmed dish. These plates could compete with the kitchen table for oldest thrift-store find.

"She's only thinking about herself," Mom began again. "She can't focus on school if she's worried about how she looks and what underwear she's wearing for her boyfriend. I told your Harshna *Mami* that Sujata should come home before something bad happens. *Bichari,* Sujata. Poor girl. He probably made her sleep with him too, and now who is going to marry her, *hunh?* The boys get what they want, and then they're finished. One mistake and your good life is gone. Remember that."

Whatever I could say to help defend Sujata would reveal what I knew, so I stayed quiet. I wanted to eat in peace, but knew Round Two was coming. Never knew a tornado to touch down without wind damage.

She poured chai into her mug and shook her head. "Going with someone white. What is she thinking?" she muttered.

"God! How is her whole life ruined because everyone's afraid of a white guy?" I was really pushing it, but I couldn't stop the hope from spilling out. If I knew what was good for me, I'd plug up the leak.

She slammed down her mug. "You always think everything will be okay. We didn't sacrifice for you so you can become some— some waitress or cashier for all your life. It takes *one* night to ruin

84

everything. No, not even one night. Five minutes!" She wagged her finger toward the Lord Krishna clock hanging on the wall.

Five minutes? *I guess Sujata made Michael stick around longer. Good for her.*

"Your Harshna *Mami* made a mistake letting Sujata go so far to the Georgetown. You will be going somewhere close, *hunh?* You can go here to the UNC and come home every weekend."

I didn't think North Carolina had an accelerated med school program, but I wasn't going to mention that. Bringing up their dance program was even stupider. If only I knew how much my Princess Fund held. I had no fantasies about it being a huge amount, but maybe it would be enough to help pay my way for a short time if I moved in with Sujata. I idly wondered how much I'd need if I went to a university in Ireland. I sighed.

The clatter of dishes thrown together in the sink sliced at my nerves. I couldn't argue about UNC right now. My courage was running on empty. So I kept quiet, finished my breakfast, and escaped upstairs.

Chai in hand, Mom stopped me by the front door before I left. She was dressed for work in her travel agency's uniform—a maroon, knit polo and khaki pants. Her hair was now in a long braid, and button-earrings set off her earlobes, the distinctive brassy color of the twenty-two karat gold announcing her Indianness to everyone.

Her post-tirade ambush at the door meant a soft lecture was coming, one where the tone was more motherly, but the tidings neurotic and smothering. *Just more wind damage.*

"*Beta*, you know all I want is for you to be successful and happy, *hunh?* We didn't come all the way here for you to throw away everything we sacrificed. That's why you need to be a doctor. You will have a good life, good husband, and a big house. You won't need anything else."

How about love?

"Don't let anyone ruin your schooling," she said. "If you don't get a good match, your education is your security. Don't be like me, *hunh*? Young boys, they have no responsibility. Their hormones are too strong, and they will do anything to sleep with you."

Right. And we girls didn't have hormones. If she only knew how my body reacted when Liam was near me. If I even imagined him touching my skin, my breathing sped up.

Oh yeah, girls had no hormones.

She turned back toward the kitchen. "And, Laxshmi? I don't want you talking to him."

"*What?*" I rushed after her.

"Mrs. Robertson says he's a handsome boy, and I don't want you getting involved with him."

"Mom, we have two classes together, and he's our neighbor. I can't just avoid him."

"*Choop.* You've argued with me enough today. Just do as I say."

Ugh. I stormed out, slamming the front door and blinking back tears of anger. A quick peek up and down the street told me I'd be heading to school alone. Liam's absence was both a disappointment and a relief. If Mom saw me walking with him, I might as well move to Chernobyl.

Not talk to him? I snorted.

Liam wasn't at the lockers either, and the hard knot in my chest grew. How could I be this miserable without him? *It's just the*

anticipation getting to you, Laxshmi. Chill.

The little girl between my locker and Liam's closed hers, revealing her newly decorated door. Pink Hawaiian flowers. Ugh. I wanted to yank the stickers off, rip off the petals, and flush them down the toilet.

I scanned the main artery one more time before standing off to the side, pretending to go through my bag while looking up through my lashes and scanning the hallway. *I can't believe I'm doing this.* Pathetic didn't begin to describe me. A horde of cheerleaders was probably entertaining him in the parking lot at this exact moment. While I stood there, students filtered around me like I had a radioactive sign attached to my forehead.

Jack's unmistakable greeting rose above the clamor around me. "Laxshmi! *Wassup?*" He exaggerated each syllable, knowing it annoyed me. *Oh yay. Make me stand out even more.*

Liam wasn't with him, and I blew out a long breath. That nervous anticipation was spinning cartwheels in my chest. I shook out my hands, hoping to release some of the energy.

Jack raised an eyebrow. "Why you so fidgety?" He followed my gaze. "You waiting for someone?"

"Me? Um, no."

"By the way." He crossed his arms. *Great.* It was his go-to big-brother pose. "Is something going on between you and Liam?"

My attention darted away. "Uh … what makes you think that?"

"Just be careful. I know how you and Piggy think. She couldn't stop talking about him yesterday. '*Oh my God, did you hear his accent? Oh my God, can we go to Ireland next summer? Oh my God, he waited for her after English,*'" he mimicked, flailing his hands around. I tried to play-punch him to defend Shiney, but he leaned away.

Liam flew through the stairwell doors and paused, taking a deep breath. He strode over, throwing a nod to Jack and flashing me his dimpled grin. His presence settled deep inside me, and the excitement spread. It felt like when I'd performed my first *grand jeté* on stage.

"Sorry," Liam said to me. "I overslept."

This time, I couldn't hold back my nervous-whimper laugh. The relief at seeing him floored me. *I'm really losing my mind.*

Jack elbowed me and when I glared at him, he gave me the I-was-right look.

Shiney and I had walked across the street to a Greek café for lunch. We were on our own since Liam had been a no-show at the lockers after fourth. My heart ached at not getting to spend the free time with him. Who knew I'd be this clingy?

The Akropolis Kafe was a popular mom-and-pop place and hangout after school. At least it was healthier than fast food. Well, it would've been if I'd had an appetite. I'd forced down a few bites of my pita sandwich, and not even the garlicky sauce or the salty tang of the lamb could snap my thoughts away from Liam. After first period, Liam and I had walked together between classes, laughing, flirting, and sharing little bits of our lives. I was sure it meant I'd see him for lunch too. Spending the entire time in the cafeteria looking for him—like I had that morning before homeroom—would've given me an ulcer. My nerves could only take so much. Maybe it was just convenient for him to walk with me to those classes and nothing more.

Once Shiney had figured out why I was so preoccupied, she'd suggested we go out to eat. She'd been making a valiant effort at distracting me ever since.

"So anyway, then Matthew asked me out." Shiney bounced up and down in her seat at her news about her Bible study crush. Her excitement had me smiling. We talked more about her plans to meet him the Friday after Labor Day at a local pizzeria and how Jack wanted to drive Shiney there to size him up since her parents wouldn't allow her to date.

A strange tickling sensation in my head had me looking up at the front entrance. Shiney followed my gaze, but when she didn't see anyone there either, she turned back to her food. I closed my eyes and tried to clear my head. The ache in my chest eased with my next breath. This time, whatever inspired me to look at the front door pulled my attention back there. A grin stretched my cheeks and had Shiney spinning around again.

Liam walked in.

He scanned the crowd and when he saw us, he answered my smile with one of his own. By the time he walked over, my breathing became ragged. Shiney was too busy muttering under her breath about how fine Liam was to even notice my reaction.

He greeted both of us and squatted by my chair so I wouldn't have to crane my neck to see him. *God, he smells divine.* I leaned closer as discreetly as I could. He must have showered after gym class. His hair was still damp and tendrils of it stuck to his skin.

"We were late getting out of gym class," he said. The muscles around his eyes relaxed, and a small smile grew on his face while I was distracted smelling him.

I jerked upright. *Oh God.* Did he realize I was sniffing him?

He snatched a fry off my plate. "I'm sorry I'd not been able to meet you earlier." He dipped it in my ketchup and shoved it in his mouth. As platonic as the gesture probably was, I warmed at the closeness it implied. *Yeah, I was really losing it.*

"No biggie." I waved it off. "Sorry we didn't wait for you."

"I could've been texting you, but I didn't have your number."

"Uh—" Before I could reply, the horde of cheerleaders I'd worried had ambushed Liam this morning walked in. At least it saved me from having to explain how I couldn't give him my number because my mom monitored every text and call I got. She even had a tracker app for when I was out and about.

Liam had to stand to get out of the crowd's way as they made their way to the counter to order. Several of them greeted him with big smiles, and he returned the favor.

He turned to me and pointed his thumb over his shoulder. "Time for me to be ordering."

I nodded, and as he walked away, it occurred to me he didn't say if he'd be joining us. *You didn't ask him too either, Laxshmi.* Judging by how he laughed with the cheerleaders and the few football jocks in line with him, he'd found the group he was meant to be with. Jack was even with them since one of the wide receivers was his best friend.

I remembered Daddy telling me as a kid how I couldn't get burned if I swiped my finger through a candle's flame, but if I held my finger above it, I would. Even knowing this, I had an urge to keep close to the fire—an urge to hope for more with Liam.

Shiney chatted on as if nothing were wrong. I didn't want to witness Liam choosing them to sit with over me. I had to leave. *Hurry up, Shiney.* It was better if I disappeared before he left the register with his food—better if I didn't get burned.

The second Shiney tossed her napkin down, I jumped up, hoping the scrape of my chair against the floor hadn't attracted Liam's attention, and grabbed both our plates to throw away. She followed, asking what the rush was, and when the girls and Liam filtered into the dining area, her eyes widened in understanding.

"Seriously, Laxshmi? You've got nothing to worry about. He's wild about y—"

"C'mon." I dragged her by the arm, weaving us through the tables toward the exit.

"Oh, Jack?" Shiney planted her feet and called out over her shoulder. *Damn.* My escape was only ten feet away.

Jack glanced up from his seat. Between him and the table we vacated, a confused looking Liam stood with his food, a questioning look directed toward me. Chloe, a gorgeous redheaded cheerleader with a don't-breathe-your-air-on-me reputation, called Liam over, saying something about Irish people needing to stick together. When he didn't move, she got up and practically draped herself on his arm. She led him toward an empty seat next to her. My heart sank. *Get over it, Laxshmi.*

Shiney had been dragging me closer to argue with Jack about the car keys he wouldn't give her. I pulled away and stopped before I got too close, before I breached the imaginary wall around Liam and got sucked in by his magnetic pull. Jack ignored Shiney, and his gaze darted back and forth from Liam to me. Liam was answering a question from Chloe, and Jack gave me his hard I-told-you-so stare. Then he shook his head, and his eyes softened. I gritted my teeth at the pity in his eyes. He'd lectured me in fourth period biology about how I didn't know Liam well enough and how I shouldn't get sucked in by his charm. *Too late.*

"Oh, by the way." Shiney raised her voice, snapping me out of my thoughts. "Laxshmi said she'd go to Salvio's with you for pizza next Friday night."

Oh God. No, no, no, no, no. She didn't just say that in front of Liam, did she?

Jack grinned and gave Liam the side-eye before pinning me with a stare. "Cool. It's a date."

Liam's head jerked toward Jack and then to me. The dryness in my throat choked me. Something too quick for me to decipher flashed across Liam's eyes, and he looked away, his jaw popping. It made me feel like a blast of heated air was baking my skin. I checked the vents above me. No way the heaters could have kicked on. It was summer. The stress had to be getting to me.

Liam now stared at Jack, who was grinning at me. He wasn't going to like how I murdered him.

Standing there like a statue wasn't making me feel any better. I grabbed Shiney's arm again and yanked her out the door.

CHAPTER 11

Liam

A fecking date?

Shiney, with her mass of dark curls, had bounced and hummed with happiness at her announcement. She was a tiny thing, but she seemed the type to pack a bit of punch. This punch had convinced her best friend to date her brother and had doubled me over. I balled my hands into fists, digging my nails into my palms. If I wasn't ten shades of red by now, I'd soon be. I was itching to find a good enough excuse to sling Jack a hook.

How could Lucky be going on a date with this wanker? He'd been shoveling kabobs in his mouth at the other end of the table—with a smirk that needed to be wiped off with my fists. I took a deep breath to calm myself.

Lucky had been filled with embarrassment and panic at Shiney's announcement. The embarrassment—the stronger of the two—felt like coming ashore after having a strong current rip away my swim trunks, leaving me starkers. And that was how she felt about this date of hers? Maybe I had it all arsewise. Maybe she'd been embarrassed to have Jack seeing her with myself. I rested my elbows on the table and ran a hand through my hair.

I'm refusing to believe that.

When the cheerleaders had come in, Lucky had been jealous. I'd assumed she was worried about them getting my attention. She'd not been comfortable this morning with them greeting me in the hallways. I'd been intending to join her for lunch. It would've shown her she needn't feel that way, but her insecurity had taken over.

No, this wasn't about Jack.

And then she'd left without waiting for me or giving me so much as a goodbye. *Well, maybe if you'd told her you'd be sitting with her, you git.*

"Liam, are you listening?" The brutal shrill of Chloe's voice pierced my eardrum. She and her mates had been checking me out yesterday in study hall, and I'd managed to avoid her until now. Despite ignoring her, she kept up her blathering, trying to draw me into the conversation. Images of screeching falcons tore through my concentration, which I couldn't lose if I wanted to be blocking out everyone else here.

I took another deep breath. The walls were a calming blue, with a mural of a Mykonos street scene with whitewashed buildings and cerulean blue doors and shutters. We'd holidayed there one summer, and now I'd need to be drawing on those memories to regain the hold over my mental blocks. If I couldn't, I might as well be an untrained empath for all the good my experience was doing me. Never thought I'd be getting this twisted over a girl.

Before Chloe could permanently be damaging my eardrums, I jumped out of my seat and stormed toward the trash bins. It wasn't like I could be eating now anyhow.

Chloe called out an invitation for me to meet them after school. Jack's eager face awaited my answer. I reopened my mind to him. His curiosity, while not exactly an emotion, left behind the telltale feeling of being unsatisfied. Coupled with his wariness, I knew he didn't trust me. The feeling was mutual.

"Sorry, already have plans," I said. Plans that included walking Lucky home. At least, I'd be hoping they did.

Jack's eyes narrowed. Since this morning, he'd been getting more suspicious of me, and by the looks he'd been shooting Lucky, he wasn't approving of all the time we were spending together. I'd been smart to keep my mind open to him earlier today. His suspicion was impressive. It would've inspired Shakespeare.

I cut through the car park of the shopping center and across the street to the front entrance of the school. *Shite.* Study hall would be next. There'd be no escaping Jack and Chloe who shared the class with me. Controlling my temper would be more than impossible around him.

I needed to bunk study hall.

Better to land myself in some trouble for missing class than for mixing it up with Jack. And for what? Having the nerve to ask Lucky out before I'd got around to it?

Yeah, I'd bunk off, but where? While I stood there at the main entrance, the crowd flowed around me like a stream parted by a boulder. Study hall was at the end of a closed-off corridor by the auditorium and the gym lockers, so those were my closest options. I headed that way and ducked into the auditorium. Sitting in the very back row, I hid myself in the shadow of the technical booth.

The auditorium was dim and cool, surrounding me in quiet blues and grays. I sank low in my seat, inhaled deeply and opened and closed my hands. Fire still burned through my veins. Images of Lucky and Jack together reignited the anger. Lucky should be going out with me.

Well, maybe if you'd feckin' asked her first. The thought kicked me in the gut.

I wanted to be dating her.

The air escaped me in a *whoosh*. But I couldn't date her, not until I knew she was The One. There'd be no point if we had to be leaving next week. I leaned forward and buried my face in my hands.

A group of students strolled in—a theater class, probably. I closed my eyes and opened my mind completely, hoping to drown in the emotional muck of the others. I needed the distraction.

A certain ripple had me bolting upright. The purity of it felt like swimming in crystal-clear water.

Lucky.

I scanned the crowd, found her, and watched her head for a seat in the middle of the auditorium. Soon enough, I'd not have to search her out or even make eye contact to make the empathic connection—finding her would be as natural as blinking.

Bloody hell. She was a good forty feet from me. The first night I'd seen her, she'd projected from her window seat clear across to my roof. Hadn't paid it any mind at the time. Some empaths' abilities went beyond the normal reading or projecting range. If she ever broke through, maybe Lucky would be one of them.

I grabbed my bag and rushed down the aisle like the lovesick puppy I was. *Christ.* Ciarán would be so proud of me. I slipped into the row behind her and put my bag in the seat beside her. She whipped around. A smile lit up her face, warming my body like the sun had come out. The knot in my chest released, and I couldn't help but grin at her.

"What are you doing here?" she asked, keeping her voice low. She was projecting the happiness she created specifically for me. I'd sensed it for the first time at the Greek café. She was happy when I'd walked in, but when she'd seen me, the intensity had amplified. Tidal waves of it had overwhelmed me. It was different from any of the happiness I'd ever felt from her before. And I'd inspired it. Waves of it washed over me now like water from a summer-warmed ocean, making my skin tingle the way soda water did my tongue.

When the teacher wasn't looking, I climbed over the row of

seats and sat next to Lucky. Ripples of her nerves and attraction began churning around me.

"Bunked off study hall."

"Bunked off?"

"Sorry—skipped."

"In here?"

"Couldn't find another closer, quiet place." I put my bag on the floor.

"Wouldn't study hall be—Oh wait, isn't Jack there? No need to say more."

"Um, yeah, Jack can definitely ... talk." Bloody shite seemed more like what came out of Jack's cakehole.

"Very diplomatic." She let out a small laugh.

The teacher was handing out pages of some kind to a small group of students on stage. A skit assignment from the sound of it. The rest of the class drifted into their seats. At some point, the bell must have rung, but I'd not heard it.

I shifted in my seat to face Lucky. If she only knew how undiplomatic my thoughts for Jack were, she'd not be happy most likely. Focusing on Lucky held more appeal than thinking any more on Jack, so I pushed him out. I remembered how little I knew about Lucky. I'd rectify that today.

"So, uh, are you an only child?" I asked.

"Yup. What about you?"

She pulled her legs up on the seat and faced me. Her gaze was intense, and she was giving me her undivided attention. Her confidence was back too, as if she'd never been the nervous girl I'd seen earlier. No ulterior motive existed, just an interest in me.

I told her in whispers about my brother and parents and what they did, and how Mum had been born and raised in England, despite her being Irish. When I mentioned my fourteen male cousins, her eyes widened, and a far-off look crept into her eyes. Without any siblings of her own, I interpreted her loneliness as if I were the sole survivor of a shipwreck, floating on a piece of flotsam. She seemed fascinated about the family and bombarded me with questions.

"So is it my turn at last to get a word in?" I asked.

She blushed. "Sorry. Go ahead."

"What do your parents do?"

Her face fell. She turned her gaze to the stage, watching her classmates take direction for some kind of acting. A deep grief washed over me.

"Did I say something wrong, Lucky?" I scanned her emotions for some answer but only found a thick sorrow.

She cleared her throat. "No, it's just that my dad died five years ago. Five years tomorrow actually. Wow." Her brow furrowed, and her lower lip quivered. With a sharp breath, she continued. "I still feel like I'm being hit by a truck when I'm reminded of him. That's all." Her eyes were soft and vulnerable.

"I'm sorry."

"Please, don't be." She cleared her throat a second time. "I'm not upset. You didn't say anything wrong." She attempted a smile, but it kept slipping. "Well, my mom works at a travel agency, and my dad was an engineer with the city. He taught me everything I know about power tools, believe it or not."

"Really? I'd always had a workshop of me own whenever we had a garage. I've yet to set one up here, but I'm hoping to this week. Working with my hands relaxes me." Thinking of her working a jigsaw was anything but relaxing. It was oddly erotic, it was. I smiled.

"Why are you smiling?" She tipped her head to the side. "Don't tell me you think girls can't handle a power tool."

"Me? No! Absolutely they can. Some of the cousins might not be thinking that, but the aunts would soon step in to set them right. Mum's pretty proud of me, considering all."

"Something tells me she'd be proud of you no matter what.

Now, most Indian parents I know … they're a little more like control freaks and less like proud-of-anything types. Not all, but most. My mom included."

"You may be right. We're a bit more laid back in Ireland. But since Mum's English, you could say she has her own things that put her knickers in a twist—etiquette and the like."

"Ooo, too bad none of that's rubbed off on you."

The sarcastic lip suited her. And me.

I gasped playfully. "You're killing me here. Are you always this rude?"

She leaned her head back against the seat. I'd never seen such expressive eyes. She flashed me a brilliant smile, and it took all my control not to lean in and kiss her.

Up on the stage, the teacher yelled, "Action!"

Lucky's attention went to the stage.

We fell silent to watch what I'd call some poor acting. When the teacher's critique was over, he had the next group come up. Lucky, thankfully, wasn't assigned to them.

She turned and watched me until I met her eyes. We talked a bit more of family. She shared some stories about her childhood with her cousin, Sujata. I wondered what it would've been like to have a little sister or a female cousin.

"Tell me about Ireland," she whispered.

Something in her eyes made me want to blurt out my secrets. If Ciarán could hear my thoughts, he would've laughed out loud.

I waited until the teacher was absorbed in directing another small group on stage, and then angled my body toward Lucky, only to find her already facing me. She blushed and looked away. I scooted closer.

"Silence, everyone." The teacher called out.

Lucky slid down in her seat and gave me a devious smile. I sensed a playfulness coming from her. It felt like a school of fish tickling me while I swam. I crouched down and lowered my voice.

"You'll be getting me kicked out."

"Nah, Mr. Truman has a reputation for letting anyone in. Just don't talk too loud."

Smiling, I told her of the greens in the meadows on our land and our family businesses like the pub where we enjoyed raising a pint or two. I told her of my summers in Ireland and with Mum's parents in Wales. I left out that our house was an estate, that we were royalty, and that I was responsible for a clan of empaths. It wasn't as if I were lying, but even that small deception of leaving things out ate at me.

A small smile stayed on her face through my stories. Every now and then she'd bite her lip anticipating something funny, drawing my attention. It drove me mad. When she slid closer to hear me, her scent brought me back to Ireland as easily as it had at the Akropolis Kafe when she leaned in. Apparently, I'd been smelling good to her after my shower.

I spoke softer so she'd move even closer.

With our heads only inches apart, it would've taken no effort at all to lean in and kiss those lips of hers. Every time she broke into a silent laugh, she'd arch her neck back. I'd follow the lines of her throat down to her cleavage and forget where I'd left off in the telling of things. She probably thought I was a right plonker.

When I stared into those gorgeous eyes of hers, the sweep of black lashes would just about hypnotize me. She had smooth skin, and a freckle or two that would disappear when she laughed. Her skin had to be soft, and I ached to touch it. With no makeup on, her blushes showed up easy enough.

We spent the time sharing bits and pieces of our lives, but I craved more. The bell rang. I sensed her disappointment as she gathered her things, and it matched my own. The only thing I could think of now was when I'd be seeing her again.

Christ. What did all this mean?

"So, I'll catch up with you before last period, yeah?" I asked.

It'd only be for a few minutes before class, but … *damn*. I ran my hand through my hair. I was almost gone in the head for her.

Her face lit up in a smile. "Okay, but don't forget, the next question is mine."

"Greedy girl," I muttered.

I walked her out, and we ran right into Jack and Chloe leaving study hall. I flashed Jack a smile to rub it in and leaned in close to Lucky to tell her I'd see her later.

Chloe's eyes narrowed, as did Jack's. *Let them.*

I had Lucky, for now.

CHAPTER 12

Lucky

Shiney and I came out of last period English, but the door to Liam and Jack's English class was still closed. My heart pounded in my chest in anticipation. We waited in the hallway near several posters of American literary giants.

"I could still kill you for pulling that stunt, you know," I said to Shiney. "You should've asked me first."

"You would've said no! Oh, and it was so worth it. If I hadn't done it, you'd never have seen Liam's reaction."

"Yeah, but it was the way you said it, Shiney. You say he likes me, but then why let him think I'm going out with your brother? And what's with Jack calling it a date? He knows better. It feels like … like, I don't know. It's not right. I don't want to play games."

"Oh my God, Laxshmi. He skipped study hall and stayed with you—"

"He didn't know I'd be in there. It was just a coincidence."

"He didn't have to come sit with you." She crossed her arms at me and raised an eyebrow. I just rolled my eyes.

The memory of Liam sitting inches from me in drama warmed my face. I could've stayed with him all afternoon. It drove my hormones into a state of frenzy though. He smelled so good, and his dimples unbalanced me more than I already felt. I was so giddy, and even though I'd never been drunk before, I imagined this was what it felt like. He probably thought I was some giggly little ten-year-old.

The classroom door opened, and a surge of anxiety filled my chest. What if Jack came out first and started talking to me? Would that reinforce the idea Jack and I were dating in Liam's head? Wouldn't that be good if I needed to stay away from him?

Shiney winked at me and left. Great. *Put me in this bind and then bail on me.*

They came out, and Jack veered toward me as soon as he saw me. He took my elbow and led me into the empty corner a few feet away. I looked over his shoulder for Liam.

"What the hell, Laxshmi? You said you wanted to keep your distance from Liam, but you spent fifth period with him?"

I frowned. "I know. It's not like I could help it." I'd unloaded on Jack during AP Bio, telling him how hard I was crushing on Liam. We'd agreed avoidance was the best option since I didn't want any drama from my mom. That was probably what motivated him to call it a date. I'd wanted to kill him, but I had to admit, it was sweet he was trying to help.

Jack shook his head and sighed. From over his shoulder, I saw Liam watching me, his jaw clenched.

"Uh, I better go," I said. "We're walking home together."

"Yeah, I figured. He wouldn't come out to the fields with us."

I wanted to smile, but it would only aggravate Jack.

He narrowed his eyes. "Just be careful, okay? There's something about him I don't trust." He turned and walked in the opposite direction from Liam.

I joined Liam.

"So. You and Jack?" he asked.

We headed toward our lockers. For a brief moment, he looked vulnerable, like my answer could hurt him. It reminded me of when I'd first seen him on the roof, sitting in the shadows, burdened by some great weight. I didn't know how to answer. Especially since the impression Shiney's stunt had left might make it easier to avoid him—and avoid getting hurt.

"Jack's just … hard to explain."

We changed the subject to stupid stuff—the faded carpet, the color of the walls, the school mascot, and whether it would ever rain and cool off this heat wave. The awkwardness only grew, deepening the gulf between us. Liam's hand clenched and unclenched around the strap of his shoulder bag. For the first time, I felt like maybe I'd made up the whole connection between us.

I wanted to curl up in my window seat and mope.

When we were done with our lockers, he nodded toward the stairwell and led the way. When we got to the bottom, he stopped abruptly, and I caught myself on the last step, barely avoiding an awkward collision.

He turned to face me, and I marveled at how his green eyes could be so light and vivid at the same time. I had trouble catching my breath, so I swallowed hard and studied the anti-slip tape at our feet, waiting for him to do or say something. I half imagined he might kiss me, we were so close, but I shook the ridiculous thought out of my head. Thank God this wasn't the crowded, main stairwell. At least we were alone.

"So you're going on a date with Jack?"

"No!" I yelled the word a little too quickly, and my gaze snapped to his. So much for using Jack to keep my distance. Who was I kidding? "I'm keeping him company while he—" I stopped myself, not knowing if I should spill the secret Shiney had told me at lunch. "While he brings Shiney to meet a friend from her Bible study group. Since he has to wait for her, she thought I could keep Jack company." It wasn't a complete lie.

Liam let out a breath and smiled. Was that relief? Or was it my imagination?

Wait.

Why did he want to know? Could Shiney be right? My mind went into overdrive analyzing possible answers.

"Why do you—?" I lost my nerve. What if I didn't like the answer? "Are you always this nosy?" I asked instead.

A small frown appeared on his face, tugging his eyebrows together. His eyes looked flat. Was he disappointed?

"Not always. There's just something ... something about you. I just have to know. You started this whole mess, you know, by spying on me." He smiled.

"*Ugh.* Not that again." And just like that, the gulf was gone. I could see it in his eyes.

I play-punched him on his chest, but his firm torso didn't move an inch. I bounced backward instead, tripping on the step behind me. In a split second, he anchored his foot on the step above, wrapped his arm around my waist, and yanked me forward. I fell against him, then my bag swung into my hip, thumping me even closer.

Where my palms touched his arms, my skin tingled, and I gasped. The sensation spread. It was like being shocked with an unending static charge. He dropped his hands and stared at me, wide-eyed.

Okay, so he feels it too.

After he let go, an emptiness engulfed my chest. I reluctantly slid my hands off his arms, not wanting to sever the connection. Our chests were heaving as if we'd run up ten flights of stairs. I wiggled my fingers, anxious to rid myself of the lingering dizziness. The pulse on his neck was pounding. I averted my gaze to avoid any awkwardness and noticed him flexing his fingers on each hand.

"Sorry. That was some static charge," he said, breathless. I couldn't do anything more than stare at my sandals. "Lucky? Are you okay?"

"Hmm? Yeah, I'm fine. Just—no, I'm fine."

Why would there be static on a hot and humid day with no thunderstorm in sight? The intensity of the charge continued to grow and so did the ringing in my ears. Shouldn't the charge be getting weaker?

"Sorry, just dazed, I guess. Thanks for, um, not letting me fall."

The stairwell seemed stuffy and getting outside was no better. The heat radiated off the parking lot, and the tree-shaded street beyond beckoned. The branches swayed with a light breeze, and the rustling leaves slowly drowned out the ringing in my ears.

Liam still looked distracted, and I walked beside him, listening to the birds. Something about what happened in the stairwell was both comforting and unnerving, like the smile he'd given me on the roof that first night.

Once in the shade, the oppression lifted. Liam hopped off the curb, startling me, and turned around, excited like a little boy. "My question. Why don't you like being called Lucky?"

I blew out a breath. "Wow. Um, it seems a little childish now, especially considering Jack and Shiney's reaction at lunch yesterday." The truth was kind of *under*whelming actually.

"Go on with yourself. Why don't you tell me anyhow." He moved out of my way so we could continue walking.

"Well, I used to love Lucky Charms cereal, and I'd pick out all the pink and purple marshmallows before I ever finished the box. Once they were all picked out, I wouldn't want to eat it anymore, and Mom would yell at me. Dad would just dump the cereal out and buy me a new box—even though she'd get mad, calling it a waste of money." I cleared my throat, trying not to choke up. "He said he'd do anything for his lucky princess … "

"Jaysus, Laxshmi. I'm sorry." He ran his hand down his face. A deep sorrow filled his eyes. "If I'd known it'd be bringing back memories, I … "

I winced when he called me by my real name. It put a distance between us I didn't like. Before we crossed the next street, I stepped in front of him. "Liam, please don't feel bad. I actually don't mind when you say it. Honest. But just you. I'm not ready for everyone—I mean, I wouldn't want just anyone calling me that."

He searched my eyes like he was deciding what to do. Something about this bothered him more than I would've expected.

"Please believe me." My hand was tingling again, and I looked down. I'd absently placed my hand on his forearm. We both looked at his arm.

"Oh. Sorry," I said.

At the same time that I dropped my arm, he raised his and caught my hand. His thumb caressed my knuckles, and I slowly lifted my eyes to meet his.

Oh God. Oh God. Oh God. He's holding my hand.

My ribcage was straining to hold my heart back.

"Each time must have been a painful reminder—"

"No, it wasn't like that, I swear. Enough time's passed now." I squeezed his hand. "Promise me you won't stop. Please?"

"I'll not stop then, not unless you want it of me." Concern lingered on his face, and I felt an overwhelming urge to wrap him in my arms to comfort him.

He casually laced his fingers with mine and led me across the street. I was so giddy it felt like my insides were hopped up on the tingling. I bit my lips together. I needed to rein in my hope that this meant something.

"So," he said, lightly tugging at my hand, pulling me closer as we walked. "Would you ever live outside the States?"

"Uh, sure, why not? I think I'd live anywhere so long as I was blissfully happy."

A smile crossed his lips as he studied me, and my cheeks warmed. I seriously had to get my reactions under control. A jogger and her dog turned the corner, splitting us up in the process.

That had to be a sign.

Keeping control of my reactions when I was close to him was tough enough, but letting go of his hand was excruciating. The emptiness in my chest returned, and I pushed on my sternum.

We strolled the last block in silence. The idea of not seeing him until morning weighed down on me. He didn't take my hand again. The rejection I felt made me mad at myself. What was I expecting from him? I'd only known him for two days. He was probably being nice because he felt sorry for me.

Maybe he's just a hand-holder. What if it was a casual friend-thing that guys and girls did in Ireland? I crossed my arms so it wouldn't look like I was desperately dangling my hand for him to hold. When I made my hands disappear, he pocketed his.

We passed spinning garden pinwheels, the buzz of someone mowing their lawn, and a few recycling bins for tomorrow's pick up. One of the moms I sometimes babysat for was pulling out of her driveway and waved. I waved back and tried to push away a stinging fear—what if she told Mom I was walking with Liam?

I pushed the anxiety aside. I'd deal with it later.

We stopped at the sidewalk leading to my front porch. Liam used my bag strap to stop and turn me so I'd face him. "Why is it you're quiet?"

"No reason."

He chewed on his lower lip and studied my face as if deciding to believe me. Even if he did read me like a book, it wasn't like I'd be rushing to the front of the line to share these thoughts. He looked down at his feet. "I had fun today."

It was so unlike him to be shy that I burst into laughter. His head jerked up, and creases deepened on his forehead. I laughed even harder.

"I did too," I said between gasps of air. "Sorry, I don't mean to laugh, but ... "

"Is that so?" He stepped closer, smiling. All he had to do was stare at me with those amazing eyes, and my heart rate would go haywire. He flashed me those heart-stopping dimples like he knew what I was thinking.

"Why do you always do that?" I asked.

"What is it I'm doing?"

What was I supposed to say? *Your smile does funny things to my insides?* I met his gaze straight on. He was probably waiting for me to embarrass myself.

I lifted my chin. "You're using your powers for evil." There. That was vague enough.

He threw his head back and laughed. "If you only knew, Lucky. If you only knew."

Before I did something stupid like grab his hand, lean up to kiss him, or beg him to walk with me tomorrow, I stepped away, walking backward. "I should get going. See you tomorrow."

"How's seven thirty?" he asked.

"Huh?" I stopped.

"In the morning?" He tilted his head for emphasis.

"Oh. Yeah, duh." *Smooth, Laxshmi.* "Well, if that's your question, then yes, seven thirty." I squealed in my head.

He held up his fingers to say bye, and I did the same. With a turn, he jogged toward his house.

In that moment, I didn't want to think about how silly I looked, grinning like some giddy first-grader. I didn't want to think about not getting my hopes up, or how I couldn't remember a single thing we talked about. Or even that I should be keeping my distance.

In that moment, I was blissfully happy. I felt whole with him.

I shook the silly thought away.

What if Shiney was right? What if he liked me? I looked at the hand he'd held. Would I always be plagued with doubts, or would I have the courage to ask him what was happening between us?

Behind me, as if to remind me where I lived, a breeze rustled our hanging sweet potato vines and philodendrons, creaking the chains holding the baskets to the eaves.

CHAPTER 13

Liam

Aunt Finola's sharp, tinny voice floated up to my room from the dining room downstairs, broadcasting through a speakerphone. I couldn't concentrate on my schoolwork what with Aunt Finola's shrill tone piercing the air like a banshee, so I joined them.

At supper earlier, Da had mentioned his sister had sneaked out photos of certain pages of an ancient text from the Elders' restricted library—a text said to discuss soulmated empaths and their joining, something no one seemed to know anything about.

Da had rushed through his meal, eager to see the pages she'd emailed him. Once we'd cleared the table, he'd spread out ten photos of stained, yellowed parchment so he and Mum could study and translate them with Aunt Finola's help. Other papers, binders, and books covered the rest of the surface. Da had moved two of the chairs to one corner so he could maneuver left to right unhindered.

"No, no, no, Patrick." Aunt Finola's voice squeaked over the speaker on Da's mobile. "What you're seeing is one page bleeding through from the page behind it. Cuff the back of his head for me, will you, Moira?"

"So, Aunt Finola, what's this book I'll be breaking you out of prison for?" I grinned at Mum's scowling face.

"Liam, love, are you ever anything but cheeky?"

"And why would I be anything but?"

She snorted. "It's a diary you're looking at, written by an Irish monk in the sixteenth century about all things unholy—demons, witches, and the like. And if the Council comes after me, I'll show them unholy—"

"Finnie, don't you be taking risks," Da said, his face hovering inches from one of the photos.

He and Aunt Finola began arguing over her safety, so I sat near the window, snatching up a photo and scanning the lines of the page to see if I could make sense of the scribbling. *Definitely Gaelic.* But only every third or fourth word looked familiar. I'd never seen spellings the likes of what this monk had used, not that they'd had much in the way of dictionaries back then. Some Latin and Greek even peppered the margins.

Da and the others went back to debating the meanings of certain words and making guesses when a line faded away into the page. The entire exercise seemed a reason for Da and his sister to be competing for who might be the bigger nerd.

I slouched back and wondered why I'd bothered to come down at all. Several lines reiterated only what we already knew well enough—legend or not, soulmated empaths were powerful, enough so to be noticed and demonized by non-empaths. If Mum were to be believed, the threat didn't end there. Even empaths, the likes of Gagliardi, could be a threat. Jealousy and greed affected us all, I supposed.

Mum grabbed Da's arm, showing him the page she'd been working on. "Even with the double meanings, this part looks as if it should read, 'a light had marked the pair.' Page four, Finola. Three lines from the top. The rest ... I–I cannot make out."

I sat up. "Could that be about the joining then?"

"It's possible, love," Aunt Finola said. "Patrick, you and Moira, didn't you once come across a Catholic priest's account of light emanating from an embracing couple?"

"Hmm. I'll have a look at my notes later. That was nearly a year ago now. From the library at Georgetown."

"Could *light* have another meaning here?" Mum asked.

That alone took another fifteen minutes to discuss and tear apart, but they drew no conclusions. *As usual.* I sagged against the chair again, the wooden ribs digging into my back. Da soon became quiet, working on a section that had his graying, bushy eyebrows pulled together.

"What is it, Da?"

"The monk used the phrase 'heart seer.' Would you be remembering that from your history lessons?"

No empath child would've been able to avoid it, especially not me—a prince of the House of O'Connor.

Before Christianity came to the shores of Erin, they called us empaths Seers of the Heart, or truth-sayers. It was easy for the Irish to believe in psychics and empaths with a history rich in tales of the *Tuatha Dé Danann*, or faeries, and their magic. A few of my distant relations would still not bother a fairy ring, even if they'd been paid. *And now I'm their leader. Christ.*

Back then, the empath monarchy coexisted with non-empath royalty, until religious fear and bigotry ran us underground during the late fifth century. The first Group of Elders were monarchs from each of the five royal empath houses, kings of Erin, all of them, and they peacefully ushered in a new era of secrecy. An international Council of Ministers formed nearly a thousand years later to ensure a more democratic governance for our race. Now they were no more than self-important wankers as far as I could tell.

I looked at the family pictures along the opposite wall. Even Uncle Nigel could be a bloody tool.

Despite the lack of a monarchy now, no one had a mind to let go of the useless titles and traditions. We kept the feudal system to a degree, bringing empaths into communities where the royal heir became lord or lady of the demesne, offering protection and preserving our way of life. The system was modernized, of course. Our clan alone boasted over 600 members, with several thousand more spread over the globe.

"And why is being called a Heart-Seer relevant?" I asked.

"Means the monk's a sympathizer," Da said. "He's not calling them demons now, is he?"

Aunt Finola gasped. "Look at page six, halfway down, Patrick. The monk, he's talking about a dark man of God who shows himself in saffron robes."

"Hmm. Called a Hindu two lines down. Did you see that part?" Da asked.

"But what of the next line? He wants … needs?"

"Seeks," Mum said. Her face paled. She stared at the page, but her eyes seemed unfocused.

"Mum? What's wro—?"

"Ah, yes, Moira, you're in the right of it," Aunt Finola said. A bit of static echoed her words. "The first part reads, 'the Hindu seeks,' but the next is faded."

"After that, looks like, 'marked by the light,'" Da added. "So the Indian was searching for the soulmated couple?"

"Now why would he travel all that way to seek them out?" Aunt Finola asked.

Mum shifted in her seat, gripping the edge of the table with her free hand. The paper fluttered as she laid it on the table. I sent her my concern, and she met my gaze for a quick moment before lowering her eyes. A surprising need to protect Lucky flared. It pushed me out of my chair and toward the window facing the trellis on Mrs. Robertson's house. I braced my hands on either side of the window frame, staring at the weeds strangling a climbing vine and its deep purple blooms.

It was past nine when the tingling in my hand woke me. I'd dozed off with my third set of estate status reports up on my laptop. It was the second time I'd dreamt of Lucky. Her smile faded from my mind as I blinked my eyes open. I studied the shadow of my hand in the dark and wondered what the tingling meant. While it was pleasant and comforting at first, the longer we'd held hands, the more intense the sensation had become. Hard to ignore, it was. I'd never felt any tingling with the other targets. Did it mean she was my soul mate? Or was it a sign to stay the hell away? The jolt we'd got in the stairwell surely screamed the latter.

But I couldn't bring myself to believe that. If it did, was I planning on paying any heed? I let out a laugh in the dark silence around me. *Not bleedin' likely.* But it wasn't something I could explain to Lucky either. I'd have to act like I didn't feel it.

I scrubbed my face. More secrets. I sat up, set aside my laptop, and swung my legs over the edge of the bed, stretching my arms out.

I wondered if Mum and Da had made any progress in the translating of those pages.

Why had the mention of an Indian man bothered Mum so much? She'd played off her earlier reaction as nothing important and avoided my questions. After Aunt Finola rang off, Mum and Da continued translating, comparing the word usage to other documents they'd collected over the years.

A ripping noise came from downstairs, like tape being removed from a box.

Mum.

I flew down the stairs to see her in the front room, kneeling on her favorite Persian rug by two open boxes of books. A third sat off to the side and held my yearbooks, old class novels, and other rubbish I'd not ever be needing again. The entire room was lined with the built-in bookshelves my parents had fallen in love with when they'd seen pictures of the house. The shelves were nearly filled now.

Mum flipped through her older notebooks one after another, like she was searching for something.

"What was it you wouldn't mention earlier?" I asked.

"Don't forget to take your yearbooks upstairs, darling."

I leaned against the wall. "Well?"

She pulled out an old leather journal with a Celtic love knot burned into the cover and smoothed her hand over the book. It must have been what she was after. I recognized it from when I'd sneaked into her private study and peeked through its pages years ago. Along with random notes, the pages held different renditions of Celtic triskeles, bordered in Sanskrit. Other pagan symbols had been mixed with Indian motifs as well.

"Does that have something to do with the fellow mentioned in the monk's book?"

She sighed, fanning the pages. "Quite possibly. There's more about Drago's family I haven't mentioned." She stood with my help and made her way to a leather wing chair. "I always suspected his grandfather belonged to a group called the Soul Seekers. From what I've quietly gathered in my research, the symbols in this book show the evolution of their emblems over the centuries. They believe soulmated empaths pose a threat and seek to destroy them. I am quite certain the monk's use of that word—seek—was no accident. As a sympathizer, he would have known the threat the Indian traveler posed. It's my belief the first Soul Seekers originated in India. I still have not discovered why there's such a deep-rooted connection between India and the Isles."

"This Drago—did you know his grandfather, then?"

"Yes, I met him once. They said he died in his sleep of age. He was 142, after all, but Drago believed he was murdere I've always assumed Drago followed in his grandfather's footstep I could never ask directly, of course. The Seekers silence outsiders and I never could bring myself to risk my research being discovered. Not when it meant it could protect you one day."

I was frowning now. Was someone murdering Soul Seekers to save soulmated empaths? Who was protecting us? I looked up the stairs. Da had turned in early. "Does he know about them?"

She sighed. "Yes, but he stubbornly insists I leave it alone and focus on finding your soul mate. I sense there's … there's something he's holding back from me though."

I'd felt it too. He'd become more testy and insistent about our search as this past year wore on—as if he were worried something bad would happen. *Christ.* "This just keeps getting better now doesn't it?"

By the sound of it, not only did Gagliardi want to keep me out of the Council to protect his precious spot in the Line of Ascension, but he might try something more nefarious because he belonged to a narrow-minded group of arsewipes who feared change. I didn't give a shite about the Council or the Elders, but I did care what happened to Lucky. A dizzying rage flooded through me, and I balled my hands into fists. I sat on the sofa to keep from face-planting onto the floor.

If that wanker Gagliardi dared touch Lucky, I'd show him what a soulmated empath could do.

You have no bleedin' proof she's The One, Liam.

But I wanted her to be. Bloody hell, did I ever. So much for keeping my head about me.

A few deep breaths later, I looked up into Mum's narrowed eyes, which were, no doubt, reading my body language.

"I have to ask, darling. Do you think Laxshmi's your soul mate?"

Wanting her to be and knowing were two different things. "I dunno. Are angels meant to be whispering something in my ear?" I stood and threw my arms out. "How is it I'd ever be knowing the truth of it?"

"She seems to have all—"

"And what difference has that made so far in any of the others?"

The last target, Sejal, had had all the traits, for the most part, and she didn't turn out to be The One. I'd waited almost a year on her for nothing. Nearing the end of that year, I thought if she'd break through to become an empath, it'd trigger the soulmating process and finally make me feel something for her. Weeks before Da had the vision that eventually brought us to Cary, I'd begun pushing Sejal emotionally, thinking the stress would cause a breakthrough for her. It was brutal, stringing her along, hoping to get an answer one way or another while knowing the truth deep in my heart. Thankfully, it hadn't worked. If it had, if she'd become an empath, we'd have been honor-bound to stay and mentor her until another empath could take over her training. She was already well in love with me by then, and it would've been a diabolical mess and utterly unfair to Sejal. Breaking it off was hard enough on her, and I'd felt like a right pile o'shite.

Lucky already had more empath potential, and she was more receptive emotionally—could that be the key?

"This time seems different, darling. *You* seem different."

I plunked down on the sofa and leaned over my knees, holding my head in my hands. It *did* feel different this time. I liked Lucky, but what if I had to wait a year before finding out? I found myself smiling. *A year snogging with her wouldn't be murder at all.*

The sooner she became an empath the better. What if I told her about our world? Would the shock and stress push her closer to breaking through? The Elders forbade that sort of talk, of course. If they ever found out, my punishment would amount to an empath lobotomy. But the thought of what they could do to Lucky chilled

my blood even more. They could inflict an empath psychosis, making her mental and taking away her credibility. No, I couldn't risk putting Lucky through that.

Mum raised an eyebrow. "When will you tell your father about Laxshmi?"

I pushed off the sofa and took some flattened boxes out for recycling. "Throw the yearbooks in the rubbish, yeah?"

I didn't have an answer for her. Not yet.

CHAPTER 14

Lucky

Mom dished out a steaming pile of basmati rice and ladled a reddish-brown lentil *dal* over it. The scent of ginger and other spices floated up with the steam, filling my nostrils and flushing my face.

I blew on a spoonful and watched Mom serve herself. She slammed down the pot of rice on the dining room table and dropped the ladle back in the *dal*. She'd been talking to Harshna *Mami* earlier and hadn't finished making dinner till late.

Sujata had finally called to tell me about what happened the weekend she'd told her parents about Michael. After her parents drove to D.C. from Illinois—ambushing her Saturday morning and spending all day lecturing her—Michael showed up by late afternoon and asked my uncle, Dinesh *Mama,* for Sujata's hand in marriage. He finally agreed.

Ha! She's marrying a white boy.

Mama and *Mami* had waited until today to share the news to give them time to meet Michael's parents.

I closed my lips around a warm mouthful and smiled. After Sujata had filled me in on her news, I told her about Liam. She agreed with Shiney. He definitely seemed interested. She got all motherly on me afterward though, warning me to be careful.

Aside from Mom's slurping and smacking as she ate with her fingers, it was blissfully silent. Her eyebrows moved around as she ate, reflecting whatever turmoil was going on in her head. I sighed, knowing the peace wouldn't last.

It didn't.

She began with the topic of boys—evidently, Liam had been weighing on her mind all day—and moved on to accelerated med school programs.

"Premlata*ben* wants you to meet her son, Tejas," Mom said.

I snapped my head up. "What? *Premlata* Aunty? Why?"

Premlata Shah was a client of Mom's who bought tickets to England all the time. She wasn't my actual aunt, but since she'd become a family friend, I used it as a term of respect. *Aunty* and *Uncle* were just what Indians used for their elders, instead of *Mr.* or *Mrs.* She'd seen photos in Mom's cubicle of me dancing *Bharatanatyam.* Ever since, Aunty had been asking me to choreograph Indian folk dances for all the shows and festivals she helped coordinate. Mom never let me say no. Shiney suspected Aunty was test-driving me as a daughter-in-law, but I'd never met her son and had thought nothing of it.

"*Hanh.* She came to the agency today. She told me you can do the early graduation in June, and then we can talk about you both getting married. She said you can go to the medical school later if you want. She will call Tejas home soon so he can meet you. Do you want more rice, *deeku?*"

I shook my head, more in disbelief than to answer her question. The muscles around my head seemed to clamp down like a vice.

Mom raised her finger as if she'd forgotten the most important thing. "Her Tejas is studying at Duke and—"

I shot up and stumbled into the kitchen, blocking out the rest. My stomach churned. I turned on the garbage disposal and scraped the rest of my dinner down the drain. The thundering noise worsened the pounding in my head, but it was better than giving her any real estate in my thoughts.

After a minute, I turned off the disposal and the water. "I'm taking out the recycling."

I stormed out the back, letting the screen door slam behind me. The infinite darkness above me did nothing to lift the suffocating blanket of my life. I picked up the recycling bin and lugged it down to the curb, trying to control the emotions taking over. The noise of cans clanking and Styrofoam rubbing together grated on me. As I bent over to drop the bin, my hands wouldn't let go. I'd clung so hard to the edge, my muscles went stiff. I dropped to my knees and bowed my head between my arms, matching my breaths to the pulsing rhythm of the crickets' chirping, hoping to fend off the tears.

"Lucky?"

I squeaked and twisted so fast, I fell back on my butt. "Liam?" I glanced at my house to make sure Mom wasn't watching.

Liam followed my gaze and stayed between his house and Mrs. Robertson's, keeping out of Mom's view. He was holding a recycling bin filled with flattened boxes.

From the light of both porches, I could see the concern on his face.

Does he really like me?

He put down the bin and moved into the shadows of Mrs. Robertson's porch, waving me over. *How does he know not to come to me?* I looked toward my house again and got up, wiping off my backside. I walked over, and the closer I got, the lighter the oppressive veil felt. I stopped at arm's length from him, not trusting myself to step any closer.

"Praying over the recycling, were you?" he asked.

A bitter laugh came out before I could stop it. I cleared my throat. "Something like that," I whispered.

His eyes shot over to my house and then back to me. "Your mum?"

I nodded, unable to stop staring into his eyes. Before I realized what I was doing, I'd told him about Sujata, Mom's edict about marriage or med school, and Premlata Aunty's 'offer.' At the mention of Tejas, Liam cracked his neck and dipped his head, his hands hanging loosely on his hips. *Great, now I'm making him uncomfortable.*

"Anyway." Babbling would get me into trouble, so I moved toward Mrs. Robertson's back door for her recycling. Ever since her hip replacement, I'd been helping her around the house.

"Here, let me." He took the bin from my hand, stacked it on top of his and brought both of them down to the curb. Watching his muscular form move in the dark rooted me to the spot.

Boy, I have it bad.

He jogged back, grinning. *Oh God.* Had I moaned out loud or something? I looked down and mumbled a thanks. He'd stepped close enough for me to see his shoes, and I curled my fingers into my palms to keep from touching him.

"It's the least I can be doing for you, especially since I can't be helping you with your mum." He tucked his hands in his pockets. "Y–You can always talk to me, you know. It's brutal—not having a choice, that is." His words echoed what he'd said at lunch the first day of school. How could he understand what it was like to have no say in something? Somehow, I sensed he could.

A strange warmth filled my mind like feeling an ocean breeze in summer. It relaxed me, and I met his eyes.

"I'll see you in the morning then?" he asked. Even in the dim light, his eyes seemed to reflect the light like a beacon.

I nodded and began walking home. "Oh, Liam?" I turned and ducked closer to Mrs. Robertson's porch railing. "How did you know not to let my mom see you?"

"I've, uh … known some Indian girls … before. Their mums were a bit on the strict side. Thought it safe to assume yours would be too."

"Oh." Maybe that explained why he was so comfortable with me. Most white guys treated me like I was invisible, befriended me to copy off my tests, or treated me like I was related to Gandhi just because I was brown.

The thought of how close he'd been with those other Indian girls burrowed its way in. *Should I ask?* He'd asked me about Jack.

"Were any of them your girlfriends?" I asked quietly. My next thought didn't just burrow in—it barreled through, making my stomach drop. My hand gripped one of the posts under the railing.

What if I reminded him of *her*? Was that why he was spending so much time with me?

Liam took a long, slow breath and exhaled out loud. He stared off in the distance, scratching behind his ear, and a tight knot formed around my stomach. His sigh told me the answer was a big fat *yes*. He must miss her, judging by his sigh. What else could it be?

He's just another crush gone bad, Laxshmi.

I shouldn't have expected anything different. A sting pricked the back of my eyes, and I cleared my throat. His head snapped up, and I changed my expression, giving him one of Mrs. Robertson's oh-wait-till-I-tell-the-ladies-at-church look. I refused to let him know this upset me.

Liam studied my face, his expression confused. *Mission accomplished.* It didn't make me feel better though.

"Uh, that's a complicated question, Lucky." He shoved his hands back into his pockets. "To answer what seems the intent of your asking … the truth of it is no."

My intent? I didn't want to act too bothered, so I ignored my curiosity. "No biggie. Just wondering." I forced a smile and turned toward home. "Gotta get back, or she'll get suspicious."

A guy in a dark sedan, a car I'd never seen before, was parked across the street. A slight glow from the phone against his ear had caught my attention. An achy unease skittered up my spine. *Stop being so melodramatic, Laxshmi.* He was probably a neighbor's friend—a neighbor who could so very easily tell Mom they saw me talking to Liam. Would I ever remember to be more careful?

"Lucky?" Liam's voice sounded like a plea, but I refused to look at him. I threw a wave over my shoulder.

I felt his eyes on me until I turned between my house and Mrs. Robertson's, the buzz of crickets blaring in my ears again.

Dreams of Liam had kept me tossing and turning all night, and while the pit in my stomach had never gone away, I couldn't wait to walk to school with him. *Pitiful.*

Seeing him in the soft, morning light, standing down by the corner away from my house and Mom's prying eyes, my stomach did a whole Olympic gymnastics routine. It didn't dislodge the pit though. He gave me a few curious looks when thoughts of his ex-girlfriend distracted me, be we kept the conversation light on our slow walk to school.

Shiney was waiting for us at the back entrance when we got there. She gave me an apologetic look and backed out of our weekend mall plans.

"Sorry, Liam," Shiney said. "We'd invited you too, remember?"

"No worries." He held open the door for Shiney and me. The vestibule smelled like stale cigarette smoke. I held my breath and went through the inner doors, gulping in the typical, musty school air.

Shiney turned to me. "At least you'll have more time to practice. See ya."

Liam and I made our way upstairs.

"Practice?" he asked. "Like when I was up on the roof watching you dance?" I groaned. He'd seen that too, hadn't he? "Ballet, right?"

"Yeah, and modern, but not anymore. I stopped this summer to concentrate on my *Bharatanatyam*. It's an Indian classical dance."

We got to our lockers and began changing out our stuff. All around us, metal slammed against metal, and the crowd thinned.

"Why don't you tell me about this *Bharatanatyam*."

I wondered if he was truly interested, or if he was just making polite conversation.

"Well, it's a pretty rigorous dance, like ballet, but much more expressive. The dancer usually tells a religious story or a folktale."

"So if I was to go up on my roof on a Saturday, say, should I be bringing popcorn?" His eyes twinkled.

Thank God he was teasing.

"Um, no." I let out a laugh. "I don't really practice up there anyway. Not enough room. I'd love to practice in the garage, but it's filled with junk. It's perfect though. There'd be plenty of space to put up mirrors, a ballet barre, proper flooring, that kind of stuff. Doubt it'll happen though."

"I'm still trying to set up my garage workshop. I do a fair bit of woodworking in there when I've got the time." We chatted about his workshop on the way to history. He sat behind me when I took my seat. I had to bite my lip extra hard to keep from smiling. *Ugh.* Would my heart and head ever get on the same page?

He leaned forward, and my ear tingled at his closeness. "So, my question then. Can I ever get a chance to watch you practice this dancing of yours?"

I turned my head, giving him my profile. His face was so close to mine I had no choice but to stare into his eyes. "Seriously? No. Why on earth would I let you?"

"My disarming smile, remember?"

While flirting with him yesterday, I'd told him he had a

disarming smile. Now I wondered at the wisdom of that. His comment drew my attention to his mouth, making everything below my belly button somersault. I clenched my teeth to keep from groaning.

As the bell rang, Jack trudged through the classroom and threw himself into an empty seat on the other side. He gave me a look. His eyes darted to Liam and back to me, and he raised an eyebrow in that yeah-I've-heard-it-all-before way of his—a look Shiney and I were well acquainted with. He'd use it whenever we'd promise to be ready at a certain time. Naturally, we'd always be late.

I gave him a small smile and shrugged.

Liam followed my gaze. "Sure it's not a date?"

I stuck out my tongue at Liam and faced forward. He seemed to have the courage to ask whatever he wanted. I needed to get some too and ask about his ex.

When we left first period for our lockers, Jack had already beaten us there.

"What are you doing here?" I asked. "I thought you had gym."

He glanced in Liam's direction and lowered his voice. "I waited for you at my locker this morning."

Liam was getting his French books out and froze for a split second. He'd obviously heard. His face became angular and pinched. Shiney and Sujata may have been right, but at least now I knew why he was hanging around me.

"Why?" I asked Jack.

"You don't remember?"

I shook my head.

He leaned closer. My entire body stiffened. What was Liam

going to think now? God. Why should I even care?

"Laxshmi, what's the date?" Jack stared at me with his deep, dark, serious eyes.

Liam slammed his locker shut, and I snapped my head around to look at him. I didn't know whether to be flattered or irritated by the expression on his face. He looked jealous.

I turned back to face Jack. The reason why he'd waited for me this morning hit me like a fist to the chest. In less time than it took me to remember, the tears welled in my eyes, stinging and hot. Jack put his arm around me and kissed my temple. I covered a sob with my hand.

"Jack. Oh my God. I forgot. How could I forget?" I stepped back for some air, but I couldn't breathe. Liam's eyes were locked onto me, and when he made a move to come closer, Jack put his hands on my shoulders and stepped in front of Liam.

I pushed Jack aside and ran across the main artery to the girls' bathroom.

In all the excitement about walking to school with Liam, I'd forgotten it was the anniversary of my Dad's death.

The bell to start second period had rung a good twenty minutes ago, but I couldn't stop the tears long enough to leave the bathroom.

What kind of daughter am I?

I sat on the cold tile floor of the accessible stall, hugging my knees to my chest, as far away from the toilet as I could get. Skipping Spanish wasn't the worst rule to break, but I'd never skipped a class before—and even that made me cry.

Mom never grieved over Dad with me. In fact, she refused to bring up anything about Daddy. Since his death, nothing had ever been the same between us—her bitterness over Dad's dying on us became more important than me. Every year, Jack would meet me in the morning and let me cry on his shoulder, or talk about my dad, or even listen to me vent about how unreasonable my mom was being.

Jack was a better friend than I was a daughter. Before Daddy had died, he'd asked me to honor and take care of Mom, and here I was, hating her for wanting me to have a better life and refusing a career that would help me take care of her one day. School came easy to me. I could be a doctor. As much as I wanted to dance, the odds of it making me financially secure enough to take care of Mom one day were small. It would mean I'd be dependent on a husband—a husband who might leave me as bitter as Mom was.

I can't let that happen.

Would I ever find a love marriage like Sujata? Or would my husband be arranged like Mom's was? Why did Liam make me hope I could be happy one day?

"Laxshmi?" Shiney's voice echoed against the tile.

I reached up and unlocked the stall.

She crawled in next to me and let me rest my head on her shoulder. "I'm sorry you forgot," she said.

"How did you find me?" I wiped my nose with wadded up toilet paper.

"You won't believe this, but it doesn't surprise me. Liam came into our class and spoke with *Señora* Campos in fluent Spanish. He asked her to send me to you. So here I am." She squeezed me to her.

He spoke Spanish too?

My face crumpled up, and I bawled.

CHAPTER 15

Liam

Sensing the whirlpool of Lucky's sorrow when she realized she'd forgotten her da's death anniversary tore at my sanity. I felt helpless. Feckin' useless. I'd only sensed that sort of grief once before—when my Uncle Henry had lost his wife. He and my little cousin Patty hadn't been the same since.

After Lucky fled, Jack left me no doubt he held me to blame. Maybe I'd distracted her, but I'd not be regretting any time spent with Lucky. I rubbed the ache in my chest. My only wish was to find a way to comfort her.

Then I saw Shiney walking into her Spanish class, the one she shared with Lucky.

I convinced my French teacher to let me speak with *Señora* Campos, and I worked my charm to get Shiney a pass to go to Lucky—all without needing any empath manipulation. I'd have barged into the girls' toilets myself if I didn't think it'd get me suspended, separating me from Lucky for who knew how many days.

I couldn't recall what we discussed in French after that, but it took all bloody class to regain my concentration.

Since Lucky didn't come out of her second period class, I ran to our lockers, hoping to catch up with her. She was there, exchanging folders and stuffing them in the messenger bag at her feet. I stopped and watched her from a distance. A shaft of light coming from the windows fell over her in golden rays. I blew out a breath and ran my fingers through my hair. It wasn't just her scent that relaxed me anymore.

She turned and caught me studying her. Tiny ripples of her grief managed to stay undiluted within a tidal wave of her happiness and gratitude. It hit me right before she broke into a dazzling smile that had me grinning like a kid at Christmas.

I went straight to her without breaking eye contact and pulled her into a hug. "I'm sorry about your da." Her scent and the tingling made me want to groan.

Our breathing picked up, but neither one of us moved for several seconds past what would've been considered an acceptable hug between friends. My jaw rested near the top of her head. With a small turn, I could've kissed her hair. I didn't dare. Not yet. Instead, I cupped her nape and rubbed my thumb in what I'd hoped were comforting strokes. Her mind cleared like a turbulent ocean calming.

I'd never imagined I'd care that much to console someone, but it was easy with Lucky.

All too soon, she stepped back, meeting my eyes. "I'm fine now. Thanks."

Belying her words, a surge of sadness surrounded me. She took a deep breath, pushing her feelings away with a forced smile. It took her a moment, but it was enough to leave me in awe of her control. If she was nearing a breakthrough, that would also be making her hyperemotional, adding to the chaos in her head. Her neural patterns would be changing, and her brain would be in an upheaval—for better or for worse—all because of me.

She closed her locker and shouldered her bag. "My mom doesn't really like to, um … talk about it or grieve in any way, so it really snuck up on me today. Thanks for sending Shiney to me."

"Well, I'd have gone in there myself if I didn't think the entire school would label me 'that feckin' Irish boy.'"

That made her laugh, and damn if I didn't feel like I'd won a gold ring. Then her face fell, and guilt overwhelmed her.

"Lucks," I whispered, tugging her closer. The crowd had thickened around us, and I didn't want to lose the moment. "I didn't know your da, but I doubt he'd be wanting you miserable and not laughing or smiling, even on a day like today. I'm sure he knows you love him, all year round, yeah?"

Her watery eyes held mine, and waves of more emotions than I could keep track of washed over me. Her breathing picked up. *Damn my big mouth.*

I grabbed her hand and dragged her to the windows. With no lockers there, it'd give us a bit more privacy. Her attempts to push away her emotions were weakening, and she was clenching her jaw and blinking back tears.

"Lucky, close your eyes."

She did, wringing out a teardrop in the process. The urge to brush her lashes hit me like before, but I kept my hands around hers. The tingling spread through my fingers and up my arms. It wasn't the greatest place to teach her some empath control, but it wasn't like I could stand by and do nothing.

"Listen to my voice and tune everything else out, yeah?" I said. "Take a few deep breaths. Go on. Good girl. Now imagine your mind being like a rubber sheet. Stretch it out and use your hearing to pinpoint each sound around us. Do you feel them?"

Her brow wrinkled. "Feel?"

"Sorry, I, uh, meant hear. Do you hear them, sense where they are on the sheet, how they're moving?" Hopefully using her hearing instead of her underdeveloped empath senses would work for her.

She nodded.

"Good. Bring the edges of the sheet back, tune out the noise, and focus on me."

Her brow relaxed. "Okay."

"Now turn the sheet inward. Pinpoint the emotions you're trying to block, just like you did with the sounds, and cover them all up."

She nodded.

I lowered my voice, hoping to force her to focus on the soft sound. "Now push the sheet to the far reaches of your mind. Take a few deep breaths. You're doing fine."

I hadn't realized, but I'd been holding her hands against my chest. It'd not take any effort to lean over and rest my forehead against hers. I closed my eyes, enjoying the feel of her soft hands in mine.

Lucky's mind became a blank slate, and my eyes flew open. She was studying my face, her gorgeous brown eyes wide and curious. "Where did you learn that?" she whispered.

"It worked then?"

She smiled and looked down at our joined hands. "Oh my God. I'm sorry." She yanked her hands away and stepped back. Her cheeks turned red, and she brushed her hair behind her ears. "Um, thanks … for that."

I took a deep breath and nodded, feeling a burn at the center of my chest at having let her hands go.

She twisted her fingers together, fighting her nerves, and brought up other meditation techniques she'd heard about. Despite pushing away some heavy emotions, her nerves were a mess.

A strange prickling crept up my spine. My muscles tensed, and I scanned the hallway looking for … what?

"Liam?" Lucky must have seen or sensed my reaction. She stepped closer, following my actions.

My gaze turned to the window and the car park below. A good hundred feet away, a suited man leaned against the driver's door of a dark sedan. He was staring up at us. I focused on him with my heightened vision and opened up my mind, stretching it as far as it would go, but with no luck. *Damn.* A large, jagged scar marred his cheek and tanned complexion. He was a thick fellow in a tight suit. Bushy, black eyebrows shielded haunting, gray eyes, which stared right at me. A small smile curved his lips. His eyes moved a fraction of an inch over in Lucky's direction, and I shoved her behind me and glared at him. A smile revealed a gap between his two front teeth.

"*Liam!* Wha—?"

"Sorry, Lucks." I moved her away from the window. "Forgot the time. You've already missed Spanish, and I'll not have you miss another class on my account." I forced a smile, but she only narrowed her eyes.

The one-minute warning bell rang. "Go on ahead. I left my calc book in my locker."

She glanced around us and back at me. "Okay." She turned slowly and walked away, her confusion slowly edging out her unease.

I rushed back to the window, but the fellow was gone. *Shite.* Who'd be having me watched? The Elders? Gagliardi?

I pulled out my mobile and dialed Mum.

She picked up after one ring. "Liam, darling. Is everything all right?"

"Can't be knowing for sure." I described the spy, his car, and what had happened.

She muttered several *Oh dears* and became silent.

"Mum?"

"Yes, darling, I'm here. This might be related to the visit this coming weekend, but I'm not convinced it is."

Neither was I. "Will you ring Uncle Nigel and see what he can find out?" I scanned the car park below for anything unusual, but not a thing seemed out of place. The class bell had rung. I'd be late, but if I confused Mrs. Lenko by projecting a quick emotion or two, manipulating her own, she'd likely excuse me without question.

"Of course, straightaway. You needn't ask," Mum said. "Your father and I will drive around the neighborhood and the school to see if I'm able to spot anyone. You believe he was a far-reader?"

"I do. I sensed him trying to read me from a second-floor window."

When the spy's empath energy had mingled with mine, the contact was enough to be setting off warning bells. Having not been around other empaths for a time meant a new exposure would feel like smelling again after suffering a head cold. The first scent was bound to be intense.

After reminding Mum not to be telling Dad about Lucky, I made another visual pass of the car park. The memory of his smirk inflamed my need to be at Lucky's side.

I clenched and unclenched my free hand around my bag's strap. Scarface had better be smart enough to stay away.

I'd been waiting for Lucky at the lockers for almost ten minutes. We'd not made plans to meet for lunch, but surely she'd need to change out her books. I'd only been a few minutes late from gym class. Had I missed her? The crowd in the main artery thinned around me. If she'd been talking to someone, I'd have seen her by now. I left for the science hallway and peeked into the biology lab. Empty. Why wouldn't she have waited for me? She hadn't been upset after calculus—she'd even said she'd meet me by the lockers. Had Jack said something about me? I ran my hand through my hair and tugged. *He bloody well better keep to himself.*

Think, Liam. Think. Jack had mentioned a meeting with his science fair advisor. He'd not be joining us for lunch, so Lucky couldn't be with him. Scarface wouldn't be trying to get to Lucky, would he?

A growing panic replaced any common sense I had. I began jogging toward the main stairs. Maybe Lucky was in the lunchroom with Shiney. A teacher yelled for me to slow down, but I burst through the stairwell doors before I heard anything more from him. The metal door slamming into the wall echoed, sounding like an explosion. I skimmed over the steps as I flew down, matching the rhythm of my heart. Any faster and I'd have surely tripped.

Students blocked my way, forcing me to weave between their grumbling selves.

Stay easy, Liam.

At the edge of the lunchroom, I stopped, my shoulders heaving, and scanned the tables for Lucky and Shiney. I opened up my mind and stretched it as far as it could go.

No Lucky.

Bloody hell.

CHAPTER 16

Lucky

After telling Shiney I needed some time alone to recharge, I took my lunch to the benches at the edge of the school's parking lot. I told her to tell Liam I'd see him later—if he seemed to be looking for me, that is. He'd been late from gym again, so I couldn't tell him myself.

Some quiet time would help me refocus my thoughts after such an intense morning. I didn't remember a time when it had been this hard to deal with the ruckus in my head. Maybe it was because it took me by surprise.

I sat back and dug my spine into the worn, wooden slats of the bench, hoping for the pressure to distract me. Initials were carved all over the seat, and I traced the ones closest to my thigh. Like painting the spirit rock out front, carving the benches was a school tradition.

I tilted my head back to stare at the oak branches above me. The sun that filtered through the leaves warmed my face. I smiled and took a deep breath.

With my eyes drooping closed, I let my mind relax, and the first image to take over was Liam's smiling face. Confusion weighed down my head and heart. I didn't want to be a reminder of someone he'd left behind, but I felt drawn to him—physically and emotionally. When he'd held me today, it had felt so natural, so right, like finding shoes that fit without pinching or poking. *Snug.*

Like in snuggle. I giggled.

"What has you laughing?"

I let out an unladylike squeak and bolted upright. *Liam.* "You scared me."

Liam sat beside me with a recyclable to-go container like mine. His cheeks were red, as if he'd been scrubbing his face, and his hair was sticking every which way. He was running his hand through it now, but he still looked like he could teach a class on modeling for magazine covers.

"You scared *me*," he said.

"What? How?"

He shook his head as if to say never mind and opened his messenger bag to take out a water bottle. He narrowed his eyes and scanned the parking lot.

"Are you okay, Liam?"

"I should be asking that of you." He flipped open the container to reveal two slices of pizza. "I'd been worried, not knowing where you were."

There was that directness. I smiled. "Did you think I locked myself in the girls' bathroom again?"

He returned the smile and bit off a huge chunk of pizza—like half of it. *Boys.* Some of the tension lining his face disappeared. "Something like that." He swallowed. "You never know, someone could've kidnapped you." A slight wrinkle appeared on his forehead as if the threat were real, then he smoothed his expression. He pointed to my uneaten pizza. "Eat." Another chunk of his slice disappeared.

I snorted. "Who'd kidnap me? The lunch police?"

He covered his full mouth with his fist and chuckled. I wasn't hungry, but I did what he asked. His first slice was gone in two more bites. "C'mon now. Nibbling won't do."

Liam's cell phone rang. He set aside his pizza and dug the phone out of his pocket. He greeted his little cousin, Patty, and judging by the smile on Liam's face, he must have missed him. He looked over and mouthed out, *Sorry.* I waved off his concern.

Apparently, Patty wanted Liam to call his other cousin, Ian, and read him the riot act.

"No, he'll be getting ready for bed, like you should be," Liam said. "I'll ring him tomorrow, yeah?"

I entertained myself while he was on the phone by checking out his black *B.B. King's Blues Club* T-shirt, tan cargo shorts, and muscular calves. I took a sip from my water bottle. The heat was getting more intense because the cloud cover was moving off. The tree provided only so much shade.

Liam rolled his eyes at something Patty had said and fixed his gaze on me. If it were possible for cells to squirm, then mine were—all over the place.

I was in serious trouble.

"Yeah, she's a girl … I see … You want to talk to her?" He raised an eyebrow at me. I smiled, wiggling my fingers to take the phone. "Right enough, here she is."

He held the phone to his chest. "Call him Patrick, yeah?"

Knowing how personal a nickname could be, I nodded. He gave me the phone, moved his bag down to his feet, and scooted closer to me.

"Hi, Patrick." My heart raced when I heard his brogue in his sweet five-year-old voice. He filled me in on his crisis with Ian, and how Sarah at school had told him he didn't know how to talk to girls, hence the practice with me. Liam heard most of it and groaned.

"So, what's your name then?" Patrick asked.

"Lucky—I mean, Laxshmi."

"Can I not call you Lucky? That'd be easier." His question sounded like a pout.

"Well, that's Liam's nickname for me. I suppose you'd have to ask him."

Liam smiled.

"I have a nickname too," Patrick said, and a yawn came over the phone line.

"I heard. A nickname makes you feel special, doesn't it?" My cheeks warmed, realizing what I'd implied. Liam's body was shaking as he tried to laugh quietly. I backhanded his thigh.

Patrick reasoned that since I was now his friend, he should be able to call me Lucky. I told him we could skip asking Liam, but it would have to involve a fair trade, like drawing me a picture, or calling me on my birthday. His happened to be this Saturday.

"Call me Patty then," he said.

"That sounds fair."

Liam's face grew serious. *Oh crap.* Maybe the nickname was only supposed to be a family thing. He read my expression and shook his head, motioning for me to continue. He laid his arm out behind me, his hand lightly resting against my other shoulder. It was too much and not enough at the same time.

"You know," I said. "You're only one of two people in the whole world who can call me Lucky. That means you're special."

"Is Liam?"

Oh boy, is he ever.

We eventually said our good-byes, and I gave Liam his phone back.

His eyes widened. "Wow. He let you call him Patty."

"I'm sorry. I won't use it—"

"No, you don't understand." Liam explained how Patty's mom had died a year ago—she was the one who'd given him the nickname. He tucked my hair behind my ear and frowned. "After she died, Patty, uh … closed off from everyone. Sort of hid his emotions, you could say. Now he only lets a few of us call him Patty."

Now I understood why *my* nickname story had bothered Liam so much yesterday.

"Oh," I whispered. Tears filled my eyes as I grasped what sharing his name really meant, and what it had meant for me. We were moving on.

He gently cupped my cheeks and swiped his thumbs over my tears. "Don't cry. It's a good thing."

My lower lip trembled. I fought the overwhelming grief of missing Daddy and the irrational need to touch Liam. I curled my fingers into my palms and left them in my lap. Liam reached into his bag and surprised me with a red lollipop.

I laughed, tears still streaming down my face. "Do you always carry around lollipops?"

"I will if they make you smile like that." He told me his physics teacher had a basket of them on his desk. The red one made him think of me.

Is it a sign?

Daddy had always given me red lollipops so he could hear me say "led lollies" like I had as a toddler. I whispered "led lollies" to myself for old time's sake, slapping my tears away.

"I promise," I said. "I'm not always such a crybaby."

"Lucks, this is good news for Patty, yeah? What you did was amazing."

I looked down. On what little space was between our legs, I traced the initials *AB+PS* carved into the bench. "You're making it a bigger deal than it is, Liam. Sometimes it's easier to open up to a stranger."

"You hardly feel like a stranger," Liam said. He cleared his throat. "I can't be thanking you enough. From my heart. Patty's more like a little brother to me. You don't know what this'll mean to all of us." He leaned in, kissed me on the cheek, and lingered. "And thank you for letting me call you Lucky. It's not as if I don't know how special it is to you."

I clutched his arm to steady myself. His cheek was so warm against mine, and his stubble woke every nerve ending in my face. I couldn't help but nudge my cheek closer. He moved his hand to my neck, his fingers brushing against my pulse. It took everything I had to control my breathing. He kissed me again, closer to my mouth. His lips were soft against my skin, and his scent shot through my lungs like it owned the space.

His lips to mine. Could this really be?
But how do I know he's thinking of me?

I tore my face away. *I won't be someone else's shadow.* Liam pulled back, breathing heavily, like me. He looked confused and hurt, and my chest ached.

"What's wrong?" he whispered. "Why are you pulling away?"

What was I supposed to say? *I like you, but I know I'll never be more than a replacement for your ex? I'm too afraid to find out I'm right? I'll always doubt your protests?*

I slid my palms up and down my lap, avoiding eye contact with him. My gaze fell to his open bag. "I see you're reading *A Midsummer Night's Dream* in class."

"I am." He studied my face for a moment. "'My heart is true as steel,' Lucky," he quoted.

Was he telling me he liked me? I swallowed and quoted a line I hoped wouldn't apply to us, but knew it probably would. "And 'the best in this kind are but shadows.'"

I had to keep my distance if I didn't want to get hurt. I moved to stand, but he held my hand and stopped me, tracing each knuckle with his thumb. "It's no illusion, Lucks. Why do you doubt me?"

"Why do you care?" *Crap.* I couldn't bear to listen to him lie to himself. "No, no, no. Forget I asked. This is too heavy." I bolted up and grabbed my bag, missing the tingling just as quickly.

"Luck—"

"Hey, Liam!" Chloe bounced toward us from the back entrance with Jack behind her. "Ready for study hall?"

Jack stopped on the sidewalk halfway between us, his arms crossed. Liam cursed under his breath. Students were heading back inside all around us. I hadn't even noticed lunch ended.

"I've got to go. Bye." I barreled past Chloe, who didn't spare me a look. She focused her sparkling eyes on Liam. *Let her be his rebound.* The thought threatened to bring up the few bites of pizza I'd eaten, reminding me I'd left my trash for Liam to take care of. *Oops.* I'd have to apologize later.

Jack stopped me with his hands on my shoulders. He scanned my face and then glanced at Liam. "I thought you wanted some time alone to recharge. You okay?"

"Liam was worried, so he came looking for me. And yeah, I'm good."

"Good." Jack hugged me, and a growing sense of unease gathered around me like a building storm. The sensation seemed to come from behind me, where Liam stood. I looked over my shoulder. The muscles in his face were taut. He stared at Jack while Chloe yammered on about something.

Great. Now I was hallucinating. I rubbed my temples. A slow throb had begun.

Even Jack's concern felt like watching a towering purple raincloud blow toward me. Or maybe it was just that I could see the concern on his face. My head throbbed harder.

Jack glanced back at Liam and then at me. The pity was back in his eyes. "Your mom's gonna kill you if she finds out, you know. And I'll kill *him* if he hurts you."

I frowned. "No one needs to kill anyone."

Jack stayed behind to wait for Chloe and Liam, while I left for the auditorium.

Once inside, the air-conditioning cooled me off and eased my headache a touch. I put my hair up in a ponytail as I weaved through the crowd, but a man in a dark suit joined me, slowing me down. He had a visitor's tag stuck to his lapel.

"Hello. I'm visiting the school for my daughter. Do you like it here?" His accent sounded Greek.

I looked around, wondering where his faculty escort was, and then turned to answer him. He now faced me, staring with the most ethereal gray eyes I'd ever seen, but an ugly scar, carved along the length of his cheek, tempered their beauty. He cocked his head as if to study me.

"Uh, sure. I love it here." His stare felt like a jackhammer against my brain. The throbbing came back in full force. Something didn't feel right about him—all I wanted was to push him away and run. The panic bubbling up in me seemed extreme. It wasn't like he'd attack me in a hallway full of students. "I really should get to class."

I picked up the pace, but he matched it, as did my heart rate. *Chill. You're freaking out because of the scar.*

He put a hand on my upper arm, stopping me. "Nice to meet you."

I jerked out of his hold and stepped back. *Doesn't he get that he's creeping me out?*

A small smile changed the angle of his scar. "Your emotions are strong."

I bit back a *no shit*, but before I could say anything at all, he turned and blended into the crowd. The jackhammering stopped, but the throbbing and the creepy panic lingered. I pressed my palms into my eyes. *Breathe in. Breathe out. C'mon. Calm down.*

"Lucky!" Liam was pushing his way to me, his eyes darting around, searching the hallway.

I was both relieved and frustrated. How could I clear my head if I always needed him? He cupped my neck and studied me like he usually did. The tingling felt like a dampener on the pounding, and my body relaxed. *Please don't let go of me.* The creepy feeling vanished, and I felt safe. Even the crowd around us seemed to part so we wouldn't be jostled.

He scanned my face. "You were—I mean … you had a panicked look about you."

"It's nothing. Just a headache."

He narrowed his eyes, obviously doubting me. I covered his hands with mine so I could feel more of the tingling. The one-minute warning bell rang. Why was it when a guy finally seemed to like me, he came with baggage?

That was it. He only *thought* he liked me.

"You're pulling away again," he whispered.

I pulled his hands off my skin. The throbbing was gone now. *Thank God.*

"You're going to be late," I said, walking back a few steps. I turned and raced into drama, thankful for some Liam-free time to think. The lights were already dimmed, and Mr. Truman stood on stage, dressed in a tie-dyed shirt and dreads, discussing foreign accents while talking in a Jamaican one. As part of our first big assignment, we had to choose a monologue native to the country we'd be assigned and perform it using an accent.

We all came to the front, taking turns digging into a dark velvet bag to choose our country. Some cheered, others groaned, and when it was my turn, I wanted to cry.

Ireland.

CHAPTER 17

Liam

It was past four in the morning. I could still feel the impression of Lucky's face in my hands, like feeling the lingering heat after holding a warm mug. When I did close my eyes, I kept imagining us walking together in the fields back home, strolling among the wildflowers. I could hear her laugh and feel her skin against my own. I'd lean over to kiss her, but then I'd be jolted wide-eyed again by the doubt I'd see in her eyes, or the sting of having to watch Jack comfort her.

Turning over, I stared at the moon through my open blinds. The silver metallic slats reflected the moonlight, amplifying its brightness, but it still left a shroud of darkness over me. The bed felt hard as stone tonight.

How could she *not* want to know why I cared about her? Unless she thought I didn't care much at all. But how could she be thinking that? We'd been walking together whenever we could. We'd held hands a time or two, and I'd even kissed her. Sure, it hadn't been a real kiss, but the intention was clear enough. Hell,

I'd even offered to help her every day after school for her Irish assignment. I smiled. It'd taken her three tries to finally pluck up the courage to ask for my help.

I covered my head with a pillow and groaned. *Girls.* How was she turning my whole world upside down in three bleedin' days? If she wasn't The One, complicated didn't even begin to describe what my life would become.

A strange sensation crawled over me, and I sat upright, flicking on the lamp. It felt like Lucky was sitting on the bed with me.

Christ. Now I'm imagining her.

My heart was hammering in my chest. After all these years, this soul mate bollocks was wearing me down.

I planted my feet on the ground and rubbed my face, giving up on sleep. Was Lucky having trouble sleeping too? *Jaysus.* I needed to be clearing out the rubbish from my head. Tinkering with something should help. The garage was mostly unpacked. It was time I used it.

I slipped out the back door, and the humid air was just cool enough to temper the heat burning inside me. In the garage, the smell of wood, varnish, and motor oil calmed me. Each garage had its own scent to get used to, and I was liking this one. This one would mix with my things and become the smell reminding me of Cary.

After a bit of searching, I found a slice of an odd-shaped tree trunk I'd been meaning to work on. The jagged bark scraped my fingers. As I traced the rings, I thought it'd turn nicely into a small table. I began working the outer bark just enough to leave the edges rough to the touch but not serrated. I liked the idea of a rough, outer edge with a refined, smooth center. Would Lucky like it? Bringing out my safety goggles and tools, I set to work sanding the top.

An image of Lucky's eyes flashed in my mind. How would I ever know if she was meant for me? Wouldn't everything be falling into place like a puzzle if she was what I was hoping she was? I had no grand notion of romance, but wouldn't finding a soul mate be something earth-shattering?

And what if she wasn't The One? Was that why she was pulling away? Because it wasn't meant to be? Could the tingling be a warning, a sign, against her?

The top was almost level enough now. I turned off the sander, still feeling the vibration of it in my fingertips, and blew off the sawdust. I brought my face to the table to eye my work. The right side needed more smoothing. The sander's buzz filled the garage once again.

Hadn't I been ready to tell Lucky that I cared about her when she'd asked yesterday? Even without knowing if she was my soul mate.

Without knowing—or without caring?

I could hear Ciarán in my head now. *"What the feckin' hell? Shag her already, then you might know bloody more."* The idea of him sitting on the stool across from me made me chuckle. I had to be half mad, laughing to myself in a room full of power tools, but it felt good to smile.

All I knew was, soul mate or not, I was gone in the head over her.

It had only been three days. *Three days.* How was that even possible?

"Why are ya letting her mess with you?" the imaginary Ciarán asked. *"What if this and what if that and so feckin' what. Get some testicular fortitude and make up your feckin' mind."*

He was right. Wasn't it time I was about my own life?

I stopped the sander, blew off more sawdust, and inspected the top. It took a half-hour of fine sanding before the smoothness satisfied me. I'd make a table of it yet. It was six in the morning now. Aside from the imaginary conversation with Ciarán, I was feeling some sanity returning.

Despite her pulling away from me yesterday, Lucky and I had a grand time today. She was still worrying about something, but if I kept things light, she'd soon relax. She'd not talk about the intense panic she'd felt yesterday before her theater class, and it'd been nagging me the whole day. She'd been projecting her panic so loudly that I'd rushed inside to find her. I hadn't been able to sense anything around me for a few minutes. It was like being blinded by the sun after being in the dark indoors. Maybe this was a part of her breakthrough. I could only hope she'd transition quickly enough.

On our way home, I stopped by the tree where we'd met that morning and took out three books from my bag. "By the way, these are for your monologue. This first one's a short story collection by James Joyce called *Dubliners*." I handed her the book and watched her smooth her hand along the spine. "This second one is a novel by Kate O'Brien, *Without My Cloak*, and the last is my favorite book of verse. It was published about a hundred years ago."

"Oh, wow! These are great. Thank you—Wait. You have a favorite book of poetry?" She arched her eyebrows.

"That's got some of the best Irish poets. What? You're the only one who can like poetry?"

We'd eaten lunch on our own again today, and I'd discovered she liked to write. Da would love that about her, but I kept that to myself for now.

"Well, no, it's just unexpected," she said. "Nice, but unexpected."

I couldn't resist stepping closer. Her scent was clear enough that the smells of cut grass and flowering shrubs fell back and faded. She tilted her head back to look at me. The canopy-filtered sunlight danced on her face. She was a stunner. She thumbed through the poems and then read the dedication from Da.

My Dear Liam,
Find comfort in these pages
For winter ends in stages,

Have faith.
You will find The One.
Your loving father,
Patrick Whelan
2009

"Why didn't your dad finish the poem? He even left a space in the middle."

We continued walking toward her home. "I dunno. Da doesn't write poetry much. Maybe he couldn't come up with anything more."

"The first two lines have promise."

"Do you think so? He does love to recite, especially if he's been bending his elbow with a glass or two."

"Sounds like it'd be fun to watch." She flipped through the pages again. "Thomas Moore? Is he one of your favorites?"

"Uh ... why would you be asking?" Her house came into view, and I didn't want to leave her.

"A lot of his pages were dog-eared at some point." She showed me a few and looked quite smug.

"Well now, look who's the detective." I shoved her gently with my elbow.

I followed her up her porch stairs and hoped she'd invite me in. From what she'd told me, her mum worked till supper most nights. I needed this time alone with her—to find out why she'd been pulling away, and if she was ready, I needed to be telling her how I felt.

Was I really about to push aside Da's vision along with the last twelve years of searching, the past six of them away from the family? Would I be ignoring everything they'd sacrificed? I ran a hand through my hair. Ciarán had said I was always diving too deep, never caring if I surfaced.

She turned, fiddling with her keys. "We could, uh, pick out something from one of your books to work on. I mean, if you're not too busy. You probably have a lot of homework though, right?" She bit her lip. The uncertainty and hope in her eyes were enough to slay me.

"Why do you think I walked up here with you?" Just like that, I was diving deep in her bubbles of happiness—the happiness that had me hoping I was as perfect for her as she was for me.

CHAPTER 18

Lucky

Liam and I put our bags by the coffee table, and he walked around, getting acquainted with the living room. Outside of Caitlyn and Bailey, not many of my white friends had been to my house. I wondered how strange Liam would think our living room was. In the corner, on our one and only end table, Indian elephant figurines sat next to stacks of Gujarati-language newspapers. Squeezed between the elephants and a lamp was a copper *loto* she used as a vase, stuffed with shortened peacock feathers.

Flanking the end table were the east-meets-west of sofa pairings. Against the wall with the long window stood a brown, microfiber sofa. Mom fashioned pillows from red and gold Indian-patterned fabric matching the cushions on our *sankheda* loveseat. The loveseat sat under the front window and was made from tubular pieces of decorated, lacquered teak wood. Little baubles dangled between each row, fluttering like leaves whenever someone sat on its cushions. On the opposite side were two, hand-me-down armchairs from one of Mom's coworkers. They were cream with apple-green stripes and stood in front of our fake fireplace. The entire room was a culturally confused eyesore.

I quickly brought out some drinks, napkins, and a bowl of tortilla chips, leaving the cheese in the microwave to melt with the salsa. I was anxious to spend time with him and irritated that I kept forgetting to protect my heart. It'd been like this all day.

He studied the photos on the mantel between the armchairs.

"So this is your Indian dance costume?" He pointed to a photo from one of my *Bharatanatyam* performances.

"Yup."

My costume was made from emerald-green silk with an ornate, brocade border. He traced the pleated fan of fabric splayed out between my legs, which were in a *demi-plié*-like position. No one from school, other than Jack and Shiney, knew this side of me. Even Caitlyn and Bailey had never seen a performance. It was like he was getting a peek behind the curtain.

I moved to get a better look at the photo, and he blocked me in, standing inches behind me. Even without touching me, his heat seeped into my skin. He rested his hand on the mantel. I glanced over my shoulder and caught him grinning. He'd been pushing the personal-space-thing all day, acting like it was accidental. *Uh-huh.*

I was getting tired of fighting my attraction to him.

"That's quite a bit of jewelry," he said.

I steadied my breathing so I wouldn't sound shaky. "Over five pounds of it. It takes about an hour to get dressed and done up." The fake ruby, pearl, and rhinestone jewelry consisted of headpieces, earrings, a nose ring and chain, long and short necklaces, armbands, a belt, and lots of bangles. I always felt like a dancing rhinestone ad.

"What are those?" He pointed to the six-inch-wide belt I wore around each ankle.

"Those are *ghungroos*. They're rows of little bells to make our footwork audible." Mine added an extra two pounds to each ankle as well. "Not quite a tutu, huh?" I looked over my shoulder again, but he was studying the picture.

"Your expression is … stunning," he said.

"Thanks. That's high praise for a *Bharatanatyam* dancer actually." His scent filled my nostrils, and I was going to do something stupid if I didn't move soon.

"Does this dance have a meaning?"

"It's a devotional piece to Lord Krishna. I'm Radha in the dance. It shows how their love transcends all earthly bonds."

Gee, I wonder why I'm a hopeless romantic.

He was quiet for a moment. "What part in the dance was this?"

"It's near the end, after a really emotional part where she thought he'd left her. He was only hiding in the trees for fun. When she finds out though, she's overwhelmed with emotions. She's overjoyed mostly, but, as I interpreted it, she's also scared by her own, um … vulnerability." I cleared the lump in my throat. "I know I would be."

He wrapped his arms around me from behind and buried his face in my neck. His warm sigh tickled my skin. I lifted my hand, but paused before I rested it on his forearm. The moment seemed more intimate than any other time we'd touched. His posture felt as vulnerable as I was scared to become.

I ground my teeth together, mad at myself for always being scared. I'd spent all of gym class today unloading my neurotic ramblings on Shiney. She finally slapped some sense into me and told me that being afraid was a choice.

She was right.

I had to know what was happening between Liam and me. What if he was just a super affectionate guy? I would never need to ask him about his ex-girlfriend then. And if he really did like me …

I pulled out of his arms and faced him. My heart thumped in my throat, and I wondered if I'd actually be able to speak. I gripped the back of an armchair and took a deep breath. *You can do this.* "Remember what I asked you yesterday? About why you cared?"

He stepped closer and nodded. "Are you ready now to be hearing why?"

I nodded, and he broke into a glorious smile.

He held my face, and the tingling made me lean into one of his hands. "I'm mad about you, Lucky. I can't sleep. Can't think. I'm a right mess. I care about you, honest I do. And watching you pull away from me … it's tearing me up inside. Tell me what you're worrying about. Let me fix whatever it is."

Oh God. He did like me. I couldn't help but grin. He stroked my cheeks with his thumbs, holding my smile in his hands.

Then my head piped in. *But you don't know why he likes you.*

"No, Lucks, don't do this. Don't pull away."

How does he read me so well?

He rested his forehead against mine, and I clung to his T-shirt. "Jaysus, I feel so raw around you. It's like smiling with my lip split after a brawl. Talk to me. Please."

Fear is a choice.

Hard as I tried, I couldn't get the question out. I pulled away and shook my head. "I–I can't." I closed my eyes. How could he prove he was over her? If I brought it up and he realized I was just a replacement, all of this would be gone. Maybe a blissful, delusional ignorance was the best thing for me—but that meant not being honest with him or myself. My stomach burned.

"Tell me you don't like me back," he said.

My attention shot back to him. "What? How can you … don't you already know?"

He looked up at the ceiling and threw his arms out. "Thank you, Jaysus. She likes me."

My cheeks warmed. "Now you're being ridiculous," I muttered.

His smile slowly faded from his face. "Then help me to understand, Lucky."

"God, don't look at me like that. I'm not saying no, I–I'm just not sure of the why. It can't be too soon … " I whispered *for you* at the end, but that was the closest I was getting to being courageous. "I don't want to get hurt."

"Too soon? Then we'll take it slow, but how can you not be knowing why I'm off my nut for you? You're bloody amazing— your heart, your sincerity, your sense of humor. And damn, you're gorgeous." He stepped closer. "And your eyes? Your eyes are mesmerizing. They're beautiful. Those lashes too. When you're batting them at me like you are now, my insides flip something fierce. And Lucks, I don't want you to get hurt either. You've got to believe in that if nothing else."

His words were making it harder to stand. "Thank you for the compliments, but ... that's not the *why* I mean."

"What do you mean then? Please, you've got to be telling me."

"I–I need to know—" The microwave timer went off. "I'm sorry. I need time, that's all."

I fled to the kitchen and brought back the nacho cheese. "Help yourself to something to eat." I let him sit on the sofa first so I could put some distance between us. How was I supposed to figure out what this ex-girlfriend meant to him if I kept acting like nothing was wrong?

"Do you have a DVD of that performance? The one in the picture."

I bit my lips together. He *would* ask to see it.

It took some coaxing, but I eventually groaned and gave in. Seeing this side of me would really hammer home the differences between our cultures, but part of me wanted him to like this side of me too. He scooted back into the sofa, smiled, and gave me the smuggest look. *Ugh.*

I popped in the DVD and joined him, keeping my distance again. He put his arm on the back of the cushion and let his fingers play with my hair. *Damn him.* Of course he'd find a way.

While he watched, I searched for useful passages in Liam's books, but I'd sneak sideways glances to see the expressions on his face. He sat at the edge of the sofa now, leaning forward. I wiped my clammy hands on my black capris, wondering what he thought.

When it was done, he faced me, his eyes a mixture of surprise and awe. "That was incredible. You've been holding out on me."

"Thanks, but it wasn't on purpose. I usually don't share my Indian side with people at school."

"People?" He studied me for a moment and then gave me a tight smile, his eyes flat. "You're really meaning white people?"

My stomach dropped. "Oh God, Liam. I didn't mean for it to sound like that. I just meant I'm a private person, and I don't always mix my two worlds. You couldn't really understand. I mean, you're not exactly a minority, are you?" I slapped my hand over my mouth. "Liam, I'm sorry. Please don't think—I mean, yes, there are differences between us, but that's not what I meant … completely, anyway. It's different with you. You're different."

He ran his hands through his hair. He looked unconvinced.

"Liam, I–I don't want you to feel … " Could this be any more awkward? Tears pricked my eyes, but I refused to get all weepy again.

"Is that why you're pulling away?" he asked quietly. "Because I'm not Indian?"

My jaw dropped. I'd never have pegged him for being insecure. Me? Yes. Him? No. The urge to comfort him overwhelmed me, and I threw my arms around him. "No! God, no, Liam. That's not important to me, honest. I'm so sorry if I made you feel that way."

Liam inhaled deeply, and I could feel him relax in my arms. He scooped my legs up and brought me into his lap. I pressed my face against his neck and couldn't get enough of his scent, even though each breath scrambled my brain cells a little bit more.

It didn't take long for my subconscious to remind me of his sigh-inducing ex-girlfriend. I slowly ripped myself away, avoiding eye contact. I had turned in his lap so my feet were on the floor.

He rested his forehead against my back, caressing my arms. "I'm glad … glad you shared your Indian side with me."

Tell him the truth.

I pulled his arms around me, relishing the tingle and craving his comfort. He moaned, pulling us back into the sofa, his chin resting on my shoulder.

"I–I have to know if you, um … still have feelings for your Indian ex-girlfriend." Could he feel my heart pounding in my chest?

"Ah, sure, Lucky." He let out a huge breath. "Is that what's been worrying you?"

I nodded, keeping my eyes fixed on the different skin tones of our arms.

"We did date, but it wasn't like … I never developed any real feelings for her." He turned my chin and shifted me slightly so I'd meet his eyes. "She was never a girlfriend in the way you might be meaning it."

So he was just using her?

He studied my face again, narrowed his eyes, and widened them as if in understanding.

How does he do that?

"No, no, no. It's not what you're thinking. I let it go on for far longer than I should have, and it got complicated is all. Please believe me."

I closed my eyes for a moment. This was the very thing I wanted to get rid of … doubt. "Liam—?"

"No, wait. Hear me out, yeah? You don't want me comparing you to her, or replacing her with you, I get that. But if you'll give me some time, I swear to you I'll erase your doubts. Isn't that fair?"

The fact he understood and was willing to prove himself put a small smile on my face, and a huge one on his.

He moved my butt onto the sofa, bringing my legs to rest over his lap again. *Sneaky.* We were now eye to eye. With one hand cupping the back of my neck and the other my outer thigh, he'd made sure I wasn't escaping.

"And Lucky? You're not to be anyone but yourself with me, yeah? I want to know *everything* about you—Indian or otherwise. You've got my undivided attention, not some other girl."

I imagined a cool breeze blowing sand away from an ordinary mound on the beach, showing the object buried beneath, as if the breeze uncovered some hidden truth. I almost snorted at my latest hallucination. What I seemed to doubt on a conscious level, my subconscious accepted wholeheartedly—he was telling the truth.

Your truth fills the air like musical notes,
And into your words, I melt and I float.

"Lucky?" I snapped out of my quick foray into La-la Land to find Liam inches from my face. "Where did you just go?" he asked.

I covered my lips with my fingers. *Did I really just zone out in front of him?*

He raised an eyebrow. "Now I really want to know." He pulled my fingers from my lips.

My cheeks began burning. "I, uh … zoned out, that's all."

"I'm a very good human lie detector, you know. Tell me before I find something else to keep your lips busy."

I choked on my breath and coughed. "Um, a couplet kind of bubbled up."

He broke out into a grin. "So I inspired you to poetry?"

"Ugh! You are so full of yourself. You know, I change what I said. It's not about you being white—it's about you being Irish."

"Oh you're going to regret ever saying such a thing."

He launched himself on me and tickled my sides until I begged him to stop. We wrestled over the pillows, and the farther I tried to get from him, the closer I seemed to be, until we were laughing into each other's necks. We gradually stopped laughing, and when our eyes met, I knew.

I was too far gone.

We spent the next hour working on my monologue. I still couldn't string more than two words together without losing the accent, but I definitely had the cadence down because all I had to do was imagine the lilt in Liam's voice. It had been my lullaby these past few nights, after all.

"Well, I'd be smart to leave. Your mum should be home soon."

I agreed. It was almost five o'clock, and I didn't want to cut it too close. He helped me clean up, and then I stood by the door with him, unsure of what to do or how to act.

An ache formed in my chest.

"So, tomorrow?" I asked.

"On the corner." He studied my face and gently kissed my cheek.

He reached for the doorknob, but stopped. "Could I show my mum that DVD? She's sort of a self-proclaimed expert on all things Indian. She'll love it."

Warmth flooded my face at the thought of his mom watching me dance. As little Indian girls, our mothers planted daydreams in our heads about impressing our future in-laws. I couldn't help but think that way now. I turned to get the DVD and rolled my eyes at myself. "Here, if you really think she'll enjoy it."

"I know she will. Take care. Work on those vowels of yours."

I made a goofy face. "I'll try."

He skipped down the porch stairs. "Have faith, Lucky. I do."

He stopped halfway down the sidewalk, paused for a moment, and turned back to me with a shy smile. "Will you come over this Saturday for a meal with the parents?"

"Huh?"

His face lit up. "Lunch. Saturday. Mum's been asking to meet you."

I glanced to my right and left, looking for witnesses. *Is he serious?* A kaleidoscope of butterflies took off in my stomach, and his grin expanded. I watched him until he was out of sight.

Several hours later, I was beating my pillow to fluff it up just right. No matter how hard I tried to distract myself, I saw, heard, smelled, and even felt Liam with me. It didn't help when the stupid tingling kept erupting inside me. How come Sex Ed never taught us what hormones really did to us?

I got out my journal and scribbled nonsense lines, hoping to release some of my energy to the paper. I eventually silenced my thoughts, but I still couldn't sleep. I thought about dancing to tire myself out and remembered lunch with Liam today. Why did I tell him I wrote poetry or danced when I couldn't sleep? Whatever happened to my privacy filters? Neither Jack nor Shiney knew those things about me.

It was as if I were a color-by-number poster, and I didn't get fleshed out until I spoke the words out loud to Liam. With everyone else, I was someone specific—a dancer, an Indian girl, an American, a daughter—but with Liam, I was no one in particular. I was just me.

And for the first time, I had a million colors to choose from. The only problem was the giant eraser in the form of my mother downstairs.

CHAPTER 19

Liam

"Liam, I was just about to ring you. Where have you been?" Mum put a book back on its shelf.

I walked through the front room and peeked down the hall. "Where's Da?"

"Upstairs talking with Finnie."

I told her about Lucky's theater assignment and how I'd be helping her after school.

Mum nodded. "She couldn't have picked a better tutor."

I stared at her, waiting for more. She hadn't even cracked a smile. "What's wrong?" I asked. It wasn't like Mum to be distracted.

"The Council brought Finnie in for questioning earlier today."

Bloody hell. "For what? Those photos? That can't be good, can it?"

She let out a nervous laugh and sounded nothing like her usual self. "It's definitely not the attention we should be drawing to ourselves. The Council has decided to send one of the Elders with Drago to question your father this weekend."

"An Elder?" I dropped my bag and sank onto the sofa. For the

Elders to be involving themselves in a trivial administrative matter meant they were surely using Aunt Finola as a pawn—a pawn in the game where I was a king. *Bloody feckin' politics.* I scrunched closed my eyes for a moment and then stared at the ceiling. The shite I'd always wanted to avoid was beginning already.

Mum removed her reading glasses and pinched the bridge of her nose. "Drago and the Elder will now be arriving a day earlier, so you and your father must leave for Charlotte on Saturday."

I sat up. "I thought we'd be leaving Sunday morning, so I invited Lucky to spend the afternoon with us. I figured I'd spring word of it on Da Saturday morning. You did say you were needing a connection—to help protect her, yeah?"

After hearing about the scarred man in the car park, Mum wanted to be meeting Lucky sooner rather than later, whether she was The One or not. Uncle Nigel had found out next to nothing about who'd hired the spy, and Mum thought it wise to be prepared. Best case scenario, whoever hired him was waiting for history to happen, wanting to manipulate his or her way into my inner circle of influence. Worst case? Soul Seekers were trying to harm one of us—Lucky being the easier target. My chest tightened at the thought.

Mum rested a hand over her heart. "Liam, I'm more than delighted to meet Laxshmi, but your father will have to leave in the morning without you then. The less he knows before he meets them, the better. Besides, the official meeting will likely be scheduled on Sunday."

"Suits me. I can drive down Saturday after lunch." I'd no doubt be a right hand better at keeping my secrets hidden than Da, since he wasn't an empath.

"I'll have to make something special—a roast?" She muttered a few more ideas to herself.

I groaned and threw my head back on the sofa. "We're not getting married, for Chr—crying out loud. And no shrinky stuff, or we'll be spending the day at the park or the movies instead."

She came over and sat next to me. "I promise, no shrinky stuff. It's just ... you've always kept the girls as far from us as possible."

Bringing one of the targets home with me seemed pointless and cruel. It would've twisted the knife in their hearts when I moved on.

"Do you know anything yet, darling? Do you think she's—"

"Mum, I've no idea. No angels in flowing white gowns singing overhead, remember?" Some strange things *had* been happening, but were they important? Or was I just a guy reacting to an incredible girl? "How the hell am I ever meant to know? It's some answers I need." I leaned forward and pressed my forehead into my palms.

"Uh, Liam ... darling." Her hesitant tone drew my attention. "Your father never wanted me to tell you this, but, well, something specific is meant to happen. He saw it in one of his first few visions. One he wouldn't say anything about, other than that he'd had a clear seeing. When the vision comes true, he'll know with absolute certainty she's The One."

I sprang up. "Why is it I'd only *now* be finding out about this? After all these years?"

She shook her head. "He'd only just told me."

I paced between the sofa and fireplace, running my hands through my hair. How could Da be so diabolical as to hide such a bloody huge detail? Might've saved years of trouble if I'd known just what was supposed to happen when I met The One. Years of torture. For me and the targets. *Christ.*

I wanted to be punching something. After a few deep breaths, I plunked down on the other sofa. Da and I would definitely be chatting about this. I grabbed a cushion and whacked it once with my fist. My anger would have to wait.

"Liam—"

"Don't." I held up my hand.

She tried to be giving me explanations and apologies, but it was

Da who'd be needing to explain. Our lives had been ruled by these visions. It hadn't surprised me she'd kept his secret.

What could prove Lucky was The One? I pictured her, recalling how the light played on her face when she'd tilted her head back in the sun, how she smelled when she was in my arms, how she finally opened up to me. My heart rate calmed, and I remembered Lucky's performance. I turned to Mum. The apology in her eyes had me softening. I reached into my bag with a sigh and brought Lucky's DVD to the player.

"So I've something for you to watch, Mum. Have you ever felt anyone project through recorded media—both a photograph *and* video?"

"That's very rare," she said. "I've never seen it, but I have read of such cases. Why?"

"This is Lucky dancing an Indian classical dance called B-something."

"*Bharatanatyam?*" She went over to the bookshelf and chose a book, nearly shoving it into my face. *Indian Performance Art.* "Are you telling me Laxshmi projects on video?"

"In video and in a photograph, but that's on her mantel."

"Both?" Mum stood there, as gobsmacked as if I'd told her aliens had landed in our garden. She blinked, waved a finger for me to begin the DVD, and grabbed a notebook. "She'll become the toast of academia with such skills." She muttered something about how that would change Lucky's EQ assessment, as if it were a foregone conclusion she'd break through. The thought brought a smile to my face. Mum sat on the edge of the wing chair and slid her glasses back on. *Ever the scientist.* I hovered a finger over the remote's Off button in case Da came downstairs and asked what we were doing. Mum's pen scratched furiously while she watched.

At the end of the performance, she closed the book and sat back. "Liam, she's exquisite. I observed fourteen different projected emotions with multiple nuances, but not from her, just the persona she created on stage. Simply incredible, and she's not yet an empath."

"Told you."

She pursed her lips and raised an eyebrow. "You only said she was beautiful and brilliant—nothing about her grace or the purity of her projections. And through a video, no less. Does she project this well when she's not dancing?"

"Not all the time, but when she concentrates on one feeling, it's powerful. I've seen her pushing aside some pretty heavy emotions too."

Mum added something to her notes and removed her glasses, tapping the end of the frame against her lips. "By the way, your Uncle Henry rang today with an update. Patty's begun reading emotions again, but he's still keeping his mind closed off. There's no telling when he'll open up fully, but Henry is so optimistic right now. It's heartwarming. He's utterly grateful to Laxshmi."

Lucky.

I'd not been able to stay away from her today. The odd thing was, if I moved more than a few feet away from her, I'd catch her twisting her fingers together and trying to hide the anxiety filling her eyes. When I'd leave for my own class, her panic felt like a lifeboat about to tip over. I pulled out the pillow behind me and sank deeper into the sofa, wondering if this was all part of being exposed to my empathic energy, or if it was something else.

"What's worrying you?" Mum had been going over her notes, but now she stared at me from over the rims of her glasses that were back on her face.

Well, bollocks. I'd let my block slip. I projected my irritation at her for reading me.

"Don't get annoyed with me, darling. Everything has always come so easy to you, and this hasn't. Nothing worth having is without some risk—*some* risk, mind you. You'll do well to remember that." She put her notebook and glasses on the coffee table and jerked her head toward the stairs. "He's coming. Oh dear, and he's not happy."

"Moira, a pint if you please, love." Da exhaled loudly as he reached the bottom. "No, it's the breath of life itself we should be having," he called out as Mum headed toward the kitchen.

"Is Aunt Finola all right?" I asked. I'd bring up this secret test of his later.

He paced by the bookshelves. "She's shaken up, but she's tough. They're bringing her back in two weeks. They said they might be having more questions for her after having their chinwag with me." He ruffled his hair with both his hands. "Oh Finnie, Finnie, Finnie. What have I gotten you into?"

Mum handed him a glass of Bushmills. "A *second* questioning, you say?"

He took a large gulp of the whiskey and inhaled through his teeth, making a hissing sound. Whiskey wasn't his usual drink of choice. "And in front of the whole court too. They're making an example of her they are." He pointed at me, but spoke to Mum. "When he becomes soulmated and rises up the Line of Ascension, do you think they'll be giving up their spots easily? There's talk that Elder Adebayo will be turning up his toes soon—heart problems, they say. The Council will doing anything they can to embarrass us, discredit us—now, before Liam takes his place."

Not this shite again.

"Liam, boyo, you'll be needing to find your target now, get joined, and take your place on the Council. Those arselickers will be falling over themselves to be getting into your good graces once you're in their ranks. It could be the only thing to get Finnie out of this mess."

I threw the sofa cushion to the side and shot up. "I'm not looking for a lost set of keys. And what if she's not The One?"

"Are you even trying?" He thumped his fist against one of the bookshelves. "There's too much at stake!" A desperate look flashed across his eyes. He averted them to stare into his whiskey, but not before ripples of his panic leaked out from behind his block.

Too much at stake? What was he saying? Because of an administrative headache with Aunt Finnie? I turned to Mum, who looked equally puzzled.

"Patrick—?"

"Just find her, Liam!" Da moved forward and gripped the back of a wing chair, his knuckles whitening.

What was his problem? He was acting rattled again, acting like he was keeping something to himself. If it could affect me, would it affect Lucky? Whatever it was, I'd not let it.

"Then what?" I held out my arms. "Do I drag her up before a bunch of old farts in Ireland? And for what? To let them invade her mind in an initiation ceremony? Prove she's worthy? Then let them lock us up to become soulmated lab rats? What the hell are you trying to prove—that your bloody visions were right? Why is it now so important?" My blood pulsed through my neck at the idea of ripping Lucky from her life because of Da's visions.

I'll not let them touch her.

"Don't be so damned melodramatic." Da pointed at me with his glass in hand and moved around the chair. "What were you thinking all this was about—why we made all these sacrifices? Once you're joined, you'll be changing, evolving, bringing in a new era. Your enhanced powers will make you untouchable. Safe." He took a drink from his glass, then swirled the amber liquid around. "Safe," he whispered to himself.

"Safe? You know I don't give a shite about the Council and their politics. Jaysus!"

"Don't give a shite?" he bellowed. "Would ya rather put your life on the line?"

Mum gasped. She shot up from her chair and went to him. "Patrick, what aren't you telling me? What have you been hiding? Have you had another vision?"

Da scrubbed his face with his free hand. Mum yanked it

away and held his face in her hands, studying it. He hardened his expression and wrenched out of her grip, knocking into the lampshade. He turned to me. "Those Gaelic pages are the closest we've gotten to finding out about what you'll be experiencing, how your abilities will be changing. Aunt Finnie needs your help ... our help. She's put herself into trouble for you."

"I didn't ask her to go to that restricted library, so don't be blaming me when she was doing you the favor. And speaking of favors, why don't you tell me about your other vision? How is it I'll be knowing that I've found her? And how could you be keeping that to yourself?"

Da glared at Mum. She shook her head. "He has a right to know, Patrick."

"Why did you keep it to yourself, Da? Was it because *you* wanted to be the one to say 'Aha! Here she is,' or is there some other secret to tell?"

"If I wanted you to know, I'd have damned well told you," he spat, the smell of whiskey strong. He stared at me, his chest rising and falling with heavy breaths.

"My lies were leading those girls on, and for what? So we had some entertainment before your next vision? Your keeping the truth from me affected them as well." The anger heated my insides, and I fisted my hands.

He slammed his glass down on the coffee table. "What is it you're not telling me? You used to say *the soul mate* or *the target* and now it's *her* and *she*. So who is this *she*? I'll follow you to school if I must, and drag the both of you back to Ireland."

"Patrick, darling, be reasonable—"

I rushed forward and stopped within an inch of his face. "Don't you be threatening me."

"You know who she is, don't you?" His face reddened, and he searched my face as if the answer were written there.

"If I did, I'd not let you anywhere near her." Hell if I ever tell

Da about Lucky now. I'd not let him use her to manipulate me.

His eyes blazed, and he looked ready for a milling. I widened my stance. I was ready too.

"That is more than enough from the both of you." Mum shoved us apart. "Patrick, we're all worried about Finola, but how is Liam meant to find the right girl in a few days?" She turned to me and arched an eyebrow. "You *are* trying, darling, are you not?"

I glared at Da. "Of course."

Da spoke to Mum, though he returned my hard stare. "Something's not right, Moira. The new visions were clearer than ever before."

Mum jerked her attention to Da. "What new visions?"

He ignored her. "Do your job and find her."

I stepped closer. "If I do, I'll be keeping her miles away from your pussface."

"You ungrateful—"

"Enough!" Mum pushed me back to keep Da from grabbing me. "Go on, Liam. Leave us. Come back when you've had a chance to calm yourself."

I grabbed my car keys and slammed the front door on my way out. We'd never fought like that before. I exhaled and stretched my neck from side to side.

It was almost seven. *Dammit.* Lucky's mum would be at home. I stepped in her direction, but stopped, running a hand over my stubble. Her mum would never let me see Lucky, and my brain was too fried to think of an excuse. I couldn't even ring her mobile. Her mum monitored all of Lucky's calls and texts.

If she wasn't my soul mate, why did I feel this magnetic pull toward her? Ciarán would definitely say my other head was doing my thinking. Was it just hormones between us? But why would that leave me with this irrepressible urge to protect her from Da and the Elders? *More bloody questions.* I slammed my palm into the porch post and then flew down the steps.

Once in my Range Rover, I cranked up some Dropkick Murphys until the windows shook, and I sped off, away from everyone.

When I got back, it was after eleven. My ears were ringing from the music, but it had drowned out my thoughts as I'd hoped it would. Da was sitting on the sofa with family photo albums strewn about him, his shoulders slumped, his eyes bleary, red, and glazed over. Whatever talking to Mum must have given him had calmed him.

He waved a hand toward the kitchen. "Your ma left your supper in the microwave."

"Thanks." I sat in one of the wing chairs, facing him. I nodded at the albums. "What's all this?"

He pointed to a photo. "Remember this one?"

I looked less than a year old. Da was holding me at some picnic, allowing me to gum the top of a Guinness bottle.

"You were teething," he said. "The bottle was cold. You kept leaning for it to soothe your sore gums. You wouldn't let it go."

"I remember hearing the story—your brothers would tease you about wasting the good Black Stuff."

He nodded and began closing and stacking the albums on the coffee table. I handed him the ones closest to me. Resting his head on the back of the sofa, he rubbed the bridge of his nose like Mum always did.

I went to the kitchen, warmed up my supper and brought it back to the front room with a bottle of Guinness for each of us. I was more hungry than curious, so I didn't press Da on how we'd prove Lucky was The One. However this test played out, she needed me as her guardian angel, and I needed her.

The test wouldn't be changing anything.

CHAPTER 20

Lucky

Caitlyn and her boyfriend, Justin, came to pick me up early Saturday morning in his black pickup. Mom was ready for work and walked out with me as they pulled up, leaving me to explain who Justin was to her award-winning scowl. She wasn't pleased, but hardly had a choice. I had to remind her last night that I'd promised to help the girls choreograph a dance routine for Homecoming. She liked Caitlyn and Bailey, so she'd agreed to the weekend and after-school practices—as long as I wasn't on the drill team itself. "Too distracting," she'd said.

Mom eyed my outfit and in a last-ditch effort to control me, ordered me to wear a T-shirt over my razor-back sports top and yoga shorts. I groaned and ran inside. Did she think I wouldn't rip it off as soon as we started dancing? It was already eighty-five degrees.

I told Mom I'd come back after lunch and then go to Shiney's house to study. She told me to keep my cell phone on me, which meant she'd track my phone from work. I'd conveniently let the battery drain down last night—she'd be suspicious if I told her I left my phone off, but she'd only doubt me if I showed her my spent battery.

Today was too special to let her ruin it.

Caitlyn brought me back home a little after eleven. I rushed to shower and get ready. Wrapped in a towel, I stared into my wardrobe, wondering how I was supposed to dress for a Saturday afternoon lunch-homework meeting with my—what—boyfriend's parents?

Was he my boyfriend? We hadn't talked about it, but he wasn't shy about letting everyone at school know how he felt about me. He'd been more than attentive and affectionate. I smiled. I'd catch him staring at me, or vice versa, and it was almost as if the tingling could pass through us without any contact. It was comforting. It *felt* right.

I chose a white, smocked, linen dress, whose sleeves rested off my shoulders. Sujata called it my sexy-on-the-fly dress. If Mom was anywhere around, I could pull up the sleeves and cover my bare shoulders. With the richly colored floral embroidery along the edge, it looked like something handmade in Mexico.

I walked over to Liam's house, fidgeting with the hem. The dress fell mid-thigh, and where my shoulder bag rubbed it, the hem kept riding up. My wedges made no sound on the sidewalk, and I glanced down to remind myself I was actually walking because, in truth, I wanted to run—my heart was already pumping like I was sprinting anyway.

I climbed his porch steps and tried to calm my breathing. Before I could reach for the doorbell, Liam threw open the door and froze. His Adam's apple bobbed up and down, and his eyes did the same, scanning me from head to toe.

I raised an eyebrow. "I hope I didn't make you wait too long."

"Uh, no. You look ... " He opened his mouth and closed it.

I smiled and felt the warmth creeping up my neck. So he liked the dress.

He took my hand and pulled me through the doorway. His mom came up behind him, and I dropped my hand from his, reaching up to push my sleeves up a bit. I couldn't believe I was here.

"It's so lovely to meet you, darling. I'm Moira. Please come in. I nearly fainted when Liam told me he'd asked you to lunch."

Liam shot her a look, and I choked back a laugh.

She turned and winked at me. "I hope you like fish, Laxshmi. Liam, don't just stand there, take her bag."

"It's nice to meet you." I extended my hand to shake hers, but she gave me a warm, lavender-scented hug instead.

Moira seemed quintessentially English—refined and poised with an elegant accent. I instantly liked her. Even though it was Saturday, she wore a tailored, pale-blue blouse and pressed linen slacks, and loose waves of her blond hair skimmed her jawline as if she'd just had her hair done.

"Lunch smells delicious," I said.

"Thank you, darling. Make yourself at home. It should only be another moment."

Their living room had wall-to-wall built-in bookshelves, a fireplace with a flat-screen above it, and small photo frames displayed between books. A deep green-and-blue Persian rug covered the wood floor and sectioned off the seating area. No culturally confused sofas here. A soothing, latte-colored fabric covered the sofas, and across from them, two brown leather wing chairs begged to be sat in. Reading lamps hung over the chair arms, and I imagined curling up in one of them with a favorite book.

A coat of arms hung on a small section of wall near the hallway. It was surrounded by an ornate, burnished gold frame, the kind you'd see in a museum. Aside from the formal-looking rug and the museum-style frame, the room looked lived-in and casual. I studied the coat of arms, determined to learn something about Liam. It was a white shield with a row of fleurs-de-lis at the top against a splash of red. Beneath that, royal-blue diamonds sat between parallel lines cut diagonally across the front. It looked simple and strong. A small gold plaque below it declared it to be the Ancient Arms of Ó Faoláin.

We both had rich cultures, only mine didn't practice heraldry, and his didn't have a dance that was thousands of years old.

Liam stood behind me, not saying a word, not even touching me. He opened his mouth and closed it again. I didn't mind waiting for whatever he had to say because for once, I had no worries.

I walked, followed by Liam, around the perimeter of bookshelves, fingering the bindings. The topics ranged from Celtic tribes to horticulture, and psychology to the Indian government. I wished I could flip through them all. A photo of Liam and his dad caught my attention. His dad was quite handsome with his laugh lines and graying hair, and I wondered where he was and what Liam would look like in a few decades.

He cleared his throat. "You're wearing a dress."

I had to bite my lips together to keep from laughing. I turned around. "It's a wonder you're not in more AP classes."

He rubbed the back of his neck and dipped his head, but not before he smiled and his face flushed.

"Is your dad here?" I asked.

"Uh, no. He had to be in Charlotte, so he left earlier. I'll be meeting up with him later."

Liam was leaving? I took a deep breath to calm my heart. It had been like this for the past two days whenever he left me. I never thought I'd be the clingy type. Neurotic? Yes. Clingy? No.

"So how long will you be gone?"

A concerned look etched his face. "We'll be back Monday, no

worries. If your mum's working Labor Day, I'll come over, yeah?"

"She is." I smoothed the front of my dress, trying to act casual, knowing I'd be missing him like a bad sugar craving. Would he miss me? "You didn't have to leave with him this morning?" I hated the question. It sounded needy.

A full grin brought out his dimples. "And miss your dress?"

I let out a laugh. "You know, you can borrow it if you like." I glanced at it. "You seem awfully infatuated ... with the dress, I mean." I brushed past him toward another bookshelf, but he stopped me by sliding his arm around my waist. My stomach somersaulted.

He turned me to face him. "Not the dress. You." A faint redness tinged his cheeks. He swallowed hard. "You look like ... an angel. You are an angel. *The* angel." His voice was husky and awed. Goosebumps erupted all over me. He reached up to stroke my cheek.

The angel? *Don't ruin such a perfect moment with doubts, Laxshmi.*

I closed my eyes at his touch and allowed myself to believe the other Indian girl had never existed. She did, of course, but he was here with *me* now. His heart was here with me. With each stroke of his fingers, he rubbed away my resistance. Each touch told me I was never anyone's shadow. He'd said his heart was as true as steel. For the first time, I trusted him.

It had to be my imagination, but he sighed as if he were relieved.

"You let go," he whispered.

"How—?" I gasped. Tingling tore the question from my mouth. Liam brushed my bare shoulder and traced my collarbone to the dip at the base of my throat. Little sparks tickled my skin wherever his fingers trailed, and when he cupped my neck, it was like leaping off a cliff in a *grand jeté*, tutu and all. I rested my hands on his chest to balance myself, feeling his heart pound against my hand. He leaned in slowly, our eyes locking, and pressed his warm lips against mine.

A radiant bliss spread from every point where we touched, like the tingling had already created a web of highways for itself. He pulled back a fraction, nuzzled his nose against mine, then studied my eyes. Was he looking for my reaction? I gave him the reassurance he seemed to need by leaning up and returning the kiss. We both smiled against each other's lips and exhaled as if we'd been holding our breaths. He groaned and hugged me to him, lifting me up. He arched his back and then gently brought me back down, kissing my shoulder. Before I could take my next breath, he kissed me again and then exploded into one of the happiest expressions I'd ever seen him make. I couldn't help but trace his dimples, nor could I stop my overactive subconscious.

A smile I inspired, by the touch of my lips.
A moment to keep in memory's grip.

"Damn," he said. "If I'm inspiring poetry again, I need to be hearing it."

"Ugh! No way. You're too full of yourself already."

"Please?" He glanced toward the kitchen and groaned. "Too late—lunch is ready."

How did he know? *Oh God.* I looked behind me. Was his mom watching us?

He took my hand, kissed the back of it, and led the way into the kitchen before my thoughts could freak me out any more.

Moira held open the back door and smiled at us. On instinct, I pulled my hand from Liam's. He turned to me, raising an eyebrow. I shrugged. It felt surreal to be myself in front of a parent—even though I suspected that Moira would be open-minded about a public display of affection. Dating was a normal part of life for Liam, but for me, it wasn't part of our culture. Hiding my American side from Mom was an act of self-preservation, as was downplaying my Indian side in front of everyone else.

We stepped outside. A concrete patio extended past a second-floor balcony overhead, giving the Whelans a clear view of my backyard. The heat baked my skin, but a hint of a breeze reminded me autumn was coming. Liam held out my chair, and the three of us sat around an outdoor table with textured glass and a wide, sipping-in-the-shade umbrella.

Moira dished out seasoned, broiled fish over wild rice, a small green salad, and fresh fruit. Fish was a rare treat for me since we didn't cook any type of meat or seafood at home, and the school's fried fish was questionable at best.

As we ate, Moira thanked me for helping Patty. She went on and on about how much it meant to them. She reached over and squeezed my hand at one point. Her eyes glistened. I tried to change the subject several times, but it didn't work.

As usual, Liam seemed to know what I was thinking. He put his arm on the back of my chair and caressed my shoulder with his thumb.

"Mum, let's stop with the family talk, yeah?"

"You're right, darling, listen to me go on."

She changed the subject to the DVD Liam had borrowed and gushed about my dance performance. Still awkward, but at least there was no chance I'd burst into tears.

Without missing a beat, she offered me more fish. I pointed out a small portion, which she scooped onto my plate. Liam reached over and grabbed two more filets, playfully muttering about Moira's favorite son being ignored.

"And that green costume was exquisite. It's Liam's favorite color as well." She slid a bite off her fork and smiled.

Liam half-sighed, half-groaned. I held back a snort.

Moira wiped the corners of her mouth with her napkin and launched into a slew of questions about my dancing. Liam hadn't been joking—she really did love everything Indian. She'd visited India several times already, and so had Liam—three times, in fact—

176

when he was three, seven, and ten. Was that where he'd gotten his taste for Indian girls?

"One of the reasons I'm so fascinated with India," Moira continued, "is because my great-grandmother was Indian."

Wha—? I gaped at Liam. "That means you're … " I quickly did the math in my head. "One-sixteenth Indian."

Would Mom be impressed? *Yeah, right.*

"That I am." He wore a proud look on his face, and I fell for him a little bit harder. Maybe Mom's sister and brother would be impressed. I closed my eyes. *Don't get ahead of yourself, Laxshmi.*

Moira began serving up an apple tart. "My great-grandmother's name happens to have been Mahalaxshmi, and she was a courtesan dancer for one of the rajas in northern India. My Irish great-grandfather Fionn was visiting this raja and fell in love with her. He helped her escape and brought her back to Ireland. She didn't even speak English."

Chills sprinted up and down my body at the incredible story and coincidences. "Did she dance *Bharatanatyam* or *Kathak*?"

"*Kathak*," she said.

"Wow, the whole thing is so romantic." Mahalaxshmi was all by herself in a foreign country, married to a man who spoke a different language. How did they even communicate? How did they make it work? I sneaked a peek at Liam, but he was already studying me, like he always did.

While we finished eating, we watched a squirrel hang from its tail and swing toward a bird feeder on a nearby branch. We laughed at his antics, and then Liam turned to me.

He leaned in and lowered his voice. "Where there's a will—"

"There's a way," I finished, wondering if he was somehow answering the question I hadn't voiced about Fionn and Mahalaxshmi. It wouldn't have surprised me.

Moira began clearing the table, and I jumped up to help.

"No, darling. Relax and enjoy the day."

Liam helped himself to another piece of the apple tart, and I worked on mine, chewing slowly and twirling my fork.

"I'd really like to know what it is you're thinking," Liam said.

"I was wondering how your twice-great grandparents communicated, and then I thought about how you always know what I'm thinking." I shrugged. "Maybe it was like that for them."

"Not *thinking*, but feeling."

I turned to him. It was an odd thing to say, but he wasn't laughing. Instead, he had that private-joke smile of his.

The patio door opened, and I helped Moira clear the rest of the dishes, despite her protests. Liam reclined in his chair, hands linked behind his head as he chewed his last bite. With the sun washing him in light, he was the one who looked like an angel.

"The fish was delicious, Moira. Thank you." I stepped inside and placed the dishes under some running water.

"You're welcome, darling, but please leave the washing up. You two have work to do." She stroked the ends of my hair, then handed me a towel to dry my hands.

"Are you sure? With two of us, we could knock this out in a few minutes." Through the kitchen window, I saw Liam staring off into space, a small smile on his face. Could he be thinking of me?

"I'm quite certain." She followed my gaze, and I put the towel down, embarrassed. How could I be so rude? Wasn't I supposed to want to impress Moira?

She chuckled. "You know, you're the first girl Liam has ever brought home."

I snapped my head toward her. "Really?"

"Truly. I've never seen him like this. If I were you, I wouldn't worry so much. Now go to him. Just don't tell him I told you anything."

"I won't." I hugged her, overwhelmed with everything. She held me close, caressing my hair like she would a daughter's, and then scooted me out the door.

Liam and I eventually headed back to their library, or front room as he'd called it. We sat on the sofa, and I took out the books we needed to practice my monologue. After an hour, I still kept losing my accent every few words.

I leaned forward and buried my face in the book. "*Ugh.*" The musty odor tickled my nose.

"You're doing well. Honest," Liam said. "You know you'll make a good grade for trying."

"That's not good enough." I wanted to make him proud.

"If it makes you feel any better," he said. "I don't believe I'll ever be doing an American accent as well as you're doing an Irish one."

"You're just being nice."

"Can't help it." He stroked my cheek. The tingling warmed me. He moved the book off my lap and came closer, making my head spin. He kissed me and then began reciting a poem.

I'd mourn the hopes that leave me,
If thy smiles had left me too;
I'd weep when friends deceive me,
If thou wert, like them, untrue.
But while I've thee before me,
With heart so warm and eyes so bright,
No clouds can linger o'er me,
That smile turns them all to light.

We studied each other's faces, and I memorized his little quirks—the few eyelashes that curled at the ends while the others were straight, the tiny mole under the corner of his right eye, the roundness of his upper lip. Judging by the way he gazed at me, he was doing the same.

How can one moment feel like an anchor for my whole life?

"That was Thomas Moore, right?" I asked, quietly. "Page 173."

He barked out a laugh and kissed the top of my shoulder.

"You're always surprising me Lucky Kapadia." He leaned in to kiss me, but I turned my face.

"Nuh-uh. You keep distracting me. Besides, your mom's right in the next room," I whispered, glancing behind us into the kitchen.

"Now that's just a challenge." He buried his face in my neck.

"Stop!" I giggled, nudging him away.

He pulled me closer just as his phone buzzed in his pocket. I didn't know if I should be relieved or annoyed. He smiled. "It's Patty."

I curled up next to Liam, eager to take the phone when he was done. As I'd expected, Patty rambled on before Liam could get a single word in. "I'll give you over to Aunt Moira in a tic, but I've a surprise for you … Yeah, a birthday surprise … No, it's here, sitting next to me." Liam grinned. Patty must have guessed. "Here she is." Liam grabbed my jaw and pulled me in for a quick kiss before he handed me his phone.

I sighed and cleared my throat. "Patty?"

"Lucky!" His sweet Irish accent tore through my heart. How could someone so far away, someone I barely knew, have that kind of power over me? It was like he was my own sibling.

We talked and laughed, and then Uncle Henry came on the phone to thank me. After some mushy-awkward moments, I gave the phone to Moira. It wasn't long before she came back from the kitchen with the phone to her chest.

"Kyle and Bryan now insist on speaking with Laxshmi. They say they'll keep ringing back until she talks to them. They promised a quick chat."

Liam got up and muttered something about their idea of *quick* would take hours. From the stories he told me about his cousins, he was probably worried they'd embarrass him. I held back a smile.

"I'll get them to quit," Liam said. Moira handed the phone to him, and he hit what I figured was the mute button. "Lucky, I've got to take this upstairs. I'll be back in a minute, yeah?"

"Yeah, sure."

He squeezed my hand before bounding up the steps, arguing with his cousins on the way.

"Will you be all right down here on your own, darling?" Moira asked. "No doubt, he'll be down shortly, but I'll be upstairs if you need me."

"With all these books?" I waved toward the shelves. "I'll be more than all right. Thanks."

She patted my shoulder and left. I started at the nearest bookshelf and walked around the room, scanning random titles. I should have been studying calculus, but I wouldn't be able to concentrate. I hated to admit Mom was right. *How can you focus on school when you're thinking about what underwear you're wearing?* Well, not literally. I snorted. Not even Mom could ruin my mood.

I glanced back toward the stairs and pushed on my sternum. Liam's absence always felt like a big rubber band snapping back when he got too far, hitting me square in the chest. We only had two classes together—three if you counted him skipping study hall to go to drama with me—and sometimes, I'd actually feel ill when we weren't together. The hallucinations were getting out of control.

I rubbed my temples to clear my thoughts and wandered around the room. His old yearbooks were all on one shelf and tempted my curiosity. I started with his ninth-grade yearbook and opened it to the inside front cover. A sweet message from a girl named Juhi caught my attention. It was an Indian name, and I wondered if she was the girl Liam had sighed over. From three years ago? Not quite sigh-worthy. I searched for his picture, but only found his name. Maybe he'd missed picture day.

I put the book back and reached for his sophomore yearbook from Atlanta. I found two Indian girls who signed it with I-used-to-be-your-girlfriend type messages, and my lungs grew heavier. He'd dated two Indian girls in one school? Three in two years? What were the odds? Especially considering no non-Indians had written any girlfriend-type messages.

And considering he'd only mentioned the one ex-girlfriend to me.

My heart beat harder against my chest. Liam was still upstairs. I quickly indexed the girls' names to find their pictures. *Can I be any more pathetic?* Jayna was in ninth grade, and Karisha was in the tenth like Liam. I flipped between their pictures and found we all resembled each other. My hands trembled. I put the book back, and held my hand over last year's yearbook.

Do you really want to do this?

I yanked it out. I had no choice.

It was from his high school in Memphis. I scanned for his picture first and traced his face when I found it. He hadn't changed much from last year. I pushed the dread back behind a dam, but the picture next to him caught my attention.

Everything around me fell away.

Framed around a quick love note were little *x*'s and *o*'s. A shaky breath escaped from my mouth, and I bit my lower lip to stop it from trembling.

Her name was Sejal Walia. The yearbook could've been a mirror reflecting back my own image. She was prettier, although I didn't like her eyebrows much, and her smile was more like a frown. Since Liam had just moved here from Memphis, leaving her would've been a fresh wound—a slow, sigh-inducing wound. What if Liam had lied to me to spare my feelings? How could he sigh like that for someone who'd meant nothing to him? Was I a replacement for one of them? For all of them?

Them. Oh God.

We even looked alike. It was creepy. Did he have an Indian-girl fetish or something? Was he some sort of serial rapist? Was that why they moved around so much?

But even worse? I'd given my heart to the wrong guy.

Stupid. Stupid. Stupid.

I wasn't special to him. I was just a number. Joke number five.

The book slipped and plunged downward, but I caught the back cover, exposing more signatures on the inside. A large heart drawn with a red marker grabbed my attention. Everything in me was warning me to run, but it felt like my feet were glued to the floor. I read the message inside the heart through tears.

Dear Liam,
I'll always remember what we had this year. You're truly the best thing that ever happened to me. I'll never forget watching the games under the stars and the hours on the phone with you. You'll forever be a part of me. I will always love you.
Love, Sejal

She'd been in love with him. How could he have dated her for a year and have felt nothing for her? *What kind of person can do that?* Were the five of us part of some bet? Were we puppets in some sick joke?

How could I ever trust someone like him?

I swallowed the rising bile. I had to leave.

A door slammed upstairs.

"Lucky?" Liam thundered down the stairs.

God, does he read minds? I shoved the yearbook back on the shelf and slapped away the tears.

"Lucky? What's wrong?" He rushed over and wrapped me in a hug. My arms lay limp at my side. It didn't feel right to hold him anymore. He was a stranger.

I pushed past him, dropped to the floor, and shoved my books in my bag.

He fell to his knees in front of me and grabbed my face. "You're pulling away again. Why? Talk to me."

"I—I have to go." I didn't have a choice. The pain was shredding my heart into a thousand pieces.

I got up and ran out the door.

CHAPTER 21

Liam

"Lucky!" I stared at the front door.

What in the feckin' hell just bloody happened?

I turned to where she'd been standing. One of the yearbooks I'd told Mum to throw away was binding-side in. The rest had fallen, pushing over the bookend.

Cursing, I ran out the door, tearing across Mrs. Robertson's front garden. Lucky had stumbled up her porch steps before I'd caught her from behind, turning her around. She was choking back sobs.

"Lucky, I can explain the whole mess. It's not what you're thinking."

She slapped away my hands and wouldn't face me. I blocked her as she tried to push toward her front door. Her pain felt like the sting of salt water on an open wound.

"I'm begging you, Lucks. Just hear me out."

She gave up trying to get past me and turned her back to me, crossing her arms around her waist and leaning against the wooden railing. I tried touching her shoulders, but she jerked away. Her hands turned to fists, and her pain turned into roiling waves of anger. But instead of sensing it as a water metaphor, I was feeling wind blowing around in my mind for the first time. The gusts whipped up the sand on my metaphorical beach, stinging my skin, attacking me as if in anger.

Bloody hell. Is that Lucky?

I stared aimlessly around her aging porch for some sort of inspiration, not knowing how to explain any of this. I blocked my mind to her, testing her yet again, but she didn't react.

"God, I should've known," she said, gritting her teeth. "I'm so stupid."

"Jaysus, Lucky, don't say that. This is my fault, not yours."

She let out a bitter laugh. "Isn't it though? I believed what you said about your ex-girlfriend. I should've trusted my instincts. Mom was right." She swiped at her cheeks, and it tore at something inside of me. I wanted to comfort her and moved closer, but she stepped away.

"Lucks, please. Will you at least look at me?"

"I guess I asked for it, huh? I should get a T-shirt that says, 'Wanted: Guy who toys with girls who look like me—'"

"Stop it! This isn't what you're thinking."

She spun around and threw her arms out. "What else could it be? Was I just another easy target?"

I flinched at her inadvertent word choice and dipped my head down. *Christ.* What the hell could I tell her without revealing too much? With someone likely spying on us, I couldn't risk the Elders finding out she knew what she shouldn't. I'd not gamble with her sanity.

"Let me expl—"

"Are you some sicko obsessed with girls like us? Or were we replacements for some Indian girl you once loved? Huh? Am I some bet you and your cousins—?"

"Jaysus, no! Will you open your ears to me? Sit. Please. I'm begging." I grabbed her hands, but she snatched them away.

I waved toward one of the chairs on her patio, praying she'd listen. She hesitated, but took the seat, her head bowed, her arms crossed around her waist again. I dragged over another chair, placing it directly in front of her, boxing her in.

This can't end before it's barely begun.

I inhaled deeply and pushed away the tidal waves of her emotions that were threatening to drown me. "Christ, Lucky. There's so much I'm needing to tell you, but it's something I can't share. Not yet, anyhow. I'll explain as much as I can though, yeah? That's the God's honest truth. I swear to you with all my heart."

"How stupid do you think I am?" She tried to stand, but I didn't let her.

"You don't understand. I had to date them, but they never meant anything to me—"

"That's even worse!"

I cursed out loud. "Luck—"

"You don't think that sounds a *wee* bit suspicious? Creepy even? Okay, so maybe you're into Indian girls like some guys are into redheads, but then why lie about it, telling me they mean nothing to you? God, you must think I'm so naïve. Either you're a liar, or you're some sociopath—*that's* your secret!"

"I swear on Patty's life I'm not lying, and I'm not some sociopath. If I could tell you everything, you'd realize why I had to date them. But that's not the way of it with you. You're different. I *want* to be with you. You've got to believe me."

Her eyes had snapped to mine at the mention of Patty's name, and trickles of her trust dripped through my mind. It was too curious of a reaction to ignore, but I had no choice. Her fight died down with each shuddering breath, and the sandstorm in my mind settled. *Damn.* Lucky was doing that. She was controlling how I was interpreting *her* emotions. How was that even possible?

Because she was my empath soul mate. The angel I was waiting for. She belonged with me, and I belonged with her.

I ached, needing to reach out to her, but I couldn't just yet.

"Believe you?" She scrunched up her face in disgust. "How do I know you didn't say those same things to them? How can I trust you? I can't even trust my own judgment."

"I never said anything of the sort to them. Let me earn back your trust. I know you've no reason to believe a word I'm saying, but you've always been able to read me. You have since day one, so ask me anything. Call me out if I'm lying, yeah?"

She leaned over and buried her face in her hands. Wisps of her hair touched my face with the breeze, and her wildflower scent overpowered me. How had I ever doubted she was The One? I reached up, paused, and slowly brushed the curtain of hair behind her shoulder. She stiffened, but didn't move away. She only looked up. Her reddened eyes were still deep pools of hurt.

Jaysus. How am I to reach through to her?

"You say they meant nothing to you, but Sejal was in love with you. How do you date someone who means nothing to you? Four different someones? And we all look alike. What's that about?"

"Lucky, I'd never hurt anyone deliberately. You can sense that about me, can't you?"

She squeezed her eyes closed and shrugged. "Were they just conquests to you then? Some game to get them to sleep with you?"

"For Christ's sake. I'd never do that. I've never taken anyone to bed, Lucks," I added softly. I was never happier I hadn't taken Ciarán's advice.

"You dated her for a year, Liam. What kind of guy does that for no reason? Were you going to string me along too?"

"We'd met at the start of school, but we were only seeing each other for about three months. I tried to feel more than friendship toward her—toward them all—but I couldn't. Not like with you. You make me want more, Lucky. I did what I did because of a secret I have to keep, but not to be cruel."

She studied my face for a moment, her eyes narrowing. The tide of her anger and frustration gradually weakened, but then she clenched her jaw and shook her head like she was fighting what her developing empath senses were telling her. I had to give her more, or I'd lose her.

"I–I had to find out if they were The One, but none of them were. That's all I can say now."

Her eyes darted back and forth as if she was processing what I'd said. "'Have faith. You will find The One.' Your dad's inscription. You're testing me too, aren't you? How do I know I won't end up like them?"

I grabbed the arms of her chair. "Because you *are* The One, Lucky." Proof or no proof.

"What does that even mean?"

"I wish I could be telling you right now, but I can't."

"Then when?"

"I dunno, but soon. Until then, give me the chance to be proving to you how I feel. It'll all make sense once you know more. I promise."

She turned her face away from me. Her waves of anger and frustration had all but disappeared, leaving behind eddies of her confusion, curiosity, and heartache. "Do any of them know this ... this secret?"

"You're the only one I'll be telling. You just found out before it was time, is all." She'd been staring at Mrs. Robertson's house, so I turned her chin toward me. She inhaled at the mild tingle that brushed our skin, but she didn't flinch at my caress. "None of them came close to what you mean to me. Now tell me I'm lying."

Her gaze roamed my face, and settled on my eyes as if she were trying to read my mind. I tested her with another block, but she didn't respond. I wanted to smile at the way she bit her lip as she concentrated. All the years and all the shite with the other targets was fading from my memory.

The search was over.

"How long have you been doing this? Were there more than four?" she asked.

Oh, feckin' bloody hell. I sent up a quick prayer and cleared my throat. I couldn't start lying to her now. "There were six in as many years. All Indian."

She scraped her chair back and stood, eyes wide. Her breaths came in short bursts. "Oh God, Liam. I–I can't do this. I don't want to be number seven. This is all too weird."

"No, *mo mhuirnín*, please. You'll not be."

"I'm not your mu ... mu woor-neen, whatever that is!" Her voice pierced the air. She covered her eyes with her palms and shook her head. Her emotions were overwhelming both of us.

I pulled down her hands and cupped her face. The tingling shot through me, and it stunned both of us. She gasped and grabbed onto my wrists but didn't pull my hands away. "It means you are my heart. My sweetheart," I whispered, resting my forehead against hers. "I know six Indian girlfriends seems odd, but you've got to be trusting this'll all make sense soon enough. It's killing me not to be sharing this with you. You mean everything to me, Lucky. Everything."

I brushed my thumbs against her closed lashes, and the sweetest sense of *déjà vu* came over me. "Open your eyes, Lucks. Look at me and see the truth."

Trust your empath senses.

She raised her eyes. "I won't be someone else's shadow, Liam. I can't."

I smiled at the small bit of hope riding the waves of her confusion. It felt like the sun peeking through towering rain clouds.

"How can you be a shadow when you bring light to every part of me? Everything about you is beautiful and vibrant—your mind, your heart, your passion for dancing. No one else has made me feel alive like you have, Lucky. You're like poetry to me."

Her eyes relaxed, reflecting a world of both vulnerability and strength. I couldn't resist the pull between us any longer. My lips met hers, and the spark felt like touching a nine-volt battery to my tongue. I didn't know what the tingling meant, but I could never concentrate on the *whys* when I was touching her. She tasted as sweet as her scent, and even though I had no idea how we were meant to become soulmated, it couldn't happen soon enough. When she wasn't near me, it was like sailing the ocean without sails, cast adrift, only, I hadn't known what the mast was for until she came along.

She broke off the kiss and pulled away from me, holding her hands out in front of her when I moved closer. "No, don't. Please. Your touch confuses me."

I shoved my hands in my pockets and stepped back. "I'm sorry. What do you need from me, Lucks? Anything."

"I don't know. Time? Give me some time."

I nodded. "I'll wait for as long as you need. I'm done searching."

"Searching? Ah. The secret." A tinge of bitterness tainted her voice. She picked up the bag she'd dropped at the top of the stairs and fished out her keys.

I stepped in front of her, blocking the way to her door. "Give us a chance. Will you not be having a little faith in me, Lucky?"

"I don't know what to believe, Liam. I don't trust you, and yet … "

"Your, um … intuition says you can."

Lucky's eyes locked onto mine. They were clouded with uncertainty again, but they were still so bloody beautiful. She nodded slightly. Her confusion came across like a boat buffeted by several opposing currents, unable to move forward.

She opened the screen, unlocked the main door, and stepped over the threshold. With a glance over her shoulder, she cleared her throat. "'So quick bright things come to confusion'," she said, quoting *A Midsummer Night's Dream* again.

"But Lysander also said, 'The course of true love never did run smooth.' Some things truly are forever, Lucky."

"Yeah, but it could still be an illusion."

The door clicked shut behind her. A wave of sadness overwhelmed me from inside the house, matching the ache building in my chest. I put my hand on the screen door, wishing somehow I could manipulate her feelings, make her happy without corrupting the trust she needed to build in me.

I'd never be breaking her trust in me again.

That evening, I left to meet Drago Gagliardi and the Elder. There was not a chance in hell that I'd be letting them find out about Lucky now.

CHAPTER 22

Lucky

I locked the door behind me, then slid to the cold, tile floor of the entryway, a small island in a sea of carpet. The rubber band had snapped back, and the pain stabbed at me this time. Air wouldn't move into my lungs fast enough. With each breath, my heart screamed. I curled into a ball and pressed my fingers against my sternum.

Why did I let myself believe he actually liked me? Could I really be that gullible to believe some secret would magically explain everything? But what if it did? My instincts had told me something wasn't right, but I didn't have the courage to listen.

My eyes burned from crying. *I can't stay down here.* I crawled off the floor and up two flights of stairs to my room. I dropped my bag onto the ground with a soft thud, and I crumpled into the fetal position to join it, sobbing.

So much for the fairy tale romance.

What secret could explain why he'd dated girls he wasn't interested in? Who would do that unless they were just after sex? He'd said he was a virgin, but was that true? A nagging feeling told me he was being honest—about everything—but what if it was just wishful thinking?

But, God, that kiss. My first. I traced my lips. They tingled at the memory.

He'd said he was done searching for The One. The one what? The one who reminded him of his first love? The one he'd lose his virginity to? The one he'd fall in love with? What?

Six Indian girls? The Indian guys in Cary didn't even have that kind of reputation.

If four of us looked alike, all six of us probably did. I wiped the tears rolling over the bridge of my nose and dug patterns into the carpet with my fingernail. I couldn't contain my subconscious anymore.

How do I forget when I don't even believe,
And get over this pain that's making me grieve?

Well, if I didn't want to be a doctor, I could always write cheesy greeting cards.

After Mom and I had been eating dinner in silence for fifteen minutes, her eyebrows pulled together. "Laxshmi? Why aren't you eating?"

"Sorry, Mummy. I'm not hungry. Probably hormones or something." *Actually, it's because my love life sucks, I got my heart ripped out today, and I have a possible sociopath claiming I'm The One.*

"You look tired, *beta*. Don't stay up too late, okay? Go to sleep early."

I tried to chew a few more bites of the *rotli* and sprouted mung beans, but gave up. I took my plate to the sink and began wiping down the counters and putting away the extra salad and mango pickle. It was a good enough distraction.

She finished eating and came into the kitchen. "*Ruhva de, deeku.* Leave them. I'll do the dishes. Go. You sleep."

"Don't worry. You worked all day. I'll do these and then go upstairs."

She rubbed my back and frowned. Her touch weakened my defenses, but I couldn't crumble in front of her. I took a few deep breaths to regain my control.

"Don't work too hard on this drill dancing for Caitlyn and Bailey. You'll be too tired to study, okay?"

"Drill *team,* Mom. It's not that. Don't worry."

"Then?"

"I said I was tired, that's all." She scowled, but I didn't care. "How was work?"

"Good. Mr. Ambley is selling the travel agency."

What? I put down the pot I was rinsing. "Why? It's been in his family for years. Will you still have a job?"

She rotated her wrist, splaying her fingers and twisting her palm once, giving me the Indian version of a shrug. "Probably money. He said the new owner will leave everything the same, but *Bhagwan jaane.* God knows."

"Wow."

"I called your Harshna *Mami* today." She handed me the dirty spoon rest from the stove. "That boy's parents live right here in Durham."

"They're doing an Indian engagement, right?" It meant Michael's parents would host the ceremony, as was tradition, and we'd have a ton of family staying here with us. "But will Neelu *Masi* be able to come?"

"Why wouldn't she come? The ceremony is in November, and her due date is end of December."

"*At* the end of December, Mom."

She waved her hand dismissively.

Even though Harshna *Mami* was only a sister-in-law, *Mami* was more like a real sister to Mom than Neelu *Masi* was. Mom was the older one, and they didn't always get along because *Masi* was the free-spirited, romantic type who did what she wanted. She was addicted to romance novels, which Mom always thought was a silly waste of time. I loved hanging out with Neelu *Masi* though. Without any siblings of my own, it was always entertaining to listen to her argue with Mom.

With all the festivities, I'd have to go Indian clothes shopping, for sure. It wouldn't be too hard to find an emerald green *sari* or *choli* set Liam would like.

Liam.

I blinked back tears. Mom muttered something about her sister.

"Sorry. What's that about *Masi*?" I asked.

She handed me a plastic sour cream container to wash out. "She probably made this happen, talking to Sujata about romance all the time."

"What? So Sujata fell in love. At least he loves her enough to marry her." It was too hard to hold back. The tears spilled over, and I choked on a sob.

"Laxshmi! What's wrong?"

"Nothing." I pushed her hand away. "Just hormones. I told you I'm tired."

"Then go upstairs if you're bleeding—"

"God! I'm not having my period right now. I'm just PMSing." I sniffed, threw down the serving spoon I was washing, and escaped upstairs.

I called Sujata as soon as I got upstairs and cried to her for over an hour. I only had the heart to tell her about Sejal and how she looked like me. If I told her about the mysterious secret and five more Indian look-alikes, she would've told me to drop him like a bad samosa. I didn't want to hear that kind of advice right now. Apparently, I was more desperate to cling to him than I thought.

Yup. Dangle a hot guy in front of me and my logic goes out the door.

The pain in my chest was back, but worse than before. It felt like the rubber band popped back even harder, as if Liam were farther away from me. *Maybe he left for Charlotte.* I cuddled into my window seat, falling asleep with my hand on the glass as if I could touch him. I awoke in the same position several hours later, shivering.

I opened my eyes Sunday morning, flew to my window, and touched the glass. What was Liam doing? At least I'd be busy with distractions today. I had *Bharatanatyam* practice first thing at the temple and then another practice with the drill team after lunch.

Drill team practice was more productive today than Saturday morning's session had been. We created a small teaser routine we could do at Caitlyn and Bailey's annual back-to-school party this Friday night, and I was glad I could join them to perform. The only reason I'd get to go this year was because it was the same night as Shiney's date at Salvio's. I'd have to ask Jack, but I didn't think he'd mind leaving his chaperoning job to take me to the party. It would be a perfect excuse. Shiney wouldn't have to lie for me, I'd already have a ride, and Mom wouldn't be suspicious if both Jack and Shiney picked me up.

After practice, Bailey came over, wiping her face with a towel. "So is Liam coming to the party?"

"I'm, uh, not sure. It's kind of weird between us right now."

"Uh-oh. What happened?" Caitlyn asked.

I pulled the twins to the corner of their country club's aerobics room and told them about everything except the secret. They, at least, wouldn't order me to forget about him like my over-protective cousin Sujata would have.

Bailey sat on the floor and looked like she'd lost her favorite pair of shoes. "It's just not fair. How are you supposed to know if he really likes you for *you*?"

Justin must have overheard the story while he was putting away the music. "Easy. You'll know by how hard he's working to keep you. A guy'll pull out all the stops for the girl he's into. Trust me." He smiled at Caitlyn.

"Yeah, but it's still kind of strange," Bailey said.

He shrugged. "So he likes exotic girls. What's wrong with that?"

Caitlyn and Bailey burst into laughter, and I felt my cheeks warm. Why were brown girls always described as exotic? But then again, Jack had once called a hot, white girl angelic. I supposed it went both ways.

We agreed to brush up on the routine again during lunch on Tuesday and Thursday. We'd use the auditorium stage and then freshen up in the locker rooms afterward. It meant I'd have to skip two lunches with Liam, assuming he still wanted to eat with us. Maybe it would be for the best if he didn't.

I woke up Monday morning with a sigh. Liam's rooftop was empty. Had I really expected any different? Shiney had called last night to invite me over to study today—since it was Labor Day and I'd be home alone. Mom always worked the "American" holidays to help stranded travelers with reroutes and such. She said we needed the money. I'd already done my homework and studied, but I'd do it again to keep from obsessing over Liam.

From the dining room where I was eating breakfast, I heard the news show Mom was watching on TV. She sat on the *sankheda* loveseat sipping her chai. At random sounds outside, she'd pull back the sheer curtains at the window to investigate, like some nosy neighbor. The sunshine and stillness outside could only mean it would be another hot and humid day.

"Just for studying with Shiney, right? Nothing else?" Mom asked, after I'd told her about Shiney's invitation.

"Yes, and Jack. We have a biology test we have to study for." She knew Jack and Shiney were a package deal, and since I didn't mention him too much, it was easy for her to consider Jack as an innocuous threat to my virginity.

"But *with* Shiney, right?"

"Yeah, of course. Her parents will be there too." I forced another bite of my toast.

"Don't forget to take some sweets to her mother."

She went to the kitchen, got out a red cardboard box of Indian confections from the fridge, and put it on the table for me. Our parents were always playing the obligation game. Last time, Shiney's mom had sent me home with South Indian fish curry because I'd brought over fresh mangoes from Mom.

She stood, staring out the dining room window, fingering the handle of her mug for some time before she spoke again.

"Have you looked at the medical school programs?"

Not again. "No."

"When are you going to?"

"I don't know. Maybe this Christmas." *When it's too late to apply.*

"If you are not going to do it, then I mean it, okay? You will need to get married, and Premlata*ben* is ready for you to meet Tejas."

I tried to push away a tornado of dread, anger, and helplessness.

"If he wants to marry you," she said. "Then you can go to school after marriage. If not, you have to be in the medical school."

You promised Dad to take care of Mom. Angry tears clouded my vision. Forrest Gump had it right. Life was like a box of chocolates. Except for me, life was about as fair as a box with only one flavor—one I hated.

Jack and Shiney came to pick me up at nine. Shiney was a bundle of energy as usual. We both sat in the back seat, where she filled me in on her latest Matthew story. We analyzed her latest conversation with him, then chatted for a bit about what she was going to wear. She narrowed her eyes at one point, figuring out something was wrong with me, but glanced at Jack and didn't say anything. I gave her a tight smile.

Once I'd made pleasantries with Mrs. Thomas and gave her the box of sweets, Shiney dragged me into her bedroom.

"Okay, out with it. What's wrong?" She plopped down on her bed, a white, four-poster draped with yards of different shades of purple scarves and covered with dozens of pillows in similar hues. It was almost like she was going for the innocent harem look.

"Everything." I sat at the foot of the bed, leaned against one of the posts, and opened up the floodgates. The whole story came out—including Liam's excuse of having a secret.

"Of all the things for him to ask me to ignore, Shiney. I mean, come on. How am I supposed to forget he actually searches for girls like me—for a reason that's some huge secret? It screams FBI Most Wanted, doesn't it?"

Maybe I had watched too many episodes of *Criminal Minds*.

"Wow, Laxshmi." The pity in her voice was obvious. I squeezed one of her teddy bears, waiting for her to agree with me. "Did you believe his kiss, at least?"

My heart shoved aside my mind, jumping up and down like a yippy puppy asking for a treat. My lips began to tingle, and I groaned out loud, making Shiney laugh.

"God, I want so badly to believe his kiss—to believe *him*. He was so happy after the first one." I buried my face in my hands. "It's just hormones and wishful thinking, Shiney."

"Laxshmi, you know I'm on your side, right?"

"Spit it out."

"Don't pass up something out of fear. What if all those girls had been white, and he was just playing the field?"

I stopped sniveling and stared at her. If that were true, I would've been more obsessed with how inexperienced I was compared to him. *Great. More to worry about now.* "Point taken."

As much sense as she made, I couldn't let go of the fear I'd be number seven. But at the same time, a *rightness* settled around me when I thought of Liam, which made me forget why I was so upset in the first place. It reminded me how I'd gradually forgotten what Daddy had looked like before he'd died. Any images of him I conjured up now were from old photographs. No matter the memory—of Dad, or how hurt I'd felt about Liam—I couldn't stop it from fading.

"Exactly," she said, as if she were a detective solving a case. "Maybe Justin's right." She threw one of her purple pillows at me.

"How can both be right? Liam can't like exotic girls, and then not like them when he dates them."

"Maybe he dreamed about you and has been searching for you ever since. Wouldn't that be romantic?" She sighed and fell back into her pillows. "O maybee," she started in a French accent. "He cannot find hiz favoreet wizout try-eeng all ze chocolat in ze box. *Oui?*"

Either because it was really funny or I needed a different release than crying, I laughed so hard my stomach hurt.

When I finally caught my breath and wiped away my laugh-tears, I swept some pillows out of the way to hug her. "I'm so afraid of being hurt. What if—?"

"No!" Shiney said, nudging my shoulders. "No more *what ifs*. Just stop thinking about it. Take a few days to get your head straight. Once you're not emotional, the right answer will come to you. You'll either trust him or you won't." She shrugged. "Just remember, bigger risks mean bigger rewards."

Easier said than done.

"The way he looks at you … " Shiney sighed. "If you want my opinion, he's not some sick criminal."

Said the lamb about the lion.

After lunch, we dropped Shiney off at their church for a barbecue fundraiser. Jack drove up to my house and told me to wait so he could help me with my books.

He parked on the street, and we got out. I leaned back in for my books.

"Geez, Laxshmi, would you hold up? I said I'd help you."

"I got them. Don't worry."

"Hey, Liam. What's up?" Jack called out after he'd closed his door.

Liam? I jerked up and slammed the back of my head into the doorframe. "Ow!"

The books went flying out of my hands, and stars exploded in front of me. Jack came around and held my shoulders to steady me.

"Damn, girl. You're such a klutz. Let me get these." He knelt down to gather my books.

I was fighting back tears and looked toward Liam's house. He wasn't there. Was I just hearing things now?

I knelt and shoved Jack's arms away, clenching my teeth. "Just leave it, Jack."

"Fine. I won't help." He stepped away and crossed his arms.

I stood with my books and swayed a bit. "Where's—?" I couldn't even say Liam's name.

"Where's what?"

"Never mind. My books. They're all here. Sorry, Jack. My head … "

"Are you sure you're okay?" He reached for my head, but I pulled away.

"I'm sure. Thanks. See you tomorrow."

I walked up to my porch, blinking back tears again. Was I going crazy? I hadn't slept well, I'd been crying off and on like a baby, and now I was hearing things.

I turned around to make sure Jack was gone and let myself collapse onto the front steps, my books scattered around me. Wrapping my arms around my shins, I leaned my forehead against my knees and let my heartache take over.

CHAPTER 23

Liam

Lucky consumed my thoughts the entire three-hour drive to Charlotte. Images of her tear-soaked lashes and the memory of her hurt tore through me. I had to get her to forgive me. Being close to her physically was the only way her neural pathways would change enough to lead to her breakthrough. Then I could tell her about our world.

But would she trust me until then? What if I had let her believe I'd cared about all the other targets? Maybe she'd not have thought me a callous arse. Or some sociopath, as she'd said. I let out a slow breath. I couldn't have lied to her like that.

Please let me find a way to reach her.

When I pulled up at midnight, the streets around the Ritz-Carlton in uptown Charlotte swarmed with bar hoppers and tourists. I handed my car keys and a tip to the valet and dragged myself through the front doors, garment and duffel bags slung over my shoulder. Rich wood and polished stone greeted me in the lobby. Posh was a good word for it. The air smelled like fresh flowers, and the surfaces gleamed in the soft lighting.

Echoes of my footsteps followed me as I strolled to the front desk to get my room key. The desk clerk was saying something about their services, but I ignored him. All these hotels were the same. With Lucky feeling the way she did, I'd not be "enjoying the amenities."

I headed toward the lift, this time with echoes of Lucky's words in my head. "*I don't know what to believe, Liam. I don't trust you.*" She was curious about the secret though, and I prayed it'd be enough to help her overlook my strange past ... for now.

I found the room in our suite without Da's stuff and tossed down my bags. The drapes on the floor-to-ceiling window had been pulled back, revealing a stunning nighttime view with lights outlining the high-rises. The dark window reflected the entire room, including me, standing there alone. Even with the hazy reflection, my eyes looked bloodshot, and bags sat under them from barely sleeping all week. I rested my forearm against the window and surveyed the cityscape. I wished Lucky could see it. My lips tingled at the memory of kissing her.

What would she think of us—our abilities, our culture, my family's money? I'd be willing to wager she'd not care much about the money, but the culture would probably fascinate her. *Yeah, she'd adapt well enough.*

But what if she never wanted to see me again? I rubbed at the stubble on my jaw and stared at my reflection. I couldn't let that happen.

It was late, so I rang Da on his mobile to find where he was keeping himself. He'd found an Irish pub called *Rí Rá* one street over. He asked me to join him for a jar or two, but I reminded him they wouldn't serve me in the States since I wasn't twenty-one. Besides, I wasn't up for the company.

"Suit yourself," Da said. "I'll be up to the room shortly."

"How did your initial meeting go with Gagliardi and the Elder?"

"It was just a short welcome. They wanted to rest after their flight. We'll be having an official meeting at brunch come the morrow."

"Ah, savage that is. Night then."

I tossed my mobile on the bed and wondered what might be found in the minibar. With enough rum or whiskey, I'd be able to sleep through the night. I hadn't slept well since I'd met Lucky. Was she suffering too? I needed the rest, but Granddad Whelan's words rang in my ear. *"Always drink when you're happy, me boy, never when you're sad."*

So what else might be helping me sleep? I dialed the front desk. "Yes, hello? Would it be too late to have a massage therapist sent up? Oh, and I'll be needing a shirt pressed by morning too."

Hours later, Da stumbled into the suite, humming loudly as he found his bed. I sat on the floor against the window and wondered if Lucky was sleeping. When she took me back—*if* she took me back—I'd have to get her a mobile her mum couldn't control.

I took out my own. For what had to be the hundredth time, I stared at the pictures I'd snapped of Lucky today at lunch. She'd tried covering her face when she'd seen me, but even still, I captured her smile. Her ability to project through a photograph amazed me. With each shot, her happiness washed over me, but it was still a pale comparison to having the original with me. If only she hadn't seen the bloody yearbooks.

I thunked my head against the window and stared out into the night. A few hours later, I woke, grabbed the pillows from the floor, cracked my neck, and climbed into bed, dreaming of Lucky.

Da was getting ready when Housekeeping brought me back the Armani shirt and jacket I'd packed, hoping to impress. I started the coffeemaker and jumped into the shower. I hadn't been planning on looking sharp at first, but when the reality of the situation had hit me—that I had a soul mate to protect—I'd wanted to look confident and intimidating.

Dominating this meeting couldn't have been more important. From what Mum had implied, Gagliardi and I were evenly matched when it came to empathic ability. He was no looker, or so she'd said, but he was cunning. I'd do whatever I needed to protect Lucky from these old farts, who'd not hesitate to leave our lives in flitters for their own political gain.

During my summers at home, Ciarán and I would've been talking trash with the lads who could be found in the local and in the Dublin clubs. We'd learned to handle most situations with a little Whelan charm, giving us the upper hand in any pissing match with the local loudmouths. It was a tactic that had let us come out on top more often than not. I'd use some of that today.

If I could get every waitress in the restaurant downstairs drooling over me, Gagliardi would be sensing that and not much else. Along with my royal title, that emotional tactic might add the extra bit I'd need to be holding my own.

But was he one to be so easily manipulated?

When I came out of my room, I smelled more than coffee brewing. Da had breakfast spread out on the dining table. He wore a school bus yellow T-shirt and a tweed blazer, ratty enough to be from the seventies, no doubt.

"What the hell are you wearing?" I asked, pouring myself some coffee. "Were you hammered when you packed?"

"Morning to you, son. Don't be telling your mum. It's part of the plan. As far as those couple of tools care, I'm a professor more than half off my nut." He stood and bowed. The man was already theatrical. It wouldn't be much of a stretch to see him as a headcase. He waved a hand at me. "And what's with what you're wearing? Cuff links and shoes shined like you're part of the Guard now?"

"Just playing my part too, yeah?"

"Let me look at you." I moved around the table to where he was sitting and grabbed a piece of toast. "Dear merciful God in heaven. How are you letting your puppies breathe with jeans that tight?"

"The future Whelan line is in no danger. Rest assured."

"Didn't realize you could look like such a distinguished gentlemen," he said. He took a slurp of his tea and winked.

I sat next to him and made myself a plate, noticing his narrowed eyes.

"What now?" I asked.

"Are you itching for a fight, or are you meaning to protect someone?"

"Yes." I was being fiercely vague, but then thought the better of it. "I'll be needing some itch cream on the way back if I don't get my fight. Which Elder did they send after us?"

He studied me over the rim of his cup. "Claire Brennan."

My mind flashed back to the signing ceremony. "Why in all that's holy and right would she come here for this?"

He shrugged. "She wouldn't say a word yesterday, except to ask when you'd be showing your face. Brought an entourage with her, she did."

"How many?"

"Seven."

"For a two-day trip? Jaysus."

"Sure look it, she didn't become an Elder by having mush for brains. Don't you underestimate her. She's the eldest of that lot too."

I frowned. "How long has she been an Elder?"

"Seventy-five years, or so the rumor goes. The records from the time before she was appointed have gone missing, they have. It's said she was only in her seventies when she became an Elder. The youngest ever."

Damn.

What did someone of her stature find so interesting about me? Or was this only about the Elders' library and Aunt Finola?

More importantly … would she be a threat to Lucky?

We went down to the main restaurant early so I could work my magic. Da had reserved the main dining room for our group. He kept himself out in the lobby, and I sauntered over to the waitstaff. I couldn't just be paying them to act—I needed them to be genuinely charmed by me.

In a move that would've made Ciarán proud, I scoped out the shyest-looking girl and started with her, explaining how I wanted to make this lunch for my dear old great-grandmother an extra special one. I smiled, flirted, and laid it on like jam on bread. When I sensed the other two waitresses drawn to me out of curiosity, I turned to them and winked. They came over, and soon I had all three hovering while I worked my Irish charm. A simple projection to make them happy wouldn't work, nor would it last. Gagliardi wouldn't be fooled by that trick. The staff needed to be generating the emotion themselves.

"So, you'll be looking out for me then?" I flashed a smile. Giggles and smiles went round in unison, and then I set my sights on the male waiters.

The two of them were having a chat with the bus boy, and I took out a wad of cash.

"Gentlemen, can I ask a favor?" They saw the money, and I had their undivided attention. "Your uh … gorgeous coworkers over there." I glanced in the girls' direction, and they smiled. "Well, they've agreed to take pure good care of us during lunch. As eager as they are, I don't want them feeling overwhelmed."

Step one was complete. The men knew I had the ladies' attention.

"Would you be able to help out more than usual—keep things running smooth? I'm needing this to be perfect." I flicked out a fifty for each, the same as I'd given the ladies.

Step two worked like I'd hoped. I was sensing that they considered themselves beholden to me, and Gagliardi would surely pick up on that—and not much more.

Ciarán would be right proud of me.

I left to meet Da. He was talking to three middle-aged women in gray dresses, who had to be part of Brennan's entourage. Smoothing my tie, I walked over to them. One of the ladies watched me, betraying nothing on her face or in her mind. She could have been a bloody robot. *Impressive.* I was guarding my feelings, but as tired as I'd been, my concentration was shaky. Could she be reading me? I escaped to the restrooms to wash my face and find a bit of peace.

I stared at my reflection in the mirror, wondering what could happen at this meeting. Was this just about power to Gagliardi, or was he a Soul Seeker bent on destruction? What if he found out about Lucky? Would he threaten her? Hurt her? I imagined him touching her, and a rage surged and overpowered my concentration. My hands curled into fists.

I'll not be this weak.

Taking several deep breaths, I pushed out all thoughts except one—Lucky. My heart rate calmed. For her sake, I had to control my emotions. Bringing her into our world and not being able to protect her was not an option. One final deep breath and I was back in control.

I slapped on a bit of the Whelan arrogance and joined Da outside. The robot lady was watching me again. Unnerving as it was, I couldn't be distracted by her. If I could be thrown off so easily, what chance did I have in front of our VIP guests? She was drawn into a conversation with Da, and I snatched the opportunity to study her. It helped me focus, as if staring at her replaced my distractions with a dull, gray vacuum. The musculature of her right cheek changed. Was that a smile? What if this was a trap? I'd remain guarded.

Drago Gagliardi and Elder Brennan got off the lift and headed toward us. Four officers from the Empath Gendarmerie followed and surrounded our group at a discreet distance.

Gagliardi was definitely the Mediterranean man from the signing-ceremony. A chiseled nose, pencil-thin lips, and that grotesque mole on his left cheek stood out before anything else. He was slightly shorter than Brennan, and his steps were short and quick around her. He reminded me of a mousy servant chasing after his master.

She, on the other hand, seemed as regal as ever. She walked with her finely carved cane, the same as I'd seen back in Ireland, but stood tall and proud in a light-blue skirt suit that matched her shrewd eyes. Her steps were elegant and fearless, and I had a hard time believing she was over 140 years old. Maybe the rumors were just hype.

Gagliardi was the first to meet my eyes. His were piercing and looked bloody chilled and determined, reminding me of a kid ready to take a dare to prove himself. My lips curled at the idea of a challenge, and my confidence bubbled to the surface. The robot lady moved slightly. Confidence could be seen as cockiness, and I was needing to rein it in so I'd remain a blank slate like her. Elder Brennan was studying me, her lips pursed and brow slightly furrowed.

The four of us shook hands. Gagliardi gave me a cursory head bow in deference to my royalty, but I didn't have to be an empath to feel the disdain in his stiff demeanor.

"Elder Brennan would like to begin the meeting," one of her assistants said.

The hostess led the six of us to our table and sat the rest of Brennan's entourage and Gagliardi's team nearby. With dark wood floors and brown and neutral furnishings, the restaurant looked like a well-dressed wallflower. Two tables with sparkling glassware and bright white dishes had been pushed together for us. A waiter held out a chair for Brennan across from her assistant, who'd be sitting at my right. Da was at my left, facing Gagliardi, while the robot lady sat across from me.

After some time with our menus, a waitress stepped up to take our order. The assistant ordered for Brennan, which freed the Elder to watch me. I assumed she'd be waiting until later to bust through my defenses—if she'd been planning on it. She'd all but admitted to going easy on me during the test. Would she do the same now?

When it was my turn to say what I wanted, I glanced up at the waitress. "Colleen, is it? A fine Irish name. What do you have a taste for?"

The color rose to her cheeks. "My favorite is the lobster Cobb salad."

"Then how could I say no to that?"

She smiled and made her way around the table.

A male waiter came next, stood by Gagliardi's end of the table, but addressed me, asking if anyone wanted refills on the drinks we were handed not five minutes ago. The effect was marvelous. Judging by Gagliardi's raised eyebrow, the waiter's deference to me had caught his attention.

"So, Drago," Da said. "How's the wife and the little ones?" His familiarity with Gagliardi was more than disrespectful, but Da must have had that planned for sure.

Gagliardi put down his water glass. "They are fine. And Moira?" He said Mum's name like he enjoyed rolling the sound of it off his tongue. I swallowed back bile and noticed Da twisting the napkin in his lap. Gagliardi's Italian accent had that typical singsong lilt of his countrymen, but his unnatural pauses between words seemed calculating.

"Well enough," Da said. "Her research keeps her busy. Did you know she's studying the empathic abilities of dogs and their owners? Fascinating stuff. We can talk more about it later if you'd care to. It's simply incredible." Da hammed it up as if they were old pals. He shook out his napkin and tucked it into his T-shirt. It would've been embarrassing had it not been so damned funny.

Gagliardi sneered. "*Sì*. Fascinating."

I'd been watching Gagliardi, studying his facial expressions, looking for tells. He soon turned his attention to me. "So, Prince Liam, how do you like moving so much? Is it not tiring to you?"

"I'm with my family, and I get to travel. There's nothing tiring about it."

"You do not miss your brother?"

"I'd have missed Ciarán at home just the same. He's been at Trinity these past few years."

"But to have to make so many new friends." He raised an eyebrow and shrugged. The action seemed an afterthought, like he was following some instruction manual on how to appear sympathetic.

If this fishing expedition was the best Gagliardi had to rattle me, he'd have to work harder.

"But I've been blessed to have made so many, haven't I now?" I put out my arm and rested my hand on the back of Da's chair.

He patted my shoulder. "Blessed you are, son."

Now was a good time to show Gagliardi I wasn't intimidated by him or the Elders.

"Elder Brennan, I hope your flight was pleasant. I apologize for not being here yesterday."

Her assistant opened her mouth to speak, but Brennan lifted her hand.

"It was. Thank you for asking, Prince Liam."

I tipped my head. She was studying me again, and her stare was hard. I glanced at the robot lady to remember to keep focus.

Gagliardi cleared his throat. "Patrick, you know why we are here today, no?"

"The vision about my boy, yeah? He'd just turned six when I had the most glorious dream of him and his future wife. At six, mind you!"

Our food arrived, and Da babbled on with his story. He told the truth, or a version near enough to it, but he was offering such mind-numbing details, it was useless. Gagliardi asked questions along the way, but never got meaningful answers. I wondered if our guests could sense Da was holding something back, or if they'd bought into the whole professor a-touch-gone-in-the-head act.

Gagliardi finished his food and put his fork down. "Prince Liam, it has taken all this time but you have not met this girl. Frustrating, no? Do you believe in your father's sight?"

"I believe in fate and faith, *il signor* Gagliardi." I raised my glass to him.

"How can a young boy such as yourself be tempted by fairy tales?"

"Fairy tales themselves don't tempt me, but the quest for the grain of truth they hold does. If God has ordained I be joined as a soulmated empath, then not even the Devil himself could keep me from her." I stared him down, hoping the *bastardo* got my veiled threat.

He cocked his head ever so slightly, assessing me. *Yeah, he understands me perfectly.* A small voice in my head warned me not to piss him off, but it was too tempting. I'd not be letting him get the upper hand by goading me into it though.

"What will you do if you meet her?" Gagliardi asked.

I ignored him and faced Brennan. "I'd present her to you, Elder Brennan, and the other Elders, of course."

Brennan turned to me without betraying any emotion.

Gagliardi shifted in his seat. "Would you not present her to the Council first?" His tone was hard.

"Elder Brennan's presence here would indicate their interest supersedes yours. Or do you disagree?" I asked.

Da squirmed in his seat.

"No, no." Gagliardi waved his hand dismissively. "It is my wish to remind someone as young as yourself we have a protocol to honor, no? As a royal, you should know this."

I sat back, placing my forearm on the table's edge. Feigning a casual indifference wasn't easy when I wanted to schkelp that feckin' smirk off Gagliardi's face.

"I'd be more than flattered if the Council chose to send you all this way out of concern for my, um … youth. But this attention would suggest something else. Someone must think I'm a threat." I paused for effect. "Do *you* think someone as young as myself could be a threat, *signore*?"

"That depends. Do you choose to be?" A subtle tension knotted his forehead.

My disgust was right at the surface. I looked at robot lady to regroup. She had already been staring at me, as if she were waiting to be at my service. Da wiped his palms up and down his lap.

Colleen and another waitress interrupted us to ask if we cared for coffee and dessert, followed by an eager busboy who cleared the table. Gagliardi ordered an espresso, as did Da, who rarely drank the stuff. Why was he being so deferential? *Ah, right. Aunt Finola.* I took a deep breath, forcing myself to relax.

When the waitstaff left, Brennan raised her hand. We all snapped our heads in her direction. "I am here to find out if you've located her. That is all. Have you, Mr. Whelan?" She was looking at Da.

"No, we have not." He sounded dejected. "I hate that you troubled yourself by coming so far, but seeing as you're here, would it be possible to ask about my sister, Finola? She's being brought in for questioning again, and I fear it might be because of her enthusiasm in helping us. Ever the romantic, she is."

Enough of this bollocks. I turned to Gagliardi. "What my father's saying is that we're not wanting my aunt subjected to what seems to be a witch hunt."

"Well … " Da said. "I–I'd not be using those words e–exactly. I know she—"

Gagliardi leaned toward me. "If the Council and I find out she accessed the library to help you and your father—"

"What if she did?" I asked. "She's not allowed to help me find the one thing the Council and our community would celebrate me finding? Or is it that she's reminded you of something you and the Council fear?"

His fingers twitched around his napkin. "We are not afraid of anything."

"Then we have that in common, *il signor* Gagliardi."

We were staring at each other when the coffees and Brennan's dessert came. Her assistant had ordered her a pecan pie. Da opened his mouth to speak, but Brennan lifted her hand again. She didn't say anything, and I assumed she wanted to enjoy her dessert in peace. I'd have smiled if my blood hadn't been boiling.

When Brennan finished her pie, she wiped her mouth with a napkin and looked at the three of us, finishing with Da. "Mr. Whelan, I'll be looking into the matter of your sister on a condition of my choosing. Is that acceptable?"

"I'd be grateful. Thank you."

What the feckin' hell? What if Brennan found out about Lucky and asked Da to hand her over after we joined? Was he truly gone off?

The robot lady glanced at me. Her eyebrows moved together

by a fraction. Apparently she wasn't impressed with how I'd been schooling my facial features. I opened my mouth to protest when Brennan glared at me. It was enough to stop me.

"Drago," Brennan said. "I wish to have all matters regarding Finola Whelan brought to me. Is that understood?" Her gaze bored into him.

"*Sì*, Elder Brennan." Gagliardi's jaw popped. Even though it meant we'd owe Brennan something, it was satisfying to know she'd pissed off Gagliardi.

Brennan turned to her assistant, who nodded and left the restaurant.

"Thank you, again, Elder Brennan," Da said.

"You're welcome. Make no mention of it again."

He raised his espresso cup in the air to both her and Gagliardi, and drank it down in one shot.

The assistant returned and gave Brennan a small nod. She got up from the table with the help of her cane. We all stood with her.

"Prince Liam," Brennan said. "I am in need of your assistance."

"Me?" I asked. Da slapped my back and pushed me toward her. "Uh, certainly. I'll be more than happy." Was I going to end up regretting this?

I walked around to her side. She held out her forearm to wrap around mine. I glanced back at Gagliardi. His dark eyes looked like they were on fire, and Da's beamed with pride. He began telling Gagliardi about Mum's supposed research on dogs while Brennan's assistant led us out.

"You remind me of someone I knew long ago," Brennan said.

"I'm hoping there's a good memory in there."

Her face seemed serene, and a hint of a smile graced her lips. Her change in demeanor from lunch surprised me.

We strolled past the front desk and down a long hallway, where a hotel employee held open a mahogany door to a small meeting room. A gendarme had followed us and stood a few feet away.

Brennan turned to her assistant. "That will be all." The assistant bowed and left.

Once the door was closed behind the two of us, she released me and rested her cane on the back of a leather executive chair. She peered into my eyes and pointed a gloved finger at me. "You made good use of Aileen."

"Who would that be?"

She walked around a conference table for six. Side tables anchored three of the walls, topped by landscapes painted in bold palette-knife strokes. She paused to study one. The three oil paintings contrasted to the subdued style of the room. It was impressively understated, like Brennan herself.

"The lady across from you. I knew she'd serve her purpose well."

A shot of adrenaline revved up my heart and shook my mental blocks like an earthquake. How had she known? *Shite.* She just found her way into my head, hadn't she? I scrambled to strengthen my defenses.

She smiled as if she were amused. "You've made an enemy of *il signor* Gagliardi today. Do you think that was very wise of you?"

"I didn't see a way around it."

"I suppose not." She gazed at the next painting. "He was reserved today because of my presence. In other circumstances, he may not have behaved himself so well."

"I think I could've handled him—if I hadn't needed to be so reserved."

"You handled yourself … adequately, for one so young."

I crossed my arms. Was she trying to piss me off?

Another smug smile appeared again. "Where you're headed, you will need that temper and bravado."

Hell if I'd keep taking her bait. I slowed my breathing and focused on fortifying my blocks.

She had circled the room and stood in front of me again. She opened up her neck scarf, revealing a pendant at the base of her throat.

"Why did you come?" I asked.

She moved, and I glanced at her jewelry again. A pit formed in my stomach. It was a Celtic triskele etched with Sanskrit writing, similar in design to the ones Mum had drawn in her journal about the Soul Seekers. *Bloody hell.*

"You're a Soul Seeker?" I whispered.

"Perhaps."

Despite her evasive answer, something was familiar about her and set me at ease. My instincts were telling me she was harmless and trustworthy. *But how?* If she'd manipulated my emotions, I'd have felt it.

She gave me that damned smile of hers again. What was so bloody amusing? She removed her right glove. A pinkish scar marred her palm, like an oval burn mark. She stepped closer, tilting her head back so her gaze could meet mine. "It *will* get worse before it gets better."

Before I had time to react, she raised her burned hand and cupped my cheek. An instant shock of white light blinded me for a few seconds. I shook my head to clear it and thought I saw a faint, blue iridescence leave her eyes. My mind had to be playing tricks on me, but then something else caught my attention—the vulnerability and strength in her eyes, like Lucky's, but deeper, older. It tore through whatever control I had. I reached up to touch Brennan's face, and she pressed her cheek into my hand. It was like looking into Lucky's eyes.

"Lucky," I whispered. Chills ran up and down my body.

She exhaled. "Finally."

Feckin' hell. A jolt of anger rushed through me, making me stumble back. She'd read me like I was a bloody five-year-old. If she harmed Lucky in any way, took her away from me, or God knew what else, I'd snap this woman's neck in half. I didn't care if she was an Elder.

She laughed. "Good. Good. Your protective instincts are

strong, and you'll be needing them." She paused to sigh. "Time hasn't changed anything, I'm afraid."

My chest felt like a vise around my lungs. I collapsed into a chair, my head buzzing. "What did you do to me?"

"You'll be yourself again in a minute." She put on her gloves again. "I was right to put Aileen with you, or you would've given your Lucky away." A steely resolve returned to her face. All traces of Lucky's softness vanished.

I leaned forward, my head between my hands.

Shite. What have I done? If anything happened to Lucky because of me ...

"Now listen to me carefully. Here's my condition." I lifted my face to hers. "As soon as the joining occurs, you must ring me. Tell no one about this conversation. Absolutely no one. Do I make myself clear?"

I nodded, barely aware of the movement. What choice did I have?

She left her business card on the table and walked toward the door.

"Wait!" I managed to stand. "What do you know about the joining?"

She gave me a wistful smile and left.

CHAPTER 24

Lucky

The back of my head was still pounding from getting out of Jack's car. *Stupid books.* He was right though. I had my klutzy moments. Why couldn't I just let him help me like he'd offered?

"I can't be leaving you for a minute without Jack getting his hands all over you," Liam's voice said in my head. The lilt made me smile. My eyeballs were pressed against my knees, visions of spaghetti and flashing light danced on my retinas.

Wait. Was I still hallucinating?

I raised my head slowly, blinking against the sunlight. He was squatting right in front of me. "Liam?" I scrunched my eyes closed, counted to three, and opened them again. *Okay, so I'm not hallucinating.* "Liam!" I launched myself at him before I even knew what I was doing.

He managed to keep his balance while trying to stand us both up. His arms were locked around me, and he let out a large breath. "Jaysus, I missed you too," he whispered against my neck between kisses. They tingled and energized me.

What am I doing?

I ripped away from him, breathless. "I'm sorry. I–I shouldn't have done that. It's just … when you were gone, I couldn't—"

"Breathe? Me neither."

My eyes locked onto his. He meant it. He really did. It was in his red-rimmed eyes and wrinkled brow, but I felt it too, like seeing a breeze lift off a veil and uncover the object beneath.

"Don't apologize, Lucky." He brought up his hand, hesitated, and then tucked a strand of hair behind my ear.

"I heard Jack say your name, but I didn't see you. I thought I was hearing things."

"Your head? Any use where you banged it?"

I figured he was asking if I was okay, so I nodded, wanting to smile at the way Liam spoke English. I felt relaxed for the first time since Saturday. I soaked him in. "Are *you* okay? You look terrible." Dark circles smudged his eyes like he hadn't slept in days.

He stepped closer. "I'm better, now that I'm with you again. I sped back this morning and your hug was worth it." He gave me a shy smile that ignited my insides.

I averted my eyes to get my bearings, but couldn't help notice he was wearing a stained T-shirt and gym shorts. He had dirt and red Carolina clay marks all over. "Uh, what have you been doing?"

"I was helping Mrs. Robertson. She's wanting a hole dug for an azalea bush and some help wrestling out her weeds."

"Oh my God!" I slapped my hand to my mouth. "I totally forgot I told her I'd do her weeding today. But how did you end up doing it?" I grabbed my bag, shook it, and dug inside for my jingling keys. I had to change into something I could work in. No way would I let him do my job for me.

"When I drove in, she was waiting for you on her porch, ready to leave for some Labor Day barbecue at a friend's. She mentioned it to me, so I thought I'd take care of it in case you'd forgot, or um, weren't up for it."

I froze. He did it for me? "Thank you."

He shrugged. I started picking up my books, which he insisted on carrying up the stairs. He would've followed me in, but I stopped him, pointing to his dirty shoes and legs. His face fell. He must have thought I was leaving him.

I hid my smile. "I'll be right back out to help."

"Lucky, I can finish—"

"So are you saying you'd rather not spend time with me? Hmm?" I moved into the doorway and let the screen door close between us.

He put his hands on either side of the doorframe and flashed me his dimples.

On his own, Liam had weeded the entire side of the yard facing his house and gotten halfway down my side. I dropped my kneepads and garden gloves next to him and got to weeding and deadheading her flowering shrubs. We worked seriously at first, but then I caught him checking out my legs.

"You know," I said, raking under an azalea bush. "If you can't keep your eyes to yourself and get your work done, I might have to teach you a lesson. I could see how much Carolina clay it'll take to stain your hair and turn you into a ginger."

He leaned back on his arms and gave me a playful smile. "If you got that close to me, I'd have to get another hug."

"Ha. Ha." My cheeks heated at the thought. I looked into his pale-green eyes and wondered how I was supposed to meld my heart and mind together. Would I ever get past the fear of being hurt? Wasn't any relationship a risk?

He studied the blades of grass by his feet. "Tell me what you're thinking, Lucky."

"Why Indian girls?" I whispered.

He did the slow sigh again. "That's part of the secret. I wish I could tell you. Honest."

I nodded, flicking a clump of dirt off my knee and onto a dead azalea bloom. Would I be a nobody to him one day, just like the others?

I took a deep breath to ready myself for the next question. "You said you had to date them. What about me? Do you, um … *have* to date me?"

"Jaysus, it sounds like rubbish when you say it like that." He wiped the back of his hand against his chin and frowned. "Technically, yes, I would've had to." He smiled and then shook his head like he'd just realized something. "But this time no one made me start seeing you. It was only because I'd wanted to."

We both got back to work and brought up safer topics to discuss. At the mention of family, he whipped out his phone and showed me pictures of his cousins. We spent the next half-hour looking at photos and sharing funny stories, lying next to each other in the shade. He told me his family had begun breeding alpacas a few years back, which along with their expensive cars and family pubs, gave me the impression they weren't hurting for money.

Before long, he held out his hand to help me stand. I surveyed the mess we'd made. I was happy we weren't done because I couldn't imagine being anywhere else—with anyone else. After another twenty minutes of work, we finished the side of the house and moved into the backyard.

"So, uh … what did you do yesterday and, um … this morning … with Jack?" Liam asked, wearing a perfectly calm expression. A nagging feeling told me a storm brewed behind his casual inquiry. I imagined a gust of wind that kept pushing me away from something I wanted to see. These hallucinations were getting weirder and weirder.

"Well, yesterday I helped choreograph a teaser routine with the drill team. It's for the party this Friday." I casually glanced at him. "Have you heard about it?" He nodded but didn't say more. *Damn.* I should've asked if he was going. He turned his back to me and tugged on a stubborn clump of weeds. The moment seemed lost, so I kept my mouth shut. "Then today, I studied with Jack and Shiney at their house." I stood and collected the garden tools, moving them a few feet ahead of where we worked.

He made a grunting sound and then clawed at the clump of weeds with a cultivator. His words came back to me. *"I can't be leaving you for a minute without Jack getting his hands all over you."*

Huh. Was he jealous?

"Wait a minute," I said. "When I came home, you saw Jack. He called out to you. You knew I'd hurt my head."

"Your point?"

"Why didn't I see you?" My heart raced, remembering how awful I'd felt.

He yanked out the stubborn weeds with a little too much force. Dirt flew everywhere. "I knew you wanted your space. You'd not want me thumping him senseless for touching you, would you? Because that's what I'd have—"

I laughed. He *was* jealous. His reaction seemed so natural, so genuine, that I was relieved. Maybe his feelings weren't as contrived as I thought.

"And you're laughing at me now?" He jumped up and grabbed me by the thighs, throwing me over his shoulder.

"Liam!" I squealed and fell into fits of laughter as he headed toward his backyard. "No, I wasn't. I swear. Put me down."

"So this is what I should've done for you then."

The bump on my head was throbbing while I was upside down, but I couldn't stop laughing. He charged onto his patio, slid me down, but stopped before my feet touched the ground. We were face to face, and I was sure it was so I could see him wink and grin at me. I rolled my eyes. He leaned me back on one of his lounge chairs and brought my legs around.

"Sit tight, yeah?" He went inside.

The tingling faded, and the rubber band snapped back again. He returned soon enough, scrunching up a bag of frozen peas, breaking up clumps between his fingers. He sat on the edge of the lounge chair, beside my hip, and gently took out my ponytail holder. I winced as the hair tugged on the sore spot. He felt around for it. "That's some knot you're sporting." He put the bag of peas in place and leaned me against the glorious coolness. I wanted to moan. He opened a fresh water bottle for me.

"So what now?" I asked.

He was looking down, fingering the edge of my shorts. "I know you hadn't intended on spending your afternoon with me, but I'm glad you did. I've been having a good time."

"I am too," I whispered.

His fingers brushed my thigh, and I felt a jolt in my heart.

He gave me an earnest look. "If it makes a difference ... the family photos, I didn't share that with any of the others. Not one of them came home to meet my mum ... and Patty? Patty's too special. It's been brutal watching him isolate himself. I'd never have let any of the others talk to him. I didn't want him making connections and then ... well, you know."

I curled my fingers into my palm. Knowing he could use some comfort, but not giving him any, filled me with guilt.

He ran his hand through his hair and cursed under his breath. "Christ, Lucky. I'm not trying to guilt you into staying with me. That's not why I said—"

"What? No." I sat up and the bag of peas slid to my rear end. *How does he read my face so well?* "I didn't feel guilty about that. I promise." I took his hand even though I shouldn't have. "I–I felt guilty about not comforting you when you mentioned Patty. I was trying to keep my distance, that's all."

He sighed, closed his eyes briefly, and let out a laugh. "You've got a big heart, Lucky. Big as the sea itself." He kissed my hand and then repositioned the bag of peas before nudging me back. My fingers still tingled from touching him. "Stay here and ice that lump. I'll finish up, yeah?"

I didn't want him to finish up all on his own, but the ice felt good against the throbbing.

He paused before getting up, his eyes twinkling, and pointed to my icepack. "You know, eating a whole bag of thawed peas—I'd only ever do that for you."

I laughed. "I'm truly sorry. I didn't realize how bad I was torturing you."

Dimples popped onto his face, and he took my hand in his. I didn't think he realized he'd done it. "Won't be a torture if you'll stay with me for supper. I can grill some hot dogs or hamburgers to eat with the peas. It's Labor Day, after all. My mum's meeting up with me Da at Duke to see some colleagues. They'll be home much later, but if you're wanting something else, we can go out to eat, or order—"

"Hot dogs sound perfect. Mom's working late anyway."

He nodded slowly and studied my face for a moment. His eyes reminded me of silvery-green moss. When he stared into my eyes, it was like standing under the thick protective canopy of a lush forest. He leaned in, but I wasn't ready for him to kiss me.

Don't cave.

I leaped up from the lounge chair and shoved my hair back into a ponytail. I struggled to catch my breath, the rubber band snapping back hard enough to knock the wind out of me. I pressed on my sternum. "That's enough ice. I'm good now. Are you, uh ... ready ... to get back to work?" I turned around, and his cheeks looked like they'd been slapped. My heart fell.

"Sure." He gave me a tight smile, his eyes flat. He turned to get up, but I stopped him by kneeling on the lounge chair behind him and throwing my arms around his neck.

I was such a sucker.

I brought my face up next to his. "Are you going to the party on Friday?"

He leaned his head into mine. "You'll be on a date, remember?"

"Uh. No. Jack and I will have pizza with Shiney and Matthew, and then Jack will be my ride to the party." I filled him in on the real reason Shiney would be there and turned to study his facial expressions. He was smiling. "So? Are you going?"

"Since we're not officially dating, I guess I'll see you if I see you."

"Liam!" I pulled my arm against his throat to play-choke him. "You know, you're messing with powers you simply *cannot* comprehend."

"You have no idea." He reached up, cupped the back of my neck, and gave me a tender kiss on the lips. We both let out a breath.

Damn.

I stood and cleared my throat. "You better know how to dance."

He smirked. "Don't you be worrying over that."

"Come on. Let's finish. I'm getting hungry for peas." I grabbed the water bottle for a drink, hoping I could wash away the magnetic pull of the tingling.

It got hotter as the afternoon wore on, and with the setting sun aiming right at us, the sweat rolled down my back. We were about done, so Liam left to prep for dinner.

I collected the yard waste, bending, squatting, and reaching for the mess we'd made. Liam watched me from the grill with a big grin on his face. I crossed my arms and raised an eyebrow. He shrugged and let out a laugh.

With the yard cleaned up, I lay back on a shaded patch of grass with my arms outstretched and eyes closed. The blades tickled my skin, and the rich smell of clay mingled with the fragrances of Mrs. Robertson's white, purple, and pink pansies, violets, and peach snapdragons. Without a breeze, the humidity seemed to hold the scents against me like a blanket.

The sound of crunching grass came closer, and my traitorous heart stuttered. I squinted up at Liam, marveling at how gorgeous he was, even dirty and sweaty. He handed me a bottle of ice-cold water. The condensation dripped down my arm.

"Thank you." I propped myself up on my elbow and held the cold bottle against my face and neck.

His gaze roamed over my body, and he cleared his throat. "Any time." He joined me, leaning on his hand, which he placed on the other side of my hip. I sat up, hoping not to choke on my water because of how close he was.

God, I hope I don't stink.

His fingers traced a path from under my jaw to the middle of my collarbone. I froze. But his finger didn't stop. He was at the top of my cleavage, nudging a finger between the swell of my breasts. He stroked upward, brought his other hand over, and cupped his hands together. His breathing went all haywire like mine.

He opened his cupped hands, and two ladybugs crawled around inside.

My eyes jumped from my little intruders to his eyes and back. "You could've just told me." I smiled.

"And miss the opportunity to be touching you?" He shook his hand out away from us, releasing my little perverted friends.

"Aww. Were you jealous?"

"I was about to rip their little wings off."

I gasped and giggled. "You wouldn't."

"I'll not be that generous again."

I laughed again, wishing I could freeze this moment. "The rest of the insect world be warned."

"They need to know." He leaned in, his lips brushing my ear. "You're mine, and I was always poor at sharing. Just ask the cousins."

Feeling his breath on my skin, my eyes fluttered closed. He chuckled. *Ugh. So he's enjoying this, is he? Well, two can play that game.*

I touched the neckline of his T-shirt and meandered downward, knowing full well I didn't have the guts to touch him as intimately as he'd touched me, but he didn't need to know that.

He watched my progress with an eyebrow raised.

I gave him an innocent smile. "So being yours means you can touch me with impunity? I guess it's only fair I get to too, you know." I kept my eyes locked on his, and when I passed his belly button, his already flat stomach tightened. He swallowed and I had to stop myself from giggling. My finger touched the button of his shorts, and he grabbed my wrist to stop me. I kissed his cheek by his ear and lowered my voice. "You shouldn't play with fire unless you know how to put it out." I felt a surge of empowerment at being confident enough to flirt with him. It was nice.

He turned his head so our eyes met.

"And I hear a cold shower is really good for that." I let my eyes dart downward between us.

A twitch of his lips was all the warning I needed before he tickled me, kissed me, or did whatever he had planned. I flung myself onto my back and rolled away. His puppy-dog eyes made me burst into laughter. "Sorry, I've got to shower." I stood and walked backward toward my house.

He collapsed onto his back and groaned. "You're killing me."

"You'll survive, if the insects don't gang up on you first."

He leaned up on his elbows. "Don't make me wait too long."

I paused for a moment, puzzled—not at the double meaning

behind what he'd said, but at the strange sense of vulnerability I was feeling. Odd, because my mind was telling me it was coming from Liam, like at lunch by the bench the other day. It was as if a strong wind was going to rip away a tree's foliage, exposing a nest of baby birds. I rubbed at my forehead. *Not again.*

Liam bolted upright and cocked his head, but then his face fell. *Okay.* "I'll try not to." I gave him a tight smile and jogged home.

I finished drying off and dressed in white, cuffed shorts and a sheer, Caribbean-blue top with a lacy camisole underneath. The color reminded me of the ocean—and of Liam.

My instincts told me he was being honest, but I still didn't know if I could trust myself. How long would I have to wait for him to tell me the secret? I couldn't survive being in limbo for long.

A week. I'd give him a week.

I called Mom preemptively, telling her I was still working on Mrs. Robertson's garden. She warned me to stay hydrated and ended the call with her usual nagging about getting homework done.

Now I could go back to Liam. I caved to the excitement and ran out to meet him.

My blood was pounding by the time I got there. He'd showered too and stood at the grill with his back to me. His khaki cargo shorts and gray T-shirt hugged his body in all the right places, making me envy his clothes. I wondered why, with all the leggy, busty blonds he could drape over his arm, he wanted an Indian girl like me. He turned and his gaze moved over me, top to bottom and back again. He watched me walk toward him, a hint of a smile playing on his lips.

I stopped right under his nose, barely able to catch my breath.

He lifted his hand to my face and hesitated. I had to do a better job of keeping my distance, but for now, I smiled. Were my hormones that much stronger than I was? Why did all my common sense jump out the window at the promise of one touch from him? The more time I spent with him, the worse it got.

Yes. One week. No more.

He gently stroked my cheek with his thumb. His hand felt warmer than the humid air around me.

"Fine as a summer day," he whispered. "You leave me overwhelmed."

"I know the feeling." I traced the muscle ridges on his arm with my fingertip. The charge thrummed through my entire body. I wondered why some times were more intense than others.

He took my hand. "C'mon, sit. Everything's near done."

He'd rearranged the patio furniture, moving the lounge chairs to the back edge, facing the house and grill. I sat crossed-legged on one of them, leaning back on my hands. The sun was low, and it washed our backyards in light. The foliage had a lime-green brightness, and the heat seemed to radiate up through the earth. I heard a camera shutter click and turned to Liam, who slipped his phone in his back pocket.

"Liam!"

He smiled and shrugged. I wished I could keep pictures of him. We'd taken several together at lunch on Saturday, but they were all on his phone, where they'd probably stay. He plated the last of the hot dogs at the table and sauntered over.

He straddled the lounge chair in front of me, smelling like the air after a rainstorm, but warmed by the grill's heat. I couldn't help the grin overtaking my face. He responded in kind, but then his expression became serious. "I keep breaking my promise to let you have your space. If you want to cool things off, I should be honoring your wishes. Stay away, see you only in class, yeah?"

My heart slammed into my chest. I needed to cool things off, sure, but I didn't want to. A strange awareness settled into my mind as if a strong wind was pushing us apart.

"No, Liam. No. I–I mean, I should … b–but no, I don't want you to leave me." Dread built up. Something was constricting my lungs, and no matter how hard I tried, I couldn't take a deep breath. Was this a panic attack? Tears filled my eyes, clouding my view of him.

"Lucky!" He cupped my face. "Hey, relax. I'm not leaving. I thought if I was making it harder for you—"

"But I–I felt it. You were pushing me away. God, what's wrong with me?"

He pulled me into his arms. "Nothing's wrong with you, Lucks. You're perfect."

I let out an unladylike huff.

"Jaysus, you're trembling," he whispered. "I was preparing myself to be … well, noble, if I could. I'll not be going anywhere if you don't want me to."

The tingling eventually relaxed my lungs, and air filled them again, nudging the despair out of the way.

"Well, stop preparing yourself," I whispered. "I don't want you to leave."

There. I'd admitted it. I didn't understand what had come over me, but at least I knew something with more certainty. *Now what?*

He rocked me in his arms, soothing and distracting me with words that soon made me giggle. When I was finally in control of myself, we made our way to the table to eat. Liam asked me about my extended family, but since ours was so small, there wasn't much to tell. Mom had tons of first and second cousins, but they were all in India. I hardly ever saw them. And as for Dad's side, I was the last in his line.

Near the end of our meal, I pushed the peas around the plate as I thought about the panic attack. Whatever it was, it felt like I'd tapped into a different part of my brain—a part that punched the rest of me in the gut.

"You, um … look … troubled," Liam said.

"I don't know what happened. I mean before, with my little breakdown. I flipped out on you, didn't I?" *Hallucinating and now this?* I put my fork down and sat back. "I'm so sorry. I–I don't even know—"

"You got scared. That's all."

"It was more than that, Liam. I don't have panic attacks, or whatever that was. I'm different when I'm around you. Why? And please don't say it's the secret." If I hadn't thought it was related to Liam somehow, I never would've brought it up. I didn't want my maybe-future-boyfriend to think I was certifiable.

Creases appeared on his forehead, and the accompanying tiny smile made me believe he was happy, but worried.

He put down his hot dog and reached for my hand. "Think of it like putting together a puzzle without seeing the picture on the box. Until certain pieces were in place, you wouldn't see the picture even if I'd told you, yeah?"

In other words, this was also part of the secret. I sighed. Of course it was.

He laced our fingers together and kissed the back of my hand. "Lucky, is that all you're waiting on? To hear the secret?" His eyes were so hopeful. It tugged at my heart.

"It's hard to have faith when you're in the dark."

He studied me for a moment, and then finished the last bite of his hot dog. He swallowed in a hurry, washing it down with water. "Okay." He clapped and rubbed his hands together. "I want you to trust me, so I'll tell you everything I can, yeah? I never dated any of the others for longer than three months, and my intentions were always honorable. None of them were conquests. I never tried to sleep with any of them, and even though I never felt about them the way I do about you, I always treated them the best I could, with respect at the very least."

I rested my elbow on the arm of my chair and put my chin in my hand. His eyes were so soft and sincere. I believed him about being respectful. It seemed as natural to him as breathing. He was chivalrous too—carrying my books, making a path for me in a crowd, or even helping Mrs. Robertson for me. It was all knight-in-shining-armor kind of stuff. I couldn't think of an Indian equivalent to knights, but then I remembered the story of Rama saving Sita from her demon kidnapper. Liam could be my knight and my Rama.

He told me more about each of the girls. The one he'd dated in ninth grade, Nisha, he'd only dated for a week. What if he lost interest in me that quickly? I almost snorted. Wasn't I only giving him a week?

We finished cleaning and made our way back to the lounge chairs. He moved my outstretched legs over his lap and caressed my thighs. I was in heaven. This had to be what an addiction felt like.

The angle of the sun created an ethereal glow in his backyard that made his eyes luminescent. Something divine in the way he gazed at me made my ability to reason flee, leaving only the faith I didn't realize I had.

His eyes reminded of the dream I'd woken up from on the first day of school. Chills skittered up my face from the memory. I'd been floating in a vibrant blue sky, falling toward the Earth, excited to be reaching my destination. With each exhale, my lungs created the atmosphere, hugging the Earth below. I'd needed nothing more to hold in my arms in the dream, and I felt that way now—about Liam. The realization made me dizzy.

With his every touch, every exhale, I was falling deeper, and it scared the crap out of me.

"What is it?" he asked me.

I threw my arms around Liam, wrapping around him like the sky would the earth. My need for him overwhelmed me. I cleared my throat. "Nothing important. I just remembered a dream."

Liam pulled back to stroke my cheek. He seemed to search my eyes for something and then brought his lips to mine for a kiss. "I need you too," he whispered.

My heart felt like it had been cracked open.

His kiss was even better than I remembered. With every stroke of his tongue, the sparks exploded in my mouth like Pop Rocks, the candy Shiney and I devoured on sleepovers. Who knew kissing could feel like this?

We soon made up for a whole afternoon's worth of kisses, stopping only to catch our breath. It let me calm the intense tingling too, but I wouldn't bring that up. I was sure he'd bolt if he knew just how foolish I'd become. He lifted me into his lap, and I clung to his neck, giddy and smiling.

"You feel bloody incredible," he said. His lips were all red and puffy.

I leaned my forehead against his and smiled. "So do you."

Liam moved in to kiss me again, but froze, his face falling. "Holy shite," he said.

He turned around, and in the doorway to the patio stood his dad.

CHAPTER 25

Liam

"I knew it!" Da bellowed from the doorway. He didn't bother blocking his curiosity nor his anger.

Bloody feckin' hell.

Lucky bolted off my lap. Waves of her embarrassment crashed into me, no doubt because we'd been caught with our lips locked. She wouldn't have wanted that to be Da's first impression of her.

Her gaze darted back and forth from Da to me. Once she found out I hadn't told him about her, she'd think the worst. I'd be ruining all the trust I'd regained today.

I jumped up and held her face, blocking her view of Da. "Lucky, don't be cross with me just yet."

She nodded, and I rushed over to Da to be heading him off. I needed to explain things to Lucky first.

"You must be the new girl," Da called out over my shoulder.

"Da," I whispered. "We're not needing this now. Can we talk inside in a minute, yeah?"

"No," he half-growled under his breath. "I've a right to meet her, especially now that I know you've been keeping things from me." He'd lowered his voice, but I feared Lucky could still hear him.

Mum made an appearance in the doorway. She gave Da an apologetic smile and tugged on his arm. "Come away, Patrick."

He shook his head and pushed past me toward Lucky. "Hello, I'm Liam's father, Patrick. It's lovely to actually meet you." He reached out his hand to shake hers.

A hesitant smile crept onto her face, and ripples of her confusion and curiosity nipped at me. She glanced at me with a questioning look, so I nodded to say everything was all right. As pissed off as Da was, he'd be nothing but kind to her.

"N–Nice to meet you too, Mr. Whelan. I'm Laxshmi." She gifted him with a smile too sweet for what he deserved for buttin' in.

"Well now," Da said. "It's a shame I know nothing about you. You seem utterly charming." He leaned over and kissed the back of her hand, giving me the side-eye.

She blushed. "Thank you."

"Da!" I yanked his hand off hers and stood between them. "I need to talk to you *inside* if you will." I turned him around by the shoulders and pushed him toward Mum. Dealing with Lucky's confusion was my first priority, before she had time to assume the worst.

"I'm glad he's found you, Laxshmi," he yelled. "I hope you're meant for each other."

Christ. His well wishes would no doubt remind her of the others. "Are you bloody hammered?" I whispered, clenching my jaw.

"I've not touched a glass of anything."

"Keep him inside, Mum. Please. I'll be back soon as I walk her home."

"You'd best be," Da said. "I'm glad you've found the target right enough, but we'll be having some words about you keeping this from me."

I gritted my teeth. "And that would be why I didn't tell you—because it has nothing to do with her being a target."

He sputtered something, but Mum pulled him inside.

I headed back to Lucky. She was still standing by the lounge chairs and looking radiant in the setting sun. With the blue top she was wearing, it was as if she'd just stepped off a tropical beach.

"Lucks, I'm right sorry."

She tilted her head. "You didn't tell him about me?"

Damn. She'd heard. A growing worry mingled with her curiosity, taking her mind exactly where I didn't want it to go. I'd rather be dragged across a coral reef than lose the progress we'd made today.

"I told Da I hadn't met anyone special yet."

"Like the other girls in your search."

I cleared my throat and nodded. I didn't know whether to smile at how clever she was, or worry about her putting too many pieces together. "He'd have been peppering me with endless questions, and since he wasn't coming to lunch on Saturday, I, um ... put off telling him. But Lucky, it has no bearing on how I feel about you. Honest."

Her eyes scanned my face for a long moment. I resisted the urge to keep explaining. She needed to learn to trust her emerging abilities.

Her shoulders relaxed. "I know about overbearing parents. It's not fair to expect you to have told your dad. You do remember I can't tell my mom about us, right?"

I heaved a sigh and pulled her in for a kiss. We'd tell her mum eventually, but bringing up forever didn't seem a wise idea at the moment. I was still wrapping the idea around my head myself.

"Um, what did your dad mean by saying 'I hope you're meant for each other'? Is that about the secret? The search?"

My heart ached at not being able to tell her. "It is. Are you angry?"

She looked at a spot on my T-shirt. "Frustrated."

I kissed her temple and wrapped my arms around her. Raised voices floated to us from inside. Speaking of fair, I'd left Mum to deal with my mess. "I need to talk to my da right quick, but I'll be back in a few. You said your mum's coming home 'round seven, yeah?" She nodded. "Well, it's almost half six, and I want to walk you home." Some strands of hair had come out of her ponytail, framing her face. I pushed them behind her ear. "Will you wait for me?"

"Of course."

Before I turned to leave, I remembered what was in my pocket and pulled out a red lollipop. Her smile unclenched the knot in my stomach, reminding me this was all about her, about us. Nothing else mattered.

I found my parents in the front room and charged up to Da. "Mum had nothing to do with this, so I'll be thanking you to leave her out of it."

"I've a right to know—"

"Jaysus! Couldn't you let me explain before you made it seem like I'd lied to her?"

He stood. "How in perdition am I meant to know what you've been saying? I didn't even know she existed, and I'm mortified that I'm your father and knowing nothing!" He stopped to take a deep breath. "Now I know why you had your knickers in a knot in Charlotte." He paced, ruffling his hair.

"I had reasons—"

"You had a grand time pissing off Gagliardi, and it was all to protect her, leaving me in the dark. You're risking his wrath for her?"

"You did *what?*" Mum asked. "Patrick, you seem to have forgotten that detail."

Da kept his glare on me as he told Mum what he'd thought

unimportant the first time he shared the story with her. She bombarded me with questions, most of which Da answered with unfair assumptions. I'd been pacing, my impatience growing the longer Lucky had to wait.

"Enough! I'm walking Lucky home. I'll be back whenever I get back." I stormed out of the front room with Da on my tail.

"Don't you derail yourself from our ultimate goal. You're not knowing yet if she's The One."

"And I don't give a fecking damn if she isn't," I said.

That glued him to the spot. I rushed out onto the patio, hearing him yell something not worth giving my ears to. The fact that my time with Lucky was over for the day was more pressing. It'd be murder waiting until tomorrow to see her.

She'd opened up to me in a way I'd not thought possible. She needed me, and it gave me hope. The sort of hope that cured diseases and stopped wars.

I slowed and felt the tension ebb as I reached Lucky. A lullaby of crickets had soothed her to sleep. Her face was so peaceful. No doubt she was exhausted, and if she'd been losing sleep like I'd been, it was a wonder she'd had any energy left to her. My mobile must have fallen out of my pocket before Da had interrupted us, and she was clutching it to her chest. I slipped it out of her hand and snapped a photo. With the sun as low as it was, her skin took on the soft haziness of one of those vintage filters from an editing app. I couldn't help but stroke her cheek. She gave a soft moan. Could she feel the tingling in her sleep? She leaned her face into my palm, opened her eyes, and smiled. I took a diving leap into her happiness.

Sitting up, she wrapped her arms around me, burying her face in my neck. "It's time to go, isn't it?"

Ripples of her sadness nipped at me, and I squeezed her closer. Her scent filled my nostrils, reminding me she was my home now. "Only until tomorrow morning, yeah?"

Her warm lips pressed against my neck, and her attraction to me washed over like a tidal wave. Her emotions were so pure. I'd forever be addicted.

She sighed and looked up. "I'm making a mess of my needing space thing."

"You'll not hear any complaining from me."

"I bet. Anyway … is everything okay with your dad?"

I cleared my throat. "Come on, you're looking knackered."

Her forehead wrinkled, but she nodded. I scooped her up in my arms. "Liam! Wha—? You don't have to carry me. I'm not that tired."

"I know. This is for me."

She laughed and snuggled closer. "Such a sap."

This gorgeous creature in my arms was my soul mate. Even without proof, I'd do anything for her, including protect her with my life. The instinct to guard her was all-consuming. How could she not be The One? Just a week ago, I'd been pushing her buttons, cynical about the search, about being with someone for the rest of my life. Now, I couldn't see any other future for myself. I stepped into Mrs. Robertson's back garden and slowed my walking to stretch out our time.

Lucky chewed on her thumbnail, her eyes unfocused. "I've been thinking," she said. Her determination came across like a fish trying to swim upstream. "I can't deny I'm curious—about the secret—but I know myself. I don't think I can wait for long, and until then I can't act like everything's normal between us. It would hurt too much if … if … "

"Shh. I know." I kissed her forehead. "So what is it you're suggesting?"

She shrugged. "Well, touching you confuses me. It's weird, I just … I don't know." Her voice was soft, as if she were ashamed by her admission. "Would you mind if we kind of … limit it?"

"Not if that's what you need."

241

"How about this?" she asked. "Twice a day. Once in the morning and then when we say goodbye at the end of the day, until you tell me the secret and I can accept this whole thing. *If* I can, I mean," she added softly.

Her earnest gaze cut right through me. I wanted her *ifs* to be *whens*. "If that's what you're wanting."

She sighed and relaxed in my arms.

We reached her back porch, and I placed her down at the foot of the stairs. She'd left the back light on, and a swarm of insects buzzed around it. A bright, green frog clung to the gutter, standing guard over his find.

"So," she started. "Of all the places you've moved to, where's your favorite?"

"Here." I winked at her.

Her laugh lit up her face. "Such a suck-up. Seriously. Where?"

"Nothing's as fine as Ireland."

"Will you go back? After graduation, I mean." Apprehension tinged her emotions, like diving into dark, murky waters. She was pushing away her anxiety, but I felt the ripples before they receded.

Life on the estate was waiting for me. Did I want to go back? Sure. But without Lucky? I couldn't imagine it. Not now. I sat on her steps and pulled her into my lap, where she curled up against me. "I'm eighteen. I'll be staying and waiting for you to graduate." She bolted upright. Her eyes widened. I traced her bottom lip. "I'll go to university wherever you'll be going." As much as I wanted to bring her back with me, Ireland and the estate would have to wait.

"But your brother and cousins? Patty?"

I smiled. She *would* be thinking of them. "I'll not be going anywhere without you, yeah? We'll head to Ireland when you're ready." So much for not bringing up forever.

She narrowed her eyes and studied my face. "I–I believe you."

I kissed her. Her faith in me made me feel like I could swim across the ocean.

She nestled her head against my shoulder and sighed. "Ireland, huh? They'd have dance programs there, too. And medical schools," she whispered.

A car with an obvious fan belt problem squealed by, reminding me her mum would be home soon. "You should be getting yourself inside. Have a good night, will you now?"

"Doubt it. Haven't been sleeping well lately."

I unbuckled my watch and attached it to her wrist. "Try this."

"What's this for?"

"You dozed off holding my mobile. Maybe this'll help when you're not with me, yeah?"

The watch fit like a large bracelet on her arm. She pressed it against her heart and then took out the band around her ponytail, letting her hair cascade around her shoulders. I couldn't resist combing my fingers through her hair while she untwisted her ponytail holder. She stretched the simple black band over my wrist. "There. Something of mine."

"Perfect." I locked my arms around her, wishing I could have more of her. The pang of wanting to start our life together clawed at my insides. "It'll be like getting stung by jellyfish, missing you tonight."

Waves of her anxiety crested around me, and I felt like I was being pushed overboard in rough seas. She tightened her grip around me, not making any effort to leave. So I carried her up the stairs, took the house key from her pocket, and unlocked her door. Her breaths were quick against my neck. Without a word more, she tore out of my arms and rushed inside.

I let out a loud breath and dragged myself home. This wasn't like when Cousin Robert and I had hid from Da for two days. We'd been ten and had taken a photo of him in the shower to enter into a *Men of Ireland* calendar contest. We were never sure what upset him the most—the photo or the fact he didn't make the cut. I'd not be hiding from him this time around.

I braced myself to face the fire and walked inside. "I'm back."

"In here," Mum called from the dining room. They sat in front of dozens of open books scattered over the table.

"Is everything smoothed over, darling?" Mum's eyes were red, and she held one of Da's handkerchiefs bunched in her hand.

Shite. I ran a hand through my hair. "Good enough for now."

She turned back to face Da, blocking me from her feelings. These books, notebooks, and research were our life, right here, on this table. Bits of information and guesswork that had been bringing Lucky and me together, but also seeming to tear Da and me apart.

"If you've got a problem with me, let's have it out then," I said to him.

He thumbed through a notebook, tossed it aside, and reached for another one. He pulled a large binder from a stack beside him.

I banged my hand on the table. "Go ahead. Let's have this out."

"I'm done with your hard neck cheek, boyo." A vein throbbed on his forehead.

"Liam, darling, do you know yet? About Laxshmi?" Mum asked.

I sat, running a hand over my neck. I could still feel Lucky's lips on my throat. "Yeah, she's The One. I'm sure of it." She had to be.

Mum gasped. "How—?"

"I realized on Saturday. That's all you'll be needing to know."

"Lay off the likes of that blather!" Da slammed the binder shut. "She's still only a target until there's proof of more, and your bloody hormones don't mean shite." He was pointing the tips of his reading glasses at me. "Until we're knowing for a certainty, we've got to continue preparing ourselves to find the next target."

I bolted out of my seat. "Next target? You and your targets can go to feckin' hell."

Mum put a hand on my arm, her fingers cold. "Darling, you know he's just being thorough and thinking of the family."

"No, he's bloody pissed I didn't tell him." I ground my teeth together. "Have as many more visions as you like, but I'm staying here with her. With Lucky. This is my life. So it's my choice."

He stood, pushing the binder aside. "We didn't sacrifice everything just to be putting up with your gammy hormones."

"Hormones?" I grabbed the back of the chair to keep from punching something. "This isn't about me getting to shag her."

"You shouldn't have become so involved with some beour without talking about it to the both of us first," he yelled.

My anger spewed out, deepening my voice. "A beour, is she? Well, she's not just some good-looking girl. It's in love with her, I am!"

Mum and Da froze. *Shite.* Was I really in love with Lucky, or was I trying to make a point?

How can I already be in love?

I turned toward the window and saw Mrs. Robertson's trellis and the climbing vine—now free of the weeds that had been strangling it the other day. All I knew was I wanted to be with Lucky, hear her voice, feel her in my arms, and make her happy. Sure, I loved her laugh, her big heart ... her sincerity. I loved her cheeky attitude, her expressive eyes, and the way she looked at me like I was everything to her. I loved the way we needed each other, and—damn—was I ever wanting her.

It had happened piece by piece, right under my nose, just like a bloody puzzle fitting together.

I really am in love with her. The air rushed out of my mouth, and I smiled.

The sound of Mum's giggling broke through the silence. She got up from the table and hugged me. "Liam, I'm happy for you. Does she feel the same?"

"I'm not ... I don't know," I whispered. "We're taking it day by day just now."

Day by day until Lucky had an official empath breakthrough. She'd taken a step closer to it today with her panic attack. I'd blocked my mind again—several times, in fact—but she'd never sensed a single one of them. Her transition would be in limbo until she could sense one.

The sound of scratching stubble drew our attention. Da was rubbing his face. "Liam, you don't understand. We need proof … or it's another vision that'll be pushing us on."

"Patrick!" Mum looked horrified.

"Leave it, Mum. He doesn't care about a bleedin' thing but his pride."

A wild and desperate look settled into Da's eyes. "What I care about is your life! Could be she's The One, but if she's not, you'll be needing to pull up your garters and move on with us. Like they say in the States, shit happens."

"I'm eighteen. You're not choosing who I love, and with a bloody certainty you're not telling me how to live my life."

He barreled around the table, stabbing his finger in my chest. "I'll be saying it again—there's no choice in the matter," he spat. "They'll kill you if you don't find The One."

Mum gasped, and the blood drained from Da's face.

"What is it you're saying?" I whispered.

Da clutched his head, shaking it, and Mum pushed me aside. "Patrick, so help me, you had best be telling me what you're about. You've been hiding something for long enough and now you say—" Her voice choked on a sob.

I put my arm around her shoulders and led her to a chair.

Da wobbled into the one beside her. All I could do was stare at him. "Mum's right. What's this about?"

"Another vision." He closed his eyes. "It'd be a year ago now." He opened his sorrow-filled eyes and lifted them to Mum. "How could I tell you? I've never had conflicting visions—he'll find his soul mate, but he'll be murdered when he doesn't." He shook his head and shrugged.

Mum wiped away her tears and took his hand. "We will get to the bottom of this." Her voice sounded small.

Da explained the vision to us. From what clues he'd gathered, the Soul Seekers would be the ones responsible for my death.

"But Lucky is The One," I said, putting my hand on Mum's shoulder. "So no worries, yeah?"

"Liam, darling," Mum said. "This isn't just about falling in love. You can't risk your life—"

"It's *my* life. When will you both get that through your heads?"

Da stood. "Knowing what this would do to the family—to your Mum—you're still insisting on being a stubborn arse? The entire clan now depends on you, son. Who'll be protecting them if you're killed? Your cousin William? His farts couldn't move a feather."

"You're expecting me to give up Lucky because of some conflicting vision of yours? You can bet your bloody arse that won't be happening."

Da stepped closer to me. "I'll not be letting you risk everything over some mot you've got yourself. Not while there's blood in my veins." That very blood was throbbing in the vein on his forehead again. "Would she be wanting you to do such a thing? Leave your family and clan unprotected?"

A cold chill spread over my body. "Don't you dare." My muscles coiled tight, ready to be sprung. "You've no right to manipulate us."

"I'm your father, and that would be giving me every right," he spat out.

"Seems we're at an impasse. No reason for me to stay then." I left the dining room, heading upstairs to pack. If I stayed, I'd be resolving this with my fists.

"Liam," Mum called after me.

I tore up the stairs three at a time. Fifteen minutes later, I was back down with a stuffed suitcase and my school bag. I'd stay at a hotel and come over in the mornings to meet Lucky.

Mum and Da were arguing as I flew down the stairs. They paused when they heard me, and Mum rushed up to me.

"Liam, you're upset and leaving won't solve anything."

"There's nothing to be fixing, Mum. I'm trying to live my life, and he thinks he has some claim. No more. Everyone's always had a piece of me and my future, but that ends."

I'd be thick not to at least pay some heed to Da's vision. With Ciarán's help, I could set up some precautions around me—around Lucky too. The Soul Seekers would be after one or both of us whether she passed Da's test or not. My only concern was for Lucky's safety. Without me, they'd leave her alone. With me, her life was in danger.

I kissed Mum's tearstained cheek and left. It was still humid enough outside to be suffocating, even with night falling. Swaths of pink and orange were clawed into the underbelly of the western sky as the last hints of sun disappeared. My suitcase wheels scraped against the pavement as I made my way to the street where I'd parked.

I brought the bags to the back of my Range Rover and turned to see Mrs. Robertson getting out of her car, one orthopedic shoe after another. She waved and waddled up to her house while I tossed my bags into the boot. Before I drove off, I left a message for Ciarán about what had happened and read one of his stupid texts he'd sent about an hour ago. I looked at our house and then at Lucky's. Da's words ground on my already frayed nerves.

"Could be she's The One, but if she's not, you'll be needing to pull up your garters and move on with us."

I pounded the steering wheel with my hand until my palm was burning in pain. With a last look at Lucky's house, I made a U-turn to leave.

Pulling up to the stone, metal, and glass portico of The Umstead Hotel, I waited for the valet. This would be home for a bit, even though my heart was with Lucky. The ache in my chest had worsened since I'd left, and I hoped she wasn't feeling it too. Was this some sign our souls were merging? That we were joining?

My mobile rang. I thought about ignoring the call, but the ID showed it was Elder Brennan.

Could my night be any more rotten?

"Elder Brennan, late for you to be calling. Isn't it the middle of the night in Ireland?"

"I must say, I'm disappointed you'd be leaving her alone." Even through the mobile, her tone held power. "Do you not realize how vulnerable she is right now?"

Holding back a string of curses, I looked out the windows of my Range Rover. *Is that bleedin' spy back?* I pulled out of the valet line to park with a view of the hotel entrance. "I'm not leaving her, and how is it she's vulnerable?"

"My contacts have informed me *il signor* Gagliardi has been in touch with people in your area, but they're not sure why he might be taking such actions."

"What's Gagliardi's bloody game?" I managed, clenching my jaw.

"What matters more is if she's had her breakthrough. Has she?"

I wasn't sure if I could trust Brennan, but I'd take the chance if it meant protecting Lucky. "She's been sensing things, but she's not responding to my blocks."

"You need to be with her, Prince Liam. When she breaks through, she'll be in more danger of her energy being spotted, if it hasn't been already. She'll be a beacon in the dark. Once you've joined, she'll have better protections."

"Protection against the Soul Seekers? Then why not be telling me what needs to happen to make this joining come about? It's answers I'm needing."

"It's patience you're needing, young man. The answers will be in front of you soon enough."

More questions raced through my mind, but only one was critical. "Is there a good reason for me to be trusting you to mean well by us?"

Her pause felt like an eternity—an eternity where I hoped letting her find out about Lucky wasn't the biggest mistake of my life. *If Brennan does something to hurt Lucky ...* I tightened my grip on the steering wheel.

She sighed. "Go home, Liam."

"Elder Brenn—"

"Ring me back after you've joined." Her voice had taken on a commanding tone that most would dare not ignore. Before I could say anything more, she rang off.

I threw my mobile against the passenger seat and watched it bounce onto the floor. She could very well be a Soul Seeker, but her reason for contacting me seemed to be centered on protecting Lucky. I couldn't deny that. Or was this a trap?

If she wasn't to be trusted, I'd deal with her later. And if Lucky was important enough to be leaving home for, she was important enough to be returning for as well.

I took a deep breath, rolled my shoulders, and pulled out, heading for home. Halfway there, a question burned through my mind and couldn't be doused.

How did Brennan know Lucky was a non-empath?

CHAPTER 26

Lucky

Would Liam really stay in the States until I graduated? *Who does that for a girl he hardly knows?* It had been such an overwhelming declaration, I hadn't even thought to tell him how I was on track to graduate with him this June.

I pushed my fingers against my aching sternum. It had started hurting about an hour ago.

For the last half-hour, I'd sat at the kitchen table and reread the same paragraph from the short story called "Eveline" by James Joyce. It was in one of the books Liam lent me for my Irish monologue. I'd photocopied the story, along with other passages and poems, so I could return the books to him tomorrow.

I groaned and sat back in the chair, clunking against the loose backing. I pulled out Liam's watch from my pocket and held it in my hands. The inscription on the back read, *Liam, In due time, Da.* The watch was a Breitling. From what I'd read online, they could be over twenty thousand dollars. With all the money they seemed to have, why were they living in this neighborhood?

I pressed Liam's watch to my cheek and sighed.

God, I'm such a sap.

A twinge of disappointment flared in my chest, knowing I should return it. It wasn't like I could replace it if I lost it. I tucked the watch back into my pocket, closed Liam's books, and organized the photocopies. I stopped when I reached his volume of poetry. His dad's dedication begged to be finished, so I grabbed my poetry journal from my bag and came up with a few possibilities. I settled on two more lines to complete it and then penciled them into the book.

Find comfort in these pages
For winter ends in stages,
And wings that leave their cages,
Find a love to span the ages.

Have faith.
You will find The One.

It was corny, but it'd do.

The One. What type of secret would explain what that meant?

While I'd been waiting for Liam on the lounge chair, Ciarán had texted his brother. I hadn't meant to read it, but his phone had been in my hands when the text had popped up on the screen.

Ciarán: So is your soul mate an empath yet?

Could being The One mean being his soul mate? But what guy goes around searching for his soul mate like she was some missing person? And what was an empath? I figured I'd Google it later.

I tapped my pencil against my chin. If Liam had started dating each of the girls because he thought one of them could've been The One, then by his own admission, he'd been wrong six times before me. How would Liam know for sure? And when? Was gambling my heart with those odds even wise? Why couldn't falling in love be easier? I fumbled my pencil, and it dropped to the table.

Falling in love? I pushed the thought away.

I rubbed my eyes and stood to take everything upstairs. A strange sensation tickled my mind, like at the Akropolis Kafe, and I spun around, half expecting Liam to be standing behind me. The gnawing at my sternum stopped, and an imaginary breeze relaxed me with its warmth.

Liam.

I shook my head. I had to be hallucinating again.

A soft knocking at the back door stopped me from leaving the kitchen. I had no idea how I knew, but somehow I did. It was Liam. My heart began to race. I checked the stairs to make sure Mom wasn't coming down, then rushed to open the back door.

I launched myself into his arms. He squeezed me tight and hummed his appreciation. An intense tingling surged through every cell in my body, and then calmed. It felt like everything was vibrating on some Liam-frequency, and my body would never know peace unless he was near. God, was I a mess.

I pulled back. "What are you doing here?"

"I'd not been able to stay away." What he said didn't feel exactly right. I stared at him, and he smiled. "You've become a pretty decent lie detector yourself." He nuzzled my neck, murmuring against my skin. "I needed to be touching you, feeling you safe in my arms." He was holding something back. It bothered me, but unfortunately, I was also getting used to it. He rested his forehead against my shoulder and sighed, as if he knew what I was thinking. "Da and I had a bit of a row, that's all."

"A fight about us?" I gently scratched my fingernails against the back of his head. His hair was thick and soft, and his scent calmed me. He nodded against my shoulder. I leaned my head against his. "He doesn't think I'm The One?"

He jerked up, his eyes scanning mine. "He can have his doubts, but I don't. I'd told him as much. I've chosen you, yeah?" His words thrilled me and scared me at the same time. He kissed me and then groaned. "I should be heading back."

"So can we work on my monologue tomorrow morning?"

He nodded, his face still tense. "We can go to the benches by the car park."

I wanted to lighten his mood, so I broke into the best Irish brogue I could manage. "We don't call it a car park here, love. It's searching you've been for the past six years, so you ought to be knowing that by now, yeah?"

He held his fist over his mouth and shook with laughter. It was contagious. "Jaysus, the family will fall in love with you." We kissed some more before he ripped himself away to leave.

"Oh, wait, before you go. Your books." I darted inside and brought them out.

Liam was leaning against the wooden railing, looking up into the night sky. I remembered the first day of school, seeing his strong jaw, comfortable swagger, and pale-green eyes. That same guy was standing here now against a canvas of soft black, looking even more amazing with features I'd had time to explore.

He was also the same guy who stood up to his dad for me.

Would I ever have the courage to do the same with Mom? He was ready to commit to something long-term ... on faith. Faith in me.

Faith I wasn't showing in him.

He pointed to the books. "So you've got everything you need then?"

"Huh? Oh. Yeah." I cleared out my thoughts and put the books on the top step. Opening the poetry volume to the inside front cover, I handed it to him with a shrug. "I, uh ... finished it."

He angled it toward the porch light and read. A smile crept along his face. "I love it. Jaysus, Lucky, it couldn't be more perfect."

He stacked the book on top of the others, and I saw my ponytail holder around his wrist.

When he pulled me back into his arms, I snapped it, giggling. "Not very masculine, but I like it." I took his watch out of my pocket. "I, uh … I can't keep this, Liam. It's so expens—"

He cut off my words with his hand. "Yes, you can. It's a gift. No arguments."

"This isn't a gift!" I looked over my shoulder and lowered my voice. Thankfully, Mom's room was on the other side of the house. "It's a–a car, or college tuition. I can't—"

"Didn't I just say no arguments?" He smiled, his eyes playful.

"Ugh." I spun around, giving him my back, but he just held me closer, chuckling in my ear. I bit back a smile.

"Please keep it, Lucks. I'll punch some extra holes in the band tomorrow so it'll be fitting better, yeah? How else should I be warning the insect world you're mine?"

"Wow." I snorted. "You're declaring an all-out war, aren't you?"

"I'd only rip off ladybug wings for you, *mo mhuirnín.*"

I turned, play-punched him in the arm and tucked myself against him on a yawn. I hoped I wouldn't have as much trouble sleeping now that I had something of his with me.

Falling for him was becoming too easy, but how did I know it wasn't an infatuation? Sure, he was hot, and his smile would pretty much make me do anything he asked. But he was more than that. He looked after me as if I were the most important thing in the world to him. While we were weeding, hadn't he told me he'd bring me lunch during the drill team practices on Tuesday and Thursday? I would've just skipped eating. He was generous, loving, and attentive. On top of that, he was respectful, chivalrous, and intelligent. He made me laugh, and he made me see a future with him, despite Mom.

Yup. I was falling in love, with a possible one week expiration date. If he didn't tell me his secret by then, I had to break it off.

The stronger my attachment got, the more it felt like standing in front of a badly constructed dam. The longer I waited, the more water would collect behind it. And when that dam broke—if it broke—I'd either be seriously soaked or I would drown.

One week. Any longer and I'd never survive.

I hated to change the mood, but I had to ask. "Liam, how did you find out that none of the other girls were ... The One?" The words *soul mate* wouldn't leave my lips. It felt too weird to say. I tipped my head back to study his expression.

"I just knew."

I lowered my eyes. *Don't chicken out. Just ask him.* "But if you thought each of them was possibly The One, and you were wrong ... "

I glanced up and caught a look of uncertainty cross his face. As I suspected—no guarantees. I tried to step back, but he wouldn't let me go.

"No, Lucky. Don't be thinking that. There's no comparison between you and any of them." He kissed my forehead. He may have believed what he was telling himself, but somewhere inside, he knew he could be wrong. His face didn't lie.

"But—"

"I'm not saying it's not complicated right now, but I'm with you no matter what."

"Then you're saying it's your choice. I don't have to worry about this secret?"

He clenched his jaw. "Not exactly."

A lump threatened to choke me. I couldn't find the courage to ask which question he was actually answering. God forbid it was both.

I opened a new browser and typed *what is an empath* in the search bar. For the next hour, I read how New Age types defined characteristics of what I would've just called sensitive people, which included me. But then again, it felt like reading Zodiac traits. With a stretch, every birth sign could apply to me.

The deeper my search went, though, the more questionable the information became. Conspiracy sites claimed empaths were aliens from Area 51, and that the government was hiding their existence. One blogger even described how these aliens had mixed with the human population millennia ago, creating sorcerers, shamans, and truth-sayers from different cultures. Apparently, empaths weren't the only thing these aliens had made.

I was already hallucinating. I couldn't validate my insanity even more by asking Liam what Ciarán's text had meant.

I snorted.

Gee, Liam, are you and your family descendants of aliens?

CHAPTER 27

Liam

I bunked off study hall again to be with Lucky in her theater class, but a group assignment kept her from spending any time with me. It didn't matter. Even while working on calculus problems, I could sense whenever she thought of me. I'd look up, meet her gaze, and project my love to her. Her answering smile was enough. Once my calculus was finished, I glued my attention to her.

For two days now, Lucky had been breaking down the dam holding back the happiness she reserved for me and me alone. The tingling was becoming more intense the heavier things were getting between us, and I suspected it was part of the joining. It had to be, but would it happen in stages or all it once? Could I do something to push it along? And what exactly was meant to happen?

For the hundredth time in the last couple of days, I blocked her from my emotions to see if she'd notice. She didn't. I'd been projecting strong emotions to her any chance I had, but all I'd succeeded in doing was making her head ache. I felt like a shite for doing it, but if it pushed her into breaking through, it'd be worth it.

The class bell rang. We left the auditorium only to find Chloe in the hallway, watching Lucky and me walking out together. The look on Chloe's face made me suspicious, so I opened up my mind to her. She was irritated for some reason or another, but I also felt something mean coming from her.

She headed our way with a bounce in her step, crowding Lucky out when she stepped up to me. "Liam, there you are. You skipped study hall again. Who's going to help me with my math?"

I tried to move next to Lucky, but Chloe shifted and Lucky's jealousy and lack of confidence got the better of her. With a wave to me, Lucky darted across the hall.

I brushed past Chloe to catch Lucky before she fled into the girls' locker rooms. "Lucky!"

She turned around and stopped before she could be escaping inside, and I pushed my way through the shower of students to stand inches from her. *Damn her no-touching policy.* Things may have been going well, but she hadn't let go of her need to take things slow.

"You left the bouncing boobs for me? I'm touched," she said.

"Touched? Interesting choice of words you've got there."

"It is, isn't it?" Lucky gave me her shy smile, which always made me want to kiss her.

I sensed Chloe's impatience as she lingered nearby. Why the hell was she waiting for me? "You know, Lucky, it'd be simple enough to leave Chloe gobsmacked by kissing you right here."

Her eyes darted around us. "And break the rules?"

"Damn, Lucky. Let me at least be telling her we're seeing each other."

"Are we?" She broke into a smile. "Go to class already. Don't worry about her. She's not important." Lucky sounded a bit like she was convincing herself. With a turn on her heel, she disappeared into the locker room.

Chloe waited for me at the mouth of the hallway. *Grand.* I kept quiet while she prattled on about nonsense. Her class was around the next corner, so I'd not have to put up with her for too long.

By the time I got to physics, my stomach was churning. Something didn't feel right. Was it Lucky? Had that spy come for her? Mum and Da had been patrolling the area around the school when they'd been able. They'd not seen much of anything. Maybe Lucky was feeling sick, and I was mirroring her. We were connected in strange ways, so I'd not be surprised. A sinking feeling overtook me. I'd have to run down after class to catch her as she left the lockers.

Fifteen minutes passed, and my concentration became the devil's plaything. Even at this distance, our connection was strengthening, and Lucky's sadness and embarrassment were as clear as if I could see them before my eyes. I kept fidgeting in my seat, and my tablemate's irritated glance only pissed me off.

What the hell was happening? *Bloody hell.* I needed to find Lucky. The connection was now fading as if the physical distance between us were growing.

My feet were pounding the floor before the bell had finished ringing. I made it down to the locker rooms just as the girls started leaving. Shiney came out alone, her forehead creased.

I grabbed her arm. "Where's Lucky? What happened? Is she sick?" I opened my mind to Shiney.

Some giggling cheerleaders stepped out of the locker room. Shiney glared at them and pulled me to the other side of the hallway. "She went home. Coach got her signed out because she was so upset."

"Why? Shiney, you've got to be telling me, please."

"She overheard two cheerleaders saying all kinds of stuff about her. They said the only reason the drill team allowed her to help them was because Bailey was a lesbian and liked her. Then they made fun of her being Indian and wondered if she'd bring a cobra to school, saying she was a snake charmer, if you know what I mean."

I balled my hands into fists. My insides felt like molten lava. "Go on."

She bit her lips and looked down. "They made fun of your nickname for her, insinuating all kinds of things that you really meant with the word *lucky*. And they said you'd told Chloe you were just out to get *lucky* at tomorrow night's party. That if Laxshmi didn't live up to your nickname for her, you'd dump her. Chloe's apparently all ready for that to happen."

"Bloody lies, Shiney. They're all lies." I cursed under my breath and rushed toward the exit. "I'm going after her now," I called out over my shoulder.

I slipped out the side entrance and ran home. *Damn Lucky's mobile issues.* A stitch in my side burned by the time I got to her house. I rang the bell and pounded on the door. She was home—her sadness was washing over me—but she wasn't answering. Why was she hiding herself? Was she believing what they'd said about me? *Christ.* What more could bloody get in our way?

If only I'd been thinking straight, I could've borrowed Shiney's mobile—Lucky's mum would've recognized her number. I looked down the street in the direction of the school. *Should I be going back?* Lucky's pain was overwhelming. She needed me. I couldn't be leaving her alone.

I rushed to my house, grabbed the ladder, and climbed to the roof from my parents' veranda. I could see Lucky sitting on her window seat. Her sheer curtains fluttered from the open window.

I cupped my hands around my mouth. "Lucky!"

Her head jerked up in surprise, but then she threw her legs off the seat, turning her back to me. Her pain sliced me open like the jaws of a shark.

"Lucky, I know you can hear me. Talk to me, or I'll be staying here all night."

She turned to face me, resting her hand on the window, and shook her head. I focused my enhanced vision across the distance.

She had a bunched-up tissue in her hand. Even with tears and a red nose, she was stunning.

"You can't be listening to anything they said. You know they're just ignorant, jealous racists."

She covered a sob. I pressed my fists against my eyes. She didn't deserve this. When I looked at her again, she was opening her window wider. She cupped her hands around her mouth. "Not now. I can't."

If she couldn't share this with me, what did it mean? That she believed their lies?

She disappeared, closing the window and curtains. I slumped against the chimney and looked past her house toward the school. Should I go back and find the scrubbers who'd done this? I couldn't bear to leave Lucky though. If I kept sending her my love, maybe she'd not feel so bad. What else could I do?

Two hours later, Lucky's mum pulled up into their driveway, earlier than usual. At least Lucky wouldn't be on her own, but I'd have no chance to visit her now. I leaned my head into my hands.

Not but a few minutes after, the diesel engine of Da's classic Mercedes grew louder as he drew near. The car door slammed, and Da began yelling. "This is just what we've been looking for. Now where's that book, Moira? Where have you put it? Let me see the book!"

The front door slammed, and I climbed down to see why Da was sounding like there was a bit of a hooley kicking off.

Since I'd come back from the hotel, Da and I had been avoiding each other. Mostly, that meant Da packing up and researching with a colleague two hours away at Belmont Abbey College. His friend was a medieval studies professor who had an interest in Irish lore. Could they have discovered something about the joining?

I reached the front room and found Da dancing around like he'd gone off his nut, waving the book of poetry he'd given me.

"What the hell are you about?" I asked.

"Your ma told me our Laxshmi finished it."

The poem?

Before I could ask any more, Mum came down the stairs, and Da grabbed her arms, twirling her around. "Ahh, *a ghrá! A thaisce!* Where's the letter, love? We've got to get eyes on it."

"Patrick, what's this all about?" she asked, her face pink and her eyes twinkling. "What letter, darling?"

He held her closer, poetry book still in hand, and hummed a waltz. "The letter I had you hide what is it—twelve years ago now. Don't tell me you're not remembering. I mailed a letter to the house and asked for it to be hidden where I'd never lay eyes on it until the time was right. And it's right." He held up the poetry book again.

"Goodness, Patrick. I'd completely forgotten."

"What letter would this be?" I asked. Was this about getting proof?

"Liam!" Letting go of Mum, he came around the sofa and grasped my shoulders. "You did it! You did it!" He wasn't guarding his emotions, so it was hard not to get caught up in his joy.

All I could do was hug him back. "Is this about Lucky?"

Ignoring me, he stepped back to Mum, still beaming. "Moira, you're still standing when it's off to the hiding hole you should be."

"Oh, yes, I believe I tucked the note between the pages of one of my books." She ran her finger along the spines of her textbooks on psychology and pulled out a thick volume that she handed to him. "Here you are—a book you would never open in a million years."

He raised an eyebrow. "*The Psychological Considerations for the Patient-Family Dynamic in Treating Addictions?* You're slagging me."

He fanned the pages, found the envelope, and handed me a letter addressed to me.

Mum came over to my side.

"Why did he put it in a letter?" I whispered to her.

"When is he not eccentric, darling?"

I opened the envelope to find a note written in his hand. I read it aloud.

To my dear son, Liam,

It's a happy man I'll die if I can lead you to this bliss. The young lady who writes these two lines will be the one to share your joys, your sorrows, and your days.

And wings that leave their cages,
Find a love to span the ages.

Find it in yourself to push aside your fears and spread your wings.
With all the love a father could have,
Patrick Whelan
Dublin
28 August 2001

I couldn't take my eyes off the letter. "You knew about this since I was six?" I asked Da.

"I couldn't be letting anything muck this up for you, son. If you knew, you might coax a girl into writing this even if she wasn't The One, or maybe you'd let something slip and a girl too keen on you might have found out and used it, eh?" He put a hand on my shoulder. "You had the right of it all along. Your Lucky is the love of your life—your soul mate, your *mo shíorghrá*. She'll be the mother of your children—our grandchildren! What a story we'll have to tell." He left me and dashed off to the kitchen, taking Mum with him, asking how many grandchildren she was wanting.

My Lucky.

I slouched on the sofa, staring at the ceiling fan and watching the spinning blades go nowhere. How could I celebrate when Lucky was miserable and alone? My insides ached to be with her. When could we tell her mum about us? I fingered her ponytail holder.

Da came back with a Guinness for each of us. He stopped and stared at me. "Why are you pulling such a long face as that? We're celebrating. You're done, Liam. You found your soul mate."

"Lucky won't see me. I don't know what to do."

He put one of the bottles in my hand and slapped me across the back of my head. "What in bleeding blazes have you been doing to make everything go arsewise? I hand you your soul mate, and you're making a dog's dinner out of it."

"For Christ's sake, Da. I didn't do anything."

He settled next to me. "Fine. Out with it—the whole bleeding story." Holding my beer, I told him everything. He listened, sipping his Guinness and frowning. When I got to the end of it, he gave a nod. "'Who could refrain, that had a heart to love, and in that heart, courage, to make his love known?'"

"Shakespeare, Da? Really?"

He held up his Guinness. "*Sláinte.*"

We clinked our bottles and drank. He kept reminiscing, giving me highlights of the shite I'd endured over the years—as if they'd been pleasant memories. Da said he'd be staying up late to ring the family so they'd be getting the news over their breakfast tea. They'd be more than happy for us, no doubt. When Mum reminded Da to be telling them to keep the news in the family for now, Da finally shut his gob.

After a few minutes of blissful silence, he turned to me. "Saved your life, your Lucky has," he said. He raised his bottle and tapped mine. Not more than a sip passed my lips.

"And now her life is in danger," I said. The tether between my heart and hers burned, needing attention, but I had no idea how to be helping her. I'd been sending her my love, not knowing if she could sense me from this distance. It was all I could be thinking to do.

"She's a Whelan now," Da said. "We'll be protecting her like family."

The thought warmed my heart. I held out my left hand and flexed my fingers. They almost tingled just from the memory of touching her.

Da nudged my shoulder. "What's that? Imagining a wedding band on your finger, are you?"

"It's her touch I'm thinking about. When we touch, our skin tingles like we're passing some sort of charge between us. Sometimes I can be feeling it with just the thought of her. I'm wondering if it's the same for her."

He gave me his deep guttural laugh, implying more than he ever would in front of Mum. "To chemistry, son. To chemistry."

Toward the end of dinner, I'd been pushing my food around, thinking of Lucky. Mum asked Da if he'd learned any more about the joining from his latest batch of leads. That was why he'd been visiting his colleague.

He put down his fork. "Wish I could be bringing home better news, but no. Not a bit."

"I'm certain the answers will come, Patrick." She wiped her mouth with a napkin.

"A few more pints wouldn't hurt for inspiration, eh, Liam?" Da reached over and tapped his bottle to mine—the same one I'd been working on all this time. When I barely responded, he put his bottle down. "If you'll not be learning to relax, you'll explode over this whole situa—" He stood so quickly that his legs hit the table. The silverware rattled and the drinks sloshed.

Mum stood and caught his arm. "Patrick! What's wrong?"

"A charge … " he mumbled. He had that far-off look in his eyes, the one he'd get when he was thinking about his research. His face paled. He leaned over, supporting himself on the table. "Moira, pack me a weekend bag now if you please." He looked at his watch. "It's that Catholic library at Georgetown I'll be needing again."

"But that's a four-hour drive at the least. Why not leave in the morning?" She placed her napkin beside her plate.

"I'll ring Finnerty. He'll be able to get me access tonight," Da muttered. Turning to the bookshelves, he grabbed some notebooks. He pushed aside his plate and stacked the binders on the table. "Moira, please. I'd not be asking if it wasn't important."

She sighed and went upstairs.

"Da? What's this about?"

"Tingling, you say?" he asked.

I nodded. He thumbed through one of his notebooks, found whatever page he was looking for, and ran a finger down the text as he scanned it. "The sky, the Earth, the light … yes, yes." He tapped the page a few times. "I don't know as of yet. It's more details I'm needing, and Finnerty has a priest's diary from the Middle Ages that'll be a help."

"Is that the one Aunt Finola mentioned when you were translating those Gaelic pages?" I pushed back my chair and stood. "I'll drive. On the way you can tell me more."

"No, no. It's here with Laxshmi that you're needed. Besides, all I have just now are hunches, and it's time I'm needing, to piece them together."

"What am I meant to do? Knock on her door and tell her overprotective mum I need to see my soul mate?"

He came and put his hands on my shoulders. "Do something

unexpected. Listen to Shakespeare. You've the heart, now find the courage and make your love known. Every waking moment if you have to. Be a lion of a man, Liam. A lion!"

Da left in a rush, leaving me to help Mum with the dishes. We'd been clearing off the table when she stopped to rest her hand on my arm. She furrowed her brow. "Can you sense her?"

"I do now. But the connection's not as strong as earlier. It feels a bit like reading fine print now, rather than a billboard. I'll not be sleeping well tonight if I don't see her."

Mum moved her hand to my cheek and gave me a small smile. "I am quite certain that you will figure it all out. Leave this, darling." She nodded toward the table. "Go and do your schoolwork."

I headed to my room, running over what schoolwork I'd yet to finish and what I might have missed in last period, when the idea hit me upside the head.

I'm a genius.

I bolted upstairs to a shower. I couldn't smell like steak and beer when I went to Lucky's house.

CHAPTER 28

Lucky

After my awful afternoon, Mom's ranting about medical school was a good distraction. I didn't want to think any more about the catty things those cheerleaders had said. Most of it was trash talk. Chloe had designs on Liam, so it wasn't too far-fetched to think she'd get her cheer-mates to make me feel bad. It'd been the things they said about Liam using me and then dumping me that hit a nerve. It took every ounce of my faith in Liam to not fall prey to their lies. But it was the tiny smidgen of truth in what they'd said that left me with the doubts plaguing me all afternoon.

By the time dinner was done, I'd had enough of my mom. I'd made it to the second floor when the doorbell rang.

I glanced back down to see Mom answering it, leaving the screen door in place. "Yes?"

"Hello, Mrs. Kapadia, I'm Liam Whelan from two doors down. We moved in next to Mrs. Robertson."

I froze. Not even my lungs would work. What was he doing? *What if she finds out?*

"Oh, yes. You are in Laxshmi's history and math class."

She couldn't remember what drill team was called, but she remembered *that* little nugget of information. I walked halfway down the stairs. What had possessed him to come here? The fine hairs on my arms stood at attention as if anticipating his touch.

"Yes, that's right." The porch light illuminated his dimples and twinkling eyes. He must have been excited to meet her. *God, why?*

"Is there something you need?" She unlocked the screen door for him.

"I left my calculus book in my locker. I was hoping I could borrow Laxshmi's so I could finish my schoolwork."

Hearing him use my real name made me more nervous somehow. What if he slipped and called me Lucky?

I had slowly made it all the way downstairs when I realized I was in my pajamas—a tank top and teeny-tiny, boxer-style shorts. I looked down and rolled my eyes. They had little rainbows all over. Mom would freak later, of course, but I liked the way Liam's eyes roamed over me when Mom's attention was on closing the door.

"Oh, yes. Come in. Come in. Let me get her." She turned to call out my name, but stopped when she saw me. Liam flashed me a smile behind her back. Keeping myself from reacting was like trying to hold back five excited Great Danes.

"Oh, you are here," she said. "Did you finish your math? He needs your book."

"Yeah, sure, I can get it."

When Mom turned back around to invite Liam to take a seat, I shot him a what-the-hell-are-you-up-to look.

He tried to hide a smile by rubbing his cheeks.

I got to my room and scribbled a note to put inside the book. It was a pretty basic threat—I'd kill him tomorrow. I'd seen him finishing his calculus in my drama class, so why was he really here? Was he expecting to get permission to date me? A sleepover invitation from my warden of virginity?

I took out the note again and wrote an apology underneath my threat.

I'm sorry for how I kept us apart.
I miss you so much it breaks my heart.

I hid the note in the book, letting it stick out a bit, and headed downstairs. I tiptoed to the second floor and leaned down to see where Mom was. Her back was to the staircase. Liam stood by the fake fireplace, facing me. I sneaked down a few more steps and sat on the stairs to listen, well aware he could see my legs.

He asked about our family photos and picked up the picture of me dancing. "I didn't know Laxshmi took *Bharatanatyam.* Has she finished her *Arangetram?*"

My jaw dropped. *He's been doing some research.* Mom let out a giggle and discussed our plans for a graduation performance at the end of the school year.

She motioned to the armchair facing me. "Sit, sit, Liam."

She'd holler for me in another minute if I kept stalling—guaranteed. Their interactions surprised me, though, and I wanted to be the fly-on-the-wall for a little longer.

"You know, Mrs. Kapadia, my great-great-grandmother was Indian, and my mum has been to India at least a half dozen times. I've been there three times myself."

"Really?" Her tone told me she was more impressed than she would ever admit. I felt a cautious optimism. "You and your mummy-daddy must come over for an Indian dinner, *hunh?*"

"Thank you, we'd be honored." He flashed his happy smile.

I could tell he was enjoying this little victory with Mom. I wanted to hug him for even trying to impress her. Regardless of how taken she seemed to be, I had no expectations she'd spare me a lecture about him later.

She turned her head to look upward, so I began my descent.

"Oh, I was just about to call you," Mom said. "What took so long?"

"I, uh, wanted to check my homework to make sure it was all finished."

She gave a little head bob of approval. "Okay then. Liam, wait. Wait one minute. Let me give you some sweets to take with you."

"Thank you, Mrs. Kapadia. That's very generous of you. Mum will be thrilled."

She left for the kitchen, and Liam rushed to me, swallowing me whole with a kiss. I clung to him. *How can I miss him so much my body aches?* The tingling felt like being wrapped within a favorite blanket, and it brought tears to my eyes. His lips kissed them away.

He gazed into my eyes and lowered his voice. "Lucks, it kills me when you're hurting." His eyes were so different from what they'd been like with Mom. They'd softened with what looked like love and concern. He brushed my lashes with his thumbs. "Don't cry, *mo mhuirnín.*"

I sniffed and plastered on a smile. "So. Not done with your homework, huh?" I put the book down and wrapped my arms around him and squeezed, feeling his heart pounding against my own chest. Our breathing deepened as the tingling reminded me I was at home in his arms. I listened for sounds from the kitchen to make sure Mom was still there.

"Let me see your eyes," he whispered.

Mom spoke to him from the kitchen about the different sweets she was putting in a Tupperware container.

"Those sound delicious, Mrs. Kapadia."

"Why'd you risk coming here?" I whispered.

He kissed my forehead. "Isn't it obvious?"

It was.

It felt like I had a true place in his heart now, but a nagging reality distracted me. Which *me* did he have in his heart? I was two different people—Liam's Lucky and Mom's Laxshmi. I glanced toward the kitchen. She'd be coming out at any second, and I battled between which one to be.

The Tupperware snapped shut.

He gave me a heart-stopping smile. "The rainbows are cute."

Oh crap. He was trying to be funny, to lighten the mood, but Mom would flip out if she saw me standing next to him dressed like I was. I dashed to a more modest position behind one of the apple-green, striped armchairs—because that was what Laxshmi would've done.

He faked a disappointed look. I dug my nails into the armchair. Fighting back tears, I mouthed, *I'm sorry.* I was sorry I couldn't be Lucky for him all the time. I was sorry I hadn't had faith in him earlier today.

Mom came out with the container of sweets, and we walked Liam to the door, me behind Mom.

"You be sure to tell your mummy she can stop by anytime."

"I will, and thank you for the *mithai*."

It shouldn't have surprised me he knew the Indian word for sweets, but it did. Mom giggled again. *Geez.* He was such a suck-up, but I loved that it meant he tried.

"Thanks for the textbook, Laxshmi. I didn't want to be unprepared. The assignment is on page 173, is that right?"

Huh? Page 173?

I caught myself before gasping out loud. He was quoting me poetry—in secret, and I had just threatened to kill him in my note. I recalled the last stanza of Thomas Moore's poem.

But while I've thee before me,
With heart so warm and eyes so bright,
No clouds can linger o'er me,
That smile turns them all to light.

"Yes. 173." I gave him the best smile I could muster because I wanted him to be happy too. I quickly turned to the door to avoid Mom seeing me. She stepped forward to release the latch to the screen door.

"Oh, wait one minute," she said. "Let me tell you which sweets are which."

He stepped into the doorway, his body blocking Mom's view of me, and listened to her descriptions. I placed my hand on the small of his back, rubbing it with my thumb. Except for the deep breath he took, he didn't budge. Did he feel the tingle when I touched him? It wasn't the kind of thing I could blurt out without sounding foolish.

After her little tutorial, he shoved one of the sweets in his mouth. "Mmm, this one is really good," he said, chewing.

"Oh, you like the *penda*. That's Laxshmi's favorite." Luckily, it was one of the better sweets in there. I hated to think what would've happened if he popped a *mohantal* in his mouth. I would've gagged.

He kept her talking, asking about what kind of sweets she made, where the nearest Indian grocery store was, and if she liked Western cakes and pastries.

"Well, thanks again, Mrs. Kapadia." He turned to me. "And thank you, Laxshmi, for the textbook. I don't know what I'd have done if I couldn't get this."

"I'm glad you came, but, uh, you shouldn't have worried over some stupid little problems—math problems, I mean." I hoped he knew how much coming here really meant to me—to both Lucky and Laxshmi.

Mom opened the screen door, and he stepped through. "Well, I'd not have been able to sleep otherwise."

"Lucky for you I was here."

He held up the calculus book for Mom's benefit. "Lucky ... for me." He put so much meaning behind his tone, I began to choke up. As he moved away, the rubber band snapped back, leaving the familiar pain in my chest.

I cleared my throat to keep the tears at bay and locked the door behind him. How could I ever doubt him after this?

"Such a nice boy. He told me his mummy's from England and his daddy's from Ireland. The English know how to raise children with manners. I'm sure Premlata*ben's* boy is like that too."

What? Not Tejas again. I had to keep in my groan.

"I didn't know Liam's mom was English," I said. "I figured she'd be Irish. Well, good night." I climbed a few steps, hoping to get away before Liam's charms wore off her.

"Laxshmi."

Crap. I turned back to face her, trying not to let my racing heart change the pitch of my voice. "Yeah?"

"You should've worn a robe."

I acted shocked, crossing my arms to cover myself. "Oh my God! I forgot. Sorry, Mummy."

"Have you been talking to him?"

"Only in class when I have to." I put on a why-would-I-bother-with-him look.

She stood there, trying to unravel my DNA, looking for my lies. "He's a nice boy, but I don't want you talking to him anywhere else, *hunh?* Just because he's nice doesn't mean anything. Sometimes boys are *too* nice. Understand?" Not even his smile could thaw her cynical heart.

"Mm-hmm." Tears stung my eyes, and I looked down, pretending to be engrossed in pulling off a hangnail.

"Okay, good night, *beta*. Be sure to get your book back tomorrow."

"I know, Mom." I couldn't make eye contact. Clenching my jaw tight, I fought the urge to scream. I casually walked back to my room.

I took out his watch from under my pillow and squeezed it to my heart. I'd wasted my time feeding my optimism. Mom was never going to change.

I made myself wait until seven-fifteen to leave the house and head to the corner where Liam and I met in the mornings. The sun had risen about a half hour ago, but it hadn't woken the humidity yet. A few leaves broke free and drifted down in a light breeze.

Liam was already there, pacing. When he looked up, he gave me the most breathtaking smile. Every muscle froze in place, except for my heart. It was trying to rip through my chest because I could *feel* how happy he was. *How is this possible?* It had to be another hallucination.

Or was there truth to the whole empath thing?

Right—aliens and empaths. Should I believe in vampires and werewolves now too? I was simply responding to his smile. He looked happy. I was just imagining the rest.

I practically floated over to Liam. He placed my bag next to his at the base of the tree and wrapped me in the most soul-comforting hug. Admitting I was in love brought on a whole new level of complication, but it didn't feel wrong. We stood there for several minutes. I could've stayed there for days.

"I missed you yesterday too," he said, referring to my note, no doubt. "I needed to see you and feel that you were all right." He pulled back, cupped my face, and stroked my cheeks with his thumbs. His eyes did that softening thing again. "Doing better today?"

"I thought I was … until I saw you."

His thumbs paused their stroking. "Right—what did I do wrong?"

I let out a laugh. "No, no, no, I didn't mean it in a bad way. I was overwhelmed by you, that's all. I feel like I'm going crazy." I rubbed my forehead.

"I'm overwhelming you, am I?" His eyes danced. "Don't I just know the feeling. And how is it exactly that I'm overwhelming you?"

I snorted. "Like I'd tell you."

He leaned back against the tree trunk, pulling me with him. I laid my hand on his chest, feeling his heartbeat. We were laughing in each other's arms in no time, and the morning seemed to come alive.

He rested his forehead against mine. "So what's making you think you've gone mental?"

Will my craziness scare him away? Somehow, I didn't think so, but I'd leave the word "empath" out just in case. Besides, it was probably like being a hypochondriac. I needed to explain my hallucinations, and reading about empaths fit my symptoms. But who wanted to admit they'd diagnosed themselves with an imaginary "condition" off the Internet?

I shrugged. "Have you ever imagined what it would be like to feel someone else's emotions?"

"Oh, *mo mhuirnín,* you'd be more than surprised." He caressed my face. "I'm always wanting to know what you're feeling."

I conjured up another hallucination and moaned. "See, you feel like a warm breeze coming off the ocean, blowing through my hair, brushing my skin … "

"Poetic." He brought his lips to mine, speaking between kisses. "You're amazing. Sandstorms and now warm breezes."

"Sandstorms?"

A cyclist rode by, reminding me we were out in the open. *Crap.*

Liam pushed off the tree but kept his arm around me. "I'll tell you soon enough, yeah? Let's head on."

Just like that, I was okay with waiting to hear the secret without a time limit. Fear and doubt didn't pollute my heart and mind anymore. It was like the breeze made me feel loved and safe in Liam's arms, even if it was just in my head. I trusted he'd always be there for me—even if I wouldn't let him—like last night. He'd been determined to be by my side, and he'd found a way. What more could I ask for?

Wishful thinking or not, it was too hard to fight it. Maybe this was the first step to a psychotic break, but what did I care? I was addicted to this feeling, and I only hoped he'd soon feel the same way about me.

I made a conscious choice right then. I chose Liam. Despite Mom, despite my culture, despite the fear of what the secret would bring. I couldn't let anyone control this decision but me—and wasn't that what I'd wanted? To make my own choices?

It was much easier to believe he could read my expressions than to believe in aliens and empaths, so I let my eyes tell him what I was too chicken to say out loud—*I love you, Liam.*

His face lit up, and his breathing quickened. "Damn, Lucky." He spun me around and consumed my mouth in a knee-buckling, stomach-clenching kiss. *Will my hormones ever calm down around him?*

The tingling surged forward, mapping out my body like it was trying to stake its claim, but I didn't care.

CHAPTER 29

Liam

At lunch, I dragged Lucky out to the benches to make her tell me exactly what had happened yesterday with the cheerleaders. She'd skillfully dodged making mention of it all morning, conveniently distracting me with a brush of her arm, her scent when she'd lean in close, or a smile that'd make me forget what I'd been after. Her no-touching policy seemed more like a way to tease me, especially this morning. We were at the benches, stealing what private moments we could, when she broke out with one of her playful rhymes.

"You smell so good, simply divine. Lucky for me, I know you're all mine."

Whether she'd admit it to herself or not, at least a deep part of her was trusting and accepting me. Sensing her love for me for the first time this morning … there weren't enough words in any language to describe the feeling. I'd never felt an emotion so pure. It felt like seeing an HD picture for the first time.

Lucky and I were moving forward again, but I still wanted

to hear what rumors these cheerleaders were spreading. I'd had a hard enough time earning Lucky's trust. I couldn't let their lies be destroying what gains I'd made.

She'd been picking at the last of her green beans, so I collected our recyclable containers and threw them in the green bin. I joined her back on the bench. "Is it done that you are, ducking having a word with me over what was said yesterday?"

She sighed, brought up her knees, and wrapped her arms around them. "Do you know your English gets all backwards when you get all serious?"

I crossed my arms and tried not to laugh.

"Fine." She turned her face to me, resting her cheek against her knees. "It's just awkward. I mean, how would you like to share your innermost insecurities? It's not easy."

I sensed a deep vulnerability that was echoed in her eyes. "You know, Lucky, I, uh … was so nervous about coming over last night, my hands were clammy and my heart was racing. I know your Mum will never think I'm good enough." The memory alone of having to face her Mum brought back the feeling. I wiped my hands on my shorts. "I'll never be her first choice, will I? If—when you tell her about me, she'd be disappointed at the very least, and I know it'll end with causing you heartache. I can't help but wonder if one day you'd regret being with me because of your mum. How's that for having insecurities?"

Tears shone in her eyes. She uncoiled her body and climbed into my lap, locking her arms around my neck. "I'd never let her win like that, Liam." She sniffed. "I won't."

Waves of her determination buffeted me from every direction. She straightened and took a deep breath. I stroked her cheeks while she gathered her courage. The tingling was gentle and soothing. When she finally opened up, she told me everything the two cheerleaders had said. Her pain soon turned into whirlpools, but she managed to push away the hurt and clear her mind. She'd been getting better at controlling the onslaught of chaos overwhelming her. I only hoped this transition period of hers wouldn't be lasting too much longer.

"So, that's why I stayed away from you yesterday. I believed what they'd said about you at first. I was confused … and then ashamed."

"They're jealous of you, and your gorgeous eyes refuse to see that. It was nothing but lies they were giving you." I traced her lips and watched her relax. I never wanted to stop touching her.

She met my gaze and nodded. "I know that now."

"So there's something more important we should be talking about," I said. "Like what those shorts of yours were doing to me heart last night? Jaysus, Lucky. I was struggling to pay attention to your mum, and later, you had me dreaming of your legs all night." I groaned, hoping to lighten the mood.

She threw her head back, laughing, and washed me in the bubbly surf of her happiness. "I was surprised my mom didn't burn them after you left."

Lucky began projecting her love for me again, so I sent her my love back, knowing she could sense it. She hummed and grabbed my face, kissing me soundly. She might not have known *what* it meant, but I knew it was making her happy.

We left the car park and headed for her theater class. I opened up my mind fully and surveyed the area with my enhanced vision to make sure nothing suspicious was about. Uncle Nigel hadn't found out anything about the spy, and Mum hadn't sensed or seen anyone lurking nearby. How Brennan had known I'd left home the other night was still a mystery. Considering Scarface didn't seem the type

Brennan would employ, I'd wager he'd been hired by Gagliardi. There had to be someone else watching us.

"What are you lost in thought about?" Lucky asked.

I was resting my arm over her shoulder, and we had our fingers laced together. The no-touching ban was long forgotten, I hoped, and it was none too soon for me. Her touch was like a balm, soothing the frayed edges of my growing need to keep her safe.

"You," I answered.

"God, you're such a suck-up. Last night was a revelation, you know. 'Thank you for the *mithai*.'"

"You liked that, yeah? Sucking up was a survival skill I learned ages ago—especially getting into trouble like I did."

We stepped through the inner doors, and a blast of cold air greeted us along with a crowd in the hallway. Jack was waiting by the auditorium doors. He knew I'd been spending time with Lucky, and his suspicion was never far from his heart.

"Hey, Jack." Lucky gave him a smile. "What's up?"

"You tell me." His shoulders squared, and every instinct in me had me wanting to push Lucky behind me. Jack put his hands on his hips. "Shiney just told me what happened yesterday. Why didn't you say something?"

"Uh, I ... " Lucky glanced up at me and gave me a sheepish grin. "Give me a minute, Liam?"

"Sure." I kissed the side of her head and moved several feet away, but that was as far as I'd be going.

Jack pulled her aside so her back was to me. Judging by his emotions and body language, he wasn't pleased with what Lucky was telling him. He rubbed his fingers over his mouth, barely containing his anger. I couldn't help but clench my hands and ready my stance, as if I might be needing to pull her out of danger at any minute. Even though my head knew he wasn't angry with Lucky, my instincts wouldn't stand down. Each time he'd glance over her shoulder in my direction, my hackles would rise. When he put his hand on her shoulder, I thought I'd explode. I took several deep breaths to relax.

Lucky's shoulders slumped under Jack's little lecture, and when her head bobbed in a gentle roll, I knew she was rolling her eyes at him.

I focused on the ripples of her irritation ... and her affection. She truly saw Jack as a brother, but when he hugged her, he had my jealousy erupting in a way that wouldn't be listening to logic.

She finally left Jack, and I let out a long, relieved breath.

"I'll call you before we come get you tonight," Jack called out. He waved and headed toward study hall.

Once we took our seats in the auditorium, their hug kept flashing through my mind. I couldn't clear my thoughts. Two weeks ago, I'd never have said I'd be the jealous type, but then again, I'd never thought my world was upside down either—until Lucky righted it.

"You're mad," she said.

"I'm fine." I hadn't meant to snap, but it was all I could do to control my thoughts.

"Liar." She raised an eyebrow and waited for me to elaborate.

We still had a few minutes before the bell rang, and I truly didn't want to be thinking about Jack. "Did your mum say anything about me after I left last night?"

"Well, she was definitely dazed by your disarming smile."

"Was she now?" I sensed a bit of sadness from her like an ebbing tide. "What else aren't you telling me?" A pang of concern shot through me. I hadn't thought about what might have been going on after I'd left.

"Oh, not much." Lucky's eyes followed her classmates as they took their seats. Her apprehension made me feel like I was jumping into snake-infested waters. She didn't say more, and I didn't push.

There was so much more to her relationship with her mum than I'd realized, and I wanted to know about it all. A small seed of worry was also burrowing into my heart. What would her mum do if she found out about us? Would she try to keep Lucky from me? Judging by the suspicion I'd sensed from Mrs. Kapadia last night, we faced a Herculean battle, but I couldn't be worrying about that now. I needed to be getting us joined first—as soon as possible. Da hadn't rung us from DC, so I'd assumed he'd found nothing useful. I rolled my neck, reminding myself to stop borrowing tomorrow's worries. I rummaged through my bag for my schoolwork.

Lucky leaned over the arm between us and watched me. "You know he's like a brother to me?"

I grunted. *What am I? A caveman now?*

"You're jealous," she said.

"Will you be telling me now why Chloe bothers you so much?"

A flash of pain crossed her face. She sat back and brought her bag into her lap. "She and her friends are just so prissy and … smug." She kept her concentration on getting her drama scripts out of her bag.

"Mm-hmm." I leaned over the arm like she had. "*You're* the one who's jealous."

She scowled. "I am not."

"Every time she's heading for me, you run off."

"Because she irritates me." Her eyes would've shot off sparks if they could. She put down her bag and stood to join her group in the front corner of the auditorium.

I grabbed her hand, and lowered my voice. "I'm jealous of every bloody second Jack gets to spend with you, and when he's messing about with you … " She sat, her gaze locked onto mine. "I go stark ravers. When he's looking at you, I want to gouge out those eyes of his, and when he makes you laugh, I'm left feeling like I failed you." She switched to watching my thumb stroke the back of her hand. "So, yeah, I'm bloody jealous. But I trust you. These feelings are new to me, Lucky. I … "

She glanced over to Mr. Truman at the far end of the auditorium before leaning in. Her lips met mine in a soft kiss, and she nuzzled her nose against mine. "I've been jealous too. Every minute you spend with Chloe feels like I'm being stabbed in the heart. Every word you say to her, every look you give her, every time you walk with her … " She chewed the inside of her cheek, deciding something. She pulled back a bit and lifted her chin. "They're supposed to be for me, with me."

I smiled at her possessiveness. "It's all yours, *mo shíorghrá*, that I am." I felt her love for me, and I sent her mine back.

The bell rang. I leaned in for another kiss, but she stood, waving her script in my face. "Sorry. Group time." She gave me a devious smile. "I'm sure the teacher won't appreciate the I-was-being-kissed excuse if I'm late, especially since you're not really supposed to be here."

"I could always leave."

She froze, then knelt down, and looked up into my eyes. "You wouldn't, would you?"

"Not unless my mot wants me gone." She gave me a questioning look, and I kissed her before answering. "Mot means girlfriend."

A shy smile spread across her face, driving me wild. "I'll go ask her." She jumped out of reach before I could kiss her again. Her happiness crested and crashed around me over and over.

I sank into my seat. "You're killing me."

She turned back and laughed. I watched as she joined her group, feeling even that small distance between us deep in my chest. Tonight at the party, I'd be telling her how much I loved her. She was fast becoming more important to me than air. Every cell in my body wanted to join with her, but I needed to know how I could do that. Hell, I'd do anything to make it happen.

Over the past few nights, a growing sense of urgency had been tormenting me. Being away from Lucky was what I'd imagine suffering a withdrawal was like, and a gnawing need to protect her had me imagining all sorts of terrors happening when I wasn't near enough. Not being able to help her yesterday had just made it worse. I was feeling tossed around in a rip current.

I let out a slow deep breath, put in my earbuds, and played Ed Sheeran's "Photograph" on my mobile. I saw I'd missed a text earlier from Elder Brennan.

It chilled my blood.

Brennan: Gagliardi bought travel agency in Cary last week

CHAPTER 30

Lucky

We got to Salvio's and met Shiney's new beau, Matthew. She was right. He was cute, in an adorable, Bible-study kind of way. He was slightly taller than she was, wore a sweater vest, and had her same dark skin tone. His eyes twinkled when he looked at her, making Shiney melt into his side. I couldn't help but smile at how happy she was.

I pulled her to the back hallway by the restrooms while Jack and Matthew ordered our pizza and drinks at the counter. "He's perfect, Shiney."

She mouthed out a silent squeal of delight, and I hugged her, complimenting her on her denim dress.

She pointed to my outfit. "By the way, very hot."

"Green is Liam's favorite color." I shrugged, feeling my cheeks heat.

"That's *so* not predictable coming from the Irish boy." She snorted. "Oh, I didn't want to ask in front of dorkus in the car, but is it official? Are you and Liam finally dating?" She raised an eyebrow and cocked her head. "You were, um, touching him today."

I bit my lip and smiled. This time Shiney squealed out loud and squeezed me till I couldn't breathe.

"Okay, so let me see this outfit." She spun me around twice. I wore a Chinese-inspired crop top with a Mandarin collar and dark, low rise jeans. Thank God they had spandex in them, or I'd never be able to do our drill team routine. The top had an oval cutout that revealed my shoulder blades. I couldn't stop smiling when I thought about Liam seeing the outfit.

Shiney grinned. "So does your mom even know you have this? I can't imagine she'd go for the bare midriff *and* bare back."

"What? It's like some of my Indian *choli* sets."

She raised her eyebrow again. "Is that why you wore those?" She pointed to a slew of Indian bangles on my arms. "Trying to make it look like an Indian outfit?"

"Okay, fine. No, she doesn't know I have this, Miss Smarty-pants. That's why I have a cardigan in the car."

"I knew it." She burst out laughing. "Liam is going to love it, even if your outfit is nationality challenged. He can't take his eyes off you anyway, so I guess it doesn't matter."

As much as I loved Shiney, I wanted to scarf down dinner and leave. I felt like something big was going to happen tonight, and I'd been buzzing all day. With a tug of her arm, I led her back to the brightly lit restaurant and shoved her into a booth.

Jack and I soon said our farewells, and I told Shiney we'd pick her up at ten. Matthew was fidgeting quite a bit, and I got the impression he was impatient for us to leave too. Either that, or it was another hallucination.

"So, uh, you and Liam were chummy again today." Jack gave me a pointed look before the light turned green and he pressed the gas.

I sighed. He'd caught on that something was wrong on Labor Day and had wheedled out a few details from Shiney. All he knew was that Liam had dated Indian girls who looked like me, and that I didn't trust him. Jack had been encouraging me to follow my instincts all week. He obviously didn't like where they were leading me.

We sat in silence for the next few miles. I appreciated his looking out for me, but how could I explain what I was going through? He'd think I was being swayed by my feelings. Maybe I was.

"It'll be all right, Jack."

He shook his head and hit the brake a little too hard at the next red light. "If you say so."

By the time we got to the twins' country club, Justin, our amateur DJ, had already started the music, and the dance floor was filling up. A bank of windows at the far end overlooked the golf course. The walls were paneled in walnut with detailed wainscoting and large sconces sticking out like arms held upward. Two massive, iron chandeliers with at least three rows of shaded bulbs hung from a coffered ceiling. The lights had been dimmed and were accented by Justin's rotating colored lights.

The air-conditioning was set extremely low thanks to Caitlyn's aversion to sweating, and since I wouldn't be wearing my cardigan, I needed to warm up fast. Jack split off to the back room by the refreshments, and I joined some of the drill team girls near the dance floor. I couldn't see Liam anywhere, but somehow I sensed he was there. A prickling sensation ran over my skin, and the air seemed charged, as if it were waiting for us to connect.

Caitlyn came jumping over. She pointed at her watch. "It's time."

Justin announced the drill team and me, and when Caitlyn turned to blow him a kiss, I found Liam standing right next to the turntables. His gaze roamed up and down my body while he rubbed the back of his neck. I twirled around for his benefit and saw his lips form an *O*. It took all of my energy to keep from hyperventilating under my first boyfriend's approving look.

Good luck, he mouthed over the pounding bass.

As our music started, we fell into place and began our routine. Letting loose and feeling the music in my bones made me forget everything—Liam, Mom, early graduation, medical school, arranged marriages—everything.

I channeled my energy through each movement, feeling acutely aware of being alive, of being connected to something outside of myself. As our steps became more vigorous and animated, hoots and hollers from the surrounding crowd amped the vibe and fed something inside me. The noise drew people from the other rooms and created an electrifying energy around us. Our team's movements aligned perfectly, and my happiness exploded outward. The crowd roared, and I felt the warm breeze that reminded me of Liam. I'd reached my happy place, as Daddy used to call it—where the outside world didn't exist, but somehow became a part of me when I danced.

As we wrapped up the routine, Justin's voice came over the speakers and asked for a round of applause for the last sequence. A huge smile stretched across my face.

As the music changed and our routine ended, we broke off into groups to dance as the crowd joined in. Caitlyn gave me a hug, and we started grooving to the next song. I scanned the room for Liam, hoping he'd join me. When I didn't see him, I turned to Caitlyn to tell her I'd be back. Before I could say anything, Justin's voice broke over the song as he was blending the next track in.

"This one's for my girls, Caitlyn and the exotic Laxshmi."

I perched my hands on my hips and glared at him.

He smirked, wiggling his eyebrows. A remix of Calvin Harris' "I Feel So Close" began, and Caitlyn and I cheered in unison. The entire energy on the dance floor changed as more bodies packed in. Our arms were in the air and our hips began to grind to the beat. I was about to turn to find Liam when he came up behind me and synced his hips to mine. I didn't have to look. My body would've known that tingling anywhere. His left hand rested on my bare waist and the other was up in the air next to mine. I turned my head, giving him my profile.

He kissed me behind my ear. "How you feel in my arms … love it."

I leaned my head back and smiled. He smelled as good as he had the first day of school when I'd bashed my head against the lockers. If I'd thought then I'd be grinding with him at this party, I would've diagnosed myself with a concussion.

He traced his fingers over my raised arm, following it down the side of my body, all the way to my waist, where his hand lay warm against my skin. He smoothed his palms over my hips and back up to my waist. The tingling sensation trailed along. He curved his body perfectly around mine and matched my movements as if he knew my next move before I did. No matter how many different rhythms I threw at him, he kept up.

He reached across my waist and spun me to face him, melding us together. We rolled our hips in unison, our faces inches apart. His eyes never left mine, and they told me everything my mind, my heart, and my body had ever wanted to hear. It was as if his soul was talking to me.

The music changed again, and Kaskade's "Eyes" came on, as if Fate had read my thoughts.

I gently pushed off to dance in front of him. He held one of my hands, giving me freedom to move but keeping me close. He never lost eye contact, but I couldn't have moved my gaze away from him even if I'd wanted to. He looked incredible in his untucked black shirt and tousled hair. It screamed confidence, masculinity, and— *ugh*—sex appeal.

I giggled. Good little Indian girls weren't supposed to think like that. *Yeah right.*

The top few buttons and his cuffs were undone, and when my hands were on his chest, the material felt silky soft. The sleeves were taut around his biceps and shoulders, like they were part of his skin.

He was tailored for my eyes.

When the tempo changed, I held my other arm out, inviting him to join me. He moved into me like the last piece of a puzzle and locked me against him. His body was hot, but not hot enough. I yearned for something more—almost painfully—and it made me feel helpless and impatient. The center of my chest burned.

What is this?

I opened my mouth and closed it. What could I say that wouldn't sound certifiable?

He kissed me and then moved to my ear so I could hear above the music. "Shh, *mo shíorghrá.* I'm feeling it as well."

Just like that, I relaxed. I was in his arms, and I didn't have to worry.

He rested his forehead against mine and we swayed to the music. Closing my eyes at his touch, I brushed my lips against his. The rhythm of our bodies synced so well it was effortless. There would never be another dance partner who could make me as happy as I was right then.

This is freedom.

Liam and I danced in our own little world for the next hour before we decided to take a break. We were both thirsty, and as the dance floor grew more crowded, it'd become harder to move. He led me to the back room, lit only by tea light candles on long rows of skirted tables, and grabbed two water bottles from one of the ice-filled basins. The room was probably used for private dinner parties, and it was the perfect size for the small, soft-drinks bar and basins of water bottles. Behind the bar, I could see a glass-enclosed room with wall-to-wall wine racks and a table for eight.

I followed him into one of the secluded corners. Down here, Liam and I cast the only shadows on the wall. A few couples were scattered nearby, making out in the relative privacy of the dim lighting. He sat on one of the tables, leaning back on one hand, and I stood against his knee guzzling the ice-cold water.

He eventually pulled me in between his parted legs and held me from behind. I turned my head to give him my profile again, and he kissed me behind my ear, tickling me with his cold lips and hot breath. It was fire and ice together, and it made my stomach clench. He slid his hand across my bare midriff and turned me slowly. The tingling tightened around my chest, but it also made me feel like dancing in fire.

"I loved dancing with you," he said. "Remind me to get you a fake ID. I want to take you dancing more often. You felt so free."

A fake ID? How would I get out of the house? Could I sneak back in without waking Mom? Liam chuckled for some reason and stroked my cheek. None of that seemed to matter anymore. I was with him. Anything was possible.

"Do you have a fake ID?" I asked.

"Thanks to my brother."

He traced my lips with his thumb, and I tucked my hand beneath his shirt collar, resting it on his muscular shoulder. It didn't feel like enough. I craved more contact, as if I'd be sick without it. He gave me a deep kiss, making me hum. The tingling spread like warm syrup, barely letting me catch my breath, but before it became too intense, he stopped. His shoulder heaved under my hand.

"Could you really be mine?" he murmured.

"Heart and soul."

"The second your mum leaves tomorrow, I'll be over, yeah?"

I wrapped my arms around his neck, and we became one of the kissing couples in the shadows. Our bodies must have already been primed because the tingling became intense right away. I felt it clawing at my heart. When it shot up into my eyes, I was blinded by a bright white light. I gasped, but it was gone as fast as it had happened.

"Lucky? What's just happened?" He cupped my neck, his brow furrowed.

"I, uh … don't know. Something blinded me for a second." What was I supposed to say? *My hormones are so wacky a charge shoots through me every time you touch me?*

He tilted my jaw this way and that. "Does it hurt anywhere?"

"No, it was strange, that's all. I'm fine." I tucked my hand under his shirt collar again and rested my forehead against his. His body stayed tense, and the concern hadn't left his face.

The music changed into something unpopular, and the crowd began moving into our room.

He stroked my cheeks and sighed. "Maybe we should catch our breaths, yeah?" My disappointment must have shown, and he laughed. "C'mon now, if you're not home in one piece, your mum will never let you out again."

He tried to laugh it off, but I sensed something more, like a gust of wind pushing me off a cliff. My pain had frightened him.

I wrapped my arms around him tighter and ran my fingers through his hair. "Don't worry, Liam. I'm fine."

He sighed. "I'd like to be keeping it that way." He pulled back to gaze into my eyes. I felt the warm breeze all over me again. I bit my lip and did a poor job of hiding my smile. "Lucky, there's something I have to say. It's in lov—"

"Has anyone seen Laxshmi?" Jack's voice bellowed over the room's hum.

Liam's jaw clenched, and a growl vibrated in his throat. Was he going to tell me he loved me? *Don't be silly.* His English was different. That was all it was. Liam frowned in Jack's direction. I laughed and slowly stepped away with a smile. He grabbed my hand, lacing our fingers together, and gave me one last kiss before we walked toward Jack's voice.

Jack spotted us, and his gaze dropped to our hands. He jerked his eyes back up to my face. "Ready, Laxshmi?"

"I'll be taking her home," Liam said.

Did he just puff his chest out? I bit the inside of my cheek to stop myself from laughing.

Jack glanced at Liam and then looked at me. "You sure, Laxshmi?"

"Yeah, I'm good. Thanks for bringing me. Tell Shiney I hope she had a great time."

Liam pulled me in front of him, his chest against my back, and placed his hands around my bare waist. I almost jumped out of my skin. *Gee, I wonder what he's trying to tell Jack.* I'd have to make sure I spent more time reassuring Liam that nothing was going on between Jack and me. I covered his hands with mine and squeezed.

Jack nodded slowly. "Catch you guys later then."

Liam led me back to the dance floor with his hand in my back pocket, gloating.

"You need to behave," I yelled out over the music.

He flashed me his sexy dimples and pointed to his ears like he couldn't hear. *Ugh.*

We hadn't even taken a few steps forward before he stopped. He glared over my head, and I turned to see what had caught his attention.

Near the entrance to the main room stood the bitchier half of the cheerleading squad. Some of them cowered under Liam's glare.

Great. Now they'll really think he's getting lucky tonight. I sighed and pulled him away from the entrance. "Liam, don't give them anything more to talk about, okay?" I yelled over the music.

He was clenching his jaw, but when I touched his face, he calmed and his eyes softened. After a few moments of studying my face, he leaned closer. "It's only that I'm thinking about how I failed to protect you."

My heart melted. I blinked back my tears, and he brushed my eyelashes with the pad of his thumb. A sense of *déjà vu* always gave me chills when he did that. What was so familiar about that gesture? Whatever it was, it made me love him even more. With the bass pounding all around us, I began swaying my hips while in his arms. I couldn't help it. Liam laughed and led me to the dance floor.

He threw a nod at Justin, who blended in "Get Lucky" by Daft Punk and Pharrell Williams at Liam's signal. They both smiled at me, and I buried my face in Liam's chest. His chest shook with a good laugh.

"You're terrible! But I love it." *And I love you.* Liam held me tighter.

We danced our way through the throng of people and found a less crowded corner. Three girls from the drill team and their boyfriends found their way to us, and before too long, all four of the guys synchronized thrusting their hips to the beat. They had us laughing so hard we couldn't dance. We finally got it together and began our own impromptu dance-off with them. We won, of course.

The tingling increased in intensity, making me feel more alive than I thought was possible. Its seductive tendrils connected me to him somehow, but I yearned for more. At times, the physical space separating Liam and me didn't seem to exist, and it was jarring to move apart, like waking from a bad dream. Based on the concerned looks he shot me when we did, he must have felt it too. Were my hallucinations affecting him?

The crowd thinned out soon enough, and I groaned. It would be time to go soon.

"It's only ten," he said. "Plenty of time yet." He tucked a strand of hair that was stuck to my face behind my ear. I hoped I wasn't too sweaty-gross.

"Do we have to stay here?" I bit my lip, and the warmth crept into my cheeks.

He raised an eyebrow and smiled.

We said our goodbyes to Caitlyn, Bailey, and Justin. Liam's fingers were still laced with mine as we stretched in separate directions to give them hugs. He tugged at me when I took too long, and as we left, I had to practically jog to keep up with him. Out in the main lobby, with the blaring music now muffled, my jingling bangles seemed louder than the bass.

I laughed. "You know, it would be much faster if you threw me over your shoulder."

"Don't be tempting me, woman." He covered my giggles with a kiss, and we stumbled out the front doors.

We made our way through the parked cars to his white Range Rover. He opened my door for me, and like a giddy little girl, I counted the seconds before he got into the driver's seat. He was shaking his head and smiling when he got in.

"What?" I asked.

"You're more impatient than usual."

"How did you know—?"

He leaned over and shut me up with a kiss. "Strap yourself in," he whispered against my lips.

So he wasn't going to answer me. My expression was probably as loud as one of those airplane banners. *See. Aliens and empaths don't exist.*

He pulled out and drove through the quiet neighborhood. Clouds blocked the stars and created a hazy silhouette of the quarter-moon. Its light left a pale halo, refusing to be dampened.

"Tonight was perfect," I said.

"I wish it wasn't home where we had to be going."

"Why?" I turned to him. "Planning on getting lucky tonight?" I giggled again and then groaned inwardly. Since when had I become so giggly? Liam stretched his arm across the center console to caress my thigh. I wrapped my arm around his, snuggling up against his bicep.

"I plan on getting luckier," he said.

CHAPTER 31

Liam

I pulled far enough into the driveway that Lucky's mum couldn't see us even if she'd been holding vigil by their front window. The tingling had been strengthening over the last ten minutes, and letting go of Lucky's hand to come around and open her door felt like having to cut off me own arm. Except for the occasional rustle of leaves, the night felt still as death itself—even the cicadas and crickets kept from imposing. *Sharp* was the only word I'd be using to describe the air. It wasn't humid or dry, cold or hot. An arc of lightning flashed across the sky with a growing rumble of thunder following.

Helping Lucky out of the SUV, I pulled her close and shut the door. She ran a finger down the buttons on my shirt. All night long, her touch had been causing me chaos. I rested my hands on her bare waist. She gave a gasp, but I wasn't letting go. Her soft skin warmed my palms. I couldn't resist pulling her closer.

This has to be the joining.

"It's amazing you're looking tonight." The faint light from my porch was casting a pale glow on her face. She stared into my eyes, sending me her love. It felt like diving naked into an ocean of sparkling water. I groaned and leaned her back against the SUV, intertwining our legs. I sent her my love too.

"I feel like I'm floating on a breeze," she whispered.

I cupped her face and trailed kisses along her neck and jaw. I couldn't keep my lips off her any longer. "You're deadly soft," I whispered against her ear.

She shivered. "Liam?"

The soft scratching of her nails against my scalp had my eyes just about rolling into the back of my head. "Mmm?"

"I do feel lucky … that I have you."

"And I feel right lucky in love." I was sure my voice was sounding husky. Ripples of her confusion nipped at me, and I chuckled. I'd not been able to help it. The little *v* between her eyebrows was telling me *mo shíorghrá* was thinking hard on what I'd said. That dry-shite Jack had interrupted our moment earlier, but now wasn't the time to be saying more. I didn't want to be talking. I pulled her face to mine and kissed her. The tingling felt like an explosion rocking through my body. It compelled me closer to her. The charge clamped down on my heart and seemed to shoot out of my mouth and into Lucky. We both pulled back, gasping.

Lucky's curiosity about what had happened didn't last long— she was as drawn to me as I was to her. The air no longer felt sharp, but heavy and thick with an energy that kept pulling us together like magnets. The air even smelled ionized. I pressed closer to Lucky, intensifying the electricity between us.

This wasn't just hormones. This was the joining. I was sure of it.

She grabbed my hair to pull our mouths closer. Another arc of lightning lit up the sky, this time with no rumble of thunder. Another charge sizzled through me, joining with one from Lucky. The intensity blinded me, and the force of it kicked Lucky's head back against the SUV. She let out a cry.

"Jaysus, Lucky." I cradled her head. Fear began to spill out from her, and it settled well enough into my chest—only I couldn't stop craving her long enough to think straight.

"Liam, what's happening? I–I think I'm causing this."

"Both of us are," I whispered against her lips, unable to fight against the pull. Images of me drowning flashed across my mind. With each pump of my legs, I swam toward Lucky, but couldn't reach her. She was my air. Every cell in my body screamed to get closer. I needed her to save me. She was my breath, my life.

The tendrils of electricity rose through me again, jolting us wherever our skin was touching. Pulling on every ounce of strength in me, I stepped back from her. Lucky closed her eyes and growled in pain, clutching at her heart. Her legs buckled. I fell forward to catch her. Both of us were now on our knees. A second later, pain shot through me, clamping my teeth together. The taste of blood filled my mouth.

Lucky reached for my face. "Oh, God. Liam, are you okay?"

The haze cleared enough that I could see her beautiful lip, swollen and bleeding now. Tears were streaking down her face like rivulets of rain on a window. The charge was building within me again. *Shite.* I couldn't help it—I brought my head within inches of hers, but I fought the pull. I had to. How could I be hurting her like this? I wanted to be joined with her more than anything in the bloody world, but what price would she be paying for this? She was bleeding already, for Christ's sake.

Scalding hot water poured through my mind—a warning from Mum. I turned to see two silhouettes in the window, then I looked toward the street. Da's car was parked there. Had he returned with information on the joining? Would it make any sort of a difference now? I shot my irritation to Mum, a warning to stay clear. Da would keep her from stepping out here.

Lightning shot through the sky again. The ionized air was becoming stronger, sizzling around me. Would the lightning have to pass through us? Was that what the monk had meant by 'a light had marked the pair?' Or the priest's account about light emanating from an embracing couple? Was it about lightning?

Fecking hell.

I glanced at the blood on Lucky's swollen lip. With the strength it was taking to keep my distance, I'd tire sure enough and cave to the pull luring us closer. What if so few soulmated couples existed because they hadn't survived this?

I looked to the heavens. "Please, God, this can't be right. This can't be it!" I started to reach for Lucky's face, to touch her skin and feel her lean her cheek into my palm, but I balled my hands instead. "I'm sorry."

Tears welled in her eyes. She grabbed my fists and kissed them. "What's going on, Liam? I'm the one who's sorry. I think I'm doing this to you."

"No, *mo mhuirnín,* it's no fault of yours. Christ, how can I … " I choked on the intensity that was building back up, burning our hands.

"I–I need you, Liam." She brought her lips to my neck and kissed me, and the dam of desire burst. I buried my face in her neck, inhaling her scent and caving.

The charge that exploded through us flung us apart, throwing her against the SUV. I rolled from my back onto my hands and knees, pounding the grass with a growl. My vision fogged, but I shook it off and crawled back to her. She was conscious, but dazed. Bloody hell, this was killing her. I helped her crawl away from the SUV and onto the grass with me. She wanted to lean against me, but I needed to keep the charge that came from us from building itself up again. She gave a small nod as if she understood and sat back, leaning forward on her hands for support.

"Lucks?" She swayed, but didn't acknowledge me. "Lucks, can you hear me?"

With another nod, she sat up straighter. More lightning danced around us, and she leaned her head back. A light wind ruffled her hair and she hummed.

I couldn't risk her life. I'd promised to protect her. I had to stop this.

Grabbing her upper arms, I brought her to her feet with me and ripped my hands away before the touch brought us trouble. She stumbled forward, but steadied herself.

"W—We can't do this, Lucks. We can't be together anymore." I scanned the skies. "You've got to be getting yourself inside now." My voice cracked. Her stunned expression sliced through me. I couldn't let it get inside my heart. This was only the beginning of what I had to do to her.

I grabbed her hand and dragged her across the front garden to her house. She was begging me for answers, but it took all my concentration just to open my fingers and let go of the fragile hand I'd been holding. I'd stopped in front of Mrs. Robertson's porch, where Lucky's mum couldn't see us. Lucky's pain and confusion and fear were overwhelming me, battering at me like a storm. The alarm in Lucky's eyes slayed me. Jaysus, did I have the strength to be breaking her heart like this? But it was her heart or her life.

Until I could find a way to safely join with her, I had to be keeping a distance between us. And if the Soul Seekers didn't think Lucky was The One, they'd leave her alone. Sure, they'd come after me, but so be it. Either way she'd be safe. Alive. I wasn't having her hurt.

"Liam, why are you pushing me away? I don't understand." She slapped away her tears.

I swallowed hard. "Lucky, forgive me. The fault's in me."

"But why?" She choked back a sob. "Why are you leaving me after everything you said?"

In the brighter light of Mrs. Robertson's porch, I saw the sheer pain and desolation in her eyes. I ground my back teeth together. I wanted to touch her, wipe her tears, kiss the ache away from her heart and mine. My vision blurred. I took a step back and wiped the back of my hand across my mouth, hating myself. "I made a mistake. You're not—" I scrunched my eyes closed and forced out the words that were a lie. "You're not The One. I tried, but … "

"No! I don't believe you. You told me I was. I trusted you."

A tornado filled with debris flew through my mind, slicing at me. Lucky was changing how I was interpreting her feelings again. I was ready to double over from the pain, but I stood there, taking it. I deserved so much more. I sent her my love, and her face crumpled. "I can't lose you, Liam. I–I need you. After everything you said … "

Lightning lit up our surroundings and struck a tree down the street. The crack had Lucky screaming and covering her ears. I jumped in front of her as if that was enough to shield her from the flash that had already vanished. My ears rang, but I could still hear Lucky's sobs.

If the lightning had hit any closer, we'd have been killed. I turned and faced her, fixing as hard a look as I could manage. "Look after yourself, Lucky."

I walked backward, unable to tear my gaze from the agony twisting up her face. She kept shaking her head and saying *no* as if she could change the reality of what was happening. *Jaysus Christ.* My chest heaved with the weight of what I'd just done.

She held out her arms and looked into the sky. "Liam, it's your pain. I feel water stinging my skin, but how is it you?"

I clenched my hands into fists and sent her a mental block. She didn't respond. *Dammit.* We were crossing interpretations, but she still hadn't broken through. How cruel could Fate be?

Lucky looked back at me, her shock and pain coming across in a building tsunami. Before it crashed over my head, it stopped, and her mind went blank. I focused my vision on her. A change had come over her beautiful face. Her eyes hardened, her chin lifted and shoulders squared. With the same force of the tsunami, her emotions veered in a different direction. A determination I'd never thought to feel from her pounded against me. I felt like a surfer, paddling past the third line of breakers, waiting for the biggest swell of my life.

I couldn't have been more proud—or more terrified.

Her shuddering breaths calmed, and the words she seemed to speak to herself floated over to me. "I won't let you leave, Liam. I love you too much, and I know ... I know you love me too." Her face crumpled once again, and she slapped her hand over her mouth.

I was diving in oceans of her love that I wasn't deserving. I'd failed her. The pain tearing through my gut almost had me ready to collapse to my knees, but I kept walking away. All I could do was whisper my vow.

"I'll be finding my way back to you, *mo shíorghrá*."

EPILOGUE

Pietro rushed into the office of Drago Gagliardi. Their meetings were usually in the late afternoon, but apparently, Pietro couldn't wait. His dark brown hair stuck out and his thick, dark-framed glasses sat crooked on his face. He carried a thick manila file in one hand and smoothed his other hand down his wrinkled shirt as he stood in front of Drago.

No one would ever suspect he was related to the Versaces, Drago thought, putting down his espresso. If Pietro had not been the Council's best computer expert, Drago would never have paid him any attention.

"*Buongiorno.* Forgive me, *il signor* Gagliardi."

"Where is your tie, Pietro?"

He had the decency to look embarrassed. "I, uh … spilled—"

Drago held up his hand. "What is it you bring me?"

He stumbled to the desk, slapping the file down onto the keyboard. Drago raised an eyebrow. Despite his superior's irritation, Pietro grinned. "I printed them, since you like paper."

Idiota, Drago thought.

"You were right." Pietro said. "Those empath websites were visited by the same IP address. All from North Carolina. Cary."

So Prince Liam had told the Kapadia girl about our world. Drago fingered the mole on his cheek. "Has Moira Whelan registered a new empath with the Council?" Drago asked.

Pietro shook his head.

This girl had more promise than the one from Memphis. Drago savored a sip of his espresso, imagining his *nonno* would have been proud of his efforts.

"Shall I inform the Elders, *signore?*"

Drago stood, glaring at him. "What was our arrangement, eh?"

"I bring you information—"

"And that is all, no?"

Pietro swallowed hard and nodded.

Drago dismissed him and rang his assistant. "Marco? Your trip to Cary was very helpful, but it is time for me to visit my new travel agency. Make the arrangements, hmm?"

After hanging up, Drago sat back, his fingers threaded behind his head. Moira thought to thwart him again, did she? If the research he'd had copied from her computer was correct, being a soulmated empath was a genetic phenomenon. If he could become this new girl's empath mentor before Moira did, he could whisk away the lovely girl where no one would be able to find her.

Then he'd turn her into the mother of his future children—whether she wanted to be or not.

Lucky … indeed.

Soulmated – Book 1 Playlist

Mindy Gledhill – "Bring Me Close"
Splender – "Yeah, Whatever"
Dave Matthews Band – "Crash Into Me"
Ed Sheeran – "Photograph"
Calvin Harris – "I Feel So Close"
Kaskade – "Eyes"
Daft Punk and Pharrell Williams – "Get Lucky"

Don't miss Book 2 in the Joining of Souls Series. Sign up today for my private mailing list for updates and release info! Go to http://www.shailapatelauthor.com and scroll down to the sign up box.

Thanks for reading SOULMATED. If you enjoyed Lucky and Liam's story, please consider posting a review online at your favorite retailer or on Goodreads. A good review—even a one-line sentence—helps us authors more than you can imagine. Thank you!

ACKNOWLEDGEMENTS

When I started writing Lucky and Liam's story, I could only imagine what it would be like to acknowledge everyone who helped birth this book. Now that I'm here, staring at this blank page, I'm in awe of these people. They deserve more thanks than I can give, and I only hope they get back tenfold of what they've given me.

My journey started with Kirsten Cyphers, Manisha Patel, and Asha Rama. They were the first ones to read my earliest draft (they deserve an award, trust me) and give me the encouragement to continue writing, continue dreaming, and continue breathing life into Lucky and Liam. Thank you, ladies. I love you!

In no particular order, I also want to thank Amber Goodman, Kavita Srivastava, Ed Green, Jeni Burns, Sophia Henry, Tiffany Picquet, EJ Mellow, Evelyn Lopez, Kimberly Bell, Harman Kaur, Heather McGovern, Ronni Hawkesworth and her daughters Lauren and Kristen, and my CRW ladies! Every author should have a team like this. Their help, friendship, and support have meant the world to me.

There's no way I could forget Ashlynn Yuhas and Cait Spivey from Bear and Black Dog Editing. I won their Anniversary Pitch Contest, and with their help, we shaped my early draft into something more closely resembling what the story looks like today. Wow. Talk about a learning process. Thank you both because your gift gave me the courage to ruthlessly continue editing and preparing my manuscript for submission.

I kept polishing the story with the help of my beta readers and fellow authors Angela Quarles and Carla Cullen, my editor Shannon Donnelly, and my incredible agent Amanda Leuck. Whatever shine this story has is because of them. You guys are amazing. Thank you. And, Angela? You rock!

Of course, you wouldn't be reading this if it weren't for the team at Month 9 Books and Georgia McBride. Thank you, Georgia, for intimidating me into pitching my story to you. (Seriously!)

And last but not least, I'd like to acknowledge my family— my mom, sister, husband, and son. Their love sustains me, and I love them dearly. To my husband and son especially, they gave me the space and time to write, they kept me fed and sane, and they sacrificed so much to allow me to follow my dream. (I did drag them to Ireland for research, so don't feel too sorry for them!) Thank you for listening to all my plot issues, thank you for all your ideas, and thank you for loving me!

I hope you enjoyed reading Lucky and Liam's story as much as I loved writing it. Without the motivation to share this story with you, it would only be a file on my computer. Mwah!

SHAILA PATEL

As an unabashed lover of all things happily-ever-after, Shaila's younger self would finish reading her copy of Cinderella and fling it across the room—all because it didn't mention what happened next. Now she writes from her home in the Carolinas and dreams up all sorts of stories with epilogues. A member of the Romance Writers of America, she's a pharmacist by training, a medical office manager by day, and a writer by night. She enjoys traveling, craft beer, and teas, and loves reading books—especially in cozy window seats. You might find her sneaking in a few paragraphs at a red light or connecting with other readers online at:

www.shailapatelauthor.com
Facebook: https://www.facebook.com/ShailaPatelWriter
Twitter: https://twitter.com/shaila_writes

OTHER MONTH9BOOKS TITLES YOU MIGHT LIKE

SERPENTINE
MINOTAUR
NAMELESS
EMERGE

Find more books like this at http://www.Month9Books.com

Connect with Month9Books online:
Facebook: www.Facebook.com/Month9Books
Twitter: https://twitter.com/Month9Books
You Tube: www.youtube.com/user/Month9Books
Tumblr: http://month9books.tumblr.com/
Instagram: https://instagram.com/month9books

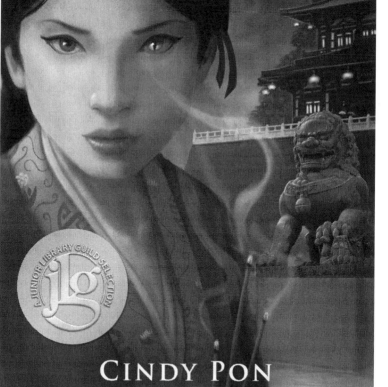

SERPENTINE

"Unique and surprising, with a beautifully-drawn fantasy
world that sucked me right in!" — **Kristin Cashore**, *New
York Times* bestselling author of **BITTERBLUE**

CINDY PON

SOON THE WORLD WILL KNOW WHAT REALLY
HAPPENED IN THE LABYRINTH.

MINOTAUR

PHILLIP W. SIMPSON

NAMELESS

JENNIFER JENKINS

She will risk
everything to stop him
from falling in love with
the wrong girl.

Emerge

TOBIE EASTON